Sleeper

Also From Lexi Blake

EROTIC ROMANCE

Masters And Mercenaries
The Dom Who Loved Me
The Men With The Golden Cuffs
A Dom is Forever
On Her Master's Secret Service
Sanctum: A Masters and Mercenaries Novella
Love and Let Die
Unconditional: A Masters and Mercenaries Novella
Dungeon Royale
Dungeon Games: A Masters and Mercenaries Novella
A View to a Thrill
Cherished: A Masters and Mercenaries Novella
You Only Love Twice
Luscious: Masters and Mercenaries~Topped
Adored: A Masters and Mercenaries Novella
Master No
Just One Taste: Masters and Mercenaries~Topped 2
From Sanctum with Love
Devoted: A Masters and Mercenaries Novella
Dominance Never Dies
Submission is Not Enough
Master Bits and Mercenary Bites~The Secret Recipes of Topped
Perfectly Paired: Masters and Mercenaries~Topped 3
For His Eyes Only
Arranged: A Masters and Mercenaries Novella
Love Another Day
At Your Service: Masters and Mercenaries~Topped 4, Coming November 14, 2017
Nobody Does It Better, Coming February 20, 2018
Close Cover, Coming April 10, 2108
Protected, Coming July 31, 2018

Lawless
Ruthless
Satisfaction
Revenge

Courting Justice
Order of Protection, Coming June 5, 2108

Masters Of Ménage (by Shayla Black and Lexi Blake)
Their Virgin Captive
Their Virgin's Secret
Their Virgin Concubine
Their Virgin Princess
Their Virgin Hostage
Their Virgin Secretary
Their Virgin Mistress

The Perfect Gentlemen (by Shayla Black and Lexi Blake)
Scandal Never Sleeps
Seduction in Session
Big Easy Temptation
Smoke and Sin
At the Pleasure of the President, Coming Fall 2018

URBAN FANTASY

Thieves
Steal the Light
Steal the Day
Steal the Moon
Steal the Sun
Steal the Night
Ripper
Addict
Sleeper

Sleeper

Hunter: A Thieves Novel, Book 3

Lexi Blake

Sleeper
Hunter: A Thieves Novel, Book 3
Lexi Blake

Published by DLZ Entertainment LLC

Edited by Chloe Vale
ISBN: 978-1-937608-69-9

Acknowledgements

I can't tell you how happy I am to get back into this world. Life and work has kept me from it for a while, but slipping into Kelsey's skin was like coming home. I want to thank everyone who helped bring Sleeper from a plan sneaking around in my mind to words on a page. This book went through several iterations as I found my way. Thanks to Kim for all the breakfast planning strategies and Kori for having to read more than one version of this book. Thanks to an amazing group of beta readers—Jennifer Zeffer, Diana Merritt and Riane Holt. Thanks to my family for their tireless support. Whenever I talk about Thieves, I have to thank the reader who was there first, a reader who became a friend and a friend who became family. I love you, Liz Berry. If no one else ever read these books, I would still write them for you!

Sign up for Lexi Blake's newsletter
and be entered to win a $25 gift certificate
to the bookseller of your choice.

Join us for news, fun, and exclusive content
including free Thieves short stories.

There's a new contest every month!

Go to www.LexiBlake.net for more information.

Chapter One

I knew the minute the world around me cracked and that horrible stench of brimstone and BO hit my nose that I'd fucked up yet again.

Eight months and I still couldn't get it right. It was frustrating as hell, but the good news was I would probably get to kill something real soon. I always feel better when I kill something.

"What the hell is that thing?" Casey backed away.

For a vampire, he was pretty freaked out by anything that wasn't human, and he was scared of some of those as well. Casey was a young vamp, having only turned two years before. In his previous life he'd been a wannabe pro skater and one of those dudes who thought he should express himself through song. While he no longer carried a skateboard around at all times, I could practically hear him writing a song about the nasty, twisting thing that had come through when my spell had gone awry.

Again.

I glanced over at the other two people who had joined me in forming the circle that should have produced the demon named Nemcox. Liv, my witch best friend, and my brother Jamie were currently on the other side of the room, forming a triangle outside the circle we'd created in an attempt to keep Nemcox trapped until I could kill him. And by kill him, what I honestly meant was slice that little fucker open, play in his entrails, and generally torture his nasty ass until his body couldn't handle it any longer.

Nemcox. I'd known him as Matthew. My father had known him as Stewart, and my former lover and brand spanking new dark prophet, Grayson Sloane, called him brother.

I was going to murder him because he was the reason my true father no longer walked the earth.

Liv shook her head, a frown on her face. Her skin had gone pale, as though the act of calling forth the demon had drained her. It probably had. Before the last few months, she'd been all about the white magic and the loving goddess and shit. I needed a bad goddess, unfortunately. "I have no idea. I might have mentioned that calling demons wasn't my major in witch school. I was really more about the white magic. That thing is definitely evil."

She wasn't wrong about that. Look, I've seen some ugly things that turned out to be quite nice. You can't always tell a book by its cover in the supernatural world. Like the troll I had to go and talk to because he was scaring the shit out of tourists in Montana. Dude was simply upset because he'd gotten kicked out from under his nice, out-of-the-way bridge in Canada. Was he twelve kinds of nasty looking? Hell, yes. But after a chat and a couple of hot dogs that I did not eat because I'm pretty sure they were actually made of dogs, he turned out to be a pretty chill guy.

The thing in front of me wasn't ever going to be anything but evil.

There was a terrible crack of thunder that seemed to shake the house to its foundation and then I heard the sound of something slap against the roof as the thing in the circle hissed and snapped its spiny tail.

Yeah, it was one fugly critter.

"Any idea what it is?" I asked, trying to view the situation from an academic standpoint. I tried to shove down the need to punch through a fucking wall. How was Nemcox managing to do this? I had his name. I should have been able to call the fucker to my hand, at which point in time I fully intended to use that hand to chop his head off and mount it on my wall.

Five attempts. Five failures. Nemcox had found a loophole in the demonic laws apparently.

"I'm trying to Google it." Jamie had to yell because it sounded like there was a hurricane outside the house. He had his phone out. My big brother was damn cool under pressure, but then he worked as a consultant with law enforcement on some of the creepiest cases they saw.

"It's an Ala!" Casey screamed. He'd gone even paler than usual. "I didn't get it until the storm started up. It's sort of a demon from Bulgaria and it likes to cause hail storms. Your insurance premiums are going to go sky-high. This is serious, Kelsey."

Since I'd begun my campaign against Nemcox, Casey had been studying up because he liked to know what was going to murder us next. He was a technophage. At least that's what I called him. Technically he belonged to a class of vampires called academics. Vampires develop talents over many years, but they tend to be born with their core talent. Some are impressive fighters. Some can control minds. Casey was incredibly talented when it came to all things electronic. He could hack most systems, fix almost anything, and in addition to those talents he could remember almost everything he ever read. It led to a remarkable amount of anxiety on his part.

You have no idea how many times I've had to explain to him that vampires can't catch Ebola.

"It won't stop," Casey insisted. "Now that it's here on this plane, it will try to build storms. It will attempt to destroy everything it can. Starting with us."

Yeah, everything always wanted to start with me.

It was one of the hazards of my job. "Can you get rid of it, Liv?"

Liv's hands were out, her eyes closed and mouth moving as she intoned in Latin. She was doing it super quietly though. It was probably one of those things where the "universe" heard her or some shit, but I had to hope the universe had some super sharp ears because it was getting loud up in here.

"What do we do if she can't get rid of it?" Casey stood behind me. He wasn't supposed to be here in the first place, and I would utterly deny his role in this party of mine if asked. Of course, the whole reason I'd selected today to try to get my kill on was the fact that my mentor and the head of the academics, Marcus Vorenus, was out of town on some kind of Council business.

Still, out of town or not, he would hear about this if the Dallas/Fort Worth area was suddenly inundated with supernatural storms. And he was smart enough to know exactly where to look. "I'll have to kill it. You go out to the car. You can't have anything to do with killing a demon."

Unfortunately, Casey was bound by the Vampire-Demon Agreement signed many years ago and set to renew soon. One of the tenets of said agreement was for vamps to stay out of demon business and demons to do the same. Casey could get into serious trouble if he got caught.

I've learned a couple of things since I took on the job of *Nex Apparatus*. It's sort of the supernatural world's equivalent of a sheriff. At least that's what Daniel Donovan would have us believe. He's the king of this plane's supernaturals, and for the most part he's pretty cool. But like I said, I've definitely learned a couple of truths about my job.

1. People are stupid and no matter how many times you tell them that calling out to a demon in some middle-of-nowhere crossroads won't make you into a fab blues guitarist, they still do it. And boy, do those dudes whine. 2. No matter how hard you scrub, supernatural blood doesn't come out of cotton. Don't wear your fave concert T-shirt when you're going to have to behead a killer shifter. And 3. This is the important one. Friends are everything. Don't get them into trouble unless it's absolutely, save-the-world necessary.

If Donovan caught Casey here, his ass would be grass.

Casey held his hands up as though giving up the fight. Which was a good thing since he wasn't a super fighter in the first place. He was a keyboard warrior, not the guy you tossed a sword to. "All right. I'll wait in the kitchen."

"It's an Ala demon," Jamie screamed. Like I said, it was pretty loud. Jamie turned his phone out as though I could see what was on the screen through the chaos of the circle that separated us. Somehow the demon had called a hailstorm right into the middle of my living room.

I was glad I'd brought this out to the suburbs because Marcus would freak if hail damaged his perfectly hand-scraped hardwoods. Of course, he'd be pissed for numerous reasons, the most important being he'd asked me to stop calling demons in the first place.

More and more, Marcus seemed disappointed in me. In the eight months since he'd turned to me and said he might be willing to share me with Gray, a distance had opened between us. He'd started traveling more and more without me. Every time he left I felt our connection thin and twist, and I worried we were almost at the breaking point.

But I couldn't think about that now.

"How do I kill it?" I shouted.

Jamie looked down at the screen again. "I don't know. I need to read the article. Hey, it's Slavic and likes to create thunderstorms."

No shit. I didn't need Wikipedia to tell me that. The fact that I had quarter-sized hail on the floor was explanation enough. And unless feeding it borscht somehow placated the fucker, I wasn't sure how knowing its region of origin helped.

So far though the circle was holding. The damage inside the house seemed to be confined there.

Luckily, I had a silver sword. I've found most things die when I cut their heads off with a silver sword. I was also wearing a shirt I didn't particularly like, so I was ready.

The last few months had been a mix of good and bad, and a

whole lot of restlessness. Grayson Sloane, my first love, the half demon I'd never been able to truly get out of my head or my heart, had turned into a dark prophet and was currently hanging out with a heavenly prophet named Jacob, and Gray had forgotten how to use a phone. I didn't know where he was or if he was okay. He was "on sabbatical" from the Texas Rangers, according to his commanding officer, and I'd been told it was an open-ended leave.

I spent my time training and working. Working and training. And worrying. A lot.

Something big was coming. I could feel it. Those contracts I talked about earlier were in an odd place. They'd technically run out, but the way they were written, they stayed in place for another year. After that, there would be nothing at all in place to keep the two factions at bay.

Daniel Donovan wanted a war, but I wasn't sure he could win it. I wasn't entirely sure Daniel's war wouldn't bring down our whole world.

Then there was the twitchy feeling I was getting deep in my soul. Marcus used to fill that place, but I'd started to feel more like my old self again, and that wasn't a good thing.

Liv was having no luck on the banishment track. It looked like I was going to have to deal with it. It was neatly contained in its circle, but it wouldn't stay that way forever.

"Y'all go." I couldn't do what I needed to do in such a small space when I was worried about Liv and my brother.

Liv's eyes came open slightly. She said nothing; didn't have to. I know a pissed-off witch when I see one.

"I have to break the circle," I shouted her way. "Do you understand what that's going to do?"

It would likely send insurance premiums in the county soaring, but it was that or let the fucker rage for days until we found a witch who could dispel it. Somehow I thought a localized, long-term hailstorm that hovered over one house might attract media attention.

If I was in hot water for calling demons, you don't even want to know what happens to weird half wolves who find themselves smiling for the evening news.

"Do it!" Jamie shouted. He'd already pulled his own sword. It was a nice weapon, but it hadn't been forged in Heaven like the one I was carrying.

One of the perks of being the *Nex Apparatus* is a handy silver sword passed down through the generations of vampires who held the title. I was the first non-vamp to piss enough people off that it was either make me a *Nex Apparatus* or execute me, so that sucker was mine now.

When Donovan had passed it to me, he'd told me a bunch of stuff about how the sword had been forged in Heaven's fire and how I had to respect it because like angels kissed it and shit.

I call her Gladys.

"All right," I shouted. "Let's do this."

I like to rip the bandage off. There are people out there who will soak the bandage and then ease it off. They're pussies and they need to stay far away from my world. In my world, if we leave the bandage on and nurse it and gently try to coax it off, it usually turns out to have been poisoned by some asshole who wants you dead. So tear that fucker off and get the fight started.

It's one of my many mottos. My therapist has me trying a few things to ease my anger issues. Needlepoint is one of them. I sewed that sucker on a pillow and I keep it close.

The Ala seemed to still as I approached. The black fog that surrounded the demon became wary, and then I could practically feel its excitement as it seemed to figure out what I was going to do.

She wanted this fight, craved it.

I kind of did, too. Like I said, the last few months had been shitty and tense, and killing a demon always made me feel better. Gladys hummed in my hand. It's what she does when she realizes demons are near.

We stared at each other for a moment. We're natural enemies, the Ala and I, according to everything I've read about my species. I'm a

Hunter, one of the rarest supernatural creatures on the Earth plane. I'm the product of a union between a lone wolf and a human. Lone wolves are a specialized form of werewolf. They're stronger, but tend to shun packs. They keep the alphas in check. That was my father, Lee Owens. My mother was a horny, lonely human. Her super powers include calling at the wrong times and constantly being on me to find a man.

If my father's place in the natural order of things was to keep the alphas in check, my own job was simple.

I'm a demon hunter. I was born to track and kill demons, to keep the balance on the Earth plane.

Which kind of sucks when you're in love with a demon.

I brought the heel of my boot down and dragged it back along the hardwood, breaking the circle.

And was immediately rewarded for letting the bitch out with hail coming down on my head. It knocked into my skull with a force it shouldn't have since it's not like I've got vaulted ceilings. Those suckers are maybe eight feet high at most. It was apparently enough for a storm cloud.

I fell back and Gladys clattered to the floor next to me. I felt the demon rush by and then glass cracking as she tried to get out of the house.

I forced myself up, got Gladys back in my hand.

"Can you keep her contained to the backyard?" I shouted over the crack of lightning that threatened to shake the walls of the small ranch house my grandmother had left me. It looked like the Ala was choosing flight over fight. It made me think less of her, and I didn't think that much of her in the first place.

Liv nodded, her eyes already closing and her hands coming out. A protection spell *was* in her oeuvre.

"Watch over her," I yelled at Jamie. Liv wouldn't be able to protect herself while she was in that state, and I really needed her to be in that state if I was going to keep the demon close. Otherwise, she would be running around causing storms, and I would likely be convicted of crimes against humanity or something.

I didn't turn around to make sure Jamie was doing his job. That was the amazing thing about my oldest brother. He was a great soldier. He took orders well, and I never had to worry about him deciding he knew better than I did. Jamie would watch over Liv and not leave his post for anything. It meant I could deal with the demon in peace.

I raced out to the kitchen where Casey was frowning my way as he shrank back from the demon.

If I thought an alarm or an electrical system would keep the demon in, I would have Casey MacGyver that sucker, but she was intent on getting out. The window that overlooked my backyard shattered and a cloud of black smoke pressed through.

I ignored Casey, who was bitching about his hair being ruined. I didn't see how it could get ruined. He did that to himself every morning when he woke up and attempted to look like he belonged in One Direction, but that was just me and I'd been told I hurt sensitive feelings when I spout off my opinions.

A blast of wind shoved me back into the house the minute I got the door open. I smashed into the dining room table, my spine knocking against the edge.

"Should I call for backup?" Casey asked.

"No." I did not need backup. "What about 'secret mission' do you not understand? Why don't you go and see if there's anyone you need to persuade that everything's perfectly normal? I saw the neighbors were prepping the grill earlier. Go and do your job."

I forced myself to move, walking against the wind. There was a hurricane going on in my backyard, but it seemed like Liv was containing the damage. I glanced to my right and Mrs. Tilman's yard looked perfect for a summer's evening. Well, with the exception of her husband, who was standing at his grill, staring into my yard like he was seeing something insane. Which he was.

Donovan had it much easier. When he'd been the *Nex Apparatus*, he'd had a magician on his team—a vamp who could form illusions so real that dudes like Mr. Tilman would never once suspect that a battle was taking place in the weird chick next door's backyard. If I'd had Chad Thomas on my team, I wouldn't have to worry about my neighbors filming me and setting up a YouTube channel. I could get in, get my kill on, and call it a day.

As it was, I had to hope that Casey got to the witness before he called in his friends.

I focused on the demon in front of me. She hovered a good foot off the ground. Though she was encased in some kind of black smoke, I could see that she had form under there somewhere. Her hands came out, feeling for the walls of her prison cell. She batted up against it all of the sudden, as though testing it for strength. She moved around, like the velociraptors from Jurassic Park, butting up against the wall she found around her, desperate to find a way out.

I couldn't let her find one. I charged, sword out, ready to take her down.

She turned and her scream became a gale force wind.

My body flew back, slamming against the side of the house. My head hit the paneling and the world went a bit woozy.

Woozy or not, I had to get back up on my feet. Luckily, I tend to heal pretty damn fast. It's the vamp blood. Marcus shares his blood with me. Even when he's not around, he leaves a stockpile behind. I've found it's pretty good in a cup of coffee, gives it a rich cream taste without the calories. Vamp blood is a universal curative. Got stabbed? Get a vamp to bleed on you and you'll be back in the club and dancing in no time. Marcus's was particularly potent. He was the oldest vampire walking the Earth plane, and his blood tended to help me take my badass status to an entirely new level.

His blood was the only reason I was able to bounce off the wall and make my run at the Ala. She'd turned away, likely believing she had me on the ropes. Most beings, she would have had time to play around with before worrying about her prey getting up. With me, she'd made a terrible mistake.

I ran at her, ignoring the wind and hail and driving rain. I reached deep into the predator part of me, the part that never, ever gave up when the kill was close. Gripping Gladys, I ran to the Ala, my feet not making a sound. Well, they probably made a sound, but no one could hear it over the storm. Not even the demon. She completely ignored me.

Until I speared her. Gladys dug deep, cutting through the smoke and biting into flesh. She was thin, but demon skin is tough and I had to put some force behind it. I planted my feet and shoved the sword in.

That was when the lightning struck.

My body seized, every muscle contracting in a symphony of pure agony. It's a bad thing to happen when you're currently murdering a demon with a sword. I was stuck, trembling like someone had shot me through with a massive Taser. The only good thing about it was my hand was wrapped around Gladys and it wasn't moving. I couldn't have made those fingers release if I'd tried.

My teeth clacked together, the force jarring, and I started to see stars.

Something struck me from the side, knocking me out of the lightning's hold. I hit the ground, my knees sinking into the rapidly softening yard. I could feel my limbs still shaking.

A low growl caught my attention and I realized that even though my day had gone to shit, there were still mighty lows to come.

A massive wolf with gray fur that was soaking wet stood over me. Wolves don't exactly have facial expressions, but Trent managed to make his irritation with me plain.

Trent Wilcox and I have an odd relationship. He's Daniel Donovan's chief lackey. At one point in time the Boston boy had helped save the queen. He'd become her personal guard, a post once occupied by Lee Owens, my bio dad. Now he both took care of the queen's security and pretty much did whatever Donovan told him to.

Stalking me was merely a hobby. I used to find it incredibly obnoxious. Now I find it a little disturbing. Eight months before, I had visited a place where all the possibilities of my life were laid out for me.

Trent played a part in some of the more sexual ones. Despite the fact that I couldn't remember it entirely, I dreamed at night of that feeling I had. There was a possible future me that really enjoyed Trent on a level that would lead to children. A boy and a girl. A half demon and a she-wolf. I dreamed of that family at night.

Which made things awkward since I had a boyfriend, and it wasn't like Trent viewed me as anything but a burden to be borne. Not that I ever told him or anything. I wasn't a complete idiot, but I worried I sometimes acted weird around him. The more and more Marcus was gone, the more I found myself seeking out Trent's company. I found it soothing to be around him, and that twitchy feeling in my gut sometimes eased when he was close to me.

Trent's normally glorious fur was soaked and he growled my way.

Yeah, I knew what that growl meant. It meant I'd fucked up again and there was going to be hell to pay.

Was it truly my fault that I found that damn growl sexy?

"Can I at least deal with the demon before you start in on the lecture?" I forced myself to my feet.

He growled again, giving me his assent.

When had I learned Trent's language? Maybe it was because the human form of Trent growled a lot, too. He leaned forward and nudged me with his perfect snout, his way of telling me to hurry the fuck up.

I struggled to my feet because she'd started up with the hail again. It seemed to have gone to golf-ball sized. It pounded against my body. My spine felt like it cracked as I gripped the sword again.

Trent howled, the sound roaring even above the demon storm. The Ala turned her attention right to that wolf. He didn't back off. Trent ran at the demon, his big wolf body a testament to predatory grace. I watched for a moment as he launched himself straight at the demon, his sharp teeth making their first appearance.

He sank them into the demon's throat and then the wind picked up again, blowing ferociously. His big body was sent rolling back but not before I saw the blood start to flow. It was a good sign. It meant I could at least banish her nasty ass back to the Hell plane. Typically, if it bleeds, the physical body can be vanquished. Doesn't work on everyone, but then I had a sword from Heaven that would help send her along.

I just had to get close enough to her to poke my sword through.

She wasn't making it easy. A blast of freezing wind shoved me back, but I planted my feet and forced myself to move forward, my sword in hand. Trent howled and charged again.

The Ala screamed as Trent proved she was more than rain and thunder. Black blood began to flow as he clamped down on the demon.

I personally don't get the werewolf's deep desire to sink their teeth into their enemies and take a taste. Werewolves don't tend to worry about things like bacteria, but they should. Even from where I stood, I could tell that wasn't good, but Trent kept chomping. If he went rabid, I would be the one who had to put him down, and I didn't want to do that. He was a pain in my ass, but he was something of a friend. And I would get in serious trouble if he came down with some weird disease.

So I needed to deal with the situation and fast.

Lightning flashed and sparked against Trent's fur. Even in the pounding rain I could see smoke as he was thrown back. The Ala seemed to think Trent was the real threat. She glided over toward him and that was when I struck.

Some people might say I'm a coward for what I did next. They might say I should have fought honorably and faced the demon down. Those people are idiots who've watched way too many movies. In the field, when you get a shot to eliminate a demon opponent, you take it.

I charged the Ala and rammed my sword through her back before she could get her hands on Trent again.

Black smoke surrounded me, blocking out the rest of the world. I was in the Ala's presence, the mist around her an actual part of her body. The rain no longer touched me and I could hear nothing but the demon's huff as the sword slid through her thin torso.

She tried to throw me off, her body bucking like a bronco not ready to be broken to a saddle. I held on for dear life because there was no way I was going to lose that sword. I wasn't sure exactly what was about to happen. Demons are odd things. Some can be killed. Others simply return back to the Hell plane damaged and weakened. Some can never die, and I have to figure out a way to keep their heads separated from their bodies for all of time.

This one was different. The black smoke encased me, becoming so thick I couldn't see out it.

That was when she turned and spoke to me.

Her body twisted, the sword moving through her as she spun around in that exorcist way and her eyes lit up. Suddenly the sword that had previously been through her back was lodged under her breast as she'd sliced through half her body to look at me. This was where dealing with demons got tricky. Sometimes with the immortal ones, you can slice and dice and still come up with nothing.

I was holding the sword so if she vanished back to the Hell plane, she couldn't take it with her. Or she'd take us both and then I would be in hella trouble.

Still, I wasn't thinking about that as she turned those endless eyes on me.

"Beware demons bearing gifts."

I frowned. It was easy because somehow she'd completely shielded me from the outside wind and rain. It was even warm in the encasement of her shadow self. The rest of the world seemed far away. Why was she suddenly giving me advice? "I need you to understand, the sword isn't a gift with purchase. Go back to Hell or I'll find another way to deal with you."

I could see her face, sunken eyes and a pointed chin. Her hair seemed to flow in blacks and grays, almost indistinguishable from the smoke around her.

"Kelsey mine, you're going to get yourself killed one of these days."

My heart nearly stopped. Only one person ever called me that. Gray. Somehow, someway, Gray was here with me. He was inside the Ala and that meant I couldn't kill her. Him. It. Why the hell was my big strong Gray inside this spindly demon? What had happened?

I knew one thing. I wasn't going to kill Grayson Sloane.

I started to pull the sword out.

A time-ravaged hand slid over my arm, stopping me. "Don't. If you do that I won't be able to control her anymore. It's the silver of the sword that allowed me to enter her. Well, that and the fact that you carry part of me with you. Your arm never changed back to wolf, did it, sweetheart?"

Before he'd become a dark prophet, Gray had donated blood to save my right arm. As a Hunter, I can change my arm into a wolf claw. Well, it's supposed to be a wolf claw. Because it had been Gray's demon blood that healed my dominant arm, when the time came for the change, I got shiny demon skin and nasty talons instead of the promised wolf form. Everyone had been certain that once Gray's blood had integrated, I would be wholly wolf again.

They'd been wrong. Perhaps it was because Gray was part royalty, or maybe because the king's blood had given it a boost, but I still sported red skin from time to time.

The Ala's hand moved over that skin as though Gray could feel the part of himself that still lived inside me. Even though the skin touching me was withered and gnarled, I couldn't help but see Gray's strong hand there, caressing me, touching me for the first time in months.

I let the sword rest in once more. "So Jacob is helping you?"

Jacob, possibly the most ancient being still walking the Earth plane. He was a prophet from the Heaven plane. He'd been the one to aid Gray in his transition from mere demon to dark prophet.

"The sword was once his," Gray explained. "He can sense when it's being used. He asked me to get a message to you. This is his prophecy, not mine."

Which was probably why he wasn't speaking in prophet talk. It's a little like a rap song, except sung by a thousand-year-old professor on a bad acid trip. The one time Gray went all prophety on me, he spoke in circles and riddles and then wondered why I ignored it all and did what I wanted to anyway. Apparently it all makes sense to the prophet.

But I got the whole beware-of-demons-bearing-gifts thing. "Okay. I promise I won't take any gifts from assholes. Now tell me where you are."

The Ala's lips curled up slightly, but the smile was a sad thing. "I'm in the world, Kelsey mine. In the world and not nearly good enough for you, but I hope you know I'm thinking of you always."

I didn't want him thinking of me. I wanted him with me. "Gray, please come home."

He reached up and touched my face. "You are my home. When I think of you, I'm there. But somehow I doubt Marcus would welcome me, and you need your trainer. You need someone who can ground you in this world and that's no longer me. I thought I could be, but I've seen the truth. I'll only bring you sadness, Kelsey mine."

Frustration welled inside me. He never listened. He could see the fates of all the planes laid out for him, with the frustrating exceptions of those close to him. And his own. Becoming a dark prophet had turned my demonic boy toy into a real Eeyore. "That's not the way I remember it. And if Jacob is telling you differently then he and I are going to have a real problem."

"I have to leave this body now," Gray whispered. "Hell is calling her home. Stop screwing around with the demons, my love. Something is happening. Something that could envelop this plane in warfare unlike anything even the ancients have seen. If you protect the man, you protect the child and the king. The crown is twofold, but one will come who thinks to unite the lower planes. A trick and a trap. It's already in place but if he ever knows how Heaven tricked him, his fury will be a thunderstorm, punishing and never ending. Convince the king. Save this world."

Yep, there he was. I could ask him a thousand questions and this was what I would get. A puzzle. Sometimes I wondered if I tried to figure it out, would it really change anything at all?

A trick and a trap.

Heaven had tricked someone who was going to be pissed.

Convince the king of what?

"Don't go," I whispered, wanting more time with him. Even if he was stuck in a desiccated demon body.

"Hell won't wait," he replied with a smile. "You should know that. Good-bye for now. Your wolf is howling and he'll bring down everything if you don't show up soon. Tell Trent to take care of you if anything should happen to Marcus."

My heart seized. "What does that mean?"

"It means the world is changing and so is he. It means…I love you, Kelsey mine. Let her go. Pull back now or she'll drag you with her. Know that I will come for you when the time is right. I'll sacrifice if need be. And beware the spawn."

The world rushed back as I stumbled, my sword coming out of the demon's body as she was pulled backward, screaming her way home to Hell.

I tumbled back on my ass, the sword falling beside me. The ground was muddy beneath me, but the moon was out again, the world back to its regularly scheduled weather. Quiet hung over the yard.

But not for long.

"What the fuck was that, Kelsey?" Trent shouted.

"Dude, clothes." I averted my eyes but only after I'd gotten a good look at the man. Despite the fact that I'd recently seen and spoken to the love of my life, who'd warned me that Marcus was in danger, I still couldn't help but admire how drool-worthy Trent was. The Boston boy was cut in all the right places. He was a big, gorgeous mass of perfectly defined muscles.

"Baby girl, if you don't want to see me like this, stop getting yourself into situations where I have to change so quickly my clothes explode. I liked those jeans, damn it," he complained.

"Trent, looking good, buddy." Liv had a sparkle in her eyes as she joined us, Jamie behind her.

I had to hope Casey had the good sense to run. While Trent was friendly, he also had a big mouth when it came to kissing Donovan's butt.

Trent didn't even blush or show the faintest hint that he was embarrassed to be caught with his impressive junk hanging out. There was a reason the dude was an alpha. "Seriously, Olivia. You're still helping her. And you, Jamie? You should fucking know better."

"I probably should and yet I don't. I'm going to go and see if I left a pair of pants you can wear." Jamie retreated as fast as he could, hauling Liv behind him.

"You're going to kill me, Owens," Trent said with a long-suffering sigh.

Not if he killed me first.

Chapter Two

"What you in for, buddy?" I slumped down into one of three chairs that lined the hall outside the king's "official" headquarters. He had a personal office. I'd seen the inside of that, too, but this time I got to do what I like to call the "sit of shame." And I was doing it looking like a drowned cat.

Trent had turned me over to the king, but he'd helpfully left my friends out of it. His gorgeous tattletale ass was currently in Donovan's office, probably making me out to be the second coming of Satan, and I was here watching the world go by.

But I wasn't doing it alone. I wasn't the only person in trouble.

"It wasn't my fault. Dustin is an asshole wolf and he deserved what I did. And he's bigger than me. He's in the sixth grade," Lee Donovan-Quinn complained. His sneakers didn't even touch the floor. He was the king's nine-year-old son. Well, one of them, but his twin Rhys didn't get into trouble the way Lee did.

I love Lee with all my heart. I can do that. I'm not his parent so I can totally play favorites, and I adore that kid in a way I simply don't the others. Don't get me wrong, I like them all, but Lee is special to me. He's named after my biological father and we have a connection I can't quite explain. It might have something to do with the fact that we both get in trouble with Daniel Donovan on a regular basis.

"What did the asshole do?" I wasn't going to chastise him. He would get enough of that soon.

Lee finally turned my way, his mouth a stubborn line. "He told me I didn't belong at school. He said I should go and hang out with the humans or I would get hurt."

Oh, maybe Dustin would get to meet me and then we'd have a talk about bullying and how it ends poorly. "So you hurt him. Did you get into a fistfight?"

It was kind of how Lee worked. He was so young and there was a shit ton of anger in him. Don't get me wrong. Lee's a happy kid, most of the time. He likes candy and playing basketball and watching movies, but there's a darkness in him I can't explain. I think sometimes that's why Lee and I fit together. Somehow Lee feels like family to me. I wish I could explain it better, but I care about him in a way I care about very few people.

"Like I said, he's bigger than me."

I had to smile because Lee was also smart. "What did you do, you little deviant?"

His lips curled up slightly. "I broke into his locker and rubbed wolfsbane all over his gym clothes."

I bet that baby wolf had howled. It was like rubbing poison ivy all over the kid's junk. It was mean and kind of brilliant. I smiled back at him. "You're in so much trouble, buddy."

"She's right." The queen was standing in the hallway, her red hair pulled back in a ponytail and a stern look on her face. Zoey Donovan-Quinn looked far younger than her thirty-six years thanks to the regular taking of the king's blood. The entire royal triad looked like they were gorgeous mid-twenty-somethings, but there was zero question that the queen was one pissed-off momma. "Let's go home. We'll talk there. Now."

Lee's face turned sullen and he shoved his body off the chair, turning and walking down the hall without another look back.

It was hard to be the only human in a family of supernaturals. His biological father was a faery prince, his other dad a vampire king. His mother and sister were companions, not the strongest of creatures but so rare and prized that they were honored everywhere they went. And his twin brother had gotten their dad's Green Man powers.

I worried it would only get worse as he grew up. What would be waiting for Lee? He would age in a way the rest of them wouldn't. He would watch everyone around him stay gloriously young and beautiful and he would be human.

"I know I don't have any right to ask you this, but go easy on him," I said as the queen frowned after her son.

She stood watching him stride down the hall and her expression softened. "I never mean to be hard, Kelsey. He's my son and I adore him. I honestly have no idea what to do sometimes. I can't make the other children accept that he's human."

"No, you can't. If you try you'll only isolate him more, but you can support him. I wasn't the world's best student. I got in trouble a lot. I remember how crappy it was to get in trouble at school because some asswipe kid started something, and then I'd go home and get in trouble all over again. I was the kid everyone else picked on. When I stood up for myself they labeled me violent and destructive. My adoptive dad would show up and agree with everything the teachers said. I would sit there and hear about how awful I was. My mom would cry and tell them she would try harder to teach me how to fit in."

The queen's mouth firmed stubbornly. "He doesn't need to fit in. He only needs to be Lee. Have I been going about this all wrong? I've been trying to work with the school. They keep telling me we have to show him a united front."

I bet they had. "Against him? I can imagine that makes him feel alone. Is he wrong to stand up for himself? For the people he loves? That sounds an awful lot like his mom and dads, and yet they're praised for it while he gets punished."

I could see tears hit her eyes and I couldn't imagine how shitty it must be to be a parent. Especially a mom. I bet no one called Donovan in and tried to make him feel bad about his parenting techniques.

"I told him he couldn't hit anyone," Zoey explained.

I shrugged. "So he found a creative solution."

"I hope that little shit still hurts."

That was the queen I knew. "He deserved it. Look, I get that you have a fine line to walk. You don't want to use the fact that you're kind of the be-all, end-all authority figure to all these people, but you're also Lee's mom. He needs to know he doesn't have to fight you, too."

I'd done that for most of my life. I love my mom, but when I was younger I heard a lot about why I couldn't be more like my brothers. Why couldn't I fit in? Why couldn't I be quieter so I didn't irritate my father?

The queen was in a shitty position, but I couldn't care about the politics of the situation. In the end, she really couldn't either. She might be the queen, but she was Lee's mom and that trumped all in my mind.

The queen looked down at me. "So I wouldn't be a horrible queen if I called that little shit's parents and explained the way of the world to them?"

I would love to listen in on that conversation. "Or I could do it."

"Where would be the fun in that? Good luck with Danny, Kelsey. I'll put in a good word for you tonight." She winked my way and then looked back down the hall. "Lee Donovan-Quinn! Let's take this home. We can talk it out over Albert's milkshakes."

I watched as the queen joined her son and took his hand.

"I've been wanting to bare my fangs at a couple of those fuckers for years now." Donovan stood in the doorway to his office, a smile on his face as he watched his wife and kid walk away. "Zoey's worried the other parents at school will accuse me of using my position to keep my kid out of trouble. What the fuck is my position worth if I can't protect my own son?"

I turned to the king, giving him my most positive, please-don't-execute-me smile. "I'm glad I could put you in a good mood, Your Highness. Might I point out that I can be helpful in many ways?"

He sighed. "Inside, Owens. Now. And don't sit on the couch. I just had it cleaned."

Luckily there was a leather chair in front of the king's desk. It wasn't like I was soaking wet. I'd dried out in Trent's truck, for the most part. After he'd put on a pair of way too small for him sweatpants and refused a T-shirt that actually was more like a crop top on him, he'd lectured me all the way back home. Jamie had driven Liv and Casey back, and Trent had kindly pretended to not notice when Casey snuck into the Jeep.

In exchange for him keeping quiet about my peeps, I got to listen to all the ways I'd fucked up. Trent is usually not a big talker, but when he's pissed off, he can seriously get going. He'd marched me right up here and left me sitting outside Donovan's office like a kid waiting to see the principal.

Trent was still here, too. He was sitting in the chair next to mine, still wearing nothing but his capri sweats. I wish I could say he didn't look superhot in them, but he's got a really nice chest. It's all muscled and he's got an eight-pack, though a whole lot of that came from his wolf DNA.

Trent wasn't the only one waiting for me.

"Kelsey, it's good of you to join us." Marcus Vorenus was wearing his customary tailored suit and polished dress shoes. My trainer glanced my way, a frown on his incredibly beautiful face. His arms were crossed over his chest as he stood in the back of the room. Behind him was a painting of some kind of wheat field with a forest in the background. Apparently it was a new addition to Donovan's office, and Marcus seemed a bit obsessed with it. Any time we were in this office in the last few weeks, Marcus stared at it as though he couldn't quite look away.

Though now I wished he would study it instead of flashing that disappointed look my way.

"I didn't know you'd gotten home." There had been a time when I would have felt it the moment he'd gotten into the city. He would have called me and put in his lunch order. Sometimes when an academic bonds with a woman he can taste what she eats when they're in close proximity. Marcus loved dark roast coffee and a nice rare steak. He hadn't asked me to eat anything lately, and I wondered if we were losing that connection between us, too.

"I flew in last night, but it was late so I stayed at a hotel. I didn't want to wake you," he said, his voice a low monotone. "Though I should have since perhaps then you wouldn't have had the energy to call a demon to your hand."

"I can explain."

Marcus frowned. "Were you or were you not calling a demon? I received a warning from a local coven two hours ago that a powerful incantation was being worked in the mid-cities area. They were able to use a spell to find the location of the magic. Would you like to guess where it was? Or are you going to give me the same story Mr. Wilcox gave me?"

Trent had told them something other than the truth? Trent was like Captain America.

He turned in his chair. "I explained that I'd driven you out to your old place because you had a neighbor complain about the fire alarm beeping. It can be hard to remember you need to change those batteries. A simple mistake. You don't actually live there anymore. It might be time for you to find some tenants."

He was good, but I feared Marcus would prove better. I looked to the king, who Trent kind of owed an oath of fealty to. He took the king's blood. I didn't want to be the reason he lost his position.

"I asked Trent to take me out there and then I called the demon when I sent him to Home Depot. You know he can get lost in there. I thought I would have enough time."

Trent's eyes rolled. "Damn it, Kelsey."

The king slapped a hand on his desk, the sound jarring. "Stop it, both of you. Trent, I know you're lying, and Kelsey, you couldn't call that demon on your own if you tried. Liv was involved and I would bet Jamie was, too. I won't even fucking mention that little academic's name because if I had proof he was there I would have to punish him severely, and I don't want to do that."

My stomach turned at the thought of getting Casey in serious trouble. If Donovan knew, then Marcus had already talked to Henri and Hugo about the incident. Henri was Casey's mentor. He would have to do something about it because Casey's behavior could blow back on him.

Why didn't I ever think?

Trent sat forward. "Your Highness, you know why she's doing this. It's nothing you wouldn't do if this were your father involved. Tell me you wouldn't have killed the fucker yourself if you'd gotten a hand on him after he murdered Lee Owens?"

"Technically, the demon Nemcox did not murder Mr. Owens," Marcus said in an altogether too reasonable voice. "He did nothing at all to the wolf. He sold a bit of information and took Neil Roberts as payment for tipping off the Council as to the whereabouts of the renegade king."

My heart twisted at his words. There was a reason we hadn't discussed this. I think I knew deep down that Marcus wouldn't see things the way I did. Marcus could be quite the politician at times. I was incapable of being reasonable about this subject. "Nemcox is the reason my father is dead."

"No, Louis Marini is the reason your father is dead," Marcus shot back, irritation flavoring his every word. I could tell he was pissed off because his Italian accent had deepened. "He is the one who fired the shot. He is dead. The queen herself killed him. You should thank her and move on with your life."

This was what we fought about. He couldn't understand why I blamed the demon I'd known as Matthew for my father's death. Apparently, since I'd never actually met my biological dad, I was supposed to shrug off the fact that Stewart/Nemcox had sold out my father to the old Council, and it had led directly to his death. It also didn't matter to my mentor that the same demonic fucker had nearly killed the king several months before. I was supposed to understand that it was all about politics and keeping the peace.

I didn't give a fuck about peace.

That twitch I felt lately was rumbling through my gut. It made me antsy. It made me remember that Marcus and I had slept in separate rooms the last few months. Oh, he claimed it was because I needed my rest, but I could feel him pulling away from me.

Yeah, that made me antsy, too.

"I think I'll keep my appreciation to myself," I replied. "And you know if you're not happy with me, you should feel free to walk out the door. Italy's that way."

I couldn't help it. Lashing out is what I do. Months of therapy had made me aware enough that I felt bad about saying it, but not bad enough to take it back. This is what I do when the beast inside me starts to hate her cage. I get mean and nasty, and if I let it go too long I get violent.

Marcus's jaw firmed and he stared at me. "What do you intend to do if you actually manage to call Nemcox to your hand? He is immortal."

"Everything dies if you cut it up enough, baby," I shot back, well aware of the nasty tone to my voice.

Marcus shook his head as if he couldn't quite believe what I was saying. "And when his family comes for you? Do you expect Lieutenant Sloane to protect you from them? I do not see him here. You are attempting to start a war you cannot win, and you're determined to bring your friends down with you. I will be the one who has to discipline Mr. Lane. I've already reached out to the head of Ms. Carey's coven and she will be dealt with as well."

"I told you they weren't with me," I lied, feeling a bit savage. Marcus was supposed to be my lover, but more and more we found ourselves on opposite sides, our tempers sparking against each other. Simply being with Marcus at one point soothed me, but I couldn't feel it now. What I could feel was something nasty building inside me.

The she-wolf who lived in my soul was restless and angry.

"It was just me and Owens." Trent stood beside me.

It was nice to have one person on my side, even though I didn't completely understand why he was doing it. Trent put a hand on my shoulder and I immediately could breathe again. I could feel his warmth even through the thin fabric of my shirt, and it seemed to work some magic on me.

Marcus's eyes narrowed, looking at the hand touching me, and Trent pulled away. I hated the fact that I immediately stiffened up again.

"I think given our lack of real evidence, we're going to have to forgo the punishment, Marcus. I'll also talk to the coven since we can't be sure Liv was with Kelsey." Donovan watched us all with a grim look on his face. "Owens, please sit down. Trent, I know why you're doing this. Believe me, I truly understand."

Trent's hands fisted at his sides. "You can't possibly."

Donovan's left eyebrow rose as he stared at Trent. "Seriously? You think it's not the same?"

They were having a whole conversation I didn't understand, but I was too busy being wicked hurt over the way Marcus dismissed my feelings.

Donovan put a hand on Trent's shoulder. "Exile is the worst punishment I would ever dole out for this particular crime and I believe I'll prove quite tolerant. Put your mind at ease. Now stop fighting. We're not at war, you and I. I am not your enemy. I'm someone who understands exactly where you are and I will help you."

Trent seemed to breathe a sigh of relief. "I'm sorry, sir."

Donovan shook his head. "No apologies necessary. Now go and put on some damn pants that fit. Keep a fresh set in your car, man. You can't run around naked. This is not the set of *Magic Mike Three*."

Trent's lips curved up. "Yes, sir. And she totally called a hurricane demon thing. You want to punish her? Feed her kale salad for a solid week."

"Hey." There are some things worse than death. "I thought you were on my side."

"I am, Owens," he said with a wink. "But I told you I loved those jeans. Unlike your boyfriend over there, I understand the need for revenge."

He turned and strode out of the office.

Marcus turned to the king. "Vengeance is meaningless in this case. It will only serve to harm my charge and to weaken our position when it comes time to deal with the situation we find ourselves in. Your Highness, this cannot be allowed to continue. You must go to the table with the demons and sign a new contract."

Donovan's eyes darkened. "You've made yourself plain, Marcus. I understand your point of view."

"And yet you do nothing," Marcus replied. "You allow the situation to fester. Have you thought of what a war would do to this plane? It's what you're courting. You're thinking about all-out war with Hell. We vampires might be stronger on the Earth plane, but there are so many more of them. You cannot keep a war between our tribes from the humans. Have you thought of that?"

"I think of everything." Donovan's voice had gone deep.

Marcus kept pushing. "Then think about the fact that since we cannot win a war with the demon plane, what you are actually doing is courting Armageddon. The Heaven plane will have two choices. They will sit back and do nothing or worse, they will take over. If you think the demons can do damage, you've never seen a vengeful angel."

Donovan's eyes narrowed, the tension in the room ratcheting up another notch. "I think I know exactly what kind of damage an angel can do. I've felt it. Marcus, if you're merely here to discuss my shortcomings as a king, you should feel free to leave."

Marcus sighed, his anger seeming to flee. "Daniel, I understand why you're doing this. I understand why she's doing what she's doing, but I can also see that it will not work. Kelsey, I will study Nemcox with you. We must find a way he is breaking our laws and then we can have him punished. Legally, honorably. Your Highness, you must push through your own emotions and do what is best for your people. We depend on you. That is all I will say on the subject. You will make your decision and we will follow. I'm going to my rooms. If either of you needs me, I will be there studying."

He turned but stopped at the sight of the painting. He was still for a moment.

"Marcus?" Donovan's anger seemed to have fled as well, replaced with worry. "Are you all right?"

"It's the painting. It calls to me. The painter was obviously a sorcerer." Marcus seemed to force himself to turn away. "The woman in the painting moves. Very slowly, but she is moving from the forest to the field. I find her…intriguing."

"Wow, I hadn't noticed that." Donovan stared at the painting for a moment. "You're right. A few days ago, she was closer to the tree line. Interesting."

"Like I said, the painter was a sorcerer," Marcus repeated, his voice dull and flat. "The story he wishes to tell will play out over several weeks. The girl in the painting…she feels familiar somehow. It will be interesting to see how she fares."

He never turned back, simply walked away.

And I was left alone with the king.

He sighed and settled back. "What am I going to do with you, Owens?"

"I'm not going to stop. Whatever you're going to do, you should do it." I can be stubborn when I want to, and I usually want to. It's my default position.

But I needed a new plan because I couldn't get Liv in trouble with her coven and I didn't want to get Casey on Marcus's bad side. He wasn't a good liar. He would wilt like a hothouse flower the minute he was questioned, and he wouldn't do well in supernatural jail. Or any jail for that matter.

Donovan groaned, his head falling back. "You're fucking just like him. You know that, right?"

"Like who?"

His head came back up, his eyes on me. "Your father. He could be the bane of my existence at times. You know we got into a fight once. It was so bad, I had to bite his ear off to get him to let go."

"You bit his ear off?" Of all the stories I'd heard about my father, this was one they'd avoided.

Donovan smiled as though remembering good times. "Zack found it and held it on your dad's head until it reconnected. He was a pain in my ass and there was no one else I would rather have watch my most precious blood. I loved your father. I didn't realize how much until he was gone. Marcus cannot understand. He wasn't there."

"I don't know that it would matter," I replied. "Sometimes I think Marcus is too practical to ever truly understand me."

"He understands you far better than you think. Better than you understand yourself. He realizes how quickly your training is progressing and he's not ready to give you up yet. The fact that you're arguing with him at all is proof that your training is moving more quickly than he would like."

I didn't completely understand the training thing. I got that it went past learning how to fight and use weapons. Marcus's presence could soothe me. He could feel when I was upset or frightened. So why couldn't he understand how I felt about the demon whose selfishness had caused my father's death?

Unless…

"He can't feel me at all anymore, can he?" He'd had to ask a coven to locate me. I was emotional this afternoon and I hadn't bothered to cover it up, yet it had been Trent who came after me, not Marcus. Marcus had been waiting here because he hadn't known where I was.

"I don't think it's completely gone yet. I think if the two of you would stop being stubborn, the spark might flare again. You can build the connection, but the fighting doesn't help."

He was slipping away from me. "I love Marcus."

"But you love Grayson Sloane more," Donovan said.

I knew Gray wasn't the king's favorite person, but I couldn't help it. I wasn't going to lie to him about it. "I don't know that I would say more. I need them for different reasons."

But I often felt the distance with Marcus more. Marcus was older than me by a couple of millennia, and I think my emotions often stumped him.

"And that is why Marcus is afraid. He thinks your need for him will fade. It's the way of Hunter and trainer."

"Not always." I'd heard stories of at least one Hunter and her trainer that had worked out. Sometimes I wanted that so badly because being with Marcus seemed like such a happy thing. When Marcus and I were in harmony, the world seemed like a perfect place. He was the kind of man I could count on for everything. Marcus was solid. I just couldn't seem to hold on to him.

"Hunters tend to end up with wolves." Donovan stared at me across his desk. "The she-wolf inside you will seek her wolf mate, and that's a relationship that tends to be for life. When wolves aren't impatient assholes, they tend to find their other half. The bond between two wolves can be something incredible, and I believe you'll find it satisfies the wolf inside you. Tell me something. Have you thought about what will happen after Sloane's contract comes due?"

It wasn't something I liked to think about. I loved Grayson Sloane. I didn't even lie to myself anymore about it. I didn't lie to Marcus. But Gray had a specific expiration date. He was a legacy, and by that I mean his mother sold his soul to the Hell plane before he was even born. She'd been a witch with some natural talent, but her true power had been given to her when she'd agreed to give birth to the child of a lord of Hell. Gray had gotten the shitty end of that stick. He'd received prophecy powers he hadn't wanted and a whole thirty-five years on the Earth plane before he was obliged to go to Hell and serve his father.

I didn't like Papa Sloane much. I liked him even less since earlier this year I'd met the man and watched as he'd gambled his son's life to turn him into a dark prophet. It had worked, but barely, and the incident had almost taken me out, too.

Besides, Papa Sloane had also sired my mortal enemy. Stewart, otherwise known as Nemcox, the asswipe who had killed my dad—no matter what Marcus said—was Gray's half brother.

"I don't know. I can't let Gray go to Hell, but I haven't found a way to stop it yet," I admitted.

"You understand the trouble you'll be in if you're not with Marcus and Gray isn't around."

The trouble with my kind is we need to be grounded. Hunters can turn extremely violent if we're not emotionally attached, and the best way to be emotionally attached is to have intimate relationships. My she-wolf liked to get her freak on in seriously physical ways. Even now, given how Marcus and I were at odds, she was twitching inside me, desperate to get what she needed. I'd ignored her up until now. I had more important things to worry about. Like revenge.

Yeah, my she-wolf liked that, too. She needed blood or sex. Either would do. Lately, I'd been placating her by running with the Dallas pack, but she wouldn't be satisfied with that forever. And if I didn't feed that part of my soul, I feared she would take over, and I wouldn't like how that scenario ended.

"I'll handle it." I said it with way more confidence than I actually felt.

Donovan shook his head. "You won't, and then you'll start taking out civilians and I'll have to put you down. I know you deserve a private life, but if you go too long without, you will literally explode and kill people."

Sometimes it was awesome to be me. "Look, if it all goes south with Marcus, I'll let you parade a bunch of himbos in front of me. I'll pick the least offensive one and ride him to sweet, sweet sanity. Can we agree on that? I won't allow inner horniness to turn me nuclear."

Donovan shook his head, chuckling. "I think we can find a proper way to handle things. I hope you and Marcus can work it out. I think he's worried about losing you."

He didn't seem worried. He seemed preoccupied. He seemed annoyed. Lately, even when we made love, he was somewhere else.

Gray was definitely somewhere else. More and more, I was alone.

"I'll try to handle it." The last thing I wanted to do was end up in some weird sex therapy the king imposed. The therapy I was already in was embarrassing enough. I didn't need more.

"We need to talk about the demon calling."

Well, of course we did. That was why I'd been called to the office in the first place. "He killed my father."

"I agree with you, but it's obviously not working, Kelsey," Donovan said. "Nemcox has got some kind of spell on him. In the last eight months you've managed to call two hell hounds, a succubus, a pissed-off satan—who is suing, by the way—and whatever hail monster came out today."

The succubus had been hard to get rid of, but Jamie had a good time. That incident had taught me I couldn't bleach my eyeballs and some things can't be unseen. I also figured out why all the girls loved big brother.

"Then I need to figure out what mojo he's working and deal with it."

"Do some research and tell me the next time you're going to try." Donovan sat back. "There are plenty of rules governing us, but what's the point of being the king if you can't bend a few?"

Sometimes Donovan wasn't such a bad guy. "I will. You're not worried about what Marcus was talking about? Gray managed to get a message to me."

A single brow rose over Donovan's eyes. "A prophecy?"

I nodded. "Yeah. You know how those go. I'm supposed to convince you to do something that will stop a war blah, blah, blah. You've got two crowns or something and some dude's trying to unite the lower planes. I'm supposed to look out for spawn of some kind."

Donovan sighed and slid a piece of paper and a pen my way. "I fucking hate prophecies. I'll need you to write everything down as well as you can remember it and I'll have some experts take a look at what Sloane said. Dev knows some people who can give us clues as to what it could mean. Spawn? Someone's having a baby and it's going to go bad?"

I shrugged and started writing what I could remember. "No idea. Apparently Heaven also tricked someone and he's going to be pissed about it. But I think I know what he's talking about when he says there will be a war unlike anything this plane has seen before."

Despite my need for vengeance, I also could see Marcus's point. We didn't need a war with Hell kind. I wasn't sure it was something we could win.

Donovan's eyes slid away from me. "I'll deal with it when I have to. For now, lay off the demon calling. It's giving me hell. And we've got other things to worry about."

Other things seemed like a good idea. Lots of other things to worry about. Things other than my sad-sack love life and the demon I couldn't manage to kill. Yeah, I was ready for other things. "Like what?"

"Like murder," Donovan said with a frown. "I got a call from the DPD an hour ago. They've been looking into a series of what they call 'odd crimes.' It's the type of thing Lieutenant Sloane would have handled, but he's gone, so I need you to call your brother and we'll go down and meet with the police department rep and take over the investigation. We'll have to report to Sloane's CO, but they're fairly certain this is one of ours."

It probably made me a bad person that a crazy corpse lightened up my day. I passed Donovan the prophecy as I remembered it. "Let's go."

My life was pretty sucky. I was ready to think about death for a while.

Chapter Three

"So you're the experts?" A big handsome dude with golden brown hair nodded as we exited the SUV.

It was me, Donovan, and Trent, who had changed into his regulation uniform of clingy black T-shirt and jeans that molded against his every muscle. He looked around as though taking in the neighborhood for every possible threat that could come our way. He pretty much did that all the time. It was his job. I bet he was hella fun at a Chuck E. Cheese's.

"I'm Dr. Donovan." The King of all Vampire was dressed down for this meeting. Not that he ever dressed up. He was a casual kind of dude. But he knew how to dress for a part. He was in a pair of khakis that would be hard to get blood out of, a button down shirt, and some glasses he didn't need because his vision was way better than twenty-twenty. "I'm with the University of North Texas. I was told you have a series of murders where the killer has left messages in ancient languages. That's my specialty."

Donovan was actually crazy good with languages, but he tended to need to hear them. According to all reports, the king could go into a country, surround himself with native speakers, and be one of them within a day or two. Non-spoken languages took him a bit more time, but he'd explained along the way that he'd been using his free time to learn some of the more ancient languages from Marcus and Henri. It was a vampire talent that manifested particularly well in academics. Most wolves I knew barely spoke English. Trent was way better with wolfy growls.

"Lieutenant Derek Brighton, DPD," the hottie with golden brown hair said, holding a hand out. He was wearing a suit and his wedding ring, the gold glinting in the late afternoon light. "This is the fourth. I called the Rangers in after the last one, but they said their expert is out of the country. When I called them today, they agreed to send a team in. I was expecting someone named Atwood."

"I'm here!" Jamie yelled as he jogged our way. My brother had changed clothes and looked fresh as a daisy. Not at all like a dude who'd recently helped call a demon. He looked over at Donovan, his head going down. "Your… Hey, Professor Donovan. Good to see you again. And your assistants."

Donovan didn't miss a beat. "Yes, my assistants. This is Trent Wilcox and Kelsey Owens. They're grad students with a vast knowledge of ancient history." He nodded back to the DPD lieutenant. "It's exciting to get out of the lecture hall. We never get called in on murders."

Trent shook his head. "Never, Professor. Just the occasional forgery attempt."

I simply nodded. I'm not good at pretending.

Brighton sighed as he turned toward the house we were standing in front of. It was a lovely suburban home with mature trees and a foreign luxury car in the driveway. It would be the perfect picture of suburban harmony if not for the multitude of cop cars jamming up the road and the distinctly horrified neighbors looking on.

"I'm not going to lie to you," Brighton said. "I'm more than happy to turn this over to the Rangers. That's a brutal scene in there, and something about it feels off to me. I don't know this is something my guys should handle. Let me know what you need from us. The forensics inspector the Rangers sent is already in there. She seemed excited about…well, you'll see. I don't understand body modification. Back when I was a kid, a tat was the height of rebellion. Whatever that dude decided to do, he was angry with his parents. Good luck. We're heading out. Miss Ward is already on the scene. She's told me she'll handle things with the Rangers from here. I'm leaving a DPD contingent to surround the scene in case you have any problems. Call in if you need anything else. And good luck."

The handsome cop strode away, looking super happy to be leaving the scene.

"Sometimes I miss Gray more than anyone can know." Jamie looked up at the house in front of us. "He handled the glad handing with the police and all I had to do was give my opinion and help kill things. With him gone, I've got paperwork to do. It sucks because it's all going to be redacted anyway. Nothing worse than writing a bunch of crap that someone's going to mark through."

"What do you know about this, James?" Donovan asked. "Sorry to call you on your day off. Were you relaxing at home? Watching the game, maybe?"

Jamie sighed. "Yeah, I was watching the game. Whichever one was on, Your Highness." He rolled his eyes my way. "You're a troublemaker, little sis."

"Born and bred," Trent said under his breath. He leaned toward Jamie. "It was the Cowboys. They're playing a preseason game with the Giants. If anyone asks. Now, what are we walking into?"

Jamie put his hands on his hips, his eyes going serious. "We've been tracking a cluster of murders. Three so far. This would be the fourth. The first three victims were all demons, though two were highborn half-bloods. We've had a rise in demons living close to the king in the last decade."

"I think it's more about the Council," Donovan said.

"You are the Council," Trent replied in a big old kiss-ass voice. "They're here to stay close to you, whether they're petitioning you or spying on you, this is all about the king and the power you've brought to Dallas."

"I've brought violence here, too." Donovan stepped up the stairs that led to the porch of the pretty, Tudor-style house ahead of us.

It was a nice neighborhood. One that shouldn't be featured on those murder shows. Still, this one wouldn't be. This particular murder would go unheralded because the DPD knew how to not freak out the public. Despite what Brighton had said about body modification, he knew damn well there was a reason the police weren't working this one. Law enforcement knew when to pull the shades closed and forget what they'd seen. The lieutenant would go back to his life and this case would disappear from the records.

My ex-honey had been the Mulder of the Texas Rangers. It looked like Jamie had taken on the liaison role between the Council and law enforcement. He stepped up, tucking his shirt in as he walked up to the porch.

"I've worked three murders in the last three weeks," Jamie began. "They were all killed in a similar manner."

"The manner being?" Trent asked.

"Complete and utter evisceration, with a side of dinner." Jamie nodded at the cop standing at the door. "By that I mean whatever killed these guys ate a piece of them, too."

"Wolf?" It wasn't that I thought wolves were killers, but they were definitely known to get hungry in the middle of a job.

"Not according to Nicole." He held the door open as the king walked through. "She found saliva on the bite marks, but it doesn't match a wolf. It's part demon, but she hasn't been able to narrow down the species. That means something. Nicole is a specialist. She's seen a lot of supernatural shit."

Nicole had worked with Gray for years. She'd been his CSI and she knew her shit. She could get a spoonful of soup and in a couple of hours discern who and what and why. If she didn't understand what was going on, I was a little scared.

"Do they have anything in common? Besides being demonic and ending up as someone's snack?" I followed behind Jamie. If Nicole was back here, she was likely to be happy to see my big bro. The last time I'd met her, she'd revealed to me that she thought Jamie was a total hottie. I couldn't see it because hey, brother, but he was single and not getting any younger. I was totally up to play matchmaker.

Maybe if Jamie got married and pushed a couple of rugrats my mother's way, she would get off my back. I'd explained to her that Marcus's baby-making days happened like a couple of millennia before, and Gray's babies might come under his legacy, therefore condoms would be used, but she kept at it. I got a couple of texts every week describing what was happening to my aging ovaries.

"Not that I can see." Jamie moved into the living room. "But I haven't delved too deep yet. Four feels like a pattern. I'll start trying to connect them."

The décor was pretty sparse. As far as I could see, the deceased demon had a couple of La-Z-Boys and a massive flat screen TV. The living room was nice and neat, with two sets of controllers left on the table between the chairs. The media stand under the TV contained almost every game console known to man, so we knew he had a hobby and very likely a friend.

Jamie moved through the house, walking down the hallway toward the back. "All three demons are halflings. Two with royal blood. The first victim was what I would call 'known to the Council.'"

"What does that mean?" I asked, following behind Trent and trying not to notice how muscular his back was. Maybe it was because Marcus had been standoffish lately, but it was hard to not see that wolf's masculinity.

Trent stopped, turning and showing off his equally muscular chest because the dude liked to buy too-tight shirts. "It means the demon had either worked for or pleaded a case to the Council. He's in our formal records."

Donovan had stopped as well, turning toward me. "We have two records. The formal and informal. Informally we keep records on absolutely everyone we come into contact with, but those are kept in my office and not the official Council chambers. Even if it's nothing but a name and some documentation. A formal record includes an interview. The first victim had dealings with the Council, serious dealings. I believe he'd come to us for protection. Which we failed at."

"We were still deciding his status when he was killed." Trent turned my way. "And it was less than half a day between his request and demise, so don't bitch at the king. We have to have some time to decide."

"We don't need time. I knew all three of them." Donovan's jaw tightened, making him look like a pissed-off superhero. He was good at that. "They were…if not friends, I would call them allies. They gave me good information and I'm sorry to see them go. If that tells you anything. Someone knows that they were passing me knowledge I could use. That's why I'm here today. I've got a small network of helpful halflings, and it's getting smaller by the day."

That answered a lot of questions. He'd been gathering intel and someone had found out. I was in the middle of a political battle. I'm going to be honest with you here. I don't love politics. I find them nasty and obnoxious, and I know they're necessary. I'm not some impractical girl who thinks everything is love and daisies. Sometimes crappy things happen and there's not a lot I can do about it.

I followed him through the house. The walls were empty, as though the owner had enough money to buy this beautiful place but nothing to truly show off. No family photos hung on the wall. No movie posters or football pennants that bespoke of a man's hobbies.

I nodded toward a DPD officer who rushed down the hall, his skin the tiniest bit green. If he saw me, he didn't acknowledge it. I think he was trying not to throw up.

Trent took a deep whiff and held up a single fist. Our entire party went still. Trent walked ahead of the king, who seemed used to his bodyguard shutting the party down for a nice smell.

He was still for a moment and I watched him, utterly fascinated. I've got a decent sense of smell, but nothing like a purebred wolf.

Werewolves aren't bitten and turned the way you see in movies. If a wolf bites you, you're simply going to die or spend some quality time in the ER. If you see too much, a nice cocktail of antipsychotics tends to help. Trent had been born a wolf, his parents' DNA informing his own. He'd always had these powers, and though he'd never once led a pack, he was all alpha.

I'd never asked him why. It seemed too intimate a conversation to have. From what I knew of Trent's history, he'd had a mate once and she'd died. He went into the Army and then later served under the king.

I had to think that was why he hadn't led his own pack. The king was right about one thing. Wolves tend to mate for life. Some will wait very long times to find the right mate. Some marry young, but it's almost always for life. Trent had lost his mate, and alphas are never single for long. They have to show their prowess by mating and having children. Never more than a few. The most I've ever heard of was three children, and even then it had happened because of Devinshea Quinn's fertility magic.

Trent was an only child, his mate dead, and he would likely spend the rest of his life without a true partner. He would take lovers when he needed to, but his heart and soul had been given already. He would be alone for the rest of his life.

Somehow that made me feel infinitely sad.

"What is it, Trent?" Donovan asked. "Past the humans and decomp. I can smell those. And at least two other demons."

Trent breathed in again, letting the scents wash over him. "Several humans, including one who takes her laundry seriously."

"That would be Nicole," Jamie said with a grin. "She always smells like fabric softener."

Trent closed his eyes and tried again. "But I'm not sure about the demons. One is dead. The decomp is attached to him. Smell again, Your Highness. And Kelsey. Open your senses. Take it in."

I shook my head his way. "I don't smell the way you do. I can follow a trail, but I can't pick out scents. It's all a jumble."

I have heightened senses. I could certainly smell the decomp, but honestly, I couldn't tell how many humans had come and gone and I couldn't say anything more than there were two demons. At some point he'd burnt microwave popcorn. That was a smell that lingered. Other than that, I was clueless.

Trent moved to my side as the king seemed to take him seriously. Donovan went still and breathed in.

"Yes." Donovan's eyes opened and he turned toward the room at the end of the hall. "I see what you're saying. I can smell demon and something else. I don't know what that is. Is it an animal of some kind? And damn, that's a lot of demon blood."

Trent stood behind me. "Close your eyes."

I frowned up at him, turning so he could see my non-amusement. It brought me into close contact with him and reminded me that my sex life had started to resemble a TV show on pause. My inner wolf immediately responded to his scent. Clean and masculine. He'd taken a shower and washed his hair before we'd come here. Not that there was much hair. He kept it high and tight. He also had that sexy half beard a lot of wolves seemed to keep. Some of them go for the full ZZ Top, and then there are wolves like my uncle who shave three times a day and look soft as a baby's butt. Trent probably shaved when he woke up, and then his wolfiness took over again and left him with that perfect scruff that kind of did something for me.

"I told you. I'm not great with the scent thing."

Donovan nodded toward Trent. "Walk her through it. She needs to get better with her senses. She can't always kill everything in her path. I'll take Jamie and go talk to the CSI."

"Or I can talk to the CSI myself and she'll tell me what's going on." I didn't see the need for a lesson.

Donovan shook his head. "Nope. Marcus said you're proving stubborn when it comes to using your full wolf senses, and you won't take a werewolf mentor. Now you've got Trent. Good luck with that. We'll talk about a training schedule when we're done. Come on, Jamie. Give your sister a minute for this particular lesson."

Motherfucker. Damn it. I had been a little stubborn about spending time with Trent, but that had a lot to do with what had happened with the visions back in January. It felt weird to be around Trent. I tried to avoid him, but he was always around the wolves in one way or another. He was either running with them or they were talking about him. The one time I'd run when he wasn't there, they'd talked about how he worked with the king and they couldn't trust him.

It pissed me off. It made me sympathize with him since he was an outsider, and I knew how that felt. I didn't want to feel for Trent. I was damned if I did and damned if I didn't, so I didn't.

It was yet another of Marcus's frustrations when it came to me.

Donovan strode away. Jamie winked my way as he went past, as though everything was a grand and glorious game, and we should simply enjoy playing.

"Close your eyes." Trent used his deep alpha voice on me.

Naturally, my she-wolf complied. Sometimes when I'm around Trent, I can feel her pacing inside me. Sometimes, like now, she stills and a certain peace settles over me. Like she knows she's with her people and she's content. My eyes slid closed. "Fine. Let's get through this."

I felt his big palms cover my shoulders. Warm. He was so warm. "Scent is a multilayered thing. It's never simple. There are always layers. Start with the beginning. What do you smell?"

"You." Because he was too close. Because he was touching me.

He chuckled behind me. "I bet you do. I hope your nose is as bad as you think it is, Kelsey. Tell me about me."

It was obvious he wasn't going away and that my lovely crime scene had gone crappy. So I breathed him in. Most living things smell warm. I know that's a weird word to use, but it's true. There's a warmth to Trent's scent. A heat, as though his blood is hotter, his skin more alive than the others around us. I could smell Donovan, though he'd left. His scent didn't have the same liveliness as Trent's. I would describe it as cool. If I put a color to it, Donovan would be blue. Jamie would be a nice orange. Jamie smelled like home and hearth.

I'm pretty sure my mom still does his laundry. There's this scent of her that lingers.

But Trent was a nice shade of red. The fiery kind. "I can smell the soap you used."

"Describe it to me."

Only a freaking wolf… "It smells soapy." When he growled, I decided to give him what he wanted. I breathed in deeply and tried to think. It's hard to peel apart the layers. I got why he was using himself as the trial. He was close to me, his body against mine, so he was the strongest scent. It washed over me and I tried to let go, to allow instinct to take over. His smell was pleasant, soothing even, as though my body recognized the alpha inside him and knew I was safe. I felt my body relax as his scent worked its way inside. "You smell like the forest."

I could practically feel his satisfaction. "Yes. The soap has a pine base. I like it. It's not too frilly. Go deeper. What else do you smell? You can tell a lot about me from my scent."

I took another breath and kept my eyes closed. He was right. It was easier to concentrate on scent without my eyes. It was easier to concentrate on him. "I can smell fabric softener and when you talk, I get the faintest hint of mint, but I think it's covering up something. Did you have a beer before we left? And you didn't offer me one?" That was rude, but he simply chuckled again. I breathed in, opening myself a little more this time. I smelled blood. Not blood really. But it had been there and now it was gone. "I think I can smell where you're healing."

"Very good, Kelsey. That demon roughed me up, but I'm almost healed. The fact that you can smell healing skin means I was right about you. I knew you had better senses than you let on, likely better than you can imagine. Your problem is you spend all your time around those vamps and you never end up testing your senses. If you spent more time with wolves, they would get a workout."

It took all I had not to relax back against him because the truth was he smelled…comfortable. Like a recliner I could sit in and know

I could sleep in for a long time and it would shelter me. I would wake up feeling totally relaxed.

I didn't relax around the wolves. I tried to stay hyperaware because the one time I had let myself go while with the DFW pack when he'd been there, I'd ended up cuddled against Trent and it had been embarrassing for both of us. He'd been twelve kinds of naked and I'd woken up with my head against his heart, my sleep informed by the beat. His arms had been around me and Marcus had been so mad when I got home because he *did* have good senses.

I hadn't done anything. I hadn't kissed Trent, though the impulse had been there.

That wasn't the point here. He was trying to teach me something and it wasn't sexual, though I could smell something earthy and male coming off him I couldn't quite describe. It made my nipples hard and I hoped Trent was enough of a gentleman to not notice.

"So you took a shower. What else should I notice? The lieutenant dude likes coffee and his wife wears a citrus scent. Or he does. But it's faint. I think it's a transfer."

"Very good." Trent's voice rumbled along my ear. "Now go further. Spread your senses out. Smell what I smell. Take a deep breath and dismiss the scents you already know. It's like turning the channel."

I took another breath and tried to do as he said. Turn the channel. I could smell all the things I'd talked about, though now there was a spicy, almost salty smell I got coming from Trent. No idea what that was. I let it go because it clung to him and I'd already catalogued him. I let my senses flow wider.

I could smell the bleach from the bathroom and the place where the owner of the home had tried to hide doggie do. That was the worst. Feces covered with a wretched fake floral scent.

Beyond that I smelled the loamy scent of decomp. That was heavy in the house. Blood. The coppery scent was there but subdued, as though it lost its scent as it aged. It matured to a low-grade metallic smell after a good while.

Trent was right. There had been more than one demon here. I caught the scent of the dead one. Death changes the regular scent, lending a gravity to it. He'd been a bit like Gray. He'd been able to take demonic form without having to possess a human. The victim could walk around and not be questioned when he was in the right form. He would look human, talk human, and when he wanted to go all demonic, he could grow horns and fangs and whatever other parts he'd been born with.

"He was royalty," Trent said, his mouth still close to my ear, as though he was trying to shut out the rest of the world and draw it all down to the two of us and our noses. "Can you tell me why I think that?"

"He had control of his form." Like Gray, whoever this demon had been, he'd had royal blood. Royalty isn't a confirmation that the demon can take human form, but it was a requirement. If the demon could take human form, he had some royal blood. Take Gray and his brother. Gray was a halfling, but he had control of his form. Despite Nemcox's full-on demon status, he could not. Nemcox required a host, hence all those *Exorcist* films.

"Very good. Now tell me what you've missed. Go deeper."

I followed the scent, allowing it to move. I left the body and tried to case the actual scene.

"I don't know what that smell is." It was slightly dirty, a bit rancid. It wasn't the body though. If anything, I would bet I was smelling saliva. "I can't tell because there are too many chemicals."

"That's Nicole at work. I wish we'd gotten here first." Trent breathed deep behind me. I could feel the way his body moved against mine. "There's something else. It's faint."

"The second demon." I could smell him clearly now. Or her. "Is that perfume?"

Trent chuckled behind me. "Yes. And not a particularly expensive one. It's like she's trying to cover her natural pheromones with fake pheromones. Although her pheromones are wow, they are quite strong."

"Eww, they had sex recently. You see, this is why I don't open my damn senses." Some smells should be private between a low-level demon and her royal lover.

He chuckled again. "Sometimes I forget how prissy you can be about sex. You weren't raised with your kind. You've got a very human view of fucking."

I winced and moved away because being that close to him might get my own pheromones going, and I did not want his wolfy senses smelling that. He'd done his job. He'd gotten me to think about the scene with more than my brain. It was way past time to move on.

"We should join the king. I think I get your point."

"Not even close, sweetheart, but you did well." He nodded toward the bedroom, allowing me to go first.

You know it's a sad day when you're relieved to get to the dead body. I strode across the well-done hand-scraped hardwoods. Everything about the place was upgraded, but there was little that seemed personal about it. It didn't feel like a home, more like a way station. I would bet the owner didn't spend the majority of his time here. This was where he came when he was spending time with the Council or other Earth plane friends. Dallas had become the hub of the supernatural world ever since the king took over nine years before. Every kind of supernatural species had an embassy here, and many of the higher-ups kept houses in town.

I walked into the master bedroom and was assaulted by the stench of stale sex, fear, and death. I had to shut my senses down it was so overwhelming. It was nicer to concentrate on the body.

He'd been caught in mid shift, horns barely starting to penetrate his thick brown hair. His skin had begun to turn and still had a slightly reddish tone, despite the fact that death had settled in. He was on his back, his mouth slightly open to show the beginnings of a nasty set of curved fangs. The king was standing over the body and Jamie was talking to a pretty blonde with a laptop in front of her. Nicole had used the top of the dresser to set up an array of weird equipment that would break down the elements of the crime. Nicole would use that equipment to figure out his species and hopefully his clan, to find the mysteries of anything left behind—and there was always something left behind.

I personally was interested in that smell I couldn't define. If Trent wasn't sure about it, then I was interested in it. There weren't many smells in the world Trent hadn't gotten a whiff of. He'd been Special Forces for years, and then undercover for the king. He'd put paws on almost every continent and hunted every creature known to man.

But he didn't know what this was.

"That's a lot of blood." I made sure I didn't step in the congealing pool that coated the carpet around the body.

Nicole looked up from her laptop, a grin on her face. This was like Disneyland for the CSI. "It's not all his. I'm super excited about that. I found some drops of blood near the door. I think Lester here nicked his assailant at some point and the dude bled a little, though it's easy to see who was on the receiving end of this particular fight. But you should understand, it wasn't much of a fight. It was more like a slaughter."

"Why don't you fill the *Nex Apparatus* in on what you've discovered," the king said.

Nicole's ponytail bobbed as she talked. "It's cool to hear you called that. Like you're a superhero or something. Anyway, here's what I've got. Time of death can be super hard with a demon because liver temp tells you nothing. Everything cools quickly and I think we're in the time that I can't use body temp. If I don't take it within about thirty minutes of death, the body hits room temperature and that tells me nothing. But what we do have is a police disturbance at two in the morning last night."

"A disturbance?"

Jamie took over. "Yep. According to the reports, at two in the morning the nearest neighbor saw a flash of light and felt an earthquake. I checked with the ANSS and they did not register a quake at any time in the last twenty-four hours, so it had to be incredibly localized."

North Texas had become a hotbed of minor quakes. Some people blamed fracking; others claimed we'd simply found new fault lines, previously undiscovered. Yeah, that was mostly from the gas companies.

I happened to know that certain demons kind of shook the earth when they departed or were forcibly exorcised from a host body. The effect was localized and most of the Metroplex wouldn't even notice. The rest would probably think there had been a bad crash nearby or the city had blown up a bridge to make way for new traffic patterns.

"So we think the murder occurred around two? Did the police follow up?" I asked.

"DPD drove by, but the neighbor couldn't tell them which house they thought it had happened at. According to the neighbor, it was a bright flash of light through his bedroom window and then he felt the earth shake," Nicole explained. "It doesn't help that the neighbor was absolutely certain it was an attempted alien abduction. The police weren't going to go door to door looking for Reticulan Grays, if you know what I mean."

"I do not." I have enough weird shit in my world. I don't need to know varieties of aliens. "Do we have any citizens in the area?"

"Yes." Trent had his cell phone out, scrolling through a list of all known supernatural creatures. The Council kept meticulous records and they were all probably on Trent's phone. "We have two listings within a mile radius. One is a Larissa Dymone, a halfling. She's in a condo two blocks from here. The other is a werepanther family. Greg and Maria Garcia. We'll also talk to the crazy alien man and see if he remembers anything that didn't come from space."

Sometimes my job is super fun. "Did we have any signs of forced entry?"

I glanced around the room. The bed was rumpled, the sheets askew. The pillows had fallen to the side and one corner of the fitted sheet had come undone. There were two glasses on the side table, a half drank bottle of some kind of wine there, too. Old Lester had been having a nice night it seemed. Right up until his murder.

"Not according to the police. The door was locked," Nicole explained.

"Yeah, but look up there, sis." Jamie was staring up at the wall over the French doors that led into the bedroom. The ceilings were vaulted, going up probably twelve feet high, but I could see the small disk that had been mounted about halfway between the ceiling and doorframe.

"I'm going to need a boost." I could bet what that small circle was, but I needed to see it with my own two eyes. As it looked as though it was untouched, I definitely need to inspect it.

Trent was right by my side in a heartbeat, kneeling down and offering me a lift. He cupped his hands and I slid my boot between them. It was a simple act of Lycan strength that lifted me up and allowed me to grab the ward Lester the royal demon had used in a vain attempt to secure his home.

Trent brought me back down and then it was Donovan at my side, pushing his way in.

"Is that a ward?" Donovan pulled his glasses off, leaning over for a closer inspection.

In our world you can't be too careful. Sure an alarm is awesome when it comes to scaring off the humans, and the high-pitched sounds will rattle most were creatures, but demons will blow right past one. A vampire doesn't care that you have a triple reinforced door with dead bolts. They'll punch right through the sucker. No, if you want to keep out supernatural creatures, magic is the way to go, and witches are your friendly neighborhood security advisors.

"It looks like a standard protection ward." From what I could tell it was your typical keep-out-all-ye-who-would-do-me-harm kind of thing. They were all over Ether and the building that housed the Council. There were wards that protected against violence, wards that made it hard for a person to lie, wards that kept out certain ghosts and revenants, because damn they were hard to get rid of once those suckers dug in. I suspected that this was nothing more than a ward to keep out all the uninvited.

Lester obviously had some serious cash. That meant he would go to a serious witch and the ward should have held.

"It's not broken." I inspected the whole thing. It was completely intact. It was a lovely piece of work, made of what looked like onyx with an opal inlay. The incantation was laid in some kind of a lovely white paint with gold flecks. "Can you read this, professor?"

Donovan didn't take the bait. He simply stared down at the ward. "Most of it's in an archaic form of Latin."

"Isn't all Latin archaic?" Jamie asked.

Nicole chuckled, but looked at Jamie like he was lucky he was hot. "There have been many, many versions of Latin throughout time. Languages evolve. The king is right. I'm pretty sure this is one of the first forms. It would be powerful for use in a spell. And the symbology is interesting. Not that I know a ton about witchcraft, but I think some of these come from a demon language."

"Yes." Donovan ran his hand over the disk. "This part is a combination of old Latin and Demonish. I can't read it entirely. And there's a piece on the back that I don't understand at all. Never seen that language before. I know this should have kept out anyone with bad intentions, but other than that, we're going to need some research."

Luckily, I knew some people.

Chapter Four

An hour later I found myself at the home of one Fred Mitchell Jackson, retired janitor. From what Trent had managed to pull up on him, his wife had died a few years back and they'd had no children. He lived alone in the tiny ranch house that seemed out of place amongst the mini mansions. The size alone made it incongruous. The fact that all the windows were covered in what looked like tinfoil was just a plus.

I bet he was hell on his HOA.

Unfortunately, I needed to talk to the dude because I'd noticed he had security cameras, and one of them was pointed at the street that ran in front of both his and Lester's homes. If there was one security camera, there might be more. It was a long shot, but the king wanted to figure out who was killing his friends and it was sort of my job.

Naturally, though, I wasn't allowed to do it alone.

"Should I ring the doorbell again?" Trent frowned at the door like his sheer will alone could force the thing open.

"Or you could show some patience." Somehow I didn't think that Trent's continuous knocking would work out in the long run. It was more likely to get us peppered with buckshot than a nice long talk with the dude whose whole existence reeked of paranoia.

Then again, crazy Fred also lived next to the demon Hell lord equivalent of Prince Harry, if the number of condoms he went through were any indication of his lifestyle. So Fred kind of had a right to be paranoid.

I smiled at the camera and tried to give him my most harmless look, but my brain was working overtime. "I didn't know demons wore condoms. I kind of thought they were all out to reproduce. Kind of like wolves."

Vamps didn't need condoms. Those swimmers died during the change. The rest of the body still functioned, but sperm didn't survive the transition. Gray had been kind of baby crazy when we were together. Of course, he'd also only had like five years left on the Earth plane before he joined Papa Sloane in Hell. His biological clock had been ticking and hard.

"Lots of wolves wear condoms when they have sex." Trent had gone still, sniffing the air in that way that let me know the sommelier of scents was in the house.

"That's not what I've heard." I rang the bell again and went back to showing the camera that I wasn't any threat at all. "I've heard wolves fuck like bunnies trying to reproduce as fast as they can since they don't actually reproduce the way bunnies do. Hey, why aren't there werebunnies out there?"

It made me sad that almost all the werecreatures were predatory. Sure there were weredeer and some werepigs, but I'd never met a person who turned into a chicken on the full moon. Same with sweet little bunnies.

"Because we ate them all," Trent replied with absolutely no shame tingeing his tone. "Not we, actually, but our forefathers. Apparently they were really tasty."

"That's horrible." His ancestors should be damn glad there hadn't been a werePETA organization back then.

My outrage didn't faze him at all. "And plenty of wolves suit up for sex. I wouldn't want a baby who didn't come from my mate."

"So wolves never have second marriages?" It seemed wrong that he would go through the rest of his life alone.

His eyes came open suddenly and he sent me what seemed like a suspicious stare. "Marriages, yes, true matings, no. A wolf only feels the mating call once in his life and then it's done."

And he'd already had his call. From what I understood, Trent had been just out of high school when he'd mated. He'd married a girl from his home pack and then joined the Army and served in the same unit my father had. There was a whole werewolf unit the government didn't like to talk about.

I had to think Trent's mating howl had shaken the ground.

I'd heard the mating howl once when I was with the Italian wolves. A male called out on a full moon for the female of his heart and she'd answered. It had been moving, in an emotional way. The idea of what Trent had lost made my heart kind of ache.

Sometimes I think my life was easier when I was numb. Before I'd met Gray and then Marcus, I had buried myself in a neat and tidy shell. Oh, sure sometimes my she-wolf scratched her way to the surface and I tried to murder people, but I didn't have all these pesky feelings. I didn't worry that Marcus was falling out of love with me and I wouldn't have given a crap that Trent was lonely. I would have taken another shot of tequila and not cared.

"So you don't think you'll ever have a girlfriend again?" Why was I still standing here? This dude wasn't opening the door. I reached into my bag to pull out a business card and ask him to call me, which he probably wouldn't.

I might have to work some vampy mojo on him to get him to talk. If I could catch him outside, since vampy mojo only works in person.

"Why the sudden interest in my love life, Owens?" Trent closed his eyes again and breathed deep. "He's coming and he's alone. I do smell metal though. Gun oil. Get behind me. Now, Owens."

I could handle a dude with a gun, but Trent was moving in front of me anyway.

"Who are you and what do you want?" The near shouted question came over what must be hidden speakers.

So he had the place wired for sound. Nice. I looked up and around and finally found the speaker. It was camouflaged against the dark bricks of the house. It had a nice sound, too. Very almighty powerful Oz of him.

I could play Dorothy. I waved from behind my muscular bulwark. "Hey, Mr. Jackson! I'm Kelsey Owens, a private investigator looking into the murder that happened across the street. I was wondering if you noticed anything odd last night. Maybe a bright light or a kind of booming sound, like a different plane opened up and spat out an assassin or something?"

I couldn't see Trent's eyes roll, but it was all there in his tone. "Could you try to act professional?"

I was. Mr. Jackson spoke crazy so I was giving it to him in his language. And honestly, he wasn't truly crazy. Some humans see things they can't handle and it breaks them in a way. When your eyes see something that can't reconcile with your version of reality, often you end up warped. I didn't know what had happened to the former janitor, but I was going to treat him with some respect, and that meant leveling with him where I could.

"And if I did see something? Who would believe me anyway?" There was a sorrow behind the bellow now.

"Me. I would believe you, Mr. Jackson. I'm not the cops. I'm something else entirely, and my only goal is to find out the truth of what happened, no matter how odd or surreal that truth turns out to be." I should put that on my business cards.

"And what about that werewolf with you? What's he here to do?" Jackson asked.

I heard a huff of surprise from Trent, but I felt like I'd scored. Yeah, life's so much easier when I don't have to play around. "The wolf's here because no one ever believes I can do a job on my own. There's sexism in the supernatural world, too, you know. It's exhausting and I miss my alone time."

"One day I will show you sexism," Trent muttered.

The door came open and a balding head peeked through. "You can come in, but you should know I got silver bullets. I got all the bullets to deal with your kind."

I doubted that, but I still gave him a sunny smile because I've learned that shoving down my morose side helps with twitchy clients. Like I said, even in my world it sucks to be female. If you don't smile you have resting bitch face and some jerk tells you how much prettier you would be if you would flash him a flirty grin. That's when he gets to see my active bitch face, which is way scarier.

Still, the smile seemed to work on the elderly Mr. Jackson. He let us both into his creepy hoarder house and stepped back, narrowly avoiding a stack of newspapers that looked like they went back to the 1950s. "You say you're looking into what happened to Les?"

"First of all, how exactly do you know about wolves and why would you say I'm one?" Trent was still putting his body between us, though the other dude weighed all of a hundred pounds soaking wet.

"Caught you on camera. Wereanimals' eyes shine a particular way in certain light," Jackson explained. "And I know about wolves because my pappy was a hunter back in the old days. Know about demons, too. Les was one of the decent ones."

"You aren't known to the Council." Trent managed to make that sound like the worst crime imaginable.

Jackson's hand tightened on the rifle he was carrying like it was a security blanket. "You from the Council? I won't go down easy, you know."

I held out a hand. "No one's trying to take you down, Mr. Jackson. I take it you don't hunt like your grandfather?"

He shook his head. "No. Never wanted to. I met my Jane and I wanted a peaceful life. I left it all behind, so the Council's got nothing on me."

"Humans who know about the supernatural world need to be registered," Trent insisted.

It was my turn to roll my eyes. "Don't listen to him. He's a big old Council kiss ass. I, for one, don't feel any need to tell anyone about the fact that you happen to know some crazy supernatural creatures exist. But I do need to know if you heard or saw anything last night. Your friend Lester wasn't some nobody."

Jackson's jaw squared but his shoulders came down. "I know. He was one of the high-ups, but he was a half-blood. They ain't all bad."

Didn't I know it? I nodded his way. "Half-bloods can go one of two ways. I have a royal blood friend and he's one of the best men I've ever met. I know the king. He told me Lester was a friend of his."

He hadn't exactly, but I was willing to slip some soft lies by him. It was all for the greater good.

Jackson seemed to calm a bit. "That's good to know. Les told me he was here to talk to the king about some changes he wanted to make that would help halflings and their families. The good ones."

"What happened last night?" I asked because he was relaxed and calm and seemed ready to answer some questions.

"Come on in. I think it might be easier to show you than to tell you." The hand on the rifle eased up and Jackson drew it over one shoulder. Despite the fact that he was wearing pajama bottoms and a too-big white T-shirt, somehow I got the feeling the rifle was part of his daily wardrobe.

Jackson started to move into what looked like it had been a living room at one point. Now it was something akin to command central. While there was a big old TV and a lounge chair, the rest of the room was made up of what appeared to be folding tables and an array of monitors and laptops, and some electronics I'm not even sure what they were. They looked kind of like repurposed video controllers or something. And there was lots of tinfoil. Lots.

"What the hell is this?" Trent frowned as he looked around, obviously freaked out by the tech.

Now this was one place I could have used Casey. Trent is pretty useless when it comes to technology. "I think this is his security system."

Jackson nodded. "I monitor much of the neighborhood, but I have to be real subtle about it."

"You watch for supernatural creatures?" Trent asked.

"Nah, I don't worry about those. It's the aliens you gotta watch out for," Jackson replied. "I've been in their program since I was a kid. They come every few years, and believe me, that's a probing you don't want. The good news is they don't like to pick us up in populated areas since someone might see, you know."

Okay, so he was proof positive that one could both know the truth about the world and also be super insane. I've seen a lot of crazy shit, but not once had I seen a little green man from outer space. We've got enough inner space to be afraid of, but I wasn't about to argue with the man. If he had some intel, I wanted it.

"I totally get it. So you have hidden cameras all over the place?"

Jackson stopped in front of a bank of monitors. They were all on, all in black and white. I could see one of them was pointed at the front door of our victim. Daniel Donovan was stepping outside into the late afternoon light. He settled his sunglasses over his eyes. Due to the nature of a vampire king, Donovan can daywalk like an academic. He can also fight like a super warrior, play with your mind like a minor magician, and call wolves like an animus vampire. Basically he's got the most powerful talents of all the classes. I'd heard him talk about the fact that he would give a bunch of his powers up if he could taste pizza one more time. Sharing senses is a minor talent of the academics, but one Donovan envied greatly.

Jamie stepped out beside him and the two talked for a moment.

"Do you record off these cameras or are they a live feed only?" Finally Trent was getting into the swing of things.

"I keep all the recordings. It was way harder before digital, though I don't trust digital entirely. But after I filled the guest room with VHS tapes going back twenty years, Jane insisted I go digital. Now I have a lot of hard drives."

All of this was fascinating, but I was starting to feel a tiny bit claustrophobic, and after Trent's earlier smell-a-thon lesson, I was all open to the unique smells coming out of Mr. Jackson's house. Burnt mac and cheese and body odor were not my friends. "Can we see the time in question?"

Jackson went to one of the laptops and threw a feed onto the big screen TV. "It was late, but I knew it wasn't anything like a damn earthquake. At first I thought maybe the insectoids were invading, but then I saw the light. Now see, the insectoids don't like bright light so I knew it wasn't them. When I realized where it was coming from, I figured it was demon oriented. Here it is."

I stared at the screen. It was nothing more than a night shot of the front of the Tudor mini mansion I'd recently been inside. The film was the grainy gray-green that comes with night vision. It appeared all was fine one minute, and the next the whole frame went blindingly white, like someone had thrown a flashbang into it. A searing white light scorched the screen and then was gone like it hadn't happened at all. The shot went right back to normal.

What the hell had happened? The door was closed. Nothing seemed to have moved. Just that shocking white light. "How did it feel to you?"

Jackson paused the tape. "It shook a bit, but that wasn't what struck me. It rattled the windows, but I could feel it. When that light hit, I felt a sickness shoot through me. Like a chill going up my spine, but with something behind it. I didn't shiver. I wanted to throw up. For a second I thought it was the end and then it went away. Just gone. Like it hadn't happened at all."

"Was there a second light?" Trent asked. "If whatever the hell this thing is came in a ball of light, shouldn't it have left the same way? Do you have that on tape, too?"

He pushed a key and the tape moved forward. "There's nothing at all until five minutes later. Let me see if I can find her. Les had a lot of visitors, but I'd never seen this one before. Pretty lady. God only knows what she turns into. I can tell you that she got to his place four hours before the incident and…there it is."

He slowed the tape as the door suddenly slammed opened. A woman rushed outside and then pulled the door closed hard, as though trying to hold something off. She held the doorknob for a moment and then turned and ran. The camera was too far away to get a good shot of her face, but I knew someone who could help me with that.

"Mr. Jackson, I know you like to keep your tapes, but could I have a copy of that one? I need to find that woman. She's the only real witness I have."

The older man's jaw firmed into a mulish line. "And what do I get out of it?"

Trent smiled down at him, a wolfish, predatory grin. "You get me not setting the Council on your ass. How about that?"

He could be rude, but he was also pretty effective. I, on the other hand, liked to keep the lines of communication open. Jackson was crazy, but he saw things. He knew things.

I pulled out my card and handed it to him. "How about I owe you? Do you know what a *Nex Apparatus* is?"

He took the card, his eyes going wide. "You're the *Nex Apparatus*?"

It's always helpful when your nickname roughly translates to death machine. People tend to take me seriously. Well, people who know Latin. The others kind of stare blankly at me until I pull out a sword or something.

"I'll email you a copy. And maybe you'll come help me the next time the Grays show up."

If there was a group of aliens probing the backsides of the citizens of Dallas, it kind of was my sworn duty to stop it. Also, it would be kind of cool to see an alien, but I rather thought I would spend this favor sobering the old guy up. I could do that, too. "Absolutely."

I gave him my email and thanked him.

"Come on, Kelsey," Trent said, starting for the door. "If we hurry we can catch up to the…to Donovan and let him in on what we found."

I noticed on the real-time monitor that the king and Jamie were still talking on the porch. I would have to chide the king for not realizing he was being monitored.

I followed Trent outside, happy that I had a lead, but somewhat terrified by where it might take me. I had a nasty idea in my head of where that light had come from and if I was right, we might all be in trouble.

But I wasn't going to put it out there until I could talk to our witness. I walked out the door and immediately felt better.

"Didn't like being confined, huh?" Trent took a deep breath and stretched his arms out. "That's the wolf in you. That was tight and the smells were all old and dank. Too many of 'em. So much nicer to be outside."

It was. I could feel that part of me ease as I let the breeze caress my skin. I was definitely leaving the windows down while we drove back to Ether. Not that I would hang my head out like Trent would. He didn't even pretend to not like it.

"You did good in there, Owens." He stopped at the edge of the street.

I should have known sending Trent with me was something of a test. "Good. Tell Donovan I don't need a keeper."

He looked back at me. "What fun would that be? Oh, and as to the question you asked me earlier, is it mere curiosity or something else?"

"I asked a question?"

"About wolves and condoms. You should know that some wolves are out to mate with anyone," he said, reaching for his sunglasses. "But there are some who know that their children will be strongest from a true mating. You can call us romantic or whatever, but I personally don't want a child who doesn't come from my fated mate."

Again that well of sorrow seemed to bubble up. I might need a doctor to check my hormone levels. "So you won't ever have a kid?"

He frowned and his hand came out to scratch against his neck, a distinctly wolfy gesture. "Didn't say that. Just said I would wear a condom until the right one lets me in."

"But you were married."

"I was married, sweetheart," he said, starting across the street. "I wasn't mated. Not all the rumors you've heard are true. When I call for my mate, I'm going to make sure she's ready to howl back. It's okay. I can be patient."

I watched him stride away and couldn't help but stare. The man had a great butt. Someday some she-wolf was going to get her hands on that.

I hurried after him, wishing I hadn't opened up the subject at all.

Chapter Five

Marcus stared at the screen, looking over Casey's shoulder, which seemed to make my tech guru super nervous.

But then Casey had always found my trainer incredibly intimidating. Casey turned slightly. "I really need a little more space to work, sir."

Marcus didn't move an inch. "You seem to be working quite well. Continue."

I had to sigh. When I'd walked into Henri's apartment it had been me and Casey, but that had quickly changed. It was a full-on academic party up in here now. Henri was in his lab/morgue playing around with what was left of the demon's body with Nicole. If there was a supernatural procedural on TV, those two would have been stars. After they'd shown up with the body, Marcus and Hugo had strode in with Donovan. They'd been studying the ward I found and trying to figure out exactly what language the back of the ward was written in. And that said something to me. Because Marcus knows all the languages, and I do mean all. Though he mostly speaks in Italian and English, he's studied them all over his two thousand years on the plane.

He was struggling with the ward, and that scared me more than anything.

"Could you not make him nervous, babe?"

Marcus turned to me, his dark eyes narrowing in obvious confusion. "I was not attempting to frighten the boy. Also, he is not a boy. He is a vampire. He can't keep flinching at everything that comes his way."

Unfortunately, Casey was good at flinching. It was one of his hobbies, along with skateboarding and making up bad songs about how hard the afterlife is. Given that he spends most of his time playing Xbox on a 110-foot screen in my apartment's media room, I thought it couldn't be all that bad. However, I desperately needed him to pull that female face off the security cam, clean it up and get me a name, so that meant prying Marcus off his back.

"So you didn't recognize the second language on the ward?" I moved back to the dining room where the ward was sitting in the middle of the table waiting for Liv to show up with her coven leader. I had high hopes that Emily would know something about the damn thing.

He sighed, a sure sign that I wasn't fooling him, but he followed along anyway. "I told you, it did not look familiar to me. One of the symbols on the front of the disc reminds me of an older version of Demonish, but other than that I'm at a loss. The Latin is nothing more than a simple warding spell. The material it's made from is unfamiliar to me as well, though the actual drawings remind me of something medieval. It's something about the lines and the type of calligraphy."

I stared at it for a moment. "Do you think that's gold in the ink? Like the monks used to copy books?"

"Perhaps," he allowed. "Perhaps it's something else. The elements are a bit different from plane to plane."

The door to the hospital wing of Henri's apartment opened and he stepped out, a light in his eyes. Henri Jacobs was a vampire who turned back in some century when there were palaces and everyone rode around in carriages. I forget. But he's Dutch. I also forget what country that's from. When I try to look up Dutchland, Marcus shakes his head and starts spewing venom about the American public education system.

Henri is one of three academics who form the team that aids in my missions. Marcus is my trainer. Henri is the specialist in medicine. And Hugo has forgotten more about law than most people ever know. If you ever get stuck in a demon contract, you want Hugo Wells on your side. And if you ever get bitten by some exotic wereanimal or get murdered by one and need a good medical examiner to autopsy you, well, you probably don't care. But Henri's the best.

"You found something?" Marcus asked.

"Something interesting," Henri replied. "Nicole is taking samples now, but I'm fairly certain that the saliva we found in the wounds is reptilian. There are only a few lounges across the world. They should be fairly easy to track."

"Lounges?" I had to ask.

Marcus adjusted his jacket, settling it back to perfection. "It's what a pack of lizards is called, though few actual lizards live together. They tend to be solitary creatures. Only about twenty of the six thousand known species alive coexist in such a fashion. Wereanimals group together for protection."

"A lounge of lizards." Science really did have a sense of humor. "Why am I seeing their base all lined in purple velvet with Frank Sinatra playing in the background?"

"Because you are a silly girl," Marcus shot back, but his lips curled up briefly before he turned back to Henri. "Do you know what kind of reptile? Are you certain it's a lizard and not a snake?"

Henri pulled off his rubber gloves, disposing of them in the trash bin near the door to the hospital wing. "Positively. They have different markers. Nicole is going to work on the DNA to narrow it down to one species."

"Are the bites what killed him?" I asked.

"Well, they didn't do him any favors," Henri said with a wink my way.

"Henri," Marcus admonished. "You've spent too much time with the young ones."

Henri shrugged. "They're quite fun, this generation. And no, the bites aren't the cause of death. The victim was a royal of high birth. Despite his halfling status, he could have survived much worse. No, I believe I've found the ultimate cause of his death. It was silver to the heart. Someone used a silver sword to pierce his heart."

"How many lizard men carry around silver swords?" It got me thinking. "How the hell would he carry it? No opposable thumbs. He would have to have gained entry, put the sword somewhere, changed to his lizard form, bitten the hell out of the victim, changed back, and then killed him with the sword."

Marcus shook his head. "The most probable theory is he killed the victim with the sword and then changed and bit him."

Henri waved that idea off. "Not at all. The bites and blood patterns indicate that the demon was alive when he fought with the lizard. We have claws marks as well. I believe you are actually looking for two perpetrators. The lizard creature would have been used to soften up the demon. As I said before, he's from a royal line and was bred for strength. He would have been quite hard to take down with a simple sword or knife. Even pushing through his demon flesh would have taken an enormous amount of strength. And pure silver swords are extremely difficult to find."

Marcus turned to me.

I held my hands up because I knew that look. "Gladys is safely in the armory. I used her today when I…polished her. She was locked up nice and tight, so if someone stole her, they put her back and cleaned her up."

"I'll have Devinshea check the security logs," Marcus assured me. "But there are more swords out there than merely the *Nex Apparatus's*, though yours would be the most powerful. You need to keep a close eye on it."

"I'll get back to you when I know more about the lizard species," Henri said. "Once we have that we can pinpoint the lounge he came from."

"And then we lure him out with martinis and swing music." I couldn't help myself. A murder of crows is cool. A pack of wolves. Even a gaggle of geese is kind of cute. A lounge of lizards sounds like something I made up.

"Are you paying any attention at this point?" Marcus's harsh tone pulled me from my thoughts.

"Of course. Gotta pinpoint that lounge of lizards. Find the one with the sword and take him down." Although… "Or we find the chick Les was partying with and see if she's got a sword on her."

"Yes." Marcus agreed with me, though he was still frowning my way. "That is much more probable. We must also figure out how the lizard was able to enter the home. The light the neighbors saw was a vehicle of sorts."

"A vehicle?" I asked.

Marcus nodded. "Yes, I believe the light and sound was a form of spell the perpetrators used to travel and to get around the warding. The woman running from the house must have seen something. Perhaps she was a part of it. If you can take the woman in alive, that would be for the best. I definitely would like to understand why someone is killing halflings. Henri, are you going to be able to inspect the other bodies?"

Henri shook his head. "They're already soup. Demons, even halflings, decompose over the course of a few days. Nicole took some samples where she could. One was found far too late. The only reason we knew it was a murder was the registration at the hotel. It pinged one of the king's systems. The hotel manager called the police so he could sue the guest for leaving such a massive mess. The EPA was about to be called in."

And the truth was the "guest" hadn't left at all. "Eww, demon soup. Yuck. What about the second guy?"

"The police called the Rangers in but by the time they got to the morgue, well, demon tissue reacts differently than human tissue. They'd put him in the refrigerator and without blood flow, that will actually accelerate demon decomp," Henri explained.

Dallas PD. They were almost certainly happy to hand off this whole mess to us. I would hate to have been the dude who had to do the paperwork on why a fresh corpse had turned into soup on the nice and chilly slab.

"All righty then. This is up to me." I was the sheriff, after all. I often wished someone would buy me a shiny gold star. No luck so far. "Henri, send the file to my office where it will sit on my desk until you come down and give it all to me in real live human language." I remembered then that something terrible was happening in my office. "Nix that. Make it the apartment. My assistant went all heart healthy on me. I've sworn not to walk in that place again until he's tossed out all the kale."

Why my vamp assistant decided to give a flip about the fact that my cholesterol was up was way beyond me.

Henri promised to meet up later and then disappeared back into the hospital.

Marcus put a hand on my elbow and led me down the hallway. "I need you to understand how serious this is. We've had a royal demon killed in a particularly brutal fashion right here in the Council's city."

"I understand, but it's not like they can blame Donovan," I replied, trying to keep up. "He doesn't tend to eat people."

"Ah, but the powers that be can find any excuse at this point to force the king into a difficult position." Marcus ushered me into Henri's masculine, super old-world office, with its ornate desk and wall full of books I would never read.

"Because of the fact that he won't meet with them?" I watched as Marcus paced the floor behind the desk.

"Yes, this is exactly the problem. The king refuses to do his duty by not meeting with the demons."

I tried not to think about it too much, but there was a day of reckoning coming and I wasn't sure what the king planned to do. Gray had made that plain to me earlier in the day. The only thing that was absolutely certain was if there were no contracts in place to tell the demons what they could and couldn't do, they would likely go a little crazy. It had been millennia since humans had to deal with demons gone wild. I got it. The king blamed a demon for my father's death, and more importantly for the queen's forced marriage to the shitty vampire who used to head the Council. But Marini was dead, killed by the kick-ass queen who hadn't been at all happy about the nonconsensual marriage, and a rapey one at that, and now the only one he could really blame was the same asswipe I was intent on murdering. "Would he sign a deal if he knew Nemcox was dead?"

A long sigh came from Marcus. "I don't know. I believe at this point he blames all demons, though at least lately I've gotten him to talk to some halflings. I've met with a few royal halflings in an attempt to find someone who can speak sense to the king."

"So you called on some friends?"

"No, *bella*. I called on Grayson and had him put me in touch with some people he thought could be helpful. One of them is our deceased. Your Mr. Sloane has been helpful when it comes to attempting to bridge the gap between the Council and demonkind."

He'd called Gray? Marcus hated Gray. "Why didn't you tell me you were talking to him?"

"You show no interest in politics and that is all we were discussing. I have to make certain I do everything I can in order to maintain the balance here on this plane. You have no idea how important it is. I'll work with anyone to avoid what could happen. Besides, Sloane and I do have a few things in common."

Me, mostly, though before I came around Marcus and Gray had actually worked together. Marcus had been Gray's contact with the Council when it came to his Ranger work. Something about Marcus's gravity, however, made me focus on the nonpersonal things he was saying. "What do you mean, what could happen? Are you talking about all-out warfare?"

It was what kept me up at night. I could handle the skirmishes we dealt with now, but I feared a world where demons routinely went after humans. It threatened us all.

"I'm talking about something far worse. I'm talking about another faction getting involved, one that has stayed out of the situation for millennia because we've had deals in place, because we've handled things here."

"Another faction?" Somehow I didn't see the Fae jumping into this particular fray. I've been told there are lots of other planes of existence, but they would likely lock down in case of Armageddon.

"Heaven, *bella*." He spoke the words quietly, as though he didn't want to be overheard.

"Are you talking about angels? I'm supposed to be afraid of white winged angels over a bunch of vamps and demons?"

He chuckled, but it wasn't an amused sound. "Oh, my darling girl. You should fear angels over everything you've ever seen. You haven't seen power until you've faced one. You haven't seen pure power until one turns on you. I fear Heaven far more than Hell. Hell has never destroyed the world before. Heaven is quite proficient at it."

"Are you telling me the biblical, washed-away-Noah thing was real?" I've seen a lot of crazy shit, but somehow the idea of one being having that much power scared me more than anything.

"If you had met an angel, you wouldn't question that Heaven can destroy that which it finds unacceptable. I worry if the king does not handle the demons, Heaven will step in and then we're all in trouble."

"Have you talked to the king about this? Does he understand what kind of threat the angels pose?"

"Since one nearly incinerated him with a mere sweep of his wings a few years ago, I can assure you that the king understands the threat."

I had to take a long breath. Somewhere in the back of my head I did understand angels were real. I'd been forced to take a class taught by Devinshea Quinn on how to identify supernatural creatures. He'd told me I would know the angel by the glowy attraction I felt and that I should understand that if he or she wanted me dead, I would be smiling when I went.

But having to really think about the fact that there was a whole plane full of them and a dude who created and destroyed at will was something else.

"All right, then, why are you so against me killing Nemcox?" It didn't make sense. "I kill him, maybe Donovan is satisfied. He won't have had a hand in it so he's clean on the demon side. I'll admit what I've done and they can come after me if they like."

"And they will kill you," Marcus hissed between clenched teeth. Fangs was a better word. I could see them poking out. He was emotional and I'd done this to him.

"They'll try." I wished he would understand or at least attempt to. Sometimes I think Marcus has seen far too much of the world to be able to truly live in it. "Look, I'm sorry you're mad at me, but I can't let it go. Well, I can for now because I need to figure out why we're losing demon allies. You're right. This should come first, but you need to think about the fact that Nemcox might be the key to turning this thing around."

"You mean you could be the sacrificial goat." Marcus frowned down at me. "Do you hate your life so much you're willing to die to get out of it? Do you honestly believe this is what your father would want? I knew Lee Owens. He was a good man. He would not wish his only child to die in a vain effort to avenge his death."

He couldn't possibly understand. "He was my father. I never got the chance to know him because of Nemcox. You honestly expect me to let it go? You think I can live knowing that asshole is walking around in the world?"

Marcus went a shade of red I'd never seen him go before. His hands came up as though he couldn't stand the thought of unintentionally touching me. "Nemcox didn't kill your father. He didn't negotiate to kill your father. Nemcox chose to give up the queen in order to secure his mate. Mr. Owens chose to stand his ground."

He was pushing my every button. Like it was my father's fault he died. "He was the queen's guard. Of course he stood his ground."

"Louis was never going to kill the queen," Marcus insisted.

"Louis wanted her too much and everyone knew it. Your father believed in death before dishonor. Not even the king stayed behind. Do you understand that? The king left his precious blood behind because he knew Louis wouldn't kill her. I understand that what Zoey had to do to survive was horrible, but she would have lived. She was smart and capable, and her own husband knew to run."

That was news to me. But then…how had I thought Donovan survived? I'd focused so much on my father's fate I hadn't asked for more information. "What do you mean the king ran?"

"Your uncle knew what the protocol was. He got the king out of there and he was smart enough to leave the queen and Devinshea behind. Every single one of them should have run and regrouped later on to save the queen. Do you think we did not have plans? Trent was embedded in the Council. He was there waiting for her. We had our Magician in the Council stronghold waiting for his chance. He would never have allowed Zoey to die."

Tears blurred my eyes and I felt my head shaking. "My father wouldn't let her go because he was her guard. He wasn't going to let her be raped."

Marcus's jaw tightened. "Do you honestly believe the queen wouldn't have spread her legs to save him? Do you think she doesn't feel his death every single day? Your father died because he was too stubborn to run, because deep down he wanted to die and this gave him an excuse. You have the same damn death wish. It kills me. I can see so plainly what will happen to you if you are allowed to go down this path. It's written there in your DNA."

I took a step back, that information washing over me like an ice cold bath. Since I knew I had a dad who wasn't a piece of shit, I'd been told the story that Lee Owens was a hero.

Had my uncle left my dad behind? Why would he have done that? Why would Donovan have run? Somehow I'd always thought they'd gotten cut off. In my mind, Donovan and my uncle had been away from the fight, unable to help at all.

I'd blamed Nemcox for months. Had I been wrong?

No. I knew one thing in life and that was when some asswipe gets your dad horrifically murdered, you deal with it. The same way I expected Jamie to avenge my death if I got gutted and left to bleed.

Except I didn't, I realized. Jamie would die. Jamie was human and even if he wasn't, would I want him to? I loved Jamie. I loved my other brother, Nate. Would I want either one of them to give up their lives to avenge me?

And yet I felt a deep need to understand why he'd died.

Marcus stood there and he seemed so far from me. "You won't stop, will you? You're going to play this out until the end. Is this why you've pulled away from me? Is this why you neglect your training? So it will be easier to sacrifice yourself in the end?"

I was so confused and I didn't want to talk about it anymore. "I don't know. I'm not trying to die here. I just know that Nemcox took something precious from me and I can't let it go."

Marcus stepped back, smoothing out the lapels of his suit. He took a deep breath, as though resolving himself. "We won't solve anything by talking at this point. I'll go and help Hugo. He's going through everything the police had on the other three crimes. It's not much, but we might find something. You should stay with Casey. In the morning, the witches will be here to inspect the ward and we'll know more then."

I reached out to him, my hand catching on his arm. "Marcus, please don't leave like this."

He put a hand on mine. "I'm afraid I'm leaving like this a lot lately." He was quiet for a moment. "I do miss you, *bella*. Work has kept you far from me. Among other things."

Those other things mostly being Nemcox and my stubborn obsession with ending his ass. But I so missed Marcus. The desperate need to be close to him had faded. I'd been told that would happen with time, but the truth is I'd liked how we couldn't seem to be apart in the beginning.

In the beginning, we'd formed a connection like I'd never felt before. His voice could soothe me, but I didn't feel the roll of worry I had from Gray. It was simple with Marcus. When he would touch me I would feel a hum, as though some piece of me settled.

I was beginning to think he spoke to that other part of me. The wolf. He'd had some magical power over her in the beginning and the human part of me had felt that as well. I'd needed Marcus to bring the two of us together, but we were starting to have different desires.

My human soul longed for Gray.

And my wolf…she wanted to howl in the way wolves howl. She wanted a true mate.

Still, I went up on my toes and brushed my lips against Marcus's, warmth heating me through.

His hands came up, catching my arms and holding me still. He deepened the kiss, his tongue demanding entrance. I softened and gave it to him.

It's wrong for me to call us separate. It's the only way I can make someone understand, but you should know that when I talk about my wolf, we're together. She twitches inside me, but she's half of me. When I would be in bed with Gray, the hours ticking by like decadent years, she was there. When she runs and hunts, I am with her. We fought at first, our dual nature forcing us to rip our singular soul to shreds, and only this man has been able to piece us together.

We loved Marcus. We'd needed Marcus.

Soon, we would mourn Marcus, we feared.

But for now, we softened against him, wolf and human still needing his touch but feeling the call of something stronger.

I let my soul mesh together, the way he'd taught me, and I kissed him with my whole being.

"I have…oh, sorry." Casey stood in the doorway, proving a vampire can flush when he wants to.

Marcus sighed and still kissed me again, though this time there was nothing but affection in his touch. "Not at all, Mr. Lane. Kelsey must do her job and I must do mine. Go. Be safe, *bella*."

I nodded, too emotional to give him words. We both felt it. We were coming to an end and it lent a certain sweetness to every kiss.

Every caress. I vowed to stop fighting him. I would take what we were given and then move on with love in my heart for him.

Marcus had given me that.

He reached up, brushing his thumb over my cheek. "Do you know how proud I am of you? I miss you already, *bella*. Don't waste all this beauty and all this strength on vengeance. It isn't what your father would want."

He kissed my forehead and walked away, but not before I saw a sheen of tears in his eyes.

I took a deep breath and forced back my emotions. Yeah, Marcus had taught me how to do that, too. I forced a smile and turned to Casey. "Did you get that face off the tape?"

He nodded. "I did. I thought I'd walk it around and see if anyone knows who she is. I didn't recognize her, though she's pretty hot." Casey sobered a bit, leaning against the desk next to me. "You know, I've had some rough times with lovers, too. You could talk to me about it."

The last thing I was going to do was discuss my love life with Casey, whose deepest relationship seemed to be with his skateboard. "Just get me that name."

"As soon as I can," he promised. "But while you're waiting, you have someone in your office. Justin called and asked you to come down."

I frowned. "Did he say anything else?"

Casey sighed. "Yeah, he threw out the vegan shakes. He restocked your fridge with beer."

Now we were cooking with gas. I got up. It was going to be a long night.

Chapter Six

I strode into my little office, and by little I mean big for any other place. It contained a lobby, a break room, a tiny storage room, and my actual office, that had been decorated to look like the set of some kind of high-end noir film. The king's…I never know what to call Devinshea Quinn. He was the king's partner, the queen's lover. He was almost certainly the king's lover as well. Though he and Donovan eschewed the PDA, the heat between the two was palpable and something I fantasized about on a regular basis. I had to wonder what it would be like to have two men to meet my every need.

Then I thought about the fact that the queen didn't have to do her own laundry and shut that shit down.

Anyway, it had been Quinn who decorated my office. If it had been up to me, this space would consist of a big comfy couch, a fridge full of beer, and not a lot else. It certainly wouldn't be the gorgeous stained glass door I pushed through with its stenciled sign reading *Kelsey Owens: Private Investigator*.

I shared the floor with some of the other Council-approved businesses. This part of Dallas contained two apartment buildings for supernaturals, and this high-rise, which started underground with the club Ether and went up twenty stories to the king's penthouse.

"Boss, you showed up." My Council-approved assistant was sitting at his desk. It did not escape my attention that his workspace was decorated in pure geek. He had several of those Funko Pop figurines cluttering his space, and I won't even talk about the bobbleheads.

Justin Parker was a vampire. I like to call him a Veek. Geek turned vamp. There were tons of them lately.

"Do I have beer here now?" I stopped in front of his desk, putting my hands on my hips and giving him absolutely my most dour stare.

He sighed and sat back. "Yeah. It wasn't me. It was my wife. Angelina works for the doc. She saw your cholesterol numbers and tried to switch up your diet. I know you think it's horrible, but she's a wolf and they all love you."

Angelina Parker was a member of the Dallas pack. She was sweet and funny and weird, which I liked. She was totally up for bucking tradition, which she proved by falling in love with and marrying a vamp. Stupid, stupid friendships. "Fine. I'll try the protein bars, but don't you dare take my freaking beer again. Are we clear?"

Like I said. Life was easier when I didn't care.

A smile slid across Justin's face. "We are, NA."

My eyes rolled of their own accord. "Nope. That makes me sound like I'm doing coke. Don't call me NA or *Nex* or *Apparatus*. Kelsey or Owens. Maybe boss, because that's kind of cool. That's all. Who's in my office?"

A weird, happy smile crossed his face. It was so dopey that it made me wonder if Justin had somehow gotten into my beer. "She's pretty. Like gorgeous."

"Angelina needs help?" Justin was super into his wife. His desk was covered with pictures of her.

He shook his head. "Nah. Angie's out shopping with her sister." He frowned. "Please don't tell my wife. It's not my fault. I can't help how I feel. She's so lovely."

I heard the door behind me open and turned. Felix Day strode in, a serious look on his normally placid face. Felix is my shrink. Well, he's kind of everyone's shrink. He has the office three doors down from mine and beyond his therapeutic practice, he also serves as a sort of advisor to the Council on all things metal health. He was married to one of the most powerful witches in the world, and I'd been told he'd done a little time on the Hell plane.

Still, he didn't usually storm into my office during business hours.

"Kelsey, I need you to wear this." He held out some kind of weird necklace/art project thingee. It was seriously held together by a string I was pretty sure he'd gotten from a craft store.

Maybe the shrink needed help, too. "It's lovely, Felix. Did your daughter make it?"

He shook his head as though trying to figure out what I meant. That was when I realized that he was wearing one of the weird homemade-in-the-absolute-worst-of-ways things, too. He had a big old medallion pinned to his chest and it looked like it was decorated in symbols with some red paint…

"Dude? Is that blood?"

Felix's movie-star worthy jawline tightened. "Put it on, now."

The door to my office opened and a beautiful soft light spilled into the lobby. It was weird because that light seemed like something I could touch and smell and see as a real, tangible thing. That light rolled over me like a blanket, the softest, warmest blanket I'd ever had wrapped around me. I found myself turning and smiling and welcoming that light.

Which turned out to be a chick. A hot, beautiful, amazing chick with honey blonde hair and pillowy lips that I was totally bi-curious about.

Justin stepped up beside me. "See. I'm going to marry her."

"Hello, brother. I thought I felt you close." The stunning blonde walked toward Felix.

She did look a bit like Felix, though he wasn't anywhere near as hot as this woman. They had the same color hair, though hers was long and wavy where Felix's was close cropped. Her skin glowed in a way his never could.

"Brother," a musical voice boomed through the office and the male version of Miss Universe times ten strode into the room. Jesus. There were two of them. This man exuded confidence. I could follow him. My wolf was deep inside, thumping her tail happily because we'd finally found the real alpha.

"Brother." Contestant number three walked in and I could feel the drool starting. He was slightly smaller than the first male, his hair coloring a bit lighter, and if I had to guess I would say he was a few years younger.

Tears rolled down my cheeks because as this man walked in, I realized how beautiful I was. I was precious. Every cell in my body, every drop of blood. I was unique and lovely and precious and so were all the creatures around me. I felt a groundswell of confidence beneath my feet, rolling over me like a wave of faith. Everything was going to be all right. It would be better than all right. I would do all the things I needed to do. I could make things better. Gray was going to come home and Marcus was going to be happy. Marcus would find everything he'd looked for all these years. Trent would have his mate.

I would be his mate.

"Please hold it, Kelsey." Felix was getting into my space and it irritated me. I was happy and he was trying to force his weird crap on me.

"Truly, Felix?" There was a bright sheen of tears in the woman's eyes and I hated that she was crying. She shouldn't cry. "You would ward against us? We were your family."

"I will ward against you when you come into my home on my plane and blind my friends." Felix was saying a bunch of words, but I was lost in an ocean of pure emotion. "What did you come to do, sister? Did you come to talk or to make slaves?"

Felix forced the ward around my neck, and the minute it touched my skin I felt the ocean recede and I was back in the real world.

I took a deep breath and forced myself not to cry because that place I'd been in was beautiful.

And then a cold fear threaded through me because Marcus was right. Angels were far scarier than any demon, and I found myself facing three of them.

* * * *

"Would someone like to explain to me why Heaven needs a PI? And might I suggest another one than myself. There are tons of PIs who don't drink the way I do. Also, serious with the potty mouth." I sat back, trying to make myself look way more confident than I was.

It was thirty minutes later and we'd all settled in. I'd learned that angels enjoyed tea. I don't have any fucking tea and my assistant drinks blood, so I'd been forced to make an emergency call. The queen had been more than happy to show up with her butler and a full-on rolling buffet of tiny treats she called "high tea." I wondered if that meant there was something herbal in the brownies, but she assured me it was a normal thing that rich people, British people, and angels do.

So now I had the queen, her seven-foot halfling butler who made those horns of his work with a tux, Felix, and the Days, who apparently always came in threes, sitting in my office. Well, Albert was kind of standing to the side, but he was totally there.

Justin was out in the lobby trying to find a proper marriage counselor because he was sure Angie would divorce him. He's a sensitive dude.

Felicity Day leaned forward, smiling. Even after she'd thrown the dimmer switch on her angelic mojo, she was still stunningly beautiful. "There is no other private investigator in the world we would rather hire."

"And I've got quite the potty mouth myself, thank you very fucking much." Oliver Day softened his words with a wink.

The queen laughed, sitting back in the chair that had been brought in for her. "He really does. I was shocked when I found out angels could be so foul mouthed."

But she grinned Oliver's way. Once more I felt like there was some story I didn't quite understand. "Are you sure there isn't some alcoholic version of tea?"

"You don't need the alcohol," Jude Day promised me. "Not anymore. You're quite strong enough now. Almost strong enough to break away and be your own woman. You are going to change the way this world works, Kelsey Owens."

He smiled at me like a proud father despite the fact that he looked like a freaking nineteen-year-old kid.

And I felt the edge again. The edge of that cloud of faith he'd brought with him tickled at my mind, whispering that I would be happier if I tore that ward off.

"They can't help themselves." Felix stood behind me. "It could work even better if you place your hand on the ward. Try to keep your skin in contact with it."

"The one you made with blood?" Still trying to deal with that fact.

Felicity shook her head. "You didn't need that, brother. I'm sorry. When we felt you, our souls responded. That's why our presence was pronouncedly stronger. Well, and perhaps we're having a bit of trouble, but that's the reason we're here."

I shoved the ward under my shirt, allowing it to touch my skin. There. That was so much better. I felt so much more like myself and wondered if I would have to walk around with the worst jewelry ever from now on because I wasn't about to allow myself to get caught without it.

The queen smiled my way and lifted her arm. There was a small tattoo on her wrist. "I'll set up a time for you. Dev and I both had them done a few years ago. This one is against angelic presence, and there's one on the small of my back to fight demonic influence. Unfortunately, we haven't figured out how to tat up the wolves. When they change the ink goes away."

A fierce frown crossed Oliver's face. "You did that to your

body?"

If the queen was fazed by that intimidating tone, she didn't show it. She simply picked up a tiny tart. "Sure did. Love ya like family, Ollie, but I can't allow myself to be influenced by Heaven or Hell. I have to serve this plane."

Oliver's face turned a florid red, but Felicity's hand on his seemed to calm the dude a bit.

Yeah, I was so getting that tat ASAP. "What's the problem you seem to be having, Ms. Day?"

Felicity set her teacup down. "We've had some problems with an artifact. An important artifact. You see, we come down to the Earth plane from time to time. We have to watch over our charges, naturally."

Because there really were guardian angels. That freaked me out a little. I need my private time. I wanted to ask them how often they like checked in, and if I could hang a mental sock on my doorway to let them know not to pop in at certain times. "So you come down and hang out at the local Starbucks?"

Jude's lips curled up. "Only if the charge is serious about his or her caffeine. It's important to our kind to keep in touch with the physical plane we watch over, though some of us take it more seriously than others."

Felix hadn't sat down the whole time. The normally peaceful shrink was pacing around the office, not touching a bite of the excellent buffet Albert had managed to put together on the fly. Sometimes I wondered if Albert was like Cinderella and he called birds and shit to help him when he was in a tight spot. Not that a bird helper would stop me from reaching for my third tartlet. What's a little bacteria when those things taste so good?

"He's talking about the fact that sometimes angels fall," Felix said with a frown. "Sometimes we get too attached to our charges and it becomes plain that our time in Heaven is done and we need to learn new things."

"Or that there are sometimes mistakes made," Jude replied. "Not by our maker, of course, but in the assignment of souls. There is nothing higher for a soul to be than angelic. Hence, we call it falling. There are no new things for a truly angelic soul to learn."

So Jude was kind of an asshole.

"That's very narrow-minded of you, brother." Felix turned and looked out into the night.

I'd read about Felix's history, but now I had to wonder about it. Felix Day is one of the few creatures in the world who knows what all three biblical planes are like. He'd been an angel. He allowed himself to be dragged to Hell and tortured because he loved a witch named Sarah. And he knew what it meant to be human because Sarah returned his love and he'd allowed himself to fall.

"And yet it is true." Jude sat back.

I stood up because I had all the answers I needed. Also, I liked Felix. He was patient with me, and that's saying something. So I didn't like anyone making him feel like shit. I clapped my hands together. "Excellent. Angels know everything and are the highest form of being. You totally don't need me. There, I saved you my fee. Thank you for your time."

Three blank faces stared up at me. Apparently angels aren't used to being dismissed.

The queen, however, shot me a brilliant smile. "Well played." She shrugged the Days' way. "Sorry, I'm all team Earth plane. I have the T-shirt and everything. Jude, you need a lesson in Earth plane diplomacy. We don't like being told we're lesser beings."

Jude started to open his mouth, but Felicity put a hand on his. She sat between her "brothers" and it was obvious who the mom of the group was. Jude closed his mouth and relaxed back.

Unfortunately that left Oliver, whose jaw tightened and he stood, pointing my way. "You dare refuse me? I come to ask your aid after everything I've done for this plane and you refuse me? Do you think I don't see the sin inside you? You fornicate with demons and vampires and yet your mind is on the dog. Do you enjoy playing the whore?"

I could feel the room tense around me. Every eye was on me, but

I'd been called worse. Way worse. Some angelic asshole wasn't going to harsh my calm. Now, if he'd tried to take away my tartlets, we would have some issues. "I don't accept money for my whoredom." Although I kind of did. "Well, I guess you could call the apartment payment. So yes, I often enjoy my whoring. Except with the demon. I totally enjoyed that, but there was not a dime between us."

That had been all about love, and I wasn't ashamed.

Despite Felicity's pleadings, Oliver wasn't done with me, and now I could see his skin start to glow. "I can see inside that filthy mind of yours. Even as you long for your demonic beast, even as you spread your legs for that vampire, you want another. It's never enough for you, whore."

Zoey's eyes were wide, but she was perfectly calm as she watched me. "Please tell me who he's talking about, Kelsey. Albert, we're going to need some tequila. Momma wants some gossip."

The queen's calm informed my own. This was how you dealt with a bully. You didn't feed him, didn't let him know he was bugging you. Something felt off about the way Oliver was behaving, and I wasn't going to make it worse by giving in. Not that I wanted to. My sex life was actually pretty cool. I didn't feel any real shame about it. Though I was embarrassed by one aspect.

I wasn't about to out myself for daydreaming about Trent Wilcox. "I do have a weird Chuck Todd fetish. Seriously, Marcus makes me watch all those Sunday morning news shows and the guy just does it for me. When he starts in on polling numbers, I get a little hot."

Oliver opened his mouth, probably to spew more vitriol my way, but he stopped as suddenly as he'd started. His face went pale and he stepped back. "I'm so sorry. I didn't mean to say any of that."

"Really?" The queen kept up her cheery smile, as though she was deeply enjoying the drama. "You didn't apologize when you called *me* a whore." Zoey stepped beside me, giving me a jovial elbow to the side. "He's good with the sexual guilt."

Felix had stopped pacing and looked at his "brother." "What's gone wrong?"

"Well, your brother's kind of an asshole." It seemed obvious to me.

Felix shook his head and closed the distance between himself and Oliver. "He's not like that. Oliver personifies the idea of justice, but when he's properly balanced, that justice is kind and compassionate."

Zoey leaned against my desk, her eyes turning worried. "Felix is right. Ollie's been awesome to deal with since Jude came around. When an angelic triad is properly aligned, they all function with great kindness. They also tend to be humble. Well, Ollie isn't, but Jude seemed to be. What's happening? Please tell me Ollie isn't thinking about falling. I don't have any more unattached friends. I'm not running a dating service, you know."

"It's not like that this time," Felicity explained as she helped Oliver to his seat. "But we have become unbalanced. It's why we're here in the first place. We aren't allowed to work on this plane the way we would in Heaven. We need boots on the ground, so to speak."

"In order to do what?" I didn't want to get enlisted into some sort of heavenly warfare.

Jude came to stand behind Oliver, putting a hand on his shoulder. "To find the Sword of Justice. It was stolen three weeks ago. It's Oliver's and without it, we're all coming unbalanced."

Well, I knew exactly where to look.

The queen was already holding up her hands. "I didn't do it."

We would see about that.

Chapter Seven

I strode back into Henri's apartment two hours later, the queen and Felix Day hard on my heels. I wanted to be alone, but it looked like I wasn't going to get that. I was edgy after the meeting with the angels, like my skin was on a bit too tight.

"How are we going to start?" Zoey asked. "I have some thoughts about the investigation."

That was so not happening. Though I would give her a job. "I think you should stick close to our angelic guests. You know, in case they need anything."

She stopped, putting her hands on her hips and giving me a look that was almost guaranteed to freeze anyone else in their tracks. "They went back to the Heaven plane. Oliver feels better there."

Yeah, I bet he did. I wish I had some otherworldly plane that I could go to.

Unfortunately for the queen, I didn't intimidate easily and I wasn't about to back down. Though I hadn't minded having her in the meeting, had found her quite helpful, I was beginning to resent her interference. Random thoughts ran through my head. The queen had everything. Why should she think she could come in and run roughshod over me, too? She couldn't leave me one place where I got to be queen? It was almost as though all the confidence and love I'd felt when I'd been near Jude had turned into nasty insecurity. "But they could come back and they seem to like you a lot. After all, you're the queen of the supernatural creatures on this plane. Consider yourself an ambassador. Felix, I need everything you know about the Sword of Justice. Unless they blanked your brain when you fell."

Felix was watching me as though trying to figure something out. "They didn't blank my brain. My brain is perfectly fine and I know quite a bit."

I couldn't seem to stay still. I paced the floor, my mind whirling around the possibilities. "Could the sword kill an immortal demon?"

I needed to work.

Marcus walked from the back of the apartment and I immediately went to him.

"*Bella*? The angels unsettled you?" He put his hand on my arm as though trying to take stock of where I was on a soul level. He frowned, his jaw tightening, and I realized I didn't feel the warmth I normally did.

I stepped away from him. It wasn't working. I needed his touch and it didn't work anymore.

Felix stared at us as though he could sense something was wrong. "Of course. It's one of several that can, though none should be found on the Earth plane. The sword that now serves as the weapon of the *Nex Apparatus* has lost much of its power simply by spending so much time on this plane. I don't think stealing it helped the sword's disposition."

"It was stolen?" the queen asked.

She was kind of missing the point. I needed to focus. "Are you trying to tell me Gladys has feelings?"

"Also, how was it stolen?" Zoey wasn't one to let go.

"*Feelings* is such a human term." Felix began to pace like a professor giving a lecture. "The swords we forge in Heaven know their purpose."

"Is that why Gladys soaks in the blood she spills?" It always fascinated me that no matter how much blood I got on the sword, I never had to wipe her down. The blood would be gone in seconds, soaked into the silver until it was shining and clean again.

Felix's lips quirked up slightly. "You know that sword at one point was named the Sword of Light?"

"Gladys fits her better." I wasn't sure I should be the one carrying around a heavenly weapon. I might fit in better on the Hell plane. And yet if anyone thought they were taking Gladys back, they would have to think again. Was that what they'd come here to do? Had the angels come for my sword?

Marcus put his hands on my shoulders, as if trying to force me to be still.

"I'm sure it does," Felix allowed. "I wonder if the sword likes being with a female again after so very long. Tell me something. Does the sword purr in your hand? Do you feel a vibration when you touch it?"

"Yes," Zoey and I said at the same time.

The queen blushed as she started to explain. "I only used the sword once. Danny and I were in a place where he couldn't carry it easily, so I kept it for him until he needed it. I remember how right it felt in my hands. Danny couldn't actually touch it, of course. He had to wear gloves. I always thought it was odd that the *Nex Apparatus's* traditional weapon would be something a vampire couldn't handle without gloves."

I wasn't a vamp so I'd never had that problem. I touched the sword with bare hands all the time. Now that I understood a bit more, I remembered what Gray had told me when he'd been able to contact me through the sword. "It wasn't given to the vampires. It used to be Jacob's."

Felix's brows rose in surprise. "Yes, it belonged to Jacob before he became a prophet. It belonged to him when he was an angel. He was tasked to watch over a certain set of humans. Humans don't know it but they have classes like the vampires. They were created this way to maintain…"

"Balance." Zoey finished the sentence for him with the sigh of a woman who had heard that word far too many times. "It's always about balance. The universe is one big yoga studio to the creator. So Jacob got his sword stolen? Was this before or after he decided to walk the Earth plane, rapping about the future?"

The queen and I got along pretty well despite the fact that she sometimes wore a tiara and seemed to do everything in her life in five-inch heels. She was the perfect girly girl and I was the tomboy, but I'd been told the queen had gotten her hands dirty in her time.

I couldn't take it anymore. I broke away from Marcus's hold. I paced as I listened, the sound of my boots hitting the floor oddly soothing in a way.

When I looked back at Marcus, he had the saddest look on his face.

"When Jacob was chosen to become a prophet, he gave up his sword. He chose to give it to a group of warrior women in the hopes that the sword would help them maintain their independence. It did for a while until they joined with the vampires," Felix explained.

"Ah, companions," Marcus surmised. "This must have happened long before I turned. The weapon was already in our possession at the time, though when I think back, it was wielded by a companion from time to time, usually the one who was married to the head of the Council. At one point in time, our companions fought with us in battles."

"That's why it speaks to me," Zoey whispered. "Damn vamps stole our sword."

"Stole is a strong word," Felix admitted. "I believe the queen at the time gave the sword to her husband with the thought that the vampires would take over security. She was in love and the vampire in question actually thought he was doing the right thing. We all know that eventually vampires enslaved the companions."

"It happened more gradually than you would think," Marcus said as he watched me. He spoke to the room, but I could feel his eyes on me. "When we realized how rare companions were becoming, how hard it was to find one, the decision was made to protect them. Of course, it was selfish and led to all manner of abuse."

"Well, I love Danny, but he would have pried that sword out of my cold, dead hands," Zoey grumbled. "Did my ancestors not understand the words blue and balls? You put them together and your husbands tend to rethink their positions."

Yeah, I liked the queen sometimes. It was why my resentment toward her seemed so out of place. But then my hands had started to shake, so I was all funky. "I'm not a companion. Do you think it speaks to me because I'm female?"

"I suspect that's part of it," Felix replied. "The sword understands blood, DNA in a way. You're unique in the world and I think the sword knows that. You don't use that fact enough."

"Which is likely why it works when she does. She doesn't run around beating people over the head with her power. So tell me, is there any way we can use Gladys to track down the Sword of Justice?" The queen asked the exact question I'd been planning to ask.

Felix sat down. "I have to think on it. I'll request another meeting with my family and run the idea past them. I worry that Gladys has been on the Earth plane for far too long. Marcus, anything historical you can pull about either sword would be helpful."

He bowed his head. "I will endeavor to find all I can."

"I've got something, Kelsey." Casey stood in the doorway. "I've got the picture pulled but it's heavily pixelated, so I'm running it through some software. It will put together a couple of most-likely faces. It studies the geometry to bring about something we might be able to use."

I heard Casey's words, but I felt the space between myself and Marcus. It was as though there was something between us now. Some unnamed wall that kept him from me.

"Do that and let me know when we've got anything close to an ID." I needed someone who had been there, seen what had happened.

We had the witches coming in tomorrow to tell me about the ward. Casey would figure out a way to ID our witness. I would try to locate that missing sword. Because it wasn't coincidence that Heaven had lost a sword and I had demons dying here. No way. No how. "Casey, will you bring Felix up to speed on the case so far? I think the good doc is going to be deputized for this one. Whoever stole that sword is using it to kill highly placed halflings."

"Damn it." Felix sighed, his shoulders slumping. "All right. I need to see everything you have. I'll try to come up with some kind of profile."

I hadn't thought about that. I kind of had a profiler. Felix Day understood how people worked. And when I say people, I really mean creatures of all kinds.

I had a job for the queen, too. "Your Majesty, I need to know everything about the king's upcoming schedule. And I need someone with his ear to the ground. If there are more halflings coming to talk to the king, I want to know, and they need protection."

"I can get that for you. I'll have Albert ask around. He still has some connections to that world. Ether bartenders are an excellent source of information as well," the queen agreed. "But I want in on the stealing it back part. It's been too long. I need practice."

I wasn't sure why the queen needed to practice her thievery. She'd gotten out of the business long ago. "I'm planning on finding out who took it, smashing his or her face in, and then taking the fucker back. No real skill involved."

Zoey frowned. "Wolves. You're all the same, you know. You never appreciate the finer arts."

"They don't, actually." Casey crossed his arms over his chest. "She has no idea how complex this computer program is. She walks in and hands me a blur of a picture and expects the world, but do I get cookies? No. I get yelled at when the state of technology isn't moving fast enough for her."

"You can't eat cookies." Why was everyone up in my grill today?

"That is not the point," Casey replied. "A nice note would be good. Maybe a pat on the back, and not with an ax because I know that's what just went through your head."

It hadn't. Not at all. I hadn't thought of an ax. I'm not a monster. I thought of a punch to the back. That was all. Still, perhaps my management style needed some work. Justin and I were way better since I bought him a bunch of comic book T-shirts and told him to ditch the ties Dev Quinn made him wear. Sometimes a little kindness went a long way. "I promise to listen to your new songs if you give me a name."

His whole face softened. "Really? I've got a whole bunch of new ones. I'll hold you to that."

I've perfected sleeping with my eyes open and I totally was going to make Liv sit in on that concert. And I'd pretty much say anything to get out of there and find some peace. I needed to be in my room, to take a deep breath. I couldn't seem to do that.

I realized suddenly I didn't even want to be with Marcus. How was I going to get rid of him? We lived together. All the problems and issues that would come with a breakup started to shout through my head.

Before I could say anything else, the door to the hospital wing opened and Henri was escorting a patient out. Neil Roberts was accompanied by his husband, Chad Thomas. The dark-haired vamp looked like sin on a stick in dark jeans and a leather jacket. He had a hand on Neil's shoulder.

Zoey's eyes widened, and she rushed over to greet her BFF. From what I've been told, the queen and the werewolf had been friends for years. Neil had been on Zoey's "crew" along with Sarah Day and the queen's now husbands, Donovan and Quinn.

"*Bella*, what is wrong?" Marcus asked as the attention shifted from me.

I shook my head. "I'm fine."

"I can plainly see that you're not."

"Yeah, well, you can't do anything about it so you're pretty much useless to me." The words were out of my mouth before I could call them back. Cruel, mean words that fit the anger in the pit of my stomach, but the minute I saw his face change, I knew I hadn't meant them. "Marcus, I'm so sorry."

He took a long breath and his hand patted my back. "Not at all. It's certainly how I feel these days. Excuse me for a moment, *bella*. I need to make a call."

He stepped away, his cell phone already in hand. I tried to focus on anything except the fact that it felt like my whole world was crumbling around me. I turned and looked at the newcomer to the room, even as I tried to stop my mind from going to dark places.

Neil's hands were wrapped in bandages, his skin a bit pale. Neil Roberts was a werewolf, though unlike most wolves, he was quite fair. His wolf was a gorgeous arctic white with pale blue eyes. "It's nothing, Z. I had an accident. That's all."

Chad frowned his husband's way. "You're going that way, then? Explain this accident to the queen, baby."

Neil's eyes came up, looking straight at me. It was weird, but it was almost like he was afraid of me.

Maybe I was more of a monster than I gave myself credit for. Oddly, there was a piece of me that thrilled at the fear in Roberts's eyes.

"What happened?" Zoey asked again.

"Mr. Roberts burned his hands," Henri said. "It's all right. They will heal."

"They were like this when I woke up this evening," Chad explained. "It's happened a couple of times in the last few weeks. He's losing time again, Zoey."

Oh, then my every instinct was flaring and firing off. Wolves healed. They didn't heal eventually. If Neil had touched a hot pan or accidently fallen into a freaking fire pit or something, he would have healed in moments, not the hours it had been since dusk had fallen. Those hands should be back to perfection, not wrapped up like they were in a delicate state.

"What kind of silver have you been touching, Roberts?"

I would have told you the man couldn't have gone paler, but that was the moment he went a stark white and fainted.

Yeah, I made all the baby wolves faint.

* * * *

"Where did Marcus go?" I'd been waiting for Neil Roberts to come out his fainting spell for over an hour. It was all dramatic and super southern, it seemed to me. Like he was playing out *Gone with the Wind* right before my eyes. His husband had picked him up and laid him out on the nearest couch while Henri and the queen fluttered over him, checking his blood pressure and assuring themselves that he wasn't dying.

I was getting hungry. I couldn't stop pacing. I could feel something rising inside me, but there was nothing to do but carry on.

This was one of those times when I could use a nice make-out session with Marcus. Or a sparring session. Lately he'd been giving me the latter option more and more, and at this point I was fairly certain he wouldn't touch me sexually at all. I'd been mean to him. Hell, I wasn't sure it would work. As soon as I could, I needed to find someone immortal who didn't mind taking and giving a few punches.

Casey shrugged. "He said he was going to talk to the king. He was super irritated. He said something about there was no need for him to be here at all. Except he said it in Italian and under his breath. My Italian's definitely getting better. So is my Dutch. I'm not sure that's a good thing though. Now I understand when they talk about the good old days. Like the Victorian era and stuff. Weird. I need friends who don't remember the black plague."

He wasn't going to find them among the academics, that was for sure.

"He's coming around." The queen was holding a cool rag to Neil's forehead.

"Hey, babe, you okay?" Chad asked.

"Sit up slowly." Henri stood over the wolf, as though waiting to rush him into surgery if needed.

Again, Neil Roberts is a wolf. No surgery usually needed. Sometimes bones that had broken needed a reset. If a wolf got filled up with silver bullets and managed to live, a doctor would have to take them out if the wolf was too weak to dispel them. Other than that, I didn't know any wolves who spent time in a surgical unit unless they worked there.

Neil started to sit up, holding on to Zoey's hand. The way he moved caused his shirt to pull to the side, showing off a swath of what should have been clean skin.

But I saw a very familiar tat.

Werewolves don't have tats. Oh, they can sit in the chair and get one all day, but that first change will leave them with nothing but perfect skin and regrets that they wasted all that time. I'd heard some wolves tried to put a couple of drops of silver in the ink to make the tat stay, but those are the wolves who found themselves super sick and in need of Henri's help.

But it wasn't merely that somehow Roberts had a tat on his chest. Roberts had the same tat as Gray. My honey has this gorgeous dragon tattoo that covers half his chest. It hadn't been that big when we first met. It had grown over the course of our relationship, and the last time I'd seen him, that dragon had somehow responded to me. Gray said the tat had woken up when he'd met me, had become something more than a demon tribal tattoo.

That tat had come from Gray's family. Neil Roberts had been taken by Gray's brother. Yes, the one and only asshat Nemcox was raising his ugly, I-want-to-cut-it-off head again and I could feel my anger rising at the thought of him.

"Where did you get the tat?"

I probably should have moderated my tone, asked the question with a quiet curiosity instead of sounding like a police sergeant who was about to throw someone in jail. I couldn't help myself, and that should have been a big old red flag.

Roberts flushed and pulled his shirt down. His hands were

shaking. "I think I need to go rest. I'm still not feeling well."

"I need to see the tat." I had a horrible suspicion about what was lurking under that shirt. It was easy to put things together when you knew the history. My brain was working overtime, linking events and people together to form a picture I didn't like.

Roberts had been touching silver. Roberts had a connection with Nemcox. What did his tat do? Was it some way of contacting the demon?

The queen stood over her BFF, shaking her head my way. "I think the interview needs to wait."

"No." I wasn't going to give anyone time to hustle the wolf out of here and potentially fuck up my investigation. These people required me to do a job. Hell, Donovan had basically told me that I would be the *Nex Apparatus* or I would be dead. Now they wanted to tell me how to do it. It was okay for me to put my ass on the line as long as I wasn't questioning the queen's friend? They were about to figure out that I didn't play that way.

"Hey, Kelsey, you look a little…uhm…okay, you got the crazy-eyes thing down." Casey was talking and some of it was penetrating my brain.

In that moment, I was fairly certain I didn't have crazy eyes. I had justice eyes. A crime had been committed. It was my job to solve it. No one was getting in my way. "You should go play on your computer, Casey."

I didn't need the peanut gallery hanging around.

"Or you could go and find Marcus." Henri had stood up and he wasn't paying attention to the werewolf anymore. He was watching me, his hands out as though I was the dangerous creature in the room. "Kelsey, perhaps we could sit down and discuss this."

That wasn't going to happen. "The only person I'm sitting with is Roberts there. Come out, little wolf. I'm not going to bite. I want to ask you how you got that tat on your side. You know what that tat is? It's a mark of ownership. Nemcox own you, buddy? I want to know where you've been in the last twenty-four hours."

The queen's face had flushed. "Calm down, Kelsey. I'm not going to let you talk to him that way. He's been through enough."

Oh, but if he'd been doing something wrong, I was going to put him through so much more.

"Your Highness, please back away. In fact, it would be best if you left the room altogether." Felix put himself between me and Roberts. "Kelsey, I need you to push her down. Push her back down for a few moments. Marcus will be back soon and he's going to take care of you. Being around those angels unsettled you. I don't know if you noticed, but at the end of the meeting, your ward fell off. You didn't have it on when Oliver shook your hand. He's unbalanced and now you are, too. It's like a contagion for someone like you. Oliver's illness has called up your inner wolf and she's angry."

"Perhaps if I touch her," Henri began. "I'm an academic. I don't have the same connection she has with Marcus, but I might be able to help."

"I'm not unbalanced." It didn't matter that my hands were shaking and they had been ever since I'd left the angels behind. "I'm going to talk to the wolf whether you like it or not. He's been handling silver. It's the only reason his hands wouldn't have healed. Even then, a couple of hours would have done it. Unless the freaking silver he held came straight from Heaven. What about it, Roberts? How did you spend last night?"

The wolf was shaking his head. "I don't know."

That wasn't an answer I was willing to accept. I was about to explain that to everyone when Chad stepped up and got in my face.

"I'm taking him out of here now," Chad explained. "You'll let me or we're going to have trouble."

I was ready for trouble. I was fairly sure I grinned, the idea of fighting a vamp lifting my spirits high. For the first time in what felt like hours, I went still. "You're not going anywhere."

Chad turned, his shoulders squaring, and I felt the world begin to bend around me. Chad belongs to one of the rarest classes of vampire—the magicians. As far as I knew, he was the only one walking the night at this time. He could form illusions so real you could taste food, feel imaginary rain on your skin, utterly believe whatever he wanted you to believe. I'd come up against him before. I might be one of the only people in the world who could see through him.

"It won't work," I said calmly as reality seemed to go dark and I heard the hissing of snakes all around me. "Do you not remember what happened the last time you pulled this shit on me? It took three tranqs to take me down. I don't think you have those on you today."

"I won't need them." Chad lifted his hand and the world shifted.

"Holy shit," Casey said, climbing up on his desk. "What the fuck is happening?"

Snakes were happening. They were crawling from the woodwork, twitching and hissing my way. The fibers of the carpet beneath my feet lengthened and formed more snakes until they were a menacing mass, threatening everyone in the room.

Well, except for Chad, who had lifted his husband into his arms and prepared to take him away.

I let my wolf loose a bit. She knew this was all an illusion. That primitive part of my brain that Chad was accessing, the lizard brain that merely wanted to survive, was taken over by the wolf inside me. The alpha wolf didn't want mere survival. She wanted to dominate, and that meant seeing past fear, trusting her instincts over what her eyes perceived.

The minute I opened the door, I felt her surge through me.

"I'm not letting you go. I can't. I'm conducting a murder investigation, and I believe your boy here just became my prime suspect." My hands twitched, eager for a fight, and I realized how long it had been since Marcus and I had thrown down.

Too long. Remember that whole thing about needing sex or violence to feed my inner wolf? Well, she was hungry and there was a whole lot of violence in Chad's eyes.

I welcomed it. I could feel the need rise like a wave threatening to engulf me. This was why I had a trainer in the first place.

I gritted my teeth because Chad turned on his power. I could feel those fucking snakes climbing my legs and sinking their fangs into me. I refused to pay any attention to them despite the fact that I ached to rip the fuckers off me and toss them aside. To do that would have given the magician more power. If I bought into it, if I took my eyes off the only thing in the room that was real, I would end up like Casey, who was screaming like a girl.

"Let me pass, Hunter," Chad said.

I stood my ground like the good Gandalf I was. Except I kind of wanted to shove my nonexistent staff right up old Chad's ass, and then we would see if he sent snakes my way again.

The anger rose, rapid and quick, a flash fire coursing through me. I didn't even realize when I had reached for the fireplace poker. All I knew was it was suddenly in my hands and I was going to use it. I could see myself shoving that piece of wrought iron right through his heart. It wouldn't kill him. I would need wood for that, but then again, I didn't want the fight over so quickly.

I raised the poker, ready to start.

"Stop it, both of you." Donovan stepped in between us, but I didn't care at that moment. I hadn't felt this way in forever, not since Marcus had taken me in. I hadn't been so out of control that I didn't care who I hurt as long as I got to hurt someone. I would fuck up Donovan, too. All that mattered was seeing blood, feeling bones crush.

"You see, I told you she's far gone and I can't fix her anymore. I've called Gray and he has an idea of what to do," Marcus was saying.

I wasn't listening.

I started to bring the poker down Donovan's way, but I was stopped in mid swing. A hand held my wrist, an arm going around my middle and hauling me back against muscled flesh.

"Stop it," Trent growled in my ear. "You stand down right this second."

"Mr. Wilcox, she's too far gone," Marcus shouted.

"No, Marcus, let him," Donovan said. "Let him try."

She-wolf did not like that. She didn't want anyone to "try." I brought my boot down on his foot and heard him groan.

"Try to ease her, Trent. She wants a fight. Don't give it to her. Soothe her. Make a connection," Donovan was saying. "You're not dealing with Kelsey. You're dealing with the wolf."

He wasn't dealing with anything at all. I meant to make sure of that. I brought my elbow back and tried to hit him. He dodged, struggling to keep that beefy arm around me.

"Marcus, I don't want to hurt her," Trent shouted.

"The king is wrong. You won't be able to ease her. She's past that now. You can't hurt her when she's in this state, but she can certainly hurt you." Marcus stood to the side, watching us with an almost clinical detachment. "Treat her like the alpha female she is. Show her you're stronger. Take her down and force her to submit. It's what the she-wolf wants."

The darkness was gone, the snakes fleeing as Chad obeyed his king, but my rage kept boiling.

My wolf was pissed that she didn't get what she needed, what she'd been needing for so long. She sure as hell wasn't going to fucking submit.

"Hush, sweetheart." Trent's mouth was against my ear. I could feel the heat of his breath. "Don't fight me. There's no reason to fight."

But there was. I wanted to. That was reason enough. I let myself go still because the wolf in me knew what Trent would do. His wolf didn't want to fight. He liked me deep down. He didn't want to hurt me. He was uncomfortable with the idea.

"See, it's all right now." Trent's grip loosened a bit, his body relaxing behind me. "Let's calm you down and then we'll get a beer and talk this through."

I didn't want to talk. I could feel her raging through me and it felt good. That's the danger of my wolf. When we weren't perfectly integrated, she threatened to take over, and I wanted to let her. There was something freeing about letting her have her way. I didn't have to worry about silly things like humanity. For the wolf who lived inside me, only a few things mattered. Freedom. The hunt. The kill. Fucking. God, I missed fucking so badly and Trent smelled like heaven.

The wolf inside me opened her senses and she liked what she smelled. Trent smelled of pine and male and sex and alpha.

"That's right. It's okay. You don't need a fight," he whispered. "You need a good run. I'll give you that. We'll get in my truck and go up to Denton and run all night."

I practically growled in frustration when Trent let me go. The she-wolf didn't like the alpha telling her to run it off like what I felt was a cramp or something and I should push through. I turned on him, baring my teeth and pushing him back. "Run yourself, puppy. And you can fuck yourself while you're at it."

"You should listen to Marcus. He's right. She's too far gone." Donovan was standing in front of his wife, but seemed otherwise merely interested in the outcome of the event. He wasn't jumping in to save his bodyguard, nor was he trying to hold me down so I wouldn't hurt myself.

"This is what it's like," Marcus said quietly. "There's no treating her gently when she gets to this point."

"Which is precisely why she shouldn't have been allowed to get to this point," Trent replied, even as his eyes were gaining that otherworldly wolfy shine that would normally indicate a full change was coming. "I hope to hell Gray knows what he's doing."

But Trent proved he was as alpha as I'd thought he was. Lesser wolves had to make a complete change, but alphas, both male and female, could change single parts of their bodies. The eyes always changed though. Trent's canines lengthened, his hands becoming wicked claws.

Yeah, that did something for me, too.

I circled around him, itching for the fight to come. He wanted to use those claws on me, I could handle that. Even pain in this situation fed something inside me.

"This is far worse than she would normally be," Felix explained. "It was the angelic influence. I tried to stop it, but she got a dose at the end and it's unbalanced her. She needs to be soothed."

"No, she needs something else and Marcus doesn't feel like he can give it to her," Donovan said quietly.

"I explained it to you," Marcus replied. "I can longer serve her in this function."

Because he'd gotten sick of taking my shit. It's what happened. Gray had left me. Oh, he'd said it was for my own good, but I knew the truth. He'd walked out on me the minute it became hard. I could still see him walking away from me and leaving me to the next guy. Well, the next guy looked like he was done with me, too.

Who would the king pay to fuck me? To give me the affection I needed so much but couldn't quite seem to earn?

"Kelsey, we don't have to do it this way." Trent seemed to be the one who'd drawn the short straw when it came to taking care of me. "Let me take you someplace private."

Where he would undoubtedly try to pull some wolfy mojo to get him out of his "duty." I wasn't about to be anyone's fucking duty.

I swiped out at him, trying to catch him off guard. I needed to get out of this damn room. At some point in time that fucking magician had taken his boyfriend and gotten away. I wasn't going to let that happen.

Trent leaned back, his body graceful as he evaded me with ease.

"She's not going to let you talk her down and she won't want to run, not unless she can kill someone, and that might end up being you," the king was saying. "I told you how this was going to go."

"She's not ready and she'll hate me later." Trent spoke to the king, but his eyes were on me.

I was ready. I was beyond ready. I could smell the magician. He was getting away and he would take my prey with him. Roberts was weak. I could smell that, too. Roberts was weak, and a weak wolf would be easy to put down. I could practically feel my teeth in his neck, severing his jugular, and then he wouldn't be able to kill demons anymore. I would find the stolen sword and I would have done my job.

And then maybe I would take that run. Maybe I would run into the woods and never come out. They would undoubtedly send Trent after me, and we would see who would win that fight once and for all.

It didn't occur to me that it had been little more than an hour before or so that I'd felt perfectly fine. I hadn't felt this kind of rage swell inside me since right before Gray had left. I'd had Marcus, but he had drifted away.

Grief pressed its way up, but I had sweet rage to shove that sucker down. I didn't even fight. I gave in wholeheartedly because wrath was so much more fun than grief.

I threw myself at Trent, not wanting to draw this out longer than need be. I launched myself at him as I felt something hit my back.

"Hold her off for a few seconds more, Mr. Wilcox." Henri was yelling over someone screaming. So loud. Someone was yelling and raging. "I formulated that tranquilizer specifically for her. Hold her off and it should work."

Tranq. He'd tranqed me? Henri was supposed to be my friend. He was supposed to be on my side, but I'd forgotten what I was. I'd forgotten that I was an animal and these people were my keepers.

"Don't cry, baby." Trent held me and I couldn't seem to fight him. Whatever Henri had dosed me with was working way better than anything before.

Trent eased me down to the ground, but had enough compassion to not dump me there. He held me in his arms and I felt him pull the dart out, tossing it away. He smoothed my hair back. "I'll find a way to help you, Kelsey. I don't want it to be this way between us."

I managed to shake my head. "Just keep me out. Put me down."

Feeling this way again put me in a black hole I thought I'd gotten out of a long time ago. I'd been wrong. It wasn't gone. It had been lurking, waiting for the real me to come back out. Poor little Kelsey. She couldn't be sane if she didn't have a man, and no man really wanted her. Yeah, those were the thoughts running through my head as Trent smoothed back my hair. I wasn't sure why, but he kissed my forehead. Sympathy, I guess. Wolves can be extremely affectionate, but I'd gotten his message.

He didn't want this between us.

If I woke up, Donovan would have to let me kill something or send in someone who would only be doing his duty.

"Put me down," I whispered, the drugs making my mind hazy. All this would do was stave off the inevitable.

He hugged me so tight I almost couldn't breathe, and I felt something wet hit my skin. Was I crying? Someone was crying. I didn't want to cry.

"Never." Trent started to rock me. "I told you. I'll figure a way out of this. I'll do it for you."

I started to argue but the darkness was already around me. The last thing I remembered was breathing in his smell and thinking something about him smelling like home.

Stupid me.

Chapter Eight

I woke up to darkness but there was something soft and warm about it. The darkness I'd entered when Henri had taken me down wasn't the one I woke to. I was still on edge, but I could feel a big hand smoothing down my back, a warm mouth at my neck, and this time the scrape of teeth wasn't something to worry about. This time it was something to beg for.

I let my head rest back. Even in the confusion of those first few moments, I knew I was somewhere good. Strangely enough, though I'd been angry at the king before, I knew he would never put me somewhere bad and let me wake like this. The man might have to kill me one day, but he would do it humanely.

And Trent. Trent had promised me.

So I was either safe or I'd gone to the Heaven plane, and in that moment I didn't care which.

I sighed and smiled as the man behind me palmed my breast.

"Relax, Kelsey mine," he whispered in my ear. "I'll have you better in no time at all."

Or I was dreaming and that was all right, too. I reached back to touch my dream lover, and that was when my back spasmed. Hard.

"Easy." Gray forced me onto my belly, and I felt a big hand on the small of my back. "Apparently you went down hard."

But I hadn't. Trent had caught me. He'd been so gentle with me. "It must be where the dart hit. That hurt."

Would I hurt in a dream? That seemed wrong.

I stiffened because there *was* something wrong. I wasn't dreaming. This was real. I could sense it. I'd thought for a moment that Marcus was here, but he wasn't. I sent out that invisible thread that tied us somehow together, but I got nothing back. He wasn't here. He wasn't even close, and I knew Gray wasn't here. He couldn't actually be here with me.

The arms around me tightened. "Hush, I'm using the sword. I told you I could use the sword to contact you. A certain king managed to find me and told me I better deal with your problem or he would have me executed. I think there's a wolf who would love to carry out that particular order."

Gladys. He could contact me through her. I relaxed a bit. The king had certainly found a creative solution. "The king exaggerates. He's not all that into executions."

"I think you'd be surprised," Gray said, rubbing my lower back. "I was worried in the beginning that the king would simply use your power, but I think he's come to care about you."

I groaned at the feeling of those big hands stroking me and getting my tense muscles to relax. "He cared about my dad."

Gray moved his hands down, rubbing, and I felt some sort of spark go through me, a deep warmth that seemed to relax my whole body. "He did, but now he cares about you. I think he considers you a part of his family. Poor Donovan. Never thought he would have to deal with a demon like me. Better?"

"Yes." It came out all breathy and sexy, like I was saying yes to something other than the question he'd asked. Like I was giving him a blanket yes to anything and everything he wanted to do.

I pretty much was.

He rolled me over and snuggled against me, his body warming

mine in a way it never had before. He rested his cheek against mine and put a hand on my chest. "You feel so good. I'm going to beat the shit out of Jacob for not telling me about the unique properties of this piece of silver."

His fingers found my nipples and started to roll them, tweaking them and making my skin come to life.

That brought up another question. "How did I get naked? I mean, you're not actually here, right? We're in some weird sword place. Am I dressed in the real world?"

"Nope. You're naked. I'm definitely naked. I'm here with you. That's all that counts. I can be with you even when we're apart." He traced the shell of my ear with his tongue. "As to your gorgeous nudity, I would hope it was the queen, but suspect it was someone else. I can't be too angry with him. He's trying to help you. Why isn't Marcus here, baby? Not that I mind. I can't tell you how little I mind being here with you like this again."

"Where is here, exactly?" I was confused, but his hands on my skin were working their magic. It felt like my bed. It smelled like I was still in the room I slept in with Marcus, but Gray couldn't be here. "The last thing I remember was fighting with Trent. Henri hit me with a tranquilizer."

He scraped those deliciously curved fangs over my neck. "The way the king explained it, you got a nasty dose of angelic insanity. Jacob explained a bit of it to me. When an angel is unbalanced, he sends out some seriously bad vibes, and you picked them up. You're sensitive to them. Particularly sensitive. They toppled all your carefully placed walls like they were toys, but this is a temporary thing. Once you've fed the beast, so to speak, you'll be back to normal, though I'm going to find that vampire and kick his ass for leaving you vulnerable."

He shifted and I could feel the hard press of his cock against my side.

"Don't be mad at Donovan. I don't think even Marcus quite understood how disconnected we've become. He tried to calm me down, but it didn't work." And right that moment, I didn't care. I knew I should, but something felt so right. When I stopped worrying, when I took a deep breath, everything felt perfect. Like something had shifted and the world finally made sense.

I breathed in, the scent around me familiar and soothing. I didn't try to place it. I let it flow over me, over us, because I could feel my wolf, too. It was one of those odd moments when we were in pure sync. It happened sometimes when we were fighting, and it happened often when we threw down.

Oddly, it had never happened with Gray. Only Marcus had been able to bring us together, to soothe both sides of my fractured soul. Something had changed and I welcomed it heartily.

"Let me kiss you, Kelsey mine. It's been so fucking long."

I turned, but the room was dark and my eyes hadn't adjusted yet. I reached for him, but his hands came out, locking me down as he pressed me into the soft comfort of the mattress. His face loomed over me. Gray was the most masculine man I'd ever seen, with a perfectly square jaw and deep blue eyes. When he got passionate, they turned almost purple. And I'd forgotten about how dominant he could be in the bedroom. He leaned down and brought his mouth to mine. I didn't fight him. Why would I? I needed this. I needed him so badly and he was here somehow. His tongue stroked into my mouth, playing with mine as he made a place for himself between my legs.

I didn't care who had undressed me. I only cared that he was here and I could forget about everything else.

"Reach up and hold the railing of the headboard," Gray ordered, getting to his knees. Even in the low light, I could see his big, muscular chest. He was naked, too, his massive body making my mouth water.

"I want to touch you."

His lips quirked up in a grin that had my heart pounding. "You will, but not until I touch you. I'm not the one who went crazy, baby. I have to make sure you're okay. It's all right. I've been told I can take my time. This won't be like the first time with the Ala demon.

I've got control now. So put your hands up and grip the headboard. Let me take care of you."

I did as he asked because he was an obnoxiously stubborn ass when it came to sex. Of course it always ended in me screaming in pure pleasure, but only after he'd frustrated me in the sweetest way possible.

He stared at me for a moment, his eyes glowing in the darkness. Not in a way that would scare me. It was a low glow, showing me that his demonic self was with us, too. "You are the most beautiful thing I've ever seen. Do you have any idea how much I think about you?"

Probably as much as I thought about him. I couldn't help but ask the question. "Then why don't you come home?"

He placed a hand on my neck, running it down my body as though he could feel my soul through the skin he touched. "Because I thought I would hurt you. I thought I would keep you from what you need."

"You thought that?" I couldn't help but notice he'd used the past tense.

Again, his lips curled up. It was the most I'd seen him smile since the beginning of our relationship. "It's recently been brought to my attention that things aren't always as perfect as they seem. And that sometimes imperfect solutions are the best way."

He leaned over and kissed me again. He kissed my mouth and forehead, my cheeks and nose. He gave me the comforting weight of his body as he moved his way down. This was where I needed to be, chest to chest, limbs tangled up, him all around me. He was so warm. I loved the feel of his scruff against my skin. I hadn't noticed that he had a beard, but I could feel it rasping sweetly. Everywhere it touched me, my skin seemed to come alive.

"I thought you had everything you needed from a man who could truly take care of you, but I've seen the light," he explained. "I understand now and I won't let you down."

My whole body tightened as he kissed my breast, softly at first, but I knew what was coming. I could never forget how long and well this man had loved me. Or how kinky he could be. He licked my nipple right before I felt the fine edge of his teeth. I hissed as he bit down lightly, keeping it on the right edge of pain. That sensation sizzled through my system, made me whimper and want more. I could already feel my body heating, softening and making me ready for him.

"I don't understand."

He moved to my other breast, tormenting it in the same manner. "You don't have to. You only have to believe that everything is going to be all right. I'll be here for you. I'll find a way to make it work. Even after…I'll make it work."

After. I hated that word because I knew what he meant. His contract would be up in a few years and he would be lost to me. He would have to live on the Hell plane with his father, but I'd hoped deep down that becoming the plane's dark prophet would mean something, would buy him time. "Your father is still coming after you?"

He rested his face between my breasts before he started kissing his way down. "He'll always come after me, but this sword works across the planes, Kelsey mine. Even if I'm stuck in Hell, I can find you. I can have some small bit of comfort even if he has you."

He? I wasn't sure who "he" was if he wasn't talking about Marcus, but I didn't have a chance to ask because Gray had moved down my body, and I could feel the heat of his breath on my most feminine of parts.

"I'll share you if it means you get what you need. It's the only way I would ever do it. God, I missed you. I missed your silky skin and the way you feel against me, and damn it all, I missed the way you taste. I would sell my soul for this. Only ever for this." He put his mouth on me.

I was glad I was holding on to the headboard because I needed something to hold on to as he spread my legs and settled in. He didn't hold back. He didn't have any shame. He ate me like I was the best dessert he'd ever had.

"Let it all go, baby. Don't hold anything back on me. You need this. You have no idea how good it feels to know you need me." His words rumbled on my skin, the growl he gave sending tremors through me. "You taste so fucking perfect. I think about how you taste all the time. Better than any meal I've ever had. I want to die with the taste of you in my mouth."

He speared me with his tongue and that was it.

I nearly screamed, so great was the pleasure coursing through me. He licked at me and I went straight over the edge. That was how intense my need was. I hadn't realized how much I'd ached for this.

Something was different. I could feel it, but I wasn't sure what it was. Maybe it was the magic surrounding the sword, but I was calmer. My wolf was happy. She was practically dancing inside me, as though she'd finally gotten everything she'd wished for. She'd always been quiet when Gray was touching me, as though she'd known he was mine, but now she woke up and when we were together, there was nothing in the world better. I was more me in that moment, more at peace than I'd ever been.

I could feel her practically purring, meshing us together and taking the pleasure to greater heights than I'd ever been before. I didn't resent her. I sometimes did because she seemed so much stronger than me at times. But in that moment I realized that she was me and I was her, and we didn't work without the other. It was all right to have this. It was good to have this.

"Please, Gray." I was ready to beg. I needed him. Somehow he'd managed to bridge the two parts of me and I was something new and different. It was more than what Marcus had made me feel. Then I was two parts, both happy with themselves, but in that moment I was one. I was one with the wolf, one with my own soul. One with him.

"Touch me." He was on his knees, between my legs. He stroked his cock. "This is the strongest wolf in the fucking world, I swear. I'm not sure how this is working, but god, it's good. It's so fucking good."

I wasn't sure when he'd started calling his cock a wolf, but I was way too far gone. All I cared about was Gray getting inside me. He'd let me off the leash and I reached for him, eager to get my hands on him and that dragon.

I touched his tattoo and he groaned, pushing my hands back.

"Baby, not today. Oh god, I felt that, too." He sat back on his heels.

"Gray?" What had I done?

"It's fine now. Be gentle with me, baby." He stroked himself again and then he covered me with his body and I felt his cock nudge me. "Take me. Take me now."

He pressed inside me, filling me up and making me squirm in the best possible way. I wrapped my legs around him, holding him tight. I loved the fight. He pressed in and held close. When he pulled back, I tilted my pelvis up, not wanting to lose him for a single second. He fucked me hard, every single thrust bringing me closer and closer to the edge. I lost myself in him, in his touch and smell and the feel of his body driving into mine. I gave as good as I got, holding him and finding the savage rhythm he set.

"Sorry about this, baby. I'm afraid he's quite insistent. We all have our instincts."

I thought he was talking about his cock, about coming too soon, but that wasn't what happened. He leaned over and bit me hard on the shoulder. The pain bloomed and then I went wild as pleasure seemed to flood my veins. I'd never felt anything like it before and I howled like the wolf inside me.

Gray growled and I felt him flood me as he gave in and took everything I was willing to give him.

But I swear, somewhere in that moment, I heard another howl. Somewhere in the distance, a wolf had heard me and returned my call.

Gray dropped down beside me, shifting back to his left side. He stared down at me, his arms still wrapped tight. "Better?"

Better? I was perfect. Still, that wasn't what he was asking. I closed my eyes and breathed in deep, centering myself easily now. "I'm good. Whatever the angelic influence did, it's gone now."

He leaned over and kissed me. "I love you so much, Kelsey

mine."

I reached for his hand, my body still thrumming with postcoital afterglow. "Don't go. I know this sounds stupid, but I have questions. Not about us. It's about an investigation."

Now that my head was clear, the only thing I wanted to do beyond fuck again was deal with what I'd learned. That tattoo was important. The fact that Neil Roberts had the same tat as Gray meant something, and I was currently in bed with the only person in the world who might give me answers.

"Of course it is." He kissed me lightly, his mouth moving over my skin. "Ask away, but I need to go soon. Not because I don't want to be here."

Because the magic was wearing off. This was how my life would be. Fleeting hours of passion. I couldn't work up the will to be bitter. I was too happy to still be in his arms. To have that familiar smell and feel of home around me. I cuddled close because I loved how warm he was. Funny that I didn't remember him being so warm. "I need to ask you about the tat."

I hated that I couldn't feel it here. Something about the sword bringing us together meant the tat on his body didn't respond to me. He didn't want me to touch his left side at all. He hissed and moved away from me when I got close. I'd liked how the dragon would shimmer on his skin and I could feel the vibration of his flesh.

"I've told you about it," he replied. "It appeared on my chest the first time my father took me to the Hell plane. It's grown since then. It's a symbol of my family."

"What would it mean on someone not born into your family?"

He stopped for a moment and then seemed to grasp the severity of my question. He sighed, a heavy sound. "Does Neil Roberts have one?"

I nodded. "He does. I saw it earlier tonight. I think it might have something to do with a case I'm following."

He rested his head down as though he was tired and needed some comfort. "It's a sign of possession. We mark our lovers in this way.

It's tradition."

"You didn't mark me."

"I never would have. Ever, Kelsey. That tat is how my father will pull me into Hell one day. If Roberts has one, then my brother marked him and he can still control him from time to time. If he…I hate betraying him. I know you don't understand."

But I did, in a way. If either of my brothers had turned into an evil son of a bitch, I wouldn't stop loving them. I would stop them from committing atrocities though. "He's your brother."

Gray nodded. "And he's also the one who sold me out to our father. He's the one who led your father to his death. I know all of that and yet I still care about him. Fuck. If Roberts has that tat, you have to treat him like the enemy."

I'd known there was something about it I didn't like. "He's been back on this plane for nine years."

"He's a sleeper. That's how my brother would use him. Roberts might not realize it, but there's no way Nem isn't fucking with him."

I glanced down, trying to get a look at the tat on his side. I didn't try to touch it. Somehow, while the sword's magic was working, it hurt him. "Is it how your father fucks with you?"

"No, it's different for me. I've got my father's blood, so on me it's merely a brand, so to speak. Proof that I belong to him and his house. But it's also a part of me. The reason it responds to you is my love for you. The tat is actually attached to the soul, not the skin. It sees my soul's mate and loves her. It's also why…well, I've been told to let that play out."

"Let what play out?" I was still getting used to him talking in riddles. It was so odd because my Gray, the Texas Ranger, had been so forthcoming. The dark prophet Gray confused me sometimes.

"Let's just say my dragon sees things I don't. He isn't bound by insecurities or social inhibitions. He can ease the way for what should be uncomfortable. Because he knows it's right. The reason the tattoo doesn't go away when Roberts changes is because it's not truly on his skin. It was branded and bonded to his soul."

"So I have to kill him to break the bond." I was sure that would make me persona non grata at the next family dinner.

"Or kill the man who branded him. Incapacitation would work as well. Of course, if…"

"If what?" I wanted anything I could get in order to not have to kill the queen's bestie. It would put her in a shitty mood and then I would be in the doghouse. According to Donovan and Quinn, it wasn't a nice place to be.

"If Roberts remembered the invocation, the actual binding words, he might be able to break the bond, but keep the dragon. The only way to kill the dragon is to kill Roberts. Even then, the dragon would follow his soul. He has to come to peace with it. That's the only way to win. If he can remember the invocation, he can break Nemcox's hold on him. If he can find peace with the dragon, it can't hurt him again. The dragon would belong to him and not Nem."

"He doesn't remember those times. Or so I've been told." It wasn't like I'd ever been allowed to question the wolf. He was too close to the royals and they protected him. They would have to let me handle him now.

"There are always ways around that," Gray said enigmatically. "Those memories live inside him. They might not be reachable by hypnosis, because they're buried deep. If I know my brother, he veiled the memories. He buried them so deep that only a powerful spell could bring them back. They'll be buried in the connection that holds the dragon to the wolf's soul. You'll find it there. It might also be the first step in unbinding Roberts from my brother. I hate this. I love my brother."

"I know you do." And yet he was still talking to me. He was still here with me when he knew what I had to do.

"But I also know him." Gray looked down at me. "I choose you, Kelsey mine. Always you. I thought that would be hard, but it isn't. Being good enough for you…that's the hard part. Risking you is the hard part, but I think it might be easier because I trust him. I don't know why, but I do. Maybe it was how passionate he was about you."

"Marcus?"

"Marcus is gone. Perhaps not today, but his path is set and this is the true reason your bond is broken so early. He won't come back unless you force him. He'll go to find his fate soon." His eyes turned back in his head, leaving me with the eyes of the prophet. "A trick and a trap. You'll solve the mystery and never see the evil coming for you. The world will fold and bend in on itself and you will be left on the wrong side. Years will pass. Your wolf will howl but he will remain steadfast. Hell will come and you will weep, but never leave the path. Hold fast. The magician will rule but you can win. Take back the plane. Don't believe the myth that there can be only one. There is strength in numbers. So much strength in the blood. Don't let them forget. History plays itself out again and again, mothers and fathers giving more than mere advice to their children. They give blood so the story continues. The path is set. Summer is almost here."

Yep. That was my man. "Don't leave the path and buy sunscreen. Got it. The summer stuff, though, has totally been used. Although it was winter is coming. You should watch it. I'm pretty sure that's trademarked, baby. Simply changing up the season isn't very creative."

His eyes were back to blue and he shook his head. "I think I've finally figured this stuff out. My prophecies aren't meant to stop events from occurring. You won't see it until it's happening. But remember the things I've said. They're more like warnings. And Marcus won't leave forever. He'll play his part in the coming months but, my love, that will not include taking care of you."

I did not want to start playing word games with a prophet. "Where will he go?"

A sad smile played at his lips. "I told you."

And that was all I would get. At some time in the future Marcus would leave me to get some sun and there was a path. Nice. I had other things to worry about besides my wayward lover.

I had to deal with the sleeper and hope someone hadn't been waking him up for a little murder spree.

"I love you, Kelsey mine." He leaned over and kissed me.

I wanted to beg him to come home, but I relaxed beneath him as he loved me all over again.

When I woke, soft light filtered through the windows. Normally, Marcus hit the button that closed all the blinds before we went to bed, but he hadn't been here last night. I wasn't sure I'd been here last night. Not in a literal sense. My body likely hadn't left this bed, but I'd been somewhere else. Somewhere Gray could touch me.

I lay there for a moment and took stock. It was something Marcus had taught me to do when I was feeling unstable or worried I might be. I breathe in and start at my toes, trying to sense any tension in my body, locating it and releasing it.

I was a happy mess of rubbery goo. There wasn't a tense muscle in my body. And my soul. Oh, it was at peace, too.

How could I be at such peace without Marcus to hold me together?

This was who he wanted me to become. I would always need nights like the one before, but something had changed and I was more than I'd been.

The next time wouldn't be so hard. I could see that now. The next time wouldn't surprise me and I would handle it.

I could handle being myself.

"Kelsey, please…"

I sat straight up, clutching the sheets to my breasts. That was when I realized I wasn't alone.

Trent lay beside me in the bed, Gladys impaled in his left side.

He looked up at me, his eyes so damn weak. "I can't. I'm not strong enough to pull it out. Please. It hurts."

So much of what Gray had said made sense now. When he'd come to me the first time, he'd been inside the Ala demon. At the time, all I'd seen was the Ala, but apparently Gray had figured out how to make me see him last night—even though he'd been inside

Trent's body.

They'd been one the night before. That had been the difference.

"What did you do?" I asked the wolf, trying to wrap my mind around why he would put himself through hours and hours of torture. And embarrassment. "How much did you see?"

Despite the fact that he was impaled on a sword that could poison him, his lips curled in a sexy grin. "I was there the whole time. Told you I would find a way. Keep you safe. Give you what you need. Don't hate me. Can't stand it if you hate me."

Hate him? I scrambled because I wasn't about to let him die on me. He'd done something extraordinary. I couldn't hate him. Ever. I didn't bother with clothes. He'd seen it all before and it was all right for him to see me. I could feel it.

What wasn't right was that sword in his belly. He'd held that sword for hours and hours while his body had been used to heal my soul.

"I'll get Henri."

Trent shook his head. "Just take it out and I'll change. I have the king's blood. I took a big old dose before our adventure. I'll change and that will help the healing process along. You know what we have to do with Roberts, right?"

I had to call in some witches. Luckily, they were coming over today anyway. "I'll get Liv started on finding the right spell."

Trent was flat on his back, staring up at me with weak eyes, but I could hear the will in his voice. "Kelsey, we're partners in this now. Marcus can't help you anymore. I didn't get everything that big bastard said, but I got the gist. Is there a reason Gray can't give us a map?"

I sighed because that would be so much easier. "It's all in the prophet's handbook. That was as easy as it gets."

Trent growled. "I hate prophecies. I'll help you in any way I can, but I'm the one you turn to now. You understand that?"

I understood I owed him and if he wanted in on this, I would let him. "Okay." I gripped the hilt of my sword. "This is probably going to hurt."

He groaned as I pulled the sword free. The sheets were perfectly clean because Gladys didn't waste a drop of blood. Even as I pulled it out of Trent's body, I could see the blood absorbing into the silver, and then I watched as the king's blood worked its magic, beginning to heal the wound. Trent was a nasty ashen color, but I couldn't help but find him beyond beautiful in that moment.

Wolves need affection. It's how they heal. There's often nothing sexual about it. I've seen wolves sleep in large piles of naked bodies for mere comfort and warmth. There's something beautiful about it. Especially when one is sick and needs the touch of his or her brethren. That's when the wolf pack will come together and lay hands on the ill one, giving them comfort and strength. So I crawled in next to him. I did it on instinct and without that useless shame I might have felt before that night. There was a wolf part of me and Trent had become my pack. I accepted it with surprising ease. I pulled the covers over us and wrapped my arms around him.

"Kelsey, I have to," he began.

I knew what he had to do. "It's okay."

He changed in an instant, proving his incredible strength. One minute I was hugging a man and the next there was a big gray wolf in my arms. He whimpered in pain and I stroked a hand down his back.

"Go to sleep." I knew why he was fighting it, but he would find me less combative than I'd been before he'd risked his life to save my sanity. I wasn't going to let his sacrifice be for nothing. I let my hands stroke his soft fur. "Go to sleep. I'll be here. I won't leave you and I won't get into trouble until you're awake and ready to protect me."

He managed a bark that sounded something like a snort of disbelief.

But his eyes were closing.

I stayed there, watching over him as he'd watched over me.

Chapter Nine

Hours later I paced the floor of the queen's living room, but this time it wasn't an anxious thing. I was thinking and found the movement soothing. I usually forced myself to be still. I'd been told so often as a child that I should, I'd developed the habit, though it wasn't natural. That afternoon, I didn't even think about it. I let my instincts flow. I paced as Trent sat in the sunshine. He was still in his wolf form. Henri had told me he should stay that way for a few more hours. His wolf body would clear the silver more quickly than his human one. He'd woken up and growled my way when I'd asked him if he needed a walk around the block to clear out the system. Hey, I was sure someone had a pooper-scooper I could borrow.

He was not in the mood for my jokes.

"So you want a witch to come in and find a bunch of memories that Nemcox shoved into Neil's soul?" The queen sounded like I'd asked her to ride a unicorn or something equally ridiculous.

"It's not on his soul. It's in between his soul and the dragon thing that now is attached to his soul." Totally reasonable. Liv hadn't blinked when I'd called her. I'd been lying in bed petting my wolf when I'd asked Liv to talk to her coven about the Neil Roberts's situation. She was my girl. She didn't call me crazy, merely said she would get on it.

Apparently she and Sarah Day had figured something out. Now it was all about convincing Roberts to stay still long enough for the witches to whammy him.

"So the tattoo is actually on his soul." Dev Quinn sat beside his wife. The king was out for the day, meeting with someone important about something super world changing, or so I was told. Marcus had gone with him, but he'd left a note explaining that he thought it best that he go back to Venice for a while. He would talk to me about it when he returned this evening.

It hurt my heart, but the ache was somewhat bittersweet. Marcus had a path. He had a dream, maybe one he hadn't even acknowledged yet. Something about what Gray had said made me think Marcus would find his happiness. I'd written down as much of the prophecy as I could remember and the lines about Marcus had struck me as hopeful.

All the world would crumble, too, but I was focusing on the positive.

So this afternoon it was me, the queen, Devinshea Quinn, my two witches, one super sullen Neil Roberts, and Trent, who did that thing where he walked in circles three times before lying his wolf body down so he could watch the fireworks. His head was on his paws as he looked up at me.

He was awfully cute in his wolf form, even if he was a bit grumpy. If he was going to follow me around in wolf form, I was totally going to start stocking my pockets with treats. Maybe a Snausage or two would get his tail wagging.

I was still processing the fact that I'd kind of had sex with Trent. It had been Trent's body that had moved over me. And he'd done it all with a sword sticking in him. He was a motherfucking superhero in the bedroom.

It made me wonder what that man could do when he wasn't impaled.

It had been Trent my wolf responded to. I wasn't so unaware that I didn't get that. My wolf was totally into Trent and I couldn't work up the will to think that was a horrible idea at the moment.

Sarah leaned in, her hand on Neil as though she was worried if she stopped touching him, he would fade away. "Yes, Dev. Believe me, I have some insight into this. My mother sold my sister and I to Brixalnax. That tat was placed on us at birth. It didn't go away until Felix redeemed me." She looked back at me. "That was before he fell. He was still an angel. And before you ask, it's not something we can request from the Heaven plane. Felix was only able to do it because he knew he was going to fall. Angels are given one freebie before they give up the wings."

So asking for a pass from the angelic trio wouldn't help. I hadn't expected it would be that easy.

Roberts sat up, his eyes grim. "It's on my soul. I can't quite process that."

"The dragon itself isn't bad, you know." I hated how sad he looked. I was feeling far more magnanimous than I had yesterday and had apologized profusely for the whole "bad cop" play. "It's a part of you, something they use to control you, but that doesn't mean you can't take it back. Gray told me that if you found a way to accept it, you'll be much more at peace."

"I want it gone." Roberts's hand went to his side as though he could feel it.

"I can't get rid of it. We can only unbind the dragon from Nemcox. I can't take it off your soul." I'd thought a lot about the dragons while I lounged in bed. Gray's dragon might not work the same, but it was a way for his father to force him home. Still, I didn't think Gray would want me to take it off him even if I could. That dragon was part of Gray, but Roberts didn't feel the same way. "The problem is you don't remember the words of the invocation. I need them. Well, Liv and Sarah need them to perform an unbinding spell. I need some truth from you."

Zoey started to stand. Quinn put a hand on his wife's elbow.

"It's her job, my goddess. Dan wanted her in this position. She can't merely do her job when it doesn't touch our family. We need her." Quinn nodded my way. "Please continue."

"How did you get the burns on your hands?"

Roberts looked down at his palms. They were perfect now. "I don't know. I woke up yesterday morning and I was naked in a park and my hands were like that. I tried shifting, but it didn't work. I found an alley and hid behind a trash compactor until Chad woke up. We tried to use his blood, but it didn't work either. That's when we went to the hospital."

"I convinced him to take the king's blood last night," Zoey admitted. "He was already donating, so I took some to Neil and that finally worked. You think Neil used the Sword of Justice to kill the halflings?"

"I think it feels awfully coincidental to me that I've got a halfling who could only have been killed by a special sword, the same sword goes missing from the Heaven plane, and Neil here, who has a switch his ex-captor can push at any time, both loses time and shows up with burns on his hand that shouldn't be there. Well, unless he's been playing around with…yes, that's right, a sword from the Heaven plane. Is that a neat triangle bringing us back to the fact that Neil is likely a sleeper agent being activated by Nemcox, who stole the sword we're looking for? Or is it three completely unconnected dots? Anyone want to argue?"

"I've lost time a lot lately," Neil said quietly. "It wasn't only yesterday."

Zoey and Dev turned to him, obviously shocked.

"Why didn't you tell me?" Zoey asked, moving closer to him.

"How long?" Quinn's voice had gone low, but there was compassion there. "Has he been doing this to you for years?"

Roberts shook his head. "No. Not at all. I thought it was all over. It's been forever. He hasn't messed with me since that day I woke up in France and found my way to Zoey. I knew he'd done something to me, but life seemed calm. It's been good for years, and I was stupid. I thought if I didn't touch that world again, it would go away. I was wrong. He's always been out there, waiting for the right time. He'll never stop. When he's ready, he'll take me to Hell again."

"Not if this works." I needed him positive for the experience. "If this works, we could break the bond."

"And I'll remember what happened to me?" Neil seemed to shrink in on himself.

"I don't know," Sarah replied. "I'm going to try to break whatever spell is keeping that memory from you, but I don't know if you'll remember everything. Once the spell is done, Felix will try to take you through some sessions to bring out the exact invocation the demon used. Then we'll break the bond and he won't be able to come after you again."

"Especially once I cut his head off his body." I had plans. I would mount it and hang shit from his horns.

Roberts looked up at me, a fire in his eyes for the first time. "I want in on that."

All the wolves wanted in on my kill. I supposed he had even more right than I did. "I'll be happy for the help. But first, I need something else from you. Help me stop this. I know it's going to suck to remember, but we need you to. I know you didn't mean to kill those demons."

"We don't know that he did," the queen insisted.

Roberts looked back at her. "I woke up covered in blood. Demon blood, Z."

There was one problem with my scenario, and I had to admit the facts. "The forensics aren't consistent with a wolf attack. According to Henri, some sort of lizard thing bit the last victim. I don't suppose you have any lizard-shifting friends?"

The queen sat up straight, her face flushing. "Shit."

"Tell them, Z. You know you have to. I don't remember those times." Roberts put a hand over hers. "You know I can't live this way. If you know something, tell her."

Trent had gotten his furry butt up and he came to sit in front of the queen, his eyes steady on her.

She frowned at him. "Fine. Gosh, you're a judgmental wolf. I'll tell her. But don't expect any treats from me."

His tail thumped and he moved back to my side. He twirled around a few times before lying back down.

The queen's lips curled up in a smile. "Well, that didn't take long. I owe Danny twenty bucks." Trent growled and the queen moved on. "All right. I've only seen Neil change once. Not into a wolf. He does that all the time. I mean I've only seen him change into whatever the hell Nemcox forces him to change into once. I think there's some kind of failsafe involved. We were in grave danger. We were in the old Council's stronghold. It was me and Trent and Neil. We got caught doing something we shouldn't."

"Stealing shit," Neil allowed.

Zoey shrugged. "As one does. Anyway, we were trapped in a dangerous place. Our only exit was being guarded by a strong shifter. Trent tried to take him on, but it was obvious that wasn't going well. That was when Neil…he didn't change forms exactly, but he was changed."

I was getting a much better picture. "So he didn't take on some four-legged form. He would be able to hold a sword."

"Yes," Zoey replied. "His eyes changed and there was something…reptilian about him."

"Dragon-like. When he gets activated, his dragon takes over and there are some physiological changes. It's smart. No one would think a wolf would be able to hold that sword. All the forensics would come back as reptilian. He's a perfect sleeper agent," I surmised. I'd heard enough. Zoey could tell me the whole story, but I would rather hear it from the source. Unfortunately, my source had issues. "All right. I think we need to do this. Liv, are you comfortable that this spell is going to help?"

Liv gave me what I like to think of as her reassuring smile. "I'm comfortable with the fact that it won't kill him or bring about the apocalypse."

I was taking that as a win.

Forty minutes later I watched as Neil took a seat in the queen's dining room. He looked thin and slightly afraid of what was to come. Zoey was kneeling beside him, talking to him, as Liv and Sarah held a deep discussion about exactly how to deal with the spell. There had been a bunch of herb chopping and potion brewing, and they'd been debating over the proper usages of Latin.

I'd been sitting rather peacefully while Trent napped away, though I had one worry running through my mind. More than one, really, but this one stood out.

Dev strode back into the room, coming to stand beside me. "All right, here's the report on the wards."

While I was up in the penthouse, Henri and Hugo had been manning command central. Casey said he was close to getting me a name to go with that face we'd pulled off the video from the crazy neighbor. I glanced down and read the report Hugo had typed up for me. God, I loved having a team of academics on my side. The ward blocked the ill intentioned, but there were some symbols on the back that they didn't recognize. One of the witches did theorize that the language was actually angelic in origin. Angels seemed to be popping up everywhere.

"So the working theory is that ward would have been rendered useless to someone angelic or perhaps someone carrying a powerful angelic object," I murmured.

"Yes," Dev replied. "It looks like someone left an angelic back door, and that's not good for any of us."

"Would a demon know the angelic languages? I mean, I would suspect they would. After all, they descended from the Heaven plane. When an angel falls it's not always to earth." I worked through the possible scenarios in my mind. "I need to find out if anyone's fallen lately. They could have stolen the sword and gone looking for a little revenge. Nemcox would be happy to oblige. Hell, if he's working with a recently fallen angel, maybe that's how he's ducking my call."

"I don't know. We can ask Felix, but he lost his powers shortly after he chose to fall," Dev explained. "We can certainly ask him if that's possible."

One more thing on my to-do list. It was starting to get never ending.

Trent was sleeping roughly ten feet away from me. When the great spell debate had begun, he'd found a sunny spot and gone to sleep. I watched him. He sleep growled and his paws moved like he was running from time to time.

Was he running away from what had happened? From what might happen?

"If he doesn't know, we might have to ask for another angelic audience. I'd like to have that protective tat before I need to meet up with those three again," I replied in a soft tone. I didn't want to wake that wolf. There were ramifications he hadn't thought of, and I was cool with that. It was going to be damn awkward dealing with him when he was back to his normal, gorgeous man self. I wasn't sure what protocol was in this instance. He'd saved my life by having sex with me. Did I send a cookie bouquet? Or high-five him for his virility? Did I offer to pay for his therapy? Did I ask him if he wanted to go again? This time, without the sword in his gut? It was all too much. I chose to focus on what was in front of me.

"I'll bring in our tattoo artist," Dev assured me. "She's brilliant. A witch and an artist."

I was sure she was the best. Quinn always sprung for the best. "Now, I need you to do something else for me."

"Of course," Dev replied. "What do you need?"

"I need you to tell me if I'm pregnant." This was what I'd been sitting here thinking about. It hadn't occurred to me until everyone else had something to do and I'd gone over the night again in my head.

Dev put a hand on my arm, the touch oddly warming. "You're not. I did check last night to ensure that you weren't in a place where it would be a big risk. You weren't ovulating. And as for anything else, well, Trent mostly lives like a monk. Especially the last two years."

"I wasn't worried about catching a disease." I breathed a sigh of relief. Wolves didn't get venereal diseases. They could manwhore it up all they liked and never worry about the clap. They could, however, knock a chick up. "I thought I should ask if I was suddenly carrying a litter."

"You understand why he couldn't wear a condom, right?"

I could guess. "Because he had to hold that freaking sword in. Because he was a vessel and he had to do everything he could to not lose the connection to Gray."

How much pain had he been in? While I was lost in passion, Trent had been trying to keep himself impaled on something that could poison him.

I had to ask. "Why would he do that for me?"

Dev shrugged. "Why does any man do heroic things for a woman?"

I would have to think about it. Now that I'd put some distance between myself and what had happened, I was feeling guilty. I hadn't meant to cheat, but it felt like I had. Oh, I'm sure Marcus had already forgiven me given the circumstances, but sometimes it's way harder to forgive myself. Was Marcus moving out because our connection was gone or because I'd slept with another man? Two, kind of.

"He knows," Quinn said, as though he could read my mind. Given the fact that he was a Green Man and something of a sex god, he likely could. Devinshea Quinn was good at reading emotions and guessing what someone would be feeling. It was one of the reasons he was an excellent advisor to the king. "Marcus, I mean. He knows you're moving past him. I suspect it's the reason he's asked the king for permission to go to Venice for a while."

"I don't like that phrase. Moving past him. I never wanted to move past Marcus. He's been so good to me."

"All right. How about this one? He knows you need more." He

was quiet for a moment, as though trying to come up with a way to explain this to me. "I understand that some Hunters and trainers marry and they're quite happy. Not a one of them was as strong as you. I've studied up since you came to live here. I believe you're something different. Sometimes events occur and the universe aligns. We think God sits high on the Heaven plane and makes decisions, but I've learned over time that it's more like a game of chess. Whatever being we think of as God, he puts things in motion, lines up the pieces, and then allows us to rise or fall as we may. But always we're given the tools we need. I believe we are in a dangerous time. It's why Dan rose when he did and as he did."

"There hadn't been another vampire king in a thousand years before Donovan." If vampires were rare, then kings were practically nonexistent. I did get Quinn's point. I'd done some studying myself. "The old Council was corrupt. They were planning on enslaving the other supernaturals. Donovan stopped that."

"The Council wouldn't have been happy with merely enslaving the other supernaturals. They would have moved on to the humans." Quinn's eyes took on a far-off look, as though remembering that time took him there in some way. "Daniel didn't want to be king. He wanted to live a quiet life with Zoey. Instead he got the crown and the throne, and me along for the ride."

"Somehow I think he's cool with that." Though they weren't demonstrably affectionate in public, it was easy to see that Donovan and Quinn loved each other.

"Oh, in the beginning he was not, but that brings me back to what I was saying about being given all the tools we need. I am the reason Daniel walks in the light, and that was important. I serve several functions in our triad. If you take any one of the three of us away, I believe Daniel fails to take the crown and the world enters a period of darkness. I also believe we are coming up on another crisis."

"Because Donovan won't deal with the demons." Marcus believed it, too. It might be the first thing Marcus and Quinn ever agreed on.

"He's being unreasonable. Zoey doesn't want to face any of it. We've been so happy that the idea of dark times ahead is unthinkable in a lot of ways. But I figured something out. We have a secret weapon. We have you."

I held my hands up because he was wrong about a couple of things. "I'm not anyone's savior."

"Tell that to the deer herd. Tell it to my son," Quinn argued. "What you don't understand is that Daniel wasn't the one who won our war. Zoey did. It's not always the strongest or the one with the most power. It's the person who will never stop. It's the stubborn woman who has no skin in the game other than to see justice done, to ensure the safety of those around her. Daniel is caught up in his emotions and playing a dangerous game. I believe you will be the one to change things because unlike the other Hunters, you are stronger. You are more. Marcus understands that, too. And that is what I meant by you will be given what you need. When you fall, someone will be there to act heroically, to defy all the odds in order to ensure that you can do your job. All you have to do is believe and trust in yourself and accept what you need. Accept the gifts that will be given to you."

Something about the way he was talking got to me. I wasn't destiny girl. I was just me and yet, I had to ask the question. "What am I going to need? Can the other dude, like, tell me?"

His eyes shifted to a solid emerald green, the color shimmering and pulling me in. Dev Quinn was what is known in the Fae world as "ascendant." An ancient god lived inside him, the Irish deity, Bris. I'd been told there were others—Arawn, the Welsh death god, Herne the Hunter—but I'd only ever met the gentle Bris. Asking him for guidance was easier than Quinn. There was something about him that warmed me, made me infinitely comfortable.

"You need to bring the two halves of your whole together, child. That's your true desire. Beyond the sexual and sensual, more than anything, you want peace, and that means a whole and integrated you. You will not find that until the two sides of your being feel valued and needed. You think the wolf is separate, but she's not. You think she needs something different and she does, in ways, but she loves the dark prophet, too. Don't try to separate. That's where you'll make the mistake."

"So I should be with Gray."

"There's no choice here," Bris replied. "There is only your heart and what it needs. Don't try to live by the rules. Make your own. For yourself. For them. Perhaps then you can find what you truly want. What you want even more than the men themselves. What will bring your halves together in a way nothing else can."

A vision struck me. My children bouncing on the bed, giggling like the little monsters I call them. My demon son and the she-wolf I can't stop thinking of.

I'd seen them in the vision. It was one of the only things I could remember, perhaps because I clung so stubbornly to it. My children by Gray and Trent.

Sometimes before I go to sleep, I pray that I will dream of them.

"Kelsey, we're ready." Liv's voice broke through my thoughts, bringing me back to the real world.

Bris smiled at me and then he was Quinn again, his eyes changing in a blink.

"I'll go and check on the kids." Quinn put a hand on my shoulder. "Don't be too hard on Trent. He's finding his way through this, too."

"Say hi to Lee for me."

"If I can find him." Quinn looked around as though expecting something to come at him from any angle. "He's a slippery one, my human son. I know Rhys is supposed to be the powerful one, but it's Lee who can truly wreak havoc. I tried to keep him in the dark about what's happening here today."

"Oh, I'm sure he knows." Little Lee knew everything. He'd been trained by his grandfather to be a good thief, but he'd also learned at a young age that information was the most valuable thing he could steal. Hell, *I* went to Lee when I needed to know what was happening around the building. He knew all the best gossip.

But I wasn't sure hearing his Uncle Neil discuss what had happened to him in Hell was the best thing for a nine-year-old kid. Some experiences were better off left for adulthood.

Quinn kissed his wife before moving to the children's wing of the penthouse.

I watched as Neil took his seat. He drank the potion Liv gave him, complained bitterly about how it tasted, and then seemed to try to relax.

"Okay, so what this spell is supposed to do is pull back the curtain," Sarah explained. "Think of your memory as an actual part of your mind, of your soul in some ways. Everything that you are or have been is locked away in some part of you. Some witches even believe that our past lives are written onto our soul, each evolution of our being marking us in ways and helping to form a new whole."

"This is some spiritual shit. I get it. So my time on the Hell plane is like a file in the computer of my soul," Neil quipped. "While you're screwing around in there, could you pull up my time as a thirties matinee idol? Because I sometimes dream about that."

Sarah smiled, her nose wrinkling. "I'll be sure to do that. Anyway, I've altered a memory spell in order to find the deeper memories. I'm going to pull some energy from the air around me and send it through you. It won't hurt, but it should target whatever is veiling your memory. It should work quickly and it could be a bit overwhelming."

"I can handle it." Roberts took a deep breath. "It's always there anyway. It's a nagging anxiety in the back of my mind, a shadow I can't quite catch. Maybe it's better to know."

I wasn't sure about that. Sometimes ignorance was bliss, but I couldn't let him stay that way. I needed to know.

Liv brought Sarah a potion to amplify her powers. She downed it and then the chanting started.

Yep. Always chanting. There was some Latiny things I didn't understand and then it seemed like energy gathered around Sarah, starting at her feet and rising up through her. The room felt charged and that was when I noticed our intruder.

As Sarah prepped to rip that veil off her friend's memory, I caught sight of Lee. He was hiding behind one of the big comfy couches, his eyes wide as he watched the scene in front of him.

I was about to walk over and nab his ass when the energy shot right through Roberts. I heard him gasp, but I watched in horror as it didn't stop. It shot through Roberts's chest and seemed to turn like a heat-seeking missile, finding the hottest target.

My heart felt like it was going to stop as Lee took the energy bullet Sarah had fired. It sent his body flying across the room and his mother screamed.

My heart was pounding in my chest as I ran for him. "Call Henri."

I would run his body down to the hospital myself if I had to. I loved Lee.

Quinn came running at the sound of the screams, and everything was chaos as we all tried to huddle around Lee's body.

His eyes fluttered open and he frowned. "What the hell is wrong with you people? Damn it, Zoey. What's going on?" He sat up and rubbed his head. "I need a beer."

He sounded different. His voice was deeper, though still Lee's somehow.

Sarah's eyes had gone wide. "Holy shit."

Quinn started to try to pick him up. If he was upset his nine-year-old was asking for a beer, he didn't show it. "Come on, son. We need to get you down to the hospital."

Lee pushed back. "Son? Dear god, Quinn. What's gotten into you? Why is everybody staring at me like that? Wilcox? Is that you? What the hell are you doing here? And put on some goddamn pants. We're in mixed company. The faeries might be all right with your junk hanging out, but I'm not."

"Lee?" Quinn asked.

Of course it was Lee. He was right there.

"Owens?" Trent was standing behind me and he'd changed back

to his wholly masculine self.

"Yes?"

That had been said in stereo. Both Lee and I looked up at Trent, who really should have put some pants on.

I would have said something but that was the moment the queen chose to faint.

Lee stood up, looking down on his mom. "Looks like Zoey's the one who needs the doc, Quinn." He scratched his belly and then looked at his hand. He frowned and turned to the mirror behind him. "What the hell? Quinn get this damn glamour off me. Why do I always have to be the kid?"

Quinn held his wife, but he was staring at his son. "I always thought she'd dreamed up that story. I didn't believe her. Uh, that's not a glamour, Lee. That's your body now. And I'm your dad. Zoey's your mom." He turned to the witch, desperation plain on his face. "Sarah, I'm going to need my son back."

Lee was staring at himself in the mirror and I was trying to process what the hell had happened.

"Wow." Roberts had his hands on his hips. "That is Lee. The old Lee. I would know that frown anywhere. Dude, did you know you had a daughter? Owens, meet your dad."

Lee turned and stared at me, and then the softest look hit his eyes. "Well, hello there, darlin'. It's coming back to me now. Damn it all, but you look like your momma."

"Huh. I think he's right. We need a beer." It was the only way to handle this whole clusterfuck. I looked back. Trent was way too close. "Dude, clothes. Please."

"She looks like her momma, but she sounds like her dad. Come on, darlin'. Let's grab a beer and talk while the crazy people figure a way out of this." He scratched his belly again. "I remember where the kitchen is."

I stood and followed…my dad.

Chapter Ten

My head hurt. Sometimes lots of weird information being shoved into a brain will do that to a girl. Sometimes finding out that your previously dead father now lived in the soul of a kid I liked will definitely bring on the migraine.

"So when the spell was cast, it went for Lee and not Neil." I'd been given a whole twenty-minute lecture on energy flow and ley lines and veiled souls, but I kind of thought that was what had happened.

We were all sitting in the living room, the queen having been revived after her brief fainting spell. She was sitting next to her son/my dad. Quinn paced, checking his phone from time to time, and Neil seemed way more interested now that we weren't talking about him.

"Apparently the magic that holds the old soul in a new body was more interesting to the forces I was channeling than Neil's magic." Sarah was shaking her head like she still couldn't believe what had happened.

"I think it's because it was faery magic," Liv interjected. "The spell we used comes from the Fae. It's a bit similar to lifting the veil so you can see the truth of a thing. I believe the force Sarah was using more readily recognized the magic from Heaven than the magic from Hell."

"Freaking magic," Lee said with a shake of his head. He frowned up at Zoey. "I told you to stay away from faery magic. It always gets us in trouble."

Zoey stared for a moment and then she looked back to Sarah. "How long does the spell last?" She reached over and put a hand on Lee's shoulder. "Not that I'm unhappy to see you, old friend. It's just…"

"I want my son back." Quinn's whole body was tense.

The queen was a bit more tactful. "You have a soccer game Thursday night and a project due. I'm not sure how the teachers at your school are going to handle something like this."

Lee pointed to Quinn. "Don't get your panties in a wad, Quinn. It's all going to be all right. It can't last forever, right? But while I'm out, I do want to talk to both of you about your parenting skills. The boy was not lying when he told you he didn't drink the root beer. It was Rhys. Yes, sweet, everyone-adores-him Rhys drank that root beer, but no one believes me because I'm a kid and I sometimes get into trouble. Next time test his breath. My brother gets away with everything. And while we're talking, let's discuss this whole homework thing. I don't need half the crap they're teaching. I've lived a whole life and do you know what I never once used? Algebra. Cut that shit out now. The boy needs weapons training. And if that little shit wolf from the sixth grade comes after us one more time, I'm going to show him how easily his balls can get shoved up into his body cavity."

Yeah, those anger issues might have been hereditary.

Quinn stood over Sarah. "I need my sweet son back now. Right now."

Sarah held up a hand. "I have to research this, Dev. It's not as simple as doing another spell. I think Liv's on to something, but I can't just take it back. This is heavenly magic. This is an old soul in a new body. I'm at a loss."

"How does he remember the things he's done as a child this time around?" Zoey asked. "When I visited him in Heaven before I came back to this plane, they told me this was a way to give his soul peace, that he would be able to live another life free of the confines of who he was before."

"What she's trying to say is being a lone wolf sucks ass," Lee added. "The urge to be alone, to not let anyone in, it was always a war in my soul." He looked up at Zoey. "Forget what I said before, darlin'. I'm cranky about the whole soul thing. You're a good mom, Zoey. You're everything I could want and I love Rhys and Evan, too. Hell, I even…I can't. You're going to have to figure that part out on your own."

He loved Quinn. Given their history, I figured that would be hard to say.

"But I'm not at peace," Lee continued, his eyes darkening. "It's different, but the war is still…where's Donovan?"

"Your dad is in the middle of an important meeting. A representative from one of the murdered demon's family has come and demanded an audience. Marcus finally convinced Daniel he has to meet with him, but he wouldn't allow the man on this plane. He's in a neutral place and that means no cell towers," Quinn explained. It was obvious he wasn't accepting the fact that a somewhat salty lone wolf had taken over his son's personality. "He'll call us when he can. Until then, you should rest and stay in the condo until your Aunt Sarah figures out how to…put you back together properly."

"I think what Dev is trying to say is we all need to remain calm," Zoey interjected, throwing husband number two a pointed stare. "Can I talk to you for a moment, dear?"

Quinn turned and strode out, Zoey hard on his heels.

Lee reached up and scratched behind his ear, his hand moving rapidly before he sniffed and sat back, one hand on his belly. "So you're Kelsey."

Sarah and Liv went back to the kitchen, already planning their next attempts. Neil wandered in behind them. I was left alone with my father.

"Looks like it." We kind of stared at each other for a long time, the silence oddly peaceful between us. "You have to dump my mom like that?"

I didn't ask the question with a ton of bitterness. I was merely curious.

Lee shook his head and shot me a way too old for his nine-year-old body stare. "Your mama left me. She figured out I was a loner and decided I was a bad bet. My own mother had died a couple of years before and I was raising Zack on my own. I believe your mother thought I was trying to find a place to dump Zack so I could roam."

It was what loners did. Lone wolves didn't have families. They were a rare type of supernatural creature who was there to maintain balance when needed. A true lone wolf is more powerful than any alpha wolf, but has no need to form a pack or ties, so he can be used to keep powerful alphas in check. A lone wolf, if he happens to knock up some human, can also produce something even rarer.

Me.

"You might have mentioned to her that you were different." From what I understood, my father truly was different. He'd never left his younger brother behind even though the need to roam must have been overwhelming.

He stood up and walked over to me. He put his hand on my chin and forced me to look into his eyes. "If I'd had even a hint that you existed, I would have come for you. Do you understand that? Even when I'm sleeping inside this new body of mine, I know you. Even though I'm only a child right now, I still come for you, daughter."

I don't cry. Well, I rarely do, but something threatened to break inside me and I had to hold it together. Tears shimmered when I thought about the fact that somehow, someway, though we'd been robbed of one relationship, we'd found another. And he did come for me. He crept out of bed and put himself in dangerous situations so he could find me and make sure I was okay.

I shook my head, unwilling to break down. "You can't do that anymore. You're human."

"Am I?" His lips curled into a smile I'd never seen on his face before. "I don't feel human. Things aren't always as they seem. You should know that better than anyone else. Tell me why Marcus isn't here. I don't smell him anywhere on you."

He stepped back and suddenly I knew the oddity of having a nine-year-old question my life choices.

"He's with the king," I managed to say.

"He's with the king while we're in the middle of a murder investigation and we got the heavenly trio up our asses? That's when he decides to play politics again? I don't think so. I want to find that vampire and then we're going to have a talk about how he takes care of you."

"Drink." Trent walked out of the kitchen and passed me a beer, saving me for the second time in a twenty-four-hour period. He'd already taken the cap off. While I'd been getting the lowdown on how everything had gone to hell, Trent had found a pair of sweatpants and a T-shirt. He sat down beside me and I had to force myself not to lean into him. "So how did the old guy end up coming out again?"

I turned to him. "You're the only one here who doesn't seem surprised."

One broad shoulder shrugged. "Zoey always said Lee was reincarnated as one of her twins. Little Lee smells like old Lee. I've been that kid's bodyguard since the day he was born and he's always given me hell. Hey, old man, you're the worst. I mean it. I told your mom she should spank you more."

Adorable Little Lee's middle finger came up. "Fuck you, Wilcox." His mouth turned up in the smirkest grin, one I'd certainly never seen on my young friend. "Damn, it's good to see you."

They shook hands, one of those weird manly gestures. Trent leaned back, his arm going around the edge of the couch behind me. "It's good to see you, too. And Marcus isn't a bad guy, but her training is almost done. I'm going to take over much of her daily schedule. It's time she embraced her wolf side."

I heard the chime of the doorbell and wished Albert wasn't so quick. I could have rushed to open the door.

"I can understand that somewhat. Let's move on to you, son," Lee said, his tone turning serious. "You want to explain why my daughter smells like you but doesn't have your ring on her finger?"

"You can't smell him on me." My whole body had flushed. Like all of it. I could feel that embarrassment down to my toes. "I don't care that you used to be a lone wolf. Now, you're a nine-year-old and you have trouble catching a baseball. You do not have supersenses."

Lee's eyes narrowed. "Don't I? You think I can't tell that he's been all over you? That I can't see the way he's looking at you and how you almost leaned against him when he sat down beside you. There are five chairs in this room, Wilcox. Why don't you find your own?"

Trent relaxed back, crossing one leg over his knee and generally looking like the cat who ate the canary. "This one fits me so well." He turned slightly toward me. "Hey, baby, did you talk to Quinn? I couldn't use a rubber so I wanted to make sure we're not pregnant."

Lee stood up, pointing at him. "I swear to god if you get my baby girl knocked up…"

I stood up as well and turned and walked out rather than screaming at the top of my lungs. I was pretty sure every inch of my skin was flaming pink. The day had been shitty and surreal.

I made it to the hallway when I saw Casey coming my way.

He waved a printout. "Hey, boss, I found our girl and she's a hooker. It's the Larissa chick. I even found an ad for her services on the Dark Web. Apparently there's a whole underbelly of supernatural ads and shit there. Very clever, too. Larissa Dymone, erotic artist. Her tagline is *Demons do it better*. Got her address and everything. I set up an appointment for myself. I thought that might be the way we ensure she talks and all."

I pulled the paper from his hand and kept on walking.

"Uh, Kels, do you have any cash? I don't think this is why Henri gave me a Visa." Casey jogged to keep up with me. "From the looks of this, demon hookers are expensive."

I kept on walking. Sadly, a little time with a hooker would be the least embarrassing thing to happen to me all day.

* * * *

"You know a thank you would be nice." Casey had managed to catch up to me when I'd stopped off at my apartment. "Maybe a 'good job, Casey. You worked hard and that needs to be appreciated.'"

I'd stopped by my apartment to pick up a couple of guns. I'd known Marcus wouldn't be there, but I could almost see him standing in the living room, staring out over the city like he did so often.

The apartment had been completely silent, but it was changed utterly. In the few hours I'd been in the queen's penthouse, someone had moved all of Marcus's personal items out of our apartment. His clothes and books and toiletries were all gone.

It was as though he'd simply vanished, and I wondered if he even intended to say good-bye.

I hadn't been able to stay there. I needed a distraction and the best one I could think of was work. I'd headed out then and there, but I hadn't been able to get rid of Casey.

If only Casey could vanish, then I would be blissfully alone.

"Hey," he shouted as I turned the Jeep onto the street I needed. "You could also watch the hairpin turns. I don't need to die twice. What crawled up your butt and died?"

"Not died," I corrected. "Came back to life."

I wish I'd have thought to steal Liv. I needed my BFF. My life had gone topsy-turvy and she was my reasonable girl. Liv was the one who listened to me bitch and then consoled me.

"You wanna talk about it?"

I frowned his way. "No, I do not."

"Okay."

He fiddled with the radio. He was only satisfied when he'd found some whiny man rock.

"My dad came back." I have no idea why I said the words. They came out totally of their own accord.

Casey sat up. "Are you serious? Why are we running? We need to go back to the compound. We need to warn everyone. Your dad is a wanted criminal."

The man who'd raised me had many fans. That's kind of what happened when you got a name as a ruthless, merciless hunter who didn't discriminate between dangerous supernaturals and perfectly harmless ones. The man who raised me simply killed them all. "Not John Atwood. As far as I know he was never dead. I'm talking about my bio dad who seems serious about protecting my nonexistent virtue."

"Ah, he heard about you doing the nasty with Trent, huh?"

"How do you know about that?"

"I heard it from Jan, the witch who runs the coffee shop on the sixth floor, and she heard it from one of the bartenders at Ether, who I'm pretty sure heard it from the bodyguard they put on the room so no one rushed in while Trent was howling and shit."

"Howling?"

"Yeah, I guess fucking while you've got a silver sword shoved through your body hurts and stuff," Casey said with a shrug. "It got intense and some of the wolves were either worried or amused. It can be hard to tell. Turn right up here. She's in those apartments."

The thought of Trent howling in pain made my heart twist. How much had he sacrificed to save me?

"I doubt he was howling in pain," a familiar voice said.

I nearly screamed as a small body sat up in the backseat of my Jeep.

"Goddamn it, Lee. You cannot do that. You nearly gave me a fucking heart attack," I yelled and then stared Casey's way. "You didn't realize he was hiding in the back?"

"You didn't either." Casey had gone a lovely shade of paler than usual.

Lee sat up, unfolding his small body from where he'd been hiding. He held up a tiny leaf. "Magically reinforced herbs. I steal them from the apothecary on twelve. Keep a stash of them in my bedroom. Masks my scent, but only works for twenty minutes or so. You would have caught me soon enough, darlin'. Don't be upset. I just want to spend some time with you before they find a way to shove me back down deep."

I tried to focus on the road in front of me. "They're working on it."

"Sarah and Liv are," Lee replied. "I think they're going to talk to the coven about it. I don't think this happens often. They're also trying to figure out how to get Neil to remember, but I don't think that's going to work the way they hope it does."

"Why not?"

"Magic's a funny thing. A spell like this—a white one—will only really work if the person you're casting the spell on wants it to work," my dad explained. "Neil's will comes into play in a white spell. I think his will could be working against the spell."

That actually made sense to me. "You don't think he wants to remember."

"I know Neil often runs from the things that scare him. He might not even realize it, but I think he doesn't want to know what happened to him. He doesn't want to face it. I don't know that a white spell is going to work."

"We have to try something," I replied, attempting to focus on the road again. I wasn't even all that surprised that my dad had found his way into my Jeep. He didn't need to be an old soul to do that. Little Lee had been able to do stuff like that all on his own. "How did you know who I was? I get that you retained the memories of your life, but you never met me. You said it yourself. You didn't know I existed."

"But I did. I spent time on the Heaven plane. One of the things I saw there was you." He leaned forward, a small hand on my shoulder. "While I was there I saw many things. It was like my whole life and all its possibilities were all around me. I saw the people I'd been, saw what will happen to me this time. I saw it all in great detail, and I remember how it felt to know. Now it's all fuzzy, like I know I saw it, know something's waiting for me, but I can't remember anything but you. It's like I held on to that one memory because I didn't want to forget it. Because even though I knew I would be a child, I wanted so much to be your dad no matter what body I was in."

Like I could remember those children of mine. Those little monsters jumping on the bed.

"That's beautiful," Casey said. "It makes me miss my dad."

I tried to ignore him, looking at Lee through the rearview mirror. "But you remember the past."

"Yes," he replied. "Look, sweetheart, I don't know how long I have. I kind of hope this wears off at some point and I'm back to being me. There's a reason I chose to do this and it wasn't to be the old me in a new body. But if that happens and I go back to not remembering anything, there are some things I need to tell you."

"There are questions I have, too." I couldn't stop thinking about what Marcus had told me. Was I chasing after the wrong revenge? Did my father want revenge at all?

How much time did we have? God, I'd run out of that place like my pants were on fire and all because I was embarrassed. How many people got the chance to talk to their dead fathers?

"This is the apartment complex," Casey said quietly. He pointed to a nicely kept set of buildings. It looked like Larissa the hooker did pretty well for herself. "Uhm, if you two want to talk, I could go in and question the suspect."

More likely he would end up using his hour with the hooker for doing what hookers did. I knew Casey. He's a good kid and he would try, but if Larissa Dymone had half a brain and anything at all to do with killing Lester, she would see right through Casey. She would pull some big old demon eyes on him, maybe show some of her extra bits, and then stab his ass with a stake. And by ass I really mean heart.

The talk with my dad would have to wait. I pulled into the

parking lot.

I did have a job to do, after all. "Did she give you a gate code when you set up the appointment?"

"Yeah. She also told me where to park. She's organized. Pretty too. The pictures on her website are way better than the one we pulled off the security camera," Casey assured me as he passed me the code.

I pushed it in and the ornate doors began to swing open. "You mean her hooker glamour shots are better than the ones taken on the night she might or might not have killed someone? Shocking."

Casey frowned my way. "Have you considered that she could be innocent in all of this?"

"She's a hooker?" Lee asked. "Probably not so innocent."

I was with Dad on this one. And I should have known Casey would take one look at the pretty hooker and think she was nothing more than an innocent demoness trying to work her way through college.

I pulled into the slot Casey indicated and started to get out. Lee moved behind me.

Casey stopped, putting a hand on my arm. "Uh, I don't think the king's baby boy should go and hang with hookers. Like, we could get blamed for corrupting him and stuff."

"Do you have any idea how many hookers I've been around, son? Way more than you by the looks of it." Lee jumped to the ground and took a look around. "Wonder if she's got a beer."

"No beer." It didn't matter that his soul was way older than me. His liver was nine and I was returning him to his mother in pristine condition. That was my vow.

"Uh, shouldn't we be saying no hookers?" Casey asked, eyeing Lee.

I sighed. "If I try to leave him in the car, he'll find another way in. Did the whole hopping-in-the-Jeep incident not teach you what he's capable of? Besides, if he's anything like his current self, he's probably pretty good at the detecting thing."

I started toward the townhouse section of the complex. It looked like our erstwhile prostitute had her own party space. It was a nice walk-up, with plants and flowers. It looked like a spot where families would picnic, but then I supposed if she had a neon sign hanging overhead that said *get it here*, her game would be up.

I rang the doorbell as Casey and Lee joined me on the doorstep.

The door came open and the scent of something super-flowery hit my nose. It was almost sickly sweet and I tried not to cough. Casey, on the other hand, was suddenly smiling like a loon.

Larissa Dymone stood in the doorway wearing a filmy white negligee and nothing else. Her lovely face was soft, her makeup done beautifully. Her hair was on the short side, dark with a single purple streak.

"Hello," she began in a super-sexy come-hither voice. Until she truly caught sight of us. Then she frowned, her whole body language changing in an instant. "Seriously? I don't do kids. I don't know what you're thinking, but he's on the young side to be deflowered. Bring him back when he hits actual puberty. Also, my website says no girls allowed."

She started to slam the door, but I was faster. "The good news is we're not here for a session."

I forced my way in, trying to wave off whatever smell was coming from inside.

Larissa huffed and finally stepped aside, letting Lee and Casey walk in.

Casey gave her a grin. "You look so pretty."

She rolled her brown eyes and strode over to what looked like a humidifier. "I won't need this now."

"What is that?" I asked.

"It's incense," Lee said, taking a look around. "Think of it as hooker aromatherapy. It's formulated for species. If she was doing a human, there would be a lot of pheromones and stuff."

I didn't want to think about what that would smell like. "Vamps like flowers?"

She shrugged as she reached for a crystal glass. "Go figure. I don't know. I simply know it makes the vamp easier to deal with. If I were doing a demon, this place would smell like Starbucks. It's weird. Caffeine smells do it for us. And the blood of the innocent, but I find that can get the cops called in. So a single mom, her kid, and a vamp walk into a brothel. Is this the beginning of a joke?"

"No joke, and we'll be more than happy to pay you for your time," I assured her.

Casey was still smiling. "I have a Visa."

Maybe I needed one of those incense things. Might make the vamps in my life easier to deal with. "Like I said, we'll pay you for your time, but I need you to answer a few questions about what happened two nights ago."

Larissa went pale and I saw the moment she started to lose control of her form. Tiny demon horns formed, poking out from her forehead. They were dainty things, as were the claws forming on her hands. The glass she held shook and she took a long drink before setting it down. "You need to leave now."

That wasn't going to happen. "Do you deny that you spent the evening with a halfling named Lester, a member of the royal…" I had the name in my notes. It was of those crazy demon names that I'm pretty sure are the only reasons we have the letter *x* in our alphabet. I glanced down at the notepad I carried in my satchel at all times. Mostly it was doodles and reminders of shit I would still probably forget. I shuffled through it until I found the right page. "Lester, of the royal family Hixalnaxendallixxxba. Yeah, I probably got that wrong, but you get the point."

Casey smiled and said it perfectly. "It means Bringers of Death and Pain."

"I know what it means, but I have no idea why you would think I know some halfling." Larissa seemed to have gotten her moxie back. Though the horns were still poking through and her eyes had gone more black than brown, her hands had stopped shaking.

Lee stared up at her. "Mostly because we have a photo of you leaving the halfling's home shortly after he was murdered."

I felt my jaw drop. "How the hell do you know that?"

His shoulders shrugged. "I told you, math is boring. I hate it. But I'm good at hacking into Casey's system and getting all the files. Murder is way more interesting."

"You are a menace," I hissed his way because there were pictures of dead bodies in those files. What the hell was wrong with him?

Besides being a forty-plus lone wolf in a tiny human boy body.

Casey was showing our new hooker friend the picture. "You see, I had to use this software I developed to get rid of all the pixilation, but you look real pretty."

"You are not getting laid," I said to Casey as I took over. I pointed to the woman in the picture. "This is you. I have footage from a security camera across the street as well. I'm here from the Council, under the king's orders and direction, so it would help a lot if you would talk to me."

She stiffened again. "Are you her?"

"Depends on who 'her' is." Though I knew what she was asking. I softened my voice slightly. "I'm not here to hurt you. I'm here for some answers. Lester wasn't the first halfling murdered lately."

She poured herself another drink. "I know. Believe me, I know. Do you want to know the crazy thing? I was there that night to ask him to get out, to be anywhere but Dallas. I liked Les. He was a good guy."

"Why did you think he should leave?" Now that I had her attention, I could slow things down. Especially since Lee was prowling around the room now. I was sure it looked like he was checking out the art on the walls, but I knew Lee. He was looking for something. Like I said before, he's a damn fine detective. "Had you heard a rumor?"

Her head shook slightly. "No rumors, only the truth. The king is killing us. He's tricking us and we all need to get as far from Dallas as possible."

Shit. So it was about to get political. "Why do you think it was the king?"

"Do it already." She faced me, her shoulders back. "You think I don't know who you are? You're the *Nex Apparatus*. You're the death machine. If you showed up on my doorstep, it's because you missed me when your team killed Les."

There was no way to miss how she was breathing, how stiff her limbs were. This chick thought I was about to murder her and she was still standing in front of me, ready to give me hell.

Not all demons are bad. I get that more than most people. I've stood in front of the most evil ones and they don't show a ton of bravery. "You're a halfling, too, aren't you?"

Her cheeks flushed, but she didn't back down. "Yes. Not that it matters to most people. Lester and I grew up together. Needless to say his family is much more powerful than mine. We went to school together."

"Is there like a Demon *Degrassi*?" Because that would be cool.

"Something like that," she allowed. "I'm not royal but my mom has some connections. Les and I were close. He was more than some client. He was…he was a good man. He believed we could all get along. He wanted to avoid a war. That was why he was trying to meet with the king."

I could hear the conviction in her voice. My only real thought while she was talking was that I could work with her. She might tell me the truth. "I don't have a single problem with Les. I didn't know him, but I know someone who thought highly enough of him that he wanted him to sway the king in favor of peace. So now my only job is to find who killed him."

"And then what? You give him a medal?"

She was a demon with a one-track mind. "Then I bring whoever that person is to justice. And you need to understand that I'm talking about my justice. I'm an eye for an eye girl, and if I can put a little extra pain in there, I will."

Lee had turned and was giving me the biggest smile. "I'm so proud of you, darlin'."

Yeah, I wished that didn't make me feel as good as it did. I tried not to think about it, tried to focus on the issue at hand. "What did you see that night?"

She looked at me, a stubborn tilt to her chin. "Why do you care about what happens to demons?"

I needed to make myself plain. "I don't. Not to the full breeds. Look, I get you might love your momma and all that, but if she's a full breed, she can take care of herself. My job on this plane is to deal with the evil demons and protect those who want to live here peaceably. I don't give a crap about your horns. I don't care about your profession. I only care about whether or not you're here to cause trouble."

"I like your horns." Casey proved he didn't need a steady stream of what was likely part vamp aphrodisiac/part sedative. "They're cute. And she isn't here to kill you. She's pretty cool, except when it comes to acknowledging good work. Then she's shitty. As long as you don't expect a pat on the back from her when you save her ass, she's okay. Her best friend, on the other hand… Liv is a beautiful soul."

Nix the sedative. "What exactly is in that incense?"

"Liv would eat you alive, buddy," Lee pointed out.

Casey smiled and nodded. "Yes. Wouldn't that be nice?"

Larissa sighed and finally seemed to relax a bit, as though our antics made her more comfortable. "Like I said, it's formulated for vampires, though it won't work on the strongest. He must be young as hell. It's meant to protect me and enhance the experience for the client. It relaxes the vampire, makes him a bit more horny, and in some cases much more truthful."

That could come in handy. I might need a stash of that.

Lee came to stand next to me. "Can you tell us what happened to Lester? How much did you see? Also, do you have any beer?"

"No beer," I said under my breath. "You're incorrigible."

"I'm thirsty and all I've had for nine freaking years is water, milk, and some weird juice shit in a box," Lee complained. "Zoey even took away my damn Dr Peppers. I need a beer, woman. Detecting is thirsty work."

Larissa watched us like she was enjoying a tennis match. "I don't drink beer. I do have some Scotch."

"I'll take…" Lee began.

I put my hand over his mouth, happy I was dealing with the miniature version of him and not the full-grown one. "I'm so going to tell your dads what a pain in the ass you are. How about we skip the refreshments and move on to the storytelling portion?"

"He's really your dad, dude. He sounds exactly like you," Casey was saying.

Lee put his hands up and I let him go. "I'll be good, darlin'."

"I am so confused," Larissa said. "I'm starting to wonder if this isn't a weird dream, so I'm going to go with it. Okay, I went over to Lester's around nine that night. We spend time together whenever he's in town."

"Friendly time or work time?" I had to ask.

She smiled slightly. "Being with Les wasn't work. I care about…cared about him. It's so hard to think of him as being gone."

She wouldn't have thought of it because Lester should have lived a long life. "He would have been hard to kill."

Larissa's eyes glanced away, as though seeing something that wasn't there. "No. Not at all. In the end, it was simple."

"The crazy neighbor talked about a white light," Lee said.

He really did read all my notes. Trent was right. He needed to be spanked more. Or put on the payroll. One of the two. "There were reports of some ground shaking as well as the light."

"It was terrible. One minute we were happy in bed and the next… well, it was like the world was ending. That light. I don't know how to describe it. It was more than light. It felt like I was being burned by it. I suppose I felt the ground shake a little, but I was much more concerned with that light. I wondered later on how no one talked about it. How it didn't make the news."

I had my theories. "I think it was highly localized. The police thought it was a random electrical event. It didn't last more than a few seconds, so they're explaining it away as meteorological."

“Seconds?” Larissa asked. “It felt like hours. I burned for hours. When I came out of it, I couldn’t believe I was still alive.”

Shit. I knew what she was going to say next. “And when you came out of it, Lester was already dead?”

She shook her head and my hopes rose. “He was fighting something. The light receded and the world went back to normal except there was a man in the room and he had a sword.”

“A man? Not a lizard?” I was kind of hoping for lizard because I worried who that man would be.

“Eww, no lizard,” she affirmed. “But the man was kind of gross, too. He was holding a sword. It was so bright. It was like all the light in the world reflected off that sword. I couldn’t look at it, but I did see that the man holding the sword was injured.”

“His hands,” I prompted.

She nodded. “He was bleeding heavily. You know the funny thing is there *was* something vaguely reptilian about him. He had claws like a reptile and his eyes. His eyes were weird and old, and I could only think of one word when I saw them. Dragon.”

Shit. Shit. Shit. “Can you describe him?”

She shook her head, that purple piece getting tangled in her horns. “No. Not past that. I ran. I realized Lester was going to die when the man shoved the sword in his heart and I knew I was next so I ran. It was cowardly of me, but I couldn’t help him.”

Something about the way she said it made me wonder. I would have bet she was utterly truthful right up until that moment when she told me she couldn’t describe him.

Why would she be honest about everything except that? Unless this wasn’t a question of description and more one of complete recognition and fear.

I needed to figure out which one. “Why didn’t you call the Council that night? They owe you protection.”

She shook her head. “The king hates our kind. There’s no protection for us. He lumps us all in with the purebreds.”

“He doesn’t,” Lee replied. “Not really. The king talks a good game, but if you met him, you would see. My nanny is a halfling. He's a treasured part of our family."

"Well, perhaps if you knew the king before, he'll let you in, but he doesn't anymore," Larissa explained. "We all know that if this comes to a fight, there will be no choosing sides. We'll have to go in with our full-bred brethren even though no one likes what that will mean. We'll be cannon fodder on one side or merely slaughtered on the other."

This was what Donovan needed to hear. This was what Marcus and Gray were attempting to get him to understand.

"Don't call the Council then." I fished out my card, handing her several. "You or anyone else who needs help can call me."

She huffed, but took the card. "You work for the Council."

"They wish," my dad said under his breath.

"I'm associated with the Council, but I assure you if a Council member was doing something wrong, I would deal with it and I wouldn't let politics come into it, and I won't allow politics to stop me from saving you from some supe who's trying to kill you." I had to make my play here and now. "No matter how close he is to the queen."

Her eyes came up, catching on mine, and I had my answer.

Lee cursed in a way he was only supposed to if he was running from a dinosaur or being eaten by a shark. Maybe his mom would say that having his old soul reemerge was a third exception to the rule.

"What's going on?" Casey scratched his head as though trying to figure something out. Maybe the aromatherapy was wearing off on him.

"I need you to say it." I couldn't take that look on her face as fact. I needed her willing to tell me the truth, willing to be a witness. "Why didn't you call the Council that night? You know the rules of the plane. You know you were supposed to call."

Her shoulders went back and her chin came up. "I didn't call because the queen's best friend split a hole in reality, somehow managed to imprison me in light, and when I came out of it, I watched as he pierced the heart of one of the best men I've ever known. I didn't call because I figured the king himself had sent an assassin."

We were in so much trouble if all the halflings were thinking this way. War was unthinkable, but a war where the lines were drawn simply by birth, with no thought to right or wrong, seemed unimaginable to me.

I know crime. I know people, and by people I mean anything living and breathing and making conscious choices. Halflings are considered to be of the Earth plane. Even if Mom was a demon or Daddy came straight from Hell. Do you know why they're considered Earth planers? Because they won't truly be accepted by Heaven or Hell. Because we are the plane that accepts the odd, the offbeat, the forbidden. We're the last place these beings can truly call home.

And I realized that Devinshea Quinn was right.

I am their warrior.

"I think I'm going to need you to come back to the Council with me. I know you're scared, but you have to tell the king this story." I kept my tone as calm as possible because the last thing I wanted to do was terrorize her more than she'd already been, but I needed Donovan to hear her story, and not from me.

She shook her head. "I can't."

"I'm going to be beside you the whole time. I promise."

"But he's there."

I didn't have to ask who *he* was. "Would it shock you to know that he doesn't remember a thing? Neil Roberts has no idea what he's doing. He's being used and manipulated by a high-ranking demon."

"That makes it worse," she replied. "Those full breeds might not invite us home for dinner, but they're quick to punish us if they feel like we've betrayed them."

I wasn't going to force her to come in. I had the story. I believed she didn't know much else. I fished out the cash I'd brought. "If you change your mind, you know how to get hold of me. Please call me if you hear anything at all."

She looked down at the cash I was offering her, and for a second

I thought she might refuse to take it. She sighed as though realizing there was no practical reason to turn down the money. "I'll call you." She glanced over at Casey. "And next time, come for an actual appointment. I'm incredibly skilled at fellatio."

Casey perked up. "Hey, I got a Visa."

Before I could slap the back of his head, there was a knock on the door.

Larissa sighed. "It's probably my landlord. He's a massive ass and I swear he lives to block people from parking in perfectly available slots." She threw open the door and frowned. "Frank, there's no one in the parking lot at this time of day. If you tow my customers, I'll come after…"

She didn't finish the sentence because "Frank" shoved a silver knife through her heart. He moved with super-human speed. One moment he was standing there in the doorway, wearing his stained wife beater, his bloated belly straining against the fabric, and the next he was staring at me, a bloody knife in his hand. Larissa's body smoked as it started to drop to the floor.

I'd told her I would save her and she was dead. I hadn't kept my promise long.

"Hello, Kelsey." The perfect upper-crust and familiar accent chilled my blood. I knew that voice. I'd heard it many times. "So sorry about the mess, but it was unavoidable. I think we should talk. I hear you've been looking for me."

Yes. I had been. I'd been looking to kill him. Nemcox was here and I was ready for battle.

Chapter Eleven

Or not. I realized as Nemcox stepped over Larissa's dead body that I'd gotten caught without my sword. Hauling Gladys around can be a difficult endeavor. I live in an open carry state, but a chick with a silver sword running around the streets of Dallas still attracts attention unless there happens to be a handy comic book convention close by. I fit in well at those, right up to the point that I punch someone.

I had the added problem of having brought a kid into battle with my only backup being Casey. He was trying. Casey trained every day with the king's warriors, but he wasn't ever going to be a badass in the field. He was the best keyboard jockey around, but I couldn't leave him to watch over Lee. Lee would eat his lunch and fast.

Nemcox was right there, and there was nothing I could do. He wasn't even in his damn demon body. This was why I tried so hard to call him to my hand. The calling would force him into my circle in his actual body, his big, nasty demon body that I could then poke with my sword and hopefully kill. Not this time. He was possessing a human soul, so all I could manage was to kill some dude who was too quick to tow and Nemcox would find someone else to terrorize.

And somehow my wolf wasn't pounding at the cage. Somehow I

was calm. I'd looked at the situation, evaluated, and the wolf and I realized retreat was our only option, otherwise the people around us would get killed, and all for nothing. This was typically when the she-wolf decided she didn't give a shit about the humans and my hands started getting twitchy.

Apparently getting well laid by an alpha wolf did wonders for me.

"You all right, darlin'?" Lee stared up at me with far too old eyes. "You need to stay calm."

"I'm good." Except I felt truly bad for Larissa. I eyed Nemcox. "Did you have to do that? She wasn't doing anything wrong."

"Oh, I suspect she was about to." He frowned down at the body. "Loose lips sink ships and all that. Like I said, I'm only here to talk now that I've handled that particular problem. Can we agree to that, Hunter? I won't gut your little friend there or tear out that one's heart and you'll not try anything foolish."

Lee started to growl beside me. It wasn't an intimidating sound. I glanced down at him.

He shrugged. "Worked better in the other body."

Casey held a hand up. "Uhm, I vote for the not getting my heart ripped out of my chest. Is that one of those things that grows back…never mind. It sounds painful. Hard pass, Kelsey."

I could spare at least one person. "I'm not talking to you while you're wearing a meat suit. I don't care what that dude's done, the longer you're inside him, the more he suffers."

"Fine. I don't particularly like wearing him anyway. He's large and unattractive." The man smiled and then a blank look came over his face and suddenly Larissa's body was easing up off the ground and grinning my way. "Demonflesh. She's actually more than a halfling. More like three quarters or so. I don't need this flesh to be living to use it. It's got another half an hour or so before it starts to rot entirely."

Nemcox rose and turned to the landlord. "You're having a terrible dream. Far too much cheap whiskey. Walk back to your apartment and sleep this one off."

The man turned and walked away, his eyes totally unfocused.

"Is this better?" Nemcox moved into the room, shutting the door. If it bothered him that he was covered in blood, he didn't show it. He smoothed back Larissa's raven dark hair. "It certainly feels better, though you need to understand I don't tend to like drag. I'm not one of those poor boys who wants to be a girl. It's so messy being a girl. Now let's talk about why you keep trying to kill me. I've been patient so far. You're practically my sister-in-law. I don't want to upset my brother by having to lop your pretty head off. It makes for terrible family reunions."

Lee started moving and I had to grab the back of his T-shirt. Thank god my dad was small. I was fairly certain had I been dealing with Lee version 1.0, he already would have attacked.

It wasn't hard to see where I got my anger impulse issues.

Still, I couldn't let my father attack a demon. "Stop. This is not your fight."

"Hell it isn't," he shot back, his eyes on Nemcox.

And Nemcox suddenly seemed totally interested in my dad. He stood there wearing Larissa's body, but the eyes were his. They were dark, and I could see his demonic brain working out the problem. "Is that what I think it is, Hunter?"

I stepped in front of Lee, unwilling to leave him in the line of fire. "That is the king's son and none of your business. You don't want to piss off the king any more than you already have, do you? He's not happy with how you tried to help execute him last year."

"Well, it wasn't like I would have enjoyed it. Sometimes one's duty is onerous. And you stopped that, you minx." He turned his head a bit, as though still trying to get a look at the boy. "And while that may be the king's son, he's so much more, isn't he? How did you do it? Do you have any idea how well Heaven hides those old souls?"

"I don't want to talk about it. You came here to tell me to stop hunting you." I was more than willing to lie to get us out of there. "Done. My trainer already had this discussion with me."

Nemcox leaned against the granite bar, glancing down at Larissa's perfectly done nails. "I'm sure he did. That Marcus always was a practical one. It's how he's stayed alive all this time. Somehow, I don't think you're the same, though you do have a new glow about you. Did my brother finally figure out he could use that nasty old prophet's sword in fun and inventive ways?"

Nemcox had not been a fan of his brother hitting the road with Jacob. "We've worked out a few things. Gray and I are good."

"I know you won't believe me, but I'm glad to hear it. We're not too far from his contract being up," Nemcox said. "I want you to know that you are welcome to join us. You're part of the family, and an honored one. Which is precisely why you have to stop this ridiculous vendetta of yours. Tell her, wolf. It wasn't my fault you died."

Lee was right back to rage. "My daughter isn't setting foot on the fucking Hell plane and if any one of you tries, I swear I'll kill you all."

He might not growl the way he used to, but Dad can make a threat.

It was also a mistake. I knew it the moment Nemcox's pitch black eyes widened. Lee had confirmed something better left unsaid. "I knew it was you in there. Oh, how delightful and unexpected. Now that is a card I hadn't counted on having in my hand. Don't you love that? When you draw an ace you were certain was off the board entirely."

I had no real idea what he was talking about, but Little Lee was definitely having more trouble with control than I was. I needed to get him out of here because I wasn't sure Nemcox wouldn't take him out if he had the chance. "I will take your very kind invitation seriously. Thanks a lot. And no more attempted murders. Got it. So, I'll be on my way."

Nemcox's eyes narrowed. "You're almost too calm. Not even a few hours in a virtual love nest with my brother should do that for you. That wolf inside you should still be rattling the cage. Unless…"

He took a deep breath. When he opened his eyes, I could see the judgment there. "You cheated on my brother?"

See, Heaven and Hell have a few things in common. Slinging the word *whore* around is one of them. "You know Gray has to have a host when he uses that sword."

He seemed to think that through for a moment before his lips curled up. "Ah, of course. I wouldn't have gone that way, but I understand. I would have thought he would use Marcus."

"Marcus was unavailable."

Nemcox's lips curled up slightly. "Well, things happen for a reason I suppose. Once you're happily ensconced in Gray's new home, there won't be any need for a host. You'll only need to call out and your husband will be there. Can't you see? He needs you as much as you need him."

This was the true danger of listening to the demon. He could sound so reasonable. The idea of living with Gray made my heart twist. Of course, I reminded myself that our residence would likely be 666 Blood and Guts Avenue.

And that home would have no place for a baby she-wolf.

But I wasn't about to have a family session with my demonic potential brother-in-law. "I care about your brother very much and we're in a good place."

The demon glanced up at me. "You do understand that I'm not the reason your dear papa is going to have to go through puberty again?"

"I know you were there." I relaxed the tiniest bit because Lee seemed to have stopped trying to attack the demon with his nine-year-old hands. "I know you made the deal with Marini."

"Did I?" Nemcox asked. "Or was it someone else? Have you thought about the fact that perhaps I was a mere broker for the deal and not the man behind it? Things aren't always as they seem. People tend to make everything about themselves without ever looking at the bigger picture. Especially queens. Good lord, give a woman a tiara and two men and she thinks the world revolves around her."

"I was there." My dad didn't seem to know when he should stay quiet and hunker down. He stood next to me, facing down the demon in a dead body, his hands fists at his sides. "I know exactly what happened and why. For you it was all about Neil. You turned us over so you could rape my friend in Hell."

"I assure you, there was no rape involved," Nemcox replied. "Well, nothing forcible, and if a few spells are used to enhance the pleasure, I say it's all for the best. And you're wrong, wolf. My precious Neil was merely payment for doing my master's bidding."

"Yes, for turning over Zoey," Lee insisted. "For sending Zoey into that place so she could be raped and tortured."

"You do like tossing out that word, don't you?" Nemcox said with a sigh. "Zoey wasn't the end result my master wanted, though he did see the upside. Without Zoey's imprisonment, the king would have taken much longer and the war would have been bloodier. She was a side product he happened to have, and he used her to get the outcome he wanted. Think of it as a three-way trade. If country A has sugar to trade but no lines of communication to Country B who wants that sugar, and Country C has a desperate need for some companionship that only Country B can provide, they all get together and everyone is happy."

I was drawing lines I didn't like. If Zoey was sugar and Neil was companionship… "Who was Country B?"

Dark eyes stared at me. "Who do you think, Hunter? Who was the only one there who didn't get out alive?"

Lee frowned beside me. "I was a guard. No one gave a shit about me except I wouldn't let Marini take Zoey that night."

"Oh, I assure you someone cared about you very much. Someone needed you dead because he figured out that only one soul in all the world could truly harm him in the end. Only one soul in all the world could ever stand up to his magnificence." Nemcox's voice was low and reverent.

Lee stepped back as though someone had physically smacked him. His face went pale and he shook his head. "Why? Why would

Myrddin do that?"

I was confused. When all this was going down, I was in high school. "Wait. Some dude named Myrddin put a hit out on my dad?"

"Merlin." Casey stepped up. "He's talking about Merlin Satanspawn. Turns out he wasn't merely a legend. Henri forced me to read all the historical documents regarding the last ten years. He thought it might be helpful for you. The king found and revived the wizard known as Merlin. He needed Merlin's expertise to fix an issue with his heart. It was only as they were leaving the pocket universe Merlin was caged in that the former head of the Council, Louis Marini, set up a trap and kidnapped the queen and Dev Quinn and murdered your father. I read all of it, but I don't think I truly believed it. He's real?"

"Oh, yes, he's real," Nemcox replied with what sounded like adoration. "He's real and he's been learning this world. Someday he'll come back."

That didn't sound good. "Come back here?"

"Come back to the king, of course." Nemcox was back to playing coy. It was there in the wave of his hand, in the batting of a dead woman's eyelashes. "Myrddin is tied to the sword king, you know that large ornate thing the king wields from time to time? That's Excalibur, the real one, the one Camelot was built around. As Merlin mentored Arthur, so he will one day ease Daniel through his greatest test."

"Why would he want the king's guard dead?" My father had been important, but only because he was a guard and Zoey adored him. From what I understood, the king had wanted to fire him many times. And he'd been the queen's guard. My uncle Zack had been Donovan's right-hand man for years.

"I told you," Nemcox insisted. "One of the great one's skills is being able to see various paths. A bit like having prophecy talent. I acted as Myrddin's focus while we were in the pocket world. I don't know what he saw for sure, but I know he believed that the lone wolf would be his downfall. He and one other, another magician, but at the time he wasn't born. I do believe he took care of that one as well."

"He killed a baby?" I might be taking down a wizard.

"Nothing so terrible, dear. He simply sent the pregnant mother fleeing to another plane where her mewling offspring can't harm his magnificence. You know when you think about it, he was actually doing it for the king. If Myrddin is dead, who would help him in his time of need?" Nemcox bit his bottom lip and attempted to look as innocent as a blood-soaked prostitute could look. "The king shouldn't be angry with me. I was helping him. And look, you got dear papa back. So why are you after me, sister?"

"I think I would have preferred to meet my father when he wasn't nine," I shot back because my patience only went so far.

"She's not coming after you," Lee said, stepping up to the demon. "Not anymore. She has no problem with you so you should leave her alone. From now on, she'll stop all attempts to call you to her. If she does that, can we make a deal that you'll leave her be?"

"You aren't making any damn deals for me," I said quickly. "That was not a contract and I don't agree to it."

He was going to give me a heart attack. I suddenly felt so bad for his parents.

Nemcox had dropped to one knee, looking deeply into Lee's face. A long moment passed and Nemcox gasped. "Good god. Is it true? Do you know what you are? Does the king know?"

Lee stepped back, his face going blank. "Leave her alone or we'll both find out. You don't want that, do you?"

Nemcox looked shaken, as though he'd seen some kind of a ghost. "Merlin has no idea what he did, what you could become. By allowing you to die and come back, he might have fulfilled the prophecy. He thought if he killed you then, it would end the threat. But your soul came back and… What fools we were."

I got a chill. It started somewhere near the vicinity of my stomach and rushed out to every limb. This was one of those moments, one of those times when the world flipped and changed and nothing was the same. I might not understand what Nemcox was talking about, but I knew when that demon was serious. Something about Lee scared Nemcox. Somehow he thought this fragile, human version of my father was even more dangerous to his "great one" than he'd been as a strong and powerful lone wolf. It was obvious the demon felt loyal to the wizard. He'd helped kill my father once. We were in a vulnerable position. Would he do it again? Would he do it here? Or would he wait, biding his time and allowing us to forget the threat? Would he be waiting somewhere down the road to do the wizard's bidding?

"I'm ready to make a deal." I only had one way to ensure my father's safety. I had one bargaining chip the demon wanted.

Me.

Nemcox's head came up, his eyes lighting. "What?" He looked between us. "Of course, for my silence. You don't even know what I know, but you're smart enough to realize I'll use it. I'll find Myrddin and tell him. I'll be true to my master. But I'm truer to my family. Yes, that is a smart play. Perhaps you're more practical than I gave you credit for."

"Kelsey, stop it. You're not making any kind of deal," Lee insisted.

I kept my eyes on the demon. "You say this Myrddin dude killed my father once. He'll try it again, won't he?"

Lee had a hand on my wrist, tugging earnestly.

"Oh, yes." Nemcox ignored Lee entirely. "I assure you. Once I let the wizard know what's happened to his plans, he'll come after the loner again. He won't do it in such a spectacular fashion since he won't want to harm his relationship with the king, but he'll find a way. It's what he does."

"I'll talk to the king," Lee swore. "In this life, he's my father and he'll believe me. I'll tell him everything that was said here. He'll know not to trust the wizard."

"One of the things that the queen talked about was the wizard's enormous influence over the king, and even over Devinshea." Casey's shoulders had gone back, his jaw tightening as he seemed to come to some decision. "When the king was in close contact, the queen felt the wizard had some power over him. Lee was the one who couldn't be swayed by his arguments. The queen felt like her wolves were the only ones who weren't influenced by Merlin."

"The wizard is a tricky fellow. He's gotten away with many crimes in the past. I'm afraid your best bet is for me to keep my pretty mouth shut." Nemcox leaned against the bar, a smirk on his borrowed lips. "So let's deal, Hunter. You know what I'm going to want, don't you?"

It turned my stomach. I knew exactly what he would want. "You want my promise that I'll marry Gray and live with my husband after his contract is up."

In Hell. Far from Marcus. Away from Trent.

Now my wolf started rattling. I could feel her. The minute I started thinking about leaving Trent, she started to howl deep inside me.

"Darlin', I want you to take a deep breath," Lee was saying. His hand was in mine, small but reassuring. "You're shaking. This is not going to happen. There's no deal. Do I make myself clear?"

He was nine and he had a whole life ahead of him. I couldn't risk it. I'd brought him along with me. I should have driven him right back home. I'd done this. I wasn't going to let Nemcox talk and put out a hit on him. No matter what. "I need to see it in writing."

"Of course," the demon practically purred. "I'll have a satan here in no time at all, dearest sister."

"Gray won't allow this," Lee said. "And have you thought about the fact that she's a Hunter? She needs contact with wolves or she gets violent."

Nemcox smiled brightly. "That's perfect because we love violence where I come from. A little isolation-induced insanity won't bother us at all. And my brother will be grateful in the end. He'll have his wife and family with him always. He won't ever have to share her with a trainer or some random wolf. It will be as it should be. He will sit at the head of his household and she will be his obedient wife. Are you ready now?"

I started to nod my head when Casey stepped in front of me.

"I invoke the laws agreed upon at the last meeting of the Council and the Royal Guild of Demons. You are not allowed to contract with vampirekind without counsel present. The Council itself must be informed that Ms. Owens is contemplating signing a demon contract. By our own rules, set up by the queen herself, Ms. Owens must go through counseling, a class on contracts and how they work, and think about the contract for a full twenty-four hours before she would be allowed to even think about signing a contract."

Nemcox got into Casey's space, working that dead body like it was slightly snakelike. Definitely predatory and dangerous. "Ms. Owens isn't vampirekind."

Casey's voice was shaking but he stood his ground. "According to the rules, I can request a trial to determine her status. I require a medical test. If she's been taking vampire blood, she's vampirekind."

I got what he was trying to do, but this was my dad. "I'm not on vamp blood right now."

Marcus's blood should be out of my system.

"We'll need a blood test to prove it," Casey insisted. "Or I'll have you both in front of the Council for attempting to violate the laws of this plane."

"Or I could tear your heart out right here and no one has to know," Nemcox threatened.

Casey didn't move an inch. "And still your contract will not be valid. And still she will have friends who demand that the rules be enforced. You can kill me, asshole. No one's going to care. But if you take the *Nex Apparatus* by right of contract, you fucking better be sure you dotted every *i* and crossed every goddamn *t* because everyone will care. You might want a war, but most of your kind doesn't. Most of those upper-crust demons like the world exactly the way it is, and they don't want their cushy torture palaces upended by a lengthy battle. We will go to war over her. The king will never let you take her unless you've followed every letter of the law. So if you want her, you better listen to me and do your due diligence before she signs on that line."

Nemcox's mouth opened and he hissed, a nasty, evil sound. He got right in Casey's face, and for a second I worried I would see his second murder of the day. Then he backed up and looked over at me. "I won't tell. Not until we work this out. I'll send my requirements. Don't fuck me over, sister. You won't like what happens."

Larissa's body dropped to the ground like a doll whose strings had been cut.

I tried to breathe. I was in a trap and I wasn't sure how to get out. I actually believed the fucker. If there's one thing demons take seriously, it's their contracts. If Nemcox said he wouldn't tell the magician about my father's soul still walking the plane, I believed him. But at some point he would tell.

Unless I found a way to kill him.

Casey's body folded in two and he took a series of hyperbolic breaths. "Oh, my god. Holy shit. If I could pee I would have."

Lee put a hand on the baby vamp's shoulder. "You did good, son. You did good."

And I wondered if I hadn't just signed my own jail sentence.

* * * *

I pulled my Jeep into the parking garage and the first thing I saw was Daniel Donovan, standing in the middle of the space, that I'm-the-king-of-the-world-and-you've-disappointed-me frown on his face.

And naturally he wasn't alone. My uncle stood beside him, his suit perfectly pressed and unlined face still managing to convey how angry he was. Then there was Trent, and I got the feeling he was the angriest of all.

Casey shoved his wrist toward my face for the tenth time. He'd been doing it over and over and I was ready to murder the persistent fucker. He'd opened a nick on his wrist and he kept trying to force me to ingest the blood that welled there. It was annoying and super gross.

I slapped his wrist away.

"It won't do any good," Lee said from the backseat. "We need to get more than a little in her. Probably at least a full cup. I know where Henri keeps a couple of bags of Donovan's blood. We'll force that down her throat."

I slammed the car into park. "You'll do nothing of the kind. Which one of you turned me in?"

"I texted my dad," Lee said and then frowned as though he hadn't meant to say that. "I mean Quinn. I texted Quinn and he managed to get hold of Dad. Donovan, damn it."

Before I could think about what that meant, the passenger door was coming open and Casey was getting hauled out of the car by his neck. Trent was standing there, holding Casey up. "What the fuck do you think you're doing? You don't touch her."

Sleep with a guy once and he gets all shades of possessive. "He was trying to force vamp blood down my throat so I can't sign the demon contract that's going to save my dad."

Trent dropped him immediately. "You trying to prove she's vampirekind so no demon can sign a contract with her?"

Casey held his throat and nodded.

Trent whacked him on the back. "That's smart. Don't worry about it. I know where Henri keeps the king's blood. We'll force some down her throat. It'll last longer. Give her a good dose of Donovan and it'll stay in her bloodstream for months."

"That was my plan," Lee said, a frown on his face.

"You! You brat," an angry feminine voice echoed through the garage.

"Shit." Lee went a bit pale as the queen made an appearance. "Mom, I didn't do it."

The queen's heels clicked along the concrete and she pointed one righteous finger Lee's way. "You are grounded."

Lee seemed to come out of his momentary fear. "You can't ground me. I'm forty-seven freaking years old."

"Holy shit." Zack stared at Lee. "It really is you."

Lee sighed and held up a hand. "Thank god, brother. I thought I was going to miss you. Hey, buddy, remember that time I looked the other way when you were seventeen and you brought that girl home. Yeah, I'm calling that one in. I need a beer."

I was going to let the queen handle that one. I needed to talk to the king. He would see reason. He wouldn't let the damn wolves force-feed me blood. And Hugo. Hugo was the academics' law expert. I could get him to write a preliminary contract.

"Your Majesty, if I could have a moment of your time," I started.

"Gray's on his way," Trent said.

"Do you even begin to comprehend how dangerous it was what you did?" The queen was down on one knee, her hands on Lee's shoulders. The queen started in on Lee.

"What do you mean Gray's on his way?" There were other things being said that I should probably pay attention to, but Trent knew how to draw me in.

"I mean he called me and yelled at me for a long time and he's on his way. How dare you think I would allow you to do something like this?" Trent loomed over me.

"I don't think I can give you a beer, man," Zack was saying. "Maybe a root beer."

Donovan was on his cell phone. "Yes, we have him. Calm down, Dev. He's fine. Well, mostly. We have other problems to deal with. Get Hugo up to my office pronto. And take the warding off the roof. Gray says he's found someone who can transport him here. I told him the safest place to do it would be the roof. I don't want him messing up and appearing in someone's shower. Marcus is going to meet him up there."

"Allow?" I did not like that word. I stood up to Trent, which is hard to do since the man has about a foot in height on me. "You think you can allow or disallow something?"

Trent stared down at me. "I think you're crazy if you think I'm going to let you go to Hell. Have you thought about the fact that without Marcus to balance you, you need me? Gray can't do it on his own. Everyone knows that. He knows that."

"Zoey, will you take our son upstairs? Dev's waiting," Donovan said, his voice deep as though the emotion of the day had gotten to him.

"I need to talk to you, Donovan," Lee said.

Zoey had a hand on his elbow. "You can talk to your dad after he handles Kelsey's problem. You do understand that this is all your fault. If you hadn't run away like that, she wouldn't have been forced to offer herself up to save you."

"Don't you think I know that?" Lee pulled his arm away. "I won't let you treat me like a child, damn it." He stopped, his hand going to his head, and suddenly he was Little Lee again. I could see it in his eyes. He looked up and there was such confusion there. "Mom?"

Zoey got to one knee. "Lee? Baby?"

He blinked again and sighed. "No. It's me. I'm back, but something's wrong. I've got a headache. I need to talk to Donovan about something. Why can't I remember? It was right there. Dad? Where's Papa?"

Donovan picked him up. "I'm taking him upstairs. Someone call Henri and tell him to meet us. Trent, you don't let her out of your sight."

I wasn't going anywhere. "I want to be with Lee."

Donovan was already moving. "No, you'll go to my office and you'll talk to Hugo. Do you understand? Unless you want to promise me here and now you're not signing a demon contract."

I kept my mouth shut because I couldn't promise him that. Someone had to protect Lee and I was the only one who could do it.

"Then you'll talk to Hugo." Donovan disappeared, the queen following behind him.

My uncle gave me a ferocious frown. "I have to go check on Lee and make sure the witches know something's going wrong with him. If you try to leave this compound, you're going to find out how fast I can go from the fun uncle to the one who locks your ass up. Am I understood?"

I gave him a jaunty salute and wondered if I could get lost at the bar on my way up to Donovan's office.

"We're going to talk about this later," my uncle promised before turning away. He looked to Trent. "You let her get away and we'll have a problem."

"I have no intention of letting her get away or sign some damn contract. It's not happening," Trent vowed.

But there wasn't anything they could do with the exception of shoving vamp blood down my throat, and I planned to fight that. I could even contest that in the trial that would establish my status.

I wasn't going to think about the whole Hell part. I was only going to think about the fact that my dad was in trouble and I was the only one who could get him out. Nemcox wouldn't accept anyone else.

"Do you want to explain to me what the hell you think you're doing?" Trent asked. Even though he kept his voice down, the sound reverberated through the parking garage.

"Not particularly." I needed to be cold, and arguing with Trent wasn't going to keep me calm. Not when what my instincts told me to do was to wrap my arms around him and ask him to help me save my dad. There wasn't anything he could do. He didn't have anything the demon would want. "We should go up to Donovan's office. Hugo will be there soon."

Hugo would be pissed, but if he wouldn't help me, I would find another lawyer. One who was willing to go against the king. Yeah. That was going to be easy to find. I wondered if a demon lawyer would be acceptable in a Council court. Probably not.

I started walking toward the elevator that would take me to Donovan's office. That's when something Trent had said before hit me. I turned on him. "What do you mean Gray knows that? What exactly does Gray know?"

I needed to understand what the hell was happening and why Gray and Trent were all buddy buddy suddenly.

"Gray knows that you need me. That he needs me. Marcus

knows, too. Why do you think he's had me take over large portions of your training?" Trent's voice was tight, his frustration obvious.

"That was because he had some important things to take care of," I replied. That was how Marcus had explained it to me. "And you don't really train me at all. We're in the gym together at the same time."

"I was assigned to take over his duties, Kelsey." Trent was in my space, overwhelming me. "Do you get that? I was assigned to take care of you, and part of that means not allowing you to do something as stupid as signing a contract with a demon. Consider yourself on lockdown, too. You can take this time and get to know your dad because I'm not allowing you out of here either. Maybe when Gray gets here he can talk some sense into you."

"Assigned to take over what duties?" Suspicion played through my head and I did not like what I was coming up with. "Are you telling me Marcus assigned you to fuck me?"

Trent stopped, his body tensing as though ready for a fight. "I'm here in case you need me."

I had to laugh at that. So last night hadn't been a selfless act of volunteerism. He'd been instructed to fuck me sane, and Trent was always a good soldier. He was the upright guy who did what his boss needed and rarely varied from the path he'd been told to march down. Pretty much my polar opposite. I would do some stupid shit just because some authority figure told me not to. "Well, I hope you get a bonus out of it."

I moved to the elevators and slapped a hand at the button. It immediately responded and opened for me. I got in, hoping to leave Trent to catch the next one. Naturally the wolf was too fast.

"You want to explain what that's supposed to mean?" He moved into the elevator, crowding me.

The doors closed and we were all alone in a space that should have been big enough, if Trent hadn't decided to take up all of it.

Still, I'm not one to let myself be intimidated. Or to give in to the almost overwhelming need to see how he kissed. He'd kissed me the night before, our mouths mingling in long communion. But it had been Gray I saw and felt, and now I wanted to know how much of Trent had been in that kiss. "You know what I meant. Marcus doesn't want the job of putting up with my shit anymore so he's found someone else. I hope you got a nice bump in salary because I'm a handful."

He put a hand on the wall behind me as the elevator started moving. "You're not a job, Kelsey."

"A fun fringe benefit then. You know we didn't hit the button. We're not going to the right floor."

"It wasn't fun," he growled my way.

Well, I had known that. I gave him my brightest smile. "Good news for you, buddy. I won't need you again. I'm signing my contract and marrying my man."

He stepped back, his eyes going wide. "What? You're getting married?"

At least I had the upper hand in this instance. Except every word I forced out of my mouth made my wolf twitchy. I was doing exactly what Bris had told me not to do. I was shoving my wolf side into a cage and not letting her out. I had to be the human side of the Hunter if I was going to save my father. "Yes, that's what the contract is about. I'm marrying Gray and part of our marriage contract agreement will include my promise to live with him permanently. Even after his contract goes into effect."

He was quiet for a moment and there was an odd look of hurt on his face. "Why would you do that?"

"Because I love him." There was so much more but I wanted to get on with it. I didn't want to sit down and explain that it was hard to think about not seeing Trent again, that he had somehow taken a piece of me as well. I wasn't the kind of girl who said those things. Hell, I usually didn't feel them and I didn't like the sensation. Especially not when I knew Trent had been ordered to get into bed with me. What felt like devotion to me was nothing but his job.

Trent shook his head. "It doesn't make any sense. I talked to him.

He didn't mention anything about marriage. He was making plans for what happens when his contract is up."

Wow, everyone was trying to take care of me and my wretched sexual needs today. "Exactly what plans does he have?"

"Well, they sure as hell didn't include you marrying him, so I would like to know what changed."

That wasn't an answer. "What plans did he make, Trent? Plans I'm not involved in, by the way. That might have been an oversight on his part."

Trent started to pace, not that he could get much of anywhere. Two steps forward, turn, two steps back. The restless behavior of an uncomfortable wolf. "He's making plans to ensure that you're okay. That you're taken care of."

"I can take care of myself." A complete lie, but I was good at those.

He stopped, his eyes stark as he stared at me. "Since I spent the better part of yesterday with a sword in my gut, I will agree to disagree with you."

"Won't happen again. I'm a rip the bandage off kind of girl. I'll do all the queen's classes and then I'll sign my contract and you won't have to worry about me." But I was already wondering if that same issue might not come up soon because the stress of the day was wearing on me. And my wolf was starting to understand that I wasn't playing around. The rattling was turning into clawing and nipping. "I'll go to the Hell plane. I've been told my particular brand of crazy will be accepted there."

The elevator doors opened. My assistant Justin stood there, dressed in his best *The Flash* T-shirt and carrying his tablet and the thermos of blood his wife always sent with him. He smiled as he caught sight of me. "Hey, boss. I got caught up on paperwork last night and I talked to a new client."

Trent turned on Justin and growled, the sound low and dangerous. "Not now."

Justin stepped back. "I'll take the next one."

So no help from my office then. I reached out and pressed the button for the tenth floor. "Way to scare the vamps, buddy."

He reached out and slapped the button that stopped the elevator. "I want to know why Gray changed his mind."

I wanted lots of things, but I wasn't getting them. There might be one thing I could goad him into telling me. "I want to know what Gray offered you."

"He didn't have to offer me anything."

"But he did, didn't he? What did he offer you? I'll find out anyway."

"I don't care about the damn money," Trent spat. "The money and the house are only ways to help keep you safe."

With Gray, it would be a lot of money. Likely millions. He might have been a Texas Ranger at one time, the cop kind, but his bank account looked more like a left-handed ace pitcher for the other Rangers.

"Back off, Wilcox." Because if he didn't, I might do something I shouldn't. He smelled so fucking good. He smelled like safety and sex and a home I hadn't known I missed.

He shook his head. "I can't. Do you think I can't feel you? We connected on a base level last night. Maybe you're too stubborn to feel it, but I do. Do you think I can't feel how much your head is spinning right now?"

It wasn't spinning, exactly, but there was a marked uptick in anxiety. I didn't like small spaces, but beyond that, he was delaying me. If I kept moving, I didn't have to think about it. I didn't have to acknowledge that signing that contract meant giving up one of my children. It meant giving up half of myself, and all of my sanity.

What had Gray said? He'd said I should watch out for a trick and a trap. I wasn't sure about the trick, but I'd been neatly trapped.

What was the path I was supposed to stay on? I only saw one and that was the one that led to Hell.

My hands started shaking. I tried to breathe.

Trent hit the button again and moved back into my space. "Baby,

I can feel your need. Something happened last night. Something that connected us. You might not have felt it because you were so focused on Gray, but I was there, too."

His hand came down, smoothing back my hair and sending a rush of pure energy through me. Calming energy.

I tried to shake my head because I didn't need another connection. I was only going to be allowed one once I signed my contract. One connection, and I wouldn't be able to see my mom or my brothers or Liv. I wouldn't get to see Lee grow up.

I heard Trent curse and suddenly he was behind me, his arms wrapped around me. I felt the warmth of his breath on my ear. "Don't fight me, bitch. I use that as a completely affectionate term. You're my bitch and you're so strong you can fight this. You just need some help."

I gritted my teeth as his hand slipped under the band of my jeans and started moving toward my pussy. I could feel the growl in the back of my throat. There are times when I can almost feel my body shifting, as though my limbs are cracking and moving to another space, a space I understand and welcome. It doesn't ever happen in reality, but in my mind I feel the change. Being near Trent made me feel that way. My instincts were twofold—to fight and claw and make him work for me or to get to my knees and give myself to the true alpha.

"I won't take more than you want to give me, but I will give you everything you need," he promised me. "Take it. I know you won't believe this but you are my pack now. I'm on the outside with everyone else. It's a pack of two. You're the damn alpha female. This is yours. I owe you this."

His fingers slipped over my clitoris and I was utterly lost.

I gave over to my wolf, letting her have her way. I'd forced her back and down for most of the day, so now she came roaring back. My hands went around, searching for his body, for something to hold on to. If I could have, I would have broken free and jumped the man. My need was that great, but he was stronger than me. My wolf thrilled at that. She loved the fact that he was so big and rough and he could handle me.

"Do you have any idea how good you smell?" His words rumbled over my skin.

I didn't bother with a reply because I was far too busy rubbing myself against his hand like a horny teenager. I let my head fall back against his shoulder, nestling there.

"Yes, that's what I want," he whispered. "Let me take care of you. Let me be what you need."

The hand that wasn't down my jeans cupped my breast and I was completely surrounded by him. Not Gray this time. I couldn't trick myself into believing I was getting worked over hard by anyone but Trent Wilcox, werewolf sex god.

"Let go, baby. Don't fight me." His fingers found my nipple, twisting to the point of pain. A nice nip that let my wolf know he was in control. As if that wasn't enough to get me panting, he set his teeth on the back of my neck.

I shivered at the sensation. My wolf was ready to submit. No. I was ready to submit. I gave over and let him take control entirely.

He pressed down on my clit and my whole body shook. Pure pleasure washed over me and raced through my veins. I did feel the connection to him in that moment. I could feel the joy and satisfaction he got from making me come.

Except it wasn't only about sex. There was something else there, simmering below his surface. While I could feel his cock hard against the small of my back, a sense of peace emanated from him.

He was happy to be here, happy to be with me. Touching me filled something inside him.

"That's what I wanted," he whispered as he eased his touch. He was still rubbing but lightly, as though he knew I needed a moment but didn't want to lose our connection. I felt him kiss the lobe of my ear. "Do you need more? We can go to my room and I'll take care of you for hours, Kelsey. Donovan will have to understand. I make the decisions now and I won't let him come between us. You won't think about anything but your next orgasm. We'll hole up and cuddle and drink and eat and fuck for days. Better yet, let me take you away from here. We'll go out into the forest and just be for a while. You and me. We need that time."

But we wouldn't get it because the elevator shifted and before Trent could react, the doors opened.

"Hey, something went wrong with the…." Casey was standing there, his jaw dropping when he realized what he was seeing. "Holy shit."

Naturally Casey could override the elevator and put me in a position where I was caught with my pants down. Not down really, but with someone's hand in them. Unfortunately, Casey wasn't alone.

Gray was standing there and I remembered what Donovan had said. He'd said something about Gray finding someone who could transport him here. Gray was a dark prophet, but when it came to travel, he was as human as the rest of us.

His father, however, was not.

Papa Sloane stood there in his perfectly pressed suit, everything about him utterly human with the singular exception of his eyes. They turned a brilliant ruby red when he caught sight of me.

I worried for a moment that Gray's father would kill Trent. I pushed away from him, thinking to try to save him, but the attack came from a different direction. As I started to open my mouth to explain, Gray growled and threw himself in the elevator.

A hand reached for mine, dragging me out as the doors closed. Marcus looked down at me, an almost amused smile on his face. "Well, you've done it now, *bella*."

Yep. I'd fucked everything up. There was a horrible sound from the elevator and I hoped both men survived.

Chapter Twelve

"Would you like to explain yourself, slut?" Lord Sloane stared down at me like I was some kind of insect he was about to squash under his ridiculously overpriced loafers. In his human form, he opted for designer wear. He looked like a captain of industry, a man in the prime of his life, though I happened to know he was millennia old.

Marcus's shoulders squared. "You would do well to remember where you are, Lord Sloane. You are here on the sufferance of His Majesty King Daniel, and he won't take well to you calling his close circle by filthy names."

I managed to get to my feet. "It doesn't matter. I've been called worse, babe." It was so hard to change habits. "I'm sorry. I meant, Mr. Vorenus."

"Marcus will do, *bella*." He gave me an encouraging smile.

"And you wonder why I speak the truth," Sloane said with a grimace. "I want to know why a lowborn beast has my family in such upheaval that I have to leave my kingdom to ensure both my sons don't fuck up here. Nemcox doesn't even enjoy female company and yet he's so eager to put you under contract. I would like to know why."

I wasn't about to tell him. I needed Nemcox to keep his damn mouth shut. If Papa Sloane knew that he had an ace in his deck, he would use it. He wouldn't care about Gray's happiness or think to use the information to put me in a corner. He would go straight to Merlin and then I would spend the rest of my life trying to protect my father. Lee. Little Lee.

My head hurt.

Still, the red-eyed demon required some kind of an answer. "I think it's my feminine charm."

Marcus stepped in front of me as though attempting to place himself in the path of danger. "Lord Sloane, I think perhaps you should wait in the king's office while I speak to my…to Ms. Owens. You'll find Hugo Wells is already there and waiting. He has some legal questions for you."

Hugo likely had some form of lecture already planned about all the ways he could keep me from signing away my soul. Unfortunately, I couldn't allow that to happen.

"I'll need the wards kept down. I require a satan if we're going to get this contract finished." Papa Sloane straightened his tie. "I'm certainly not going to trust in some academic. If we're going to do this, I want an ironclad contract. I won't be tricked into giving the bitch access to my kingdom simply so the king can find a loophole that brings her back after she's collected enough information. A satan will ensure the validity of the contract upfront."

A satan is a class of demon. They act as the plane's lawyers and the be-all, end-all arbiters of contracts. Satans can be requested by either party and the satan's word is law. I could have Hugo draw up my contract, but it would be enforced or rejected by Hell's cutest cherubs. Though I've been told they bite.

"I doubt that will be necessary," Marcus murmured. "But you can certainly call one if it becomes so. Casey, would you escort our guest to the king's office?"

Casey's eyes went wide. "You mean the Hell lord?"

"Yes, I mean our guest, Lord Sloane," Marcus replied.

Casey swallowed and managed a nod. "This way, Lord Sloane."

When they were halfway down the hall, I turned to Marcus. "Go easy on him. You should have seen the way he stood up to Nemcox. He invoked all kinds of rights and got him to back down. He's a good kid."

Marcus sighed and shook his head. There was a terrible howling roar from somewhere below us, but Marcus ignored it completely. "I will take that into account. Now would you like to explain to me why you're planning on throwing out all your training and becoming the Sloanes' pet Hunter?"

"Nemcox knows something about Lee. Do you know what happened with the spell we were trying to use on Neil Roberts?"

"Yes." His whole face softened. "Have you enjoyed talking to your father? I suspect you see much of yourself in him."

"I loved it right up to the point that Nemcox told me the wizard guy is the one who actually ordered my father's death and that the queen's incarceration and Roberts's time in Hell were mere byproducts of what he wanted."

A long sigh issued from Marcus. "I told you he wasn't directly responsible for your father's death. My question is why would Myrddin want a bodyguard's death? How was your father important to him?"

The floor beneath me shook. "Should I go after them?"

"Not at all. Let them sort these things out. I believe Lieutenant Sloane is only now realizing what has to happen, and he's dealing with some unsavory emotions. It's one thing to accept sharing your partner on an intellectual basis, quite another to see it in action. Please go on. If I'm to help you, I need to know everything you can tell me."

The floor shook again and I wondered exactly what those two were trying to do to each other. And if they'd taken off their shirts to do it. I looked back to the man I'd seen as my savior the last few years. "You would still help me?"

"I will always help you, *bella*. Always. I'm sad that our time together is coming to an end, but I will care about you the rest of my very long life and I will forever wish you well." His eyes closed briefly as a howl shook the walls around us. There was a wry look on his face when he opened them. "I believe you will need all the good wishes in the world if you are to survive those two. I have to admit there's a part of me that delighted in seeing the lieutenant lose his cool over finding you with another man. It was certainly due."

My heart ached. Being this close to Marcus made me remember how easy it had been to be his woman. "Marcus, I'm so sorry I put you through that."

He reached out and his hand cupped my cheek, swiping away a tear I didn't know I'd shed. "No. You should never be sorry for seeking out what you need. You didn't try to hide this from me and I always knew things could go this way. I shall seek some peace and see what happens over the next few decades, but if you call me, I'll be here."

I knew what he meant. He would go to Venice and let Evangeline grow up. She was Lee's little sister and she might be Marcus's prophesized companion, the one who would take him with her when she died. Apparently immortality wasn't as cool as it sounded.

"Now tell me why you believe the wizard wanted to hurt your father," Marcus prompted. "We don't have much time. The king will be up here and he will demand explanations."

"According to Nemcox, this Merlin dude did some prophecy of his own and according to him, my dad and one other person were the only two beings in the world who could thwart his plans."

Marcus frowned. "My darling girl, I'm not sure how to handle this. My first instinct is to say Nemcox is lying. Myrddin serves the sword and the crown. Daniel has both."

"Why would he lie?" Yeah, I knew that was a stupid question the minute it left my mouth.

"He's a demon and he wants you out of the way. If you enter Hell under a contract, you'll cease to be effective here and might even be pressed into serving your new house. More than that, we all know Gray's father desires a child between the two of you. Again, if the child is born on the Hell plane, he will not only be a royal, but he will have no protections and no standing with the Council."

I tried to work through the problem, examining all of the points of contention. I came upon one truth that was incontrovertible. "But he can't lie in a contract. That would void the contract."

Marcus looked at me like he was shocked by my naïveté. "I assure you the demon will follow the letter of the contract. He will never tell the wizard that your father's soul has a new body. Nowhere in the contract will it state the reasons why this is dangerous."

I shook my head. "I don't think he's lying." I'd watched him as he'd figured out who Little Lee was, and I'd watched him figure something else out. "Is there any way Lee, the one we know now, is more than human? Nemcox was afraid of him."

I don't know that afraid was the right word. It seemed to me that it had been equal parts fear and pure wonder as Nemcox had stared at Lee.

"How could he be more? I suppose he has some faery genes. Males cannot be companions, but he could potentially have some of his father's Green Man powers." Marcus reached out, putting a hand on my shoulder. "Merlin has absolutely nothing to fear from a human child, and that is what Lee is. The demon is trying to trick you. Let's go to the king and discuss this. He'll know what to do. He'll call Myrddin and solve all of this quickly."

My heart raced. "No. I'll handle it all myself." Had I made a terrible mistake in telling Marcus the truth? Casey had told me the queen reported Donovan had an irrational love for the wizard. For Merlin…

"Is Merlin also known as Satanspawn?" That was what Casey had called him.

Marcus chuckled. "It's nothing for you to worry about. He's the product of a human woman and an incubus. That forms the demon part of his soul, hence the ridiculous nickname."

Beware the spawn.

That was what Gray had told me. I hadn't realized what it meant, but now I had a big old bet.

"Marcus, you have to promise me you won't talk to Donovan."

His brows rose. "Why would I do that?"

"Because I'm asking you to. Because this matters to me and I have to have the time to figure out what's best."

"Which is precisely why we should talk to His Majesty," Marcus insisted.

"No." I was getting desperate. If Donovan went to the wizard, there would be nothing I could do. "Please. I need time to figure a few things out. I can't have the king going to the wizard. If you're wrong and he's not lying, then my father could die."

A hand soothed down my arm. "Hush, *bella*. You have my word. I'll be silent for now, but you have to know I'll do anything to stop you from signing that contract."

And I had to do anything to save my father.

The doors to the elevator opened. I turned, terrified of what could happen next.

Gray was on one side of the elevator, his horns out. He seemed to grow larger than normal when he took his demon form. His shirt was ripped and bloody and it looked like he'd gotten bitten in several places.

There was a big gray wolf on the other side of the elevator. He looked like he'd taken a beating, too. His fur was matted with blood, but I couldn't see any open wounds.

How was I supposed to handle this? Two men were twice the anxiety and definitely double the trouble. I'd basically had sex with both of them in the past twenty-four hours and my first instinct was one I'd refined at junior high dances—I thought about running away and crying in the bathroom. They wouldn't come after me in the girls' room. I could hide out there forever. Liv could bring me food and I could sleep there. It would be a quiet life.

Trent growled, the fur on his back standing up straight.

Gray turned as though preparing to square off again. I could see the claws on his hand. They were razor sharp. "Why don't we see if all that king's blood in your system can keep you alive when I pluck your heart out of your chest and piss on it."

Marcus chuckled behind me as though this was all terribly amusing. "It's at times like this that you must ask yourself an important question."

I could think of a few. What the hell was I thinking falling for two men when I couldn't handle one? Could I live happily alone in a rain forest? Why not give lesbianism a real shot? "What's that?"

"What would Zoey do? It's really the only way to go, *bella*." Marcus stepped back.

What would Zoey do? Well, the queen sure as hell wouldn't spend her time crying in the bathroom. The Queen of all Vampire would show the boys who the boss was.

So I could run and allow them to be drama queens, or I could take control of my damn scene.

"Grayson Sloane, you are not going to urinate on Trent's heart." I moved in between them, giving them both my sternest look. "Trent, you are not going to rip out his throat. Yeah, I know what that growl meant, buddy. You will both behave."

Gray's eyes bore into mine. They were dark as night, his pupils drowning out all the white. "Or what, Kelsey mine? Or am I even able to call you that now? Tell me something. Were you trying to enjoy yourself before you're forced into monogamy? Perhaps my brother has the right idea. Perhaps only a contract will keep you faithful."

Trent growled again.

If I was stuck down in Hell with Gray, we were going to make a few things plain between us. I pointed a finger Trent's way because I was so going to be the one to handle this. "Don't you even try. You sit. Marcus, I need a few minutes alone with these two."

Marcus tipped his head, the hint of a smile playing on his lips as he backed away. "Of course, *bella*. I will go and see if Lord Sloane needs anything. Don't keep us waiting too long."

He walked away and I was left with my two bloody suitors. I pointed to the conference room where we might have some semblance of privacy. The doors were thick and warded to keep prying supernatural ears out.

Gray strode in, not bothering to look back at me. He hadn't much looked at me at all after he'd stared his fill the first time. He didn't try to touch me either. Months we'd been apart and this was what I got.

Trent sat and stared at me, his wolfy eyes narrow.

I shook my head. "I'm not apologizing to you. I'm not the one who got into a fight. Do I even want to know what happened to your pants?"

He growled again, a low sound that let me know if he wanted to he could go find them right now. He chose something different. Naturally—and yes, I see the pun there—he simply stood up and became his gorgeous man self. He put his hands on his muscled hips. "I wasn't trying to start a damn fight, Kelsey. He attacked me."

Gray turned, his back to the windows that showed a lovely view of downtown Dallas. "And I would have killed you, too. Let's see how strong you are when you're not high off of the king's blood."

Trent started to growl and then his expression collapsed into one of pure confusion. He paced the floor, one hand running over his hair. "What the fuck was that, Sloane? I thought we had a deal. How exactly did you think I was going to be able to calm her down? Did you honestly think her wolf is going to be satisfied with some handholding and girl talk? Did you expect I could ease her rage with some ice cream and a couple of rom coms? If it was that simple, you should have brought Liv into this."

I needed to take control. And to stop looking between them and wondering how the hell I'd managed to get myself in this position between two gorgeous men. "First off, sexist much? Talking about one's relationships is healthy and not contained to one gender. Which is precisely why I don't do girl talk. I drink tequila and sleep with the wrong people when I'm emotionally upset because I am not healthy and don't you forget it. Second. What the fuck is this plan of Gray's?"

"I put a plan in place to protect you when I'm gone," Gray said between clenched fangs. "The operative words being *when I'm gone*.

Trent here decided that because I needed to use his body to help you last night that he's welcome to take what he wants. I'm going to explain the situation to him. And then I'll find another damn wolf to take his place."

I watched as Trent's hands shifted slightly, claws popping out of his fingers. "You try to put another wolf in her bed and you'll have a dead wolf on your hands. I'll send you to Hell early, demon."

I noticed a couple of people who worked for the Council walking by. Beth, a witch from accounting, was almost immediately on her cell phone. Gossip. At least it was still daylight and most of the vamps were tucked away or I might have had a bigger audience.

Again, this was a time to ask what Zoey would do. She might show her boobs and bring her men together in a magical ménage that would bring harmony to the world. But then I sometimes thought light and joy probably shot out of her nipples like at a Katy Perry concert.

I did not have her spectacular boobs, so I was going to have to rely on what I did well.

Sarcasm and not giving a shit.

I sank down into one of the conference chairs and sat back, putting my booted feet right on that sucker that likely had been built by artisans from the Faery plane and cost Quinn a bundle. "Hey, if you two are going to fight again, at least make it interesting for me. Sloane, ditch the clothes and let's oil you two up."

Trent's eyes rolled, but Gray stopped for a moment as though trying to wrap his head around what I was saying. "Why would we oil up?"

Trent shook his head and moved toward the big closet where I was sure the business guys kept their extra pens and stuff. Apparently they also kept extra pairs of sweatpants. Trent pulled out a gray sweatsuit with the Ether logo on it and got dressed while he spoke. "She wants us to wrestle naked and oiled up, and she's probably going to sell tickets because she's a little pervert."

He softened that with a wink, but he was wrong about that. "I'm not a pervert. I'm thrifty. I'm about to lose my billionaire sugar daddy and mama needs some cash for beer."

Gray stared at me while Trent shook his head.

"I didn't mean to fight with him, Kelsey," Trent said, perfectly calm now. "We seem to have reached a point of misunderstanding in our agreement." He winced a little. "And I know I need to explain that to you better than I have."

"He was supposed to take care of you after I descend," Gray explained tightly. "And that is all you need to know."

"Jesus," Trent said under his breath. "And I thought I was difficult." He turned back to Gray. "Buddy, if this is going to work, you can't say things that are going to make her want to take your balls off. Do you plan on descending without your balls? You want to leave them up here on the Earth plane as a souvenir for the rest of us?"

Trent seemed to know me better than Gray, but then when I honestly thought about it, Gray and my relationship had been brief. We hadn't spent more than a week or so together before we'd been torn apart the first time. Then I'd been in Italy and he'd been walking the Earth plane.

Trent and I had been friends a lot longer. Trent didn't see me as some princess on a pedestal. Trent knew I liked burgers and beer and was capable of taking a dude's balls if he pissed me off enough.

Was it possible that he actually cared about me?

"I wasn't trying to make her angry with me," Gray said, visibly calming. "I've only ever been interested in protecting her."

"Is it protecting me or possessing me?" I had to ask the question.

Gray shook his head. "Don't even start in on that. I gave you up to Marcus when you needed him. When you needed me and I couldn't physically be with you, I allowed Trent to host me."

"With a sword in my gut," Trent complained.

Gray shook his head. "Can you leave us alone for a few moments? This should be a private discussion between me and my…between me and Kelsey."

"Absolutely not." Trent sank into one of the chairs, making himself comfy. "I'm part of this and I'm not going away. If this is going to work, we don't have secrets."

I held up a hand. "If this is going to work, I need to know what *this* is."

Gray placed his hands palms down on the table, looming over both of us. "This is a means to protect you after I descend. I've done an enormous amount of research into Hunters and how your kind functions. If not completely bonded to an academic who also has an affinity with wolves, the Hunter usually dies young. She becomes unstable and must be put down."

Yeah, story of my life. The sad truth was in the beginning I'd kind of accepted that would be my fate. It seemed fitting and honestly, life kind of sucked. Then I met Gray and Marcus. Then I moved into this place and found some meaning. I helped people. I did good.

And you know what? I fucking like beer and burgers and a good rom com, and I liked hanging with Trent.

I had to accept that at some point, I decided I want to live.

"All right, so the problem with Marcus and myself is that he doesn't have this affinity for wolves? That seems weird because he's popular among the wolf packs." Especially in Italy. They loved him there, which was odd since vamps and wolves usually were wary of each other.

"It's not the same," Gray explained. "The wolves in Italy see Marcus as a patron of sorts. He's been good to them and the wolves trust him in a way they don't trust other vampires, but that's not what I mean by affinity. The king has an affinity for wolves. He can call them, which is precisely why so many distrust him. If it weren't for Quinn and the queen performing their fertility rituals, they likely would never have joined the king's Council."

I was assuming by "call," Gray didn't mean on a cell phone. "Are you telling me Donovan can control wolves?"

"He never uses the power," Trent insisted and for the first time since we'd started this conference, he looked less than comfortable. "He's never once used it on me."

"No, you play the king's puppet because you like to," Gray shot back.

I was getting sick of his new attitude. "If you don't have anything nice to say, get your ass out of here."

He put out a hand and seemed to try to calm himself. "I'm sorry. Being near my father, it can be unsettling. When he transported me, he went through the Hell plane. I'm afraid I felt more of that than I would like."

His hand went to his side and I wondered. In some ways Gray was as two-natured as I or Trent were. Although in Trent's case, he had been born fully integrated with the wolf inside him. He didn't question or try to quell his instincts the way Gray and I did.

We were an odd lot when I thought about it. All three of us had feet planted in both worlds, but only Trent was comfortable with it. Only Trent had grown up understanding what his second nature meant.

Only Trent knew how to completely calm my wolf. He did it through touch and patience, and a nice bit of alpha-male dominance.

Gray seemed to be trying to force himself to chill. I knew how hard that could be sometimes, but Gray also had a switch that was a little bit like mine.

I stood up and moved to him. His hand was over the spot where his dragon lay inked into his skin. I wasn't planning on making a big deal out of this. I didn't want another boy fight unless I got them naked and oiled up, so I decided Gray could talk through this particular exercise. "So wolves like me tend to go crazy because we can't bond to anyone but an academic who can call wolves. Is that what you're saying? I'm going to need you to pull up your shirt."

We would get back to the whole part where Donovan could potentially make my new honey his bitch. I wasn't letting that go, but it seemed like we had other things to concentrate on for now.

Gray looked down at me. "Pull up my shirt?"

"So she can lay hands on your dragon," Trent supplied. He nodded toward me. "I think that's a good idea. He's obviously in need of comfort."

"Comfort?" Gray asked, but he did pull his shirt from his slacks.

I slid my hand over his skin and immediately felt the warmth of the dragon responding to me.

Gray gasped and his eyes closed. "Comfort. I'd forgotten."

"See, wolves never forget. Touch is healing. Touch is comfort," Trent said.

"Did you have to touch her clitoris?" But Gray didn't move and his eyes didn't come open.

Trent chuckled. "Absolutely. Her wolf requires a firm hand, my brother." He sobered a bit. "She was upset. I don't think her wolf likes the idea of being caged on the Hell plane. You understand how poorly that would go?"

Yes, there it was. Anxiety spiked through my system at the thought of never walking the Earth plane again, never feeling the moon pull at my soul. I didn't change the way a normal wolf would, but I ran on full moons. I ran like the wind and it eased my soul. I wouldn't have that on the Hell plane. I would have nothing.

Gray's hand eased over mine as though holding me to the dragon. "I will never allow that to happen to you, Kelsey mine. And yes, Trent, I can feel it in her right now. It's welling up inside like a noxious poison. Still, I never meant… I didn't think you would take her until I was gone. I thought she would be mine for a while longer."

I took a deep breath and let my head rest against Gray's back. I could feel him calming and his words had meant something to me. I loved this man. I wasn't sure why, but he was my soul's mate. I'd tried to fight it, but it never worked. No matter how much I'd cared about Marcus, my heart had always been Gray's.

And yet I wanted Trent to move in behind me, his hands going over my skin and giving me the same comfort I was giving to Gray. I wanted to be between these two men in a way I'd never considered before that day in the winter when all things had been possible. When I'd seen what we could become if we worked together.

"It doesn't have to be like that." Trent was watching us intently.

"And how would you know?" Gray asked.

"Because I see it every single day," Trent replied quietly. "Because I've been around a family like this for years and they make it work."

Gray shook his head and broke our connection. He moved away from me. "No. That wasn't my plan at all. Look, there's no happy ménage at the end of this for us. I'm going to Hell. There's no happy anything for me."

"He has to let you out," I argued. "You're a dark prophet. You have to be allowed to roam the Earth plane as well."

"Do I? I'm sure as long as I'm willing to prophesize for my father, I'll be allowed some access to the Earth plane, but have you thought about what that means, Kelsey? I would be helping my father. My father's job is to torture souls, to ensure that Lucifer makes his monthly quota, so to speak. He also would like very much to widen his influence on this plane. Did you honestly believe I would do that? Do you think I'm going to be a good little demon and help hurt others so I can maybe make it back here once a month and go on a date with you?"

"We still have time." I couldn't think about the second option, the one he was talking about. If Gray wouldn't work for his father on the Hell plane, then he would be tortured until he broke or died. Either way, he would no longer be the Gray I knew. "We still have a few years left."

Trent stood up. "Are you trying to send her into a full-on rage? She's in a delicate state. It's too early to test her like this. Come here, Kelsey. Come here right now."

He was using that alpha voice on me, the one that brooked no disobedience. Normally this was the moment when my wolf decided if she wanted to fight or fuck, but honestly, she wanted neither right this second. She did want comfort.

I walked to him, his arms going around my body and hugging me tight to his chest. His cheek rubbed against mine and I felt him sigh as though the contact soothed something in him, too.

"She needs this, Sloane. Either help me or get the fuck out. I'm here for a reason and I'm not going away. I'm here because the minute she walked in the door I knew she would be important to me. If it means anything at all to you, I knew you would be, too. It was disconcerting and confusing until she showed up. Why do you think I was so hard on you?"

"Because you're an asshole." But Gray was suddenly at my back, his chest cuddling against me. "And this means nothing except that I'm sorry. I'm sorry, Kelsey. I shouldn't have acted like a jealous ass. I was hurt."

This…oh, this felt right. This felt a lot like heaven, and I was already thinking things I shouldn't have. I was thinking about lifting my face up for Trent's kiss and seeing if I could move Gray's hand to my breast. All the crap of the day would flow away and I could lose myself for a few hours.

I felt Trent tense as though he could feel my desire.

And then Gray moved back. "Are you better?"

I turned, moving reluctantly out of Trent's arms. Gray's face was flushed, but he wouldn't quite meet my eyes. "Yes. I feel better."

"Good. Then you can tell me why my brother thinks you're signing a contract." Now his eyes found mine and there was lots of righteous judgment there.

Gray might be feeling weird about the sexual vibe thing that had gone through the room, but it was obvious he was perfectly happy to talk about all the things I'd done wrong.

I suddenly found myself staring down both men because Trent rounded on me, too.

"You are not signing a damn contract. I've already explained that to you," Trent began.

"I'm doing it for Lee."

They both stopped.

"What does the king's kid have to do with this?" Gray backed up. "I know you like the kid, but he's not your responsibility. You're certainly not about to sign away your soul for him, so I'll hand this over to Donovan and we can tell my father to go back to Hell."

"It's not that easy," Trent said. "Lee is an old soul. He's her father's soul. Her real father. So you can't expect her to step back and let Donovan handle this."

"Her real father?" Gray asked.

I was able to look at him and plead my case now that he understood. "Yes, the original. We're oddly alike. He's in there and he's got a second chance at life and everything, and if I don't sign that contract, he'll die. Your brother will make sure of it."

"What does my brother have to do with this?" Gray asked, obviously confused.

Trent looked to me for clarification, too. "Why does he want to hurt Lee? He has to know the king won't allow that to happen."

They were off and talking about all the reasons I had to be wrong and I realized I'd made a mistake bringing them in.

"Stop." There was truly only one thing I needed to know. "Gray, if your brother makes me a promise, will he keep it? Or would he try to find a way to get around it?"

"Kelsey, he's a demon," Trent replied. "You can't trust him."

Gray's eyes narrowed. "Of course, don't trust the demon. I should have known you would say that."

Trent's hands came up. "I wasn't talking about you. I know you're not a full breed and you don't take after your demon half. But Nemcox is, and I've seen the kind of destruction he can bring about."

"You don't know my brother at all." Gray turned to me, dismissing Trent. "If he made a promise to you, he'll keep it. He won't even attempt to find a way around it because in his mind, you're his family. My brother loves me. Yes, demons can feel emotions. They can love people. I'll talk to him. I'll get you out of this. Can I please know why you think he'll hurt Lee?"

I couldn't trust him with that secret. I couldn't trust Trent either. It wasn't that I thought they would try to hurt Lee. Quite the opposite. They would attempt to help, likely by going straight to Donovan, and then my house of cards would fall because Donovan would call the wizard.

Hey, Mr. Wizard, so I hear my son can possibly be one of two beings who could kill you and take your power. Just wanted to check and make sure you don't have plans to wipe him off the face of the earth...

It would be like Dumbledore calling Voldemort to make sure he was down with HP living a happy, healthy life.

"No. I won't say another word and I will be signing that contract." Unless I could figure some other way out of this.

"I won't allow it." Trent's arms wrapped around my middle and I felt him place the lightest kiss on my ear. "Not because I think you're incapable of making a proper decision, my alpha female. Merely because the thought of losing you makes me insane. I can't lose you now that I've found you. I'll do anything to keep you by my side. In front of me. Wherever you choose to stand, as long as your choice doesn't leave me behind."

It was exactly the worst thing to say to me because my whole soul softened.

He'd laid in wait for me, like the goddamn apex predator he was. He'd hidden behind acts of friendship and shrugs of nonchalance, when all along he'd plotted and planned and ached for me.

Could I believe that? I did in the moment. In the moment, his haunting voice gave me ease.

Gray intruded, looming over me. "You have to talk to me, Kelsey. You can't think for a second I'll allow you to come to Hell with me."

I felt Trent's arms tighten as though Hell was coming for me in that moment, and then the door opened, a stranger walking inside. He was dressed in an expensive suit, his hair slicked back and perfect.

"Oh, look at all this drama." I might not have recognized the vessel, but I knew that upper-crust accent. "Wolf, get your hands off my sister-in-law. Grayson, I'm shocked that you're standing here allowing that animal to paw your beloved."

Trent stepped in front of me. "You have no right to be here."

Gray sighed and sat back down. "Well, brother, I did try to tear him apart. He's quite strong and he takes the king's blood. He's probably taken it for years, so I could cut his head off and if someone held it on, it would simply grow back."

I went up on my toes, whispering in Trent's ear. "You do know there's only one actual demon hunter here and it's not you, right?"

He turned, giving me a look that required no translation.

I held up my hands in defeat. "Just checking. It's my job and stuff. And I'm pretty sure he's here to see me. Should we find another location?"

"I would be perfectly happy to host our negotiation session," the demon offered. "I'm here because Father wills it and the king requested my presence. You know I've been trying to speak with the king for years. If I'd known all I had to do was contract with one small female, I would have done it a long time ago."

"You'll do nothing of the kind." Gray sent his brother a stare that could peel paint off the walls. "You will not sign anything with her. I've told you my feelings on the subject."

"And I've explained to you over and over that you will feel differently once you're home." Nemcox faced off with Gray. "I know this better than you do. This plane affects you in terrible ways. It clouds your mind. Once you're living in your proper home, you'll understand and you will thank me."

Awesome. Gray's mind was clouded with the not pure evil of the Earth plane. He didn't look like he was being persuaded and I didn't like the thought that these brothers would hash it out. "Nemcox, your promise to me includes not discussing my reasons for signing with anyone. And that includes Gray and your family."

He put a hand on his borrowed heart, looking as innocent as an occupying demon could. "I'm wounded that you think I would do otherwise."

"Damn it, Kelsey," Trent began. "Why is this so important? What does he have on Lee?"

Nemcox *tsked tsked* my way. "Now who's the problem? Hush,

Hunter. I told you—loose lips sink ships." He stopped in the middle of the room and his whole demeanor softened as he breathed in. "Oh, there's something I haven't smelled in years and years."

I looked up and Neil Roberts was standing outside, his eyes on the demon.

I moved, putting myself between the demon and the man he'd tortured for decades and prayed I wouldn't have to decide between my father and the queen's closest friend.

Chapter Thirteen

"Trent, I need you to get Neil up to the penthouse for me." I felt like a lion tamer who suddenly found himself caught between two predators.

Roberts might look like a sweet club kid, but he turned into a killer lizard capable of taking down unstoppable demons. So I was proceeding with caution. In Nemcox's case, I wanted to keep the body count down. Nemcox could be easily killed. Well, the body he was currently inhabiting could be killed. He would merely come back in another and I would be left with cleanup duty.

"I'm not leaving you alone here." Trent did move toward the door. "But I'll talk to him."

For a moment I thought Roberts would be the reasonable one. He stood there staring, but not making the move that would bring him close to his ex-captor. Then as Trent started to open the door, the wolf made a decision and charged in.

"You have no right to be here." Roberts stopped short of getting in arm's length of the demon. "None. You've been forbidden all Council spaces." He looked toward Trent. "How is he doing this? We have the place warded against possessed beings."

That was totally my fault. "They're down for a couple of hours while I have a meeting with some hell lords. I'm sorry about this. Why don't you let Trent take you up to the penthouse? I promise this will be over in a few hours and he'll be gone again."

"You look tired, love." Nemcox hadn't moved an inch and his eyes never left Roberts. "That man isn't taking care of you properly."

Roberts ignored my very reasonable solution to the problem. "Like you took care of me, you disgusting piece of shit?"

The demon flushed but held his ground. "I generally prefer sweetheart or lover. And I took excellent care of you. Tell me something, can you feel our connection? Is it warm on your body?"

Neil frowned. "Nothing about you makes me warm."

"That tattoo does. I know it does. You lied to me back then," Nemcox insisted. "You lied because you were punishing me, but I know what it does to you. That dragon is our bond, Neil. That dragon is a piece of your soul and it knows its mate. Don't fight it anymore, puppy."

Neil stopped, his face going blank. "The dragon knows its mate? What does that mean? I thought it was nothing but a way to control me."

"It's so much more." Nemcox took a step toward him, but stopped when Neil nearly jumped back. "It's magic. Yes, I can give you power through it, but that's not why I had you marked. You wouldn't believe me that we belong together. You fought me so hard in those first days. I thought I would lose you. So I gave you the dragon. It's both a power conduit and portal to your soul. You and the dragon are one. What the dragon wants and needs is the same as you. Stop fighting it. Come home to me. It's been so long."

Neil looked over to Gray. "Is what he's saying true? Kelsey says you have one, too."

Gray nodded. "Yes. It was given to me when I was thirteen and it's grown with me ever since. It's how demonkind gives power to their loved ones, though I suspect my brother might have cheated a bit. My dragon allows me to take demonic form, but I don't lose my self-control."

"He wasn't doing anything interesting with his self-control," Nemcox complained.

Neil ignored him. "How does it work? If the person can control me, does that mean the dragon recognizes him as our mate?"

"Not at all," Gray replied. "Have you honestly never felt your dragon move?"

"Of course he has." Nemcox folded his arms over his chest, staring at his former victim. "We lived together for years. He's stubborn and he won't give me an inch."

Gray frowned. "You never touched his dragon?"

"Of course I did," his brother insisted. "I touched him all the time. I gave it every bit of my affection. He's the one who withheld. He's the one who's lying about never feeling the connection. Do you know how hard it is to love someone as much as I love him and to have him deny the truth? He even made me doubt it at times."

Oh, but there was no doubting the connection. "Gray, let me touch your dragon. I can show him what happens when the connection is real."

Gray's expression had gone stark as he looked at his brother. "You don't know? Brother, Kelsey feels when my dragon moves. He comes to life under her hand. Sometimes he glows a bit when she's around."

Neil's knees hit the floor and he covered his face with his hands.

My stomach dropped and I moved toward him. Trent was already on one knee, his hand on Neil's back.

"It's okay," Trent was saying. "You don't have to do what some tattoo says. If you think I'll let him take you, that any one of us would allow him to take you again, you're wrong. Never again. I swear."

I wondered if it was too late to make leaving Neil Roberts alone for all of eternity part of my contract because I felt so much for him in that moment. He hadn't understood what the tattoo meant and I could understand how devastating that would be if the "one" the dragon responded to was the epitome of everything evil. It was something sweet to me because Gray and I fit, because we loved each other. Somehow that dragon responding to me made things feel right. But what if I hated him or he hated me? What if we were trapped by some insane tattoo? I had to believe that because I didn't want to live in a world where Neil Roberts's destined soul mate was the same man who'd violated him for years.

"I won't let him take you," I vowed. "No matter what the tattoo says."

Neil's face came up and he was smiling. It was the most brilliant smile I'd ever seen on his handsome face. "I didn't understand. I tried to shove it down, but it's a part of me. It really is."

"Yes." Nemcox breathed the word like an answered prayer, a benediction. "Yes, listen to the dragon. He knows the truth."

"He does," Neil agreed. "Which is why I feel him move when my husband touches me." Neil laughed, a joyous sound. "I force it down, but every time Chad comes near me, it feels warm. I don't let him touch me there because it feels weird, but now I get it. There's nothing wrong with me. This thing that he put on me, it's not his. It's mine. He forced it on me, but I can make it mine. It wants to be mine and it loves who I love."

"I watched that dragon protect Zoey once," Trent said quietly. "There was no reason for you to change in that moment except the dragon on your soul loved Zoey and couldn't bear to see her hurt."

So many of the things my father had said to me mere hours before came back to me. "The dragon isn't your enemy. It's one more piece of you. Accept him and all the strength he can bring you. Accept him and you might be able to come to terms with what happened to you all those years ago."

The demon shook his head, tears running down his face. "You're lying again. How long do you have to punish me?"

Neil wiped his eyes and stood up. "I don't. I don't have to punish you at all. I don't have to punish myself." He turned to me. "I'm ready, Kelsey. I want to try the spell again. I'm ready to remember everything. I'm not scared now." He put his hand on his side as though soothing the tattoo. "Chad will be there with me and we can get through anything together."

I nodded. At least I might get to complete my last case before my descent into Hell. Closure was a good thing. "I'll let Liv know. We can try again after sunset."

Neil turned back, looking his assailant right in the eye. "I'm not afraid of you anymore, and you need to understand that the next time you try to have me do your dirty work for you, I'm going to fight. I'm going to fight you as hard as I can. I won't kill for you again."

"Kill for me?" Nemcox managed to look genuinely confused.

"I'm not stupid." Neil moved to the door, never taking his eyes off Nemcox, as though the demon would make a move at any moment. He backed up. "You've been using me for weeks to take out your father's rivals. Is that why you had me murder those demons? I don't care. I won't do it again."

He finally turned and stalked out of the room.

"Trent, I need you to watch him." It didn't feel right to have him walk off alone.

Trent's jaw tightened. "I think I should stay with you."

"Please. Let me handle this. Make sure Neil gets upstairs safely and then you can run back down here and save me from myself."

Gray looked up, his eyes weary. "I'll make sure she doesn't sign anything while you're gone. I promise."

"I'll hold you to that," Trent said before starting for the door.

"And it would be nice if you put on a shirt." Gray looked over at his brother. "I'm sorry, Nem. I didn't realize you hadn't felt his dragon under your hand."

Nemcox shook his head. "It's something Neil is doing. And he's lying about the vampire. There's no way the dragon responds to him. I placed that seal on him. I did it. He's mine."

Gray's eyes were sympathetic as he looked at Nemcox. "No, brother. It doesn't work that way. You can place the mark, but it's Neil's soul. You can't affect it. You know a soul is sacrosanct. His soul informs the dragon. They're one. The dragon will love who his soul loves. I wish it could be different for you. I know how much you care for him."

Nemcox turned to Gray, his eyes flashing red. "I love him. He's mine. Don't make less of my love than I would of your own. Do you understand what I'm doing for you, Grayson? I'm saving you a world of heartache. I'm giving you the one woman who feeds your soul. Why can't you support me taking the man who feeds mine?"

"Because he doesn't return your love, brother. It's different. I would stand up to Father if that was the problem. I would stand beside you and take what punishment would come, but this is different."

Nemcox rounded on Gray, hissing his way like a scalded snake. It made Gray start.

"It is no different. This is and always has been your problem, my weakling brother. We are royal. They are chattel. What we want, it belongs to us by right of birth and power. You want this to be soft and sweet but it is not and you will understand when you are with us fully." Nemcox turned to me. "If you don't sign that contract by midnight tomorrow our deal is done and I will speak with the spawn and he will know what to do. Enjoy your final night of freedom, whore. From here on you will understand what it means to serve your demon master. Grayson, if you don't want her alone, you'll come home early and of your own accord."

When he strode out of the room, his movements were odd. Normally the demon was polished and perfect. No one would ever suspect he wasn't exactly what he looked like—a human. But now the body he was riding had stiffened, shoulders hunching forward and back with each step. His legs moved in an odd glide, the tip of his toes coming down first.

Like they were cloven hooves.

I caught a flash of red eyes gleaming my way before he disappeared down the hall.

Gray had gone a bit ashen and I wondered if he'd seen this side of his brother before or if Nemcox had been careful. I knew Gray understood on an intellectual level that his brother was a full-born demon, but Nemcox seemed to have a unique way of allowing those around him to forget what he was capable of.

"I'm sorry, Kelsey." Gray sat back, seemingly weary. "You have to forgive him."

Yes, this was the trouble with Gray and his family. "No, I don't. He raped Neil Roberts for years."

Gray shook his head. "We don't know that."

"Oh, we do. I think I'll choose to believe Neil."

"Because he's a wolf and not a demon?"

I thought that was obvious. "Yes."

Gray stood, his expression going grim. "Well, I can see I chose well then. I'll leave you to Trent."

It took all I had not to scream my frustration. "You'll sit back down and stop acting like a butt-hurt idiot."

That seemed to stop him in his tracks. He stared at me for a moment and then the faintest hint of a smile lit his face. "Butt-hurt? This is a thing now?"

I waved him off, turning to look out the windows. Dusk was settling in over the city, a veil descending. "It's been around for a while. You're too hoity-toity to know it."

I felt him move in behind me, his hands cupping my shoulders. "Hoity-toity? I don't feel that way. I've been staying in youth hostels across the world. Jacob isn't big on five-star hotels. Says he can't find real people in them."

His lips brushed the top of my head and I couldn't help but sigh and lean back into him. "I'm sorry you had to ask your father to bring you here."

He was quiet for a moment. "I told you to beware the spawn. This has something to do with the wizard. My brother's ties to him run deep. He's out there in the world, studying and learning. I don't trust him the way Nem does. What does my brother have on you?"

I shook my head. "Something so important I won't even tell you."

His arms moved around me, encircling me. "What are we going to do, Kelsey Mine?"

I had absolutely no idea.

As the night fell, I stood in his arms, the silence my only answer.

Chapter Fourteen

The only thing worse than being stuck in a roomful of angry, complaining men who are mostly angry at and complaining about me is doing it on an empty stomach.

I sat in the middle of Donovan's big office listening as Marcus and Lord Sloane went at it about some obscure point of law concerning contracts and I stared at the painting on the wall. It was the one that seemed to fascinate Marcus. One lone woman running out of the forest and onto a massive field of wheat. Or whatever that wispy sunshine-colored plant was. I don't know why I thought she was running, but I did. And not in a get-my-cardio-in way. She was fleeing something.

Probably a bunch of talky men.

Hugo placed a document in front of me. "This will enroll you in the class you need to take. You'll need to sign where I've marked. The class will educate you in all the dangers of signing away your soul. It begins in three weeks."

"Excuse me?" Lord Sloane moved his focus from Marcus to the Brit. "A class about the dangers of contracts? That seems a bit one sided and intolerant. How can this be educational when both sides are not represented? This is why we'll eventually go to war. This king is completely intolerant."

"Three weeks?" Nemcox had been sulking in one of the corner chairs for over an hour. "That's an interesting play, counselor, but she is not bound by the queen's laws. She can sign the contract in the next twenty-four hours or our deal is void."

"I think the king will insist on a hearing to decide her status," Marcus replied.

"Her status has already been determined." Hugo stood beside Marcus, a joint academic front. "The Council voted that she is a ward of the Council. Because she's a ward of the Council, she receives all rights and has all the obligations a vampire or a companion has."

"That was the old Council," Lord Sloane pointed out. "When he formed the new Council, Donovan issued an order stating all old laws and rulings would need to be looked at again by a court to have standing in the new order."

"He was talking about archaic laws," Marcus insisted. "His decree certainly wasn't meant to cover something so solidly based in law."

"Then he should have written it better," Lord Sloane shot back.

Hugo whispered something to Marcus, whose frown deepened. He said something to Hugo in Italian but it didn't cover sex or gelato, so I couldn't translate.

I wondered where my dad was. We were in Donovan's office, but the king had yet to make an appearance. I didn't know what was going on with Neil or what was happening to my dad.

I thought I might already be in Hell. This was it. Endless rounds of men talking about the law and how I'd fucked up heartily, and no one bringing me dinner.

"Of course we can't work that quickly," Hugo was saying when I thought to pay attention again. "These things take time. We could perhaps have a full court session in two weeks."

Lord Sloane's eyes rolled and he groaned.

Gray leaned my way. "You understand what they're trying to

do?"

Of course I did. Hugo and Marcus were attempting to drag out the proceedings until I either died of hunger and boredom and then my soul went to wherever souls went that hadn't signed a contract or until I came to my senses. Like I said. This was Hell. "It's not going to work."

I stood up, moving to the windows as Lord Sloane and the academics went back to fighting over when a hearing could be had to determine everything from my status as potential Vampire property to whether or not I was smart enough to legally sign away my soul.

How many more times would I look out over the city? I'd been born in the suburbs, but I oddly loved the city. I loved the energy of all those lives around me. What would it feel like when I was surrounded by death?

"There's a simpler solution." The demon stepped in beside me, his voice low.

"Yes, you could bring me a contract. I could sign it and we could go." It made the most sense. "Once you've got me on the Hell plane, there won't be much they can do."

"My father is still attempting to force the king to negotiate. Lucifer is getting anxious," Nemcox explained nonchalantly, as though he was merely gossiping about his boss and not the original purveyor of sin. "He fears what will happen if we have no ties between us."

Politics. No matter what plane you're on, politics is probably the reason it's all fucked up. "I would think Lord Lucifer would want the chaos."

"Oh no." Gray was suddenly at my other side, his hand sliding around my shoulders. "Lucifer fully understands what could happen if he loses control of the Underworld."

It all came back to angels. "Daddy would step back in and take control?"

"If by Daddy you mean an all powerful and vindictive God, then yes," Nemcox said with a shake of his head.

I was pretty sure it wouldn't be vindictiveness on God's part. From what I could tell, whatever being claimed Heaven's throne tended to let the lower planes be. We rose and fell on our own choices. We had been given free will, and like unruly children, we sometimes broke the things our parents provided us with.

Were we about to break the world?

If even Lucifer knew how dangerous it was to have no laws or ties between the Council and Hell, how could Donovan not?

I hate it when I'm wrong. It's an actual feeling in the pit of my stomach, a sort of nauseating roll.

I was a total hypocrite. I was more than willing to give up vengeance for safety. Not for me, of course. I'd never be smart enough or practical enough to do that. But it had been simple when it came to Lee. I honestly hadn't thought about killing Nemcox in hours. All that mattered was saving my father.

Marcus was trying to save the plane and I wasn't helping him along. I looked over to my former lover. He was a stunning man, but I wasn't the right woman for him. That had been preordained. Her name was written in some big book of fate, and I suddenly had faith that she would come. She would show up and my Marcus would know what it meant to find his one true love. He would love her so much he would die when she did. It would be as though he'd walked through time to find her.

"Kelsey, you're crying." Gray's hand was on my head, stroking my hair.

Where would we be in six months? Would Gray descend early so I wouldn't be alone in Hell? Would his torture and pain end the man he was, transforming and twisting his soul?

Or could I stop it? Could the very fact that I was there give him strength?

"She's afraid," Nemcox said and he managed a bit of sympathy. "They all are. You'll have to show her it's not all blood and guts. There are pleasures to be had as well. And once you've presented Father with a child, he'll soften toward you."

I shook my head. "I think 'whore' is his affectionate name for me. I've had worse."

Nemcox faced the window, his borrowed arms crossed over a chest that wasn't his. "What did Neil mean when he accused me of forcing him to kill demons?"

He was going to play this game? "Seriously? Like you don't know about the halfling murders?"

He waved an elegant hand. "I know some highborn halflings have been missing lately. Are you saying they're dead? I couldn't care less, but their houses might take issue. Why would I want to kill a bunch of halflings?"

"Perhaps because they were petitioning the king to open the Council to demon ambassadors." It was my working theory.

Gray sighed and I got the feeling this reunion of ours was turning out to be a major disappointment for him. "Kelsey, my brother wouldn't do that. He wants to avoid a war as much as the rest of us."

"More," Nemcox explained. "I don't actually like getting dirty. And I would be on the opposite side of my love. He would be on the front lines, you know. I wouldn't mind if that pretend husband of his died in battle, but I can't stand the thought of my puppy being hurt."

Unless he was the one doing the hurting. Nemcox's love was a twisted thing and it made me appreciate Gray all the more. It certainly made me worry what would happen to him on the Hell plane. "Neil Roberts is responsible for killing the halflings. Or rather, his dragon is."

Nemcox gasped, an odd sound coming from his lips. "No. No, that's not possible."

I was starting to understand how screwed we were. If the demon was telling the truth and he wasn't controlling Neil, then who was? "Who else could use that dragon to control Neil?"

Nemcox shook his head. "No one. I'm the only one who has access to the dragon. I bound the dragon. He belongs to me. Kelsey, I would tell you if I was doing this. Well, perhaps I wouldn't if I did have some nefarious purpose, but I don't. I'm worried about him. I love him and if someone else has figured out how to use the conduit, I want them murdered and brutally. It's your job and your duty."

"Now you're concerned about my job?" I'd kind of thought he would be an old-fashioned type of demon.

"Well, you certainly won't have one when you're married," he conceded. "Obviously then you'll concentrate on your proper duties, but for now you are the *Nex Apparatus* and I demand you do your job. Find whoever is forcing my darling to commit acts of treachery."

One good thing might come out of this. "I would, but it appears I'm on a time crunch. I'm heading to Hell soon and that doesn't leave me with a lot of time to sleuth, as they say in my business. I suppose the king will name a replacement. You should probably wait and talk to that person. I'm sure he or she will be extremely helpful."

I would be busy tending my husband's home in Hell, ensuring he had a clean uniform he could torture people in and that dinner was promptly on the table at six p.m.

I saw the moment Nemcox knew I had him. He glanced over at his father. "Fine. I will allow my father to broker with the academics for a few days."

"Brother, I'm begging you to stop these proceedings. I don't want this for her." Gray started to reach out for his brother.

Nemcox stepped back. "You have no idea what you want, Grayson. You're a naïve child and I have to make this decision for you." He turned red-tinged eyes my way. "I'll be back tomorrow night for an update. I'm sure your lawyer there will find a way to draw out the proceedings, but if Neil gets hurt, everything is off, Hunter. Do you understand me?"

Yes, he was changing our bargain. If I didn't figure out who was playing around with Neil's soul, he would tell the wizard.

Luckily, I needed this bargain and I'd planned to figure out the issue with Neil. "I do."

He nodded my way. "Then you've bought yourself some time. Contact me through Gray if you need me. I'll do some digging of my own, and by digging I mean I need to torture some people for information."

The door opened and the king strode in, followed by my uncle Zack. Like Neil had before him, Donovan stopped and stared at Nemcox. The king was a lot better at the intimidating glare though.

"Nemcox, you are here only because I want to understand why my *Nex Apparatus* would lose her damn fool mind and decide to contract her soul to you." Every word that came out of Donovan's mouth was clipped and hard. "Two days ago I couldn't get her to stop trying to murder you and now she's accepting you as her demon overlord for all of time. Would you like to explain?"

"Oh, I assure you I shall hand over her reins to my brother as soon as possible," Nemcox promised. "We're going to be a family, you see. I find it odd that you who owns your companion can possibly be so intolerant."

"I do not own Zoey," Donovan replied.

Lord Sloane huffed, an elegant sound. "Not on paper, I'm sure. You're quite good at looking like the modern king, Your Highness. But deep in that soul of yours, you own them. You own your companion and Quinn, and you will kill anyone who tries to take them from you. You're no better than any of us. You simply try to hide your primal urges. Good luck with that. As to my son's plans to ensure our family harmony, they must wait. I've agreed with your lawyers to a trial tomorrow evening that will decide the legal status of Ms. Owens. I will, of course, bring my own team, so I'll need the wards down."

Donovan's eyes didn't move off the snake in the room. "And I will have a security team greet you, Lord Sloane. Now, if that's settled, I would like you to leave. I'll have Hugo send word when we'll expect you."

Thank god. Food. I could go get food.

Donovan moved to his desk. "Not you, Kelsey. Settle in. We're going to talk."

I practically whimpered. My stomach was turning in on itself.

That was when my uncle held up a bag and I smelled heavenly

burgers and fries. “I thought you might need some fortification for this meeting. I understand you’ve had a long day.”

He passed me the bag and winked before leaving again.

The academics began walking the demons out, quietly discussing what they would need for tomorrow’s trial. Gray stopped at Donovan’s desk.

“Your Highness, I know my kind is not welcome here but I’m going to ask for your hospitality. Not as a halfling but as a prophet.”

“Which side of you destroyed the fifth floor foyer?” Donovan asked. “Was that the prophet side, too? You couldn’t have given me a heads-up? I might have told Dev not to replace the floors if I’d known you were going to bash Trent’s head against them.”

Gray had the good sense to flush with embarrassment. “I believe that was the jealous lover part of me, Your Highness. I’m new to the idea of sharing a woman I love and I am not handling it well. I would like to stay with Kelsey during this time. I’ll follow any protocols you deem necessary.”

Donovan sighed and looked at Gray with what seemed to be sympathy. “Believe it or not, I do know where you are. You have leave to stay. I believe you’ll find Marcus has moved out of the apartment and there are two bedrooms in that unit. I wouldn’t mind someone watching over her. She makes poor choices.”

“Somehow I think we won’t need the second bedroom. At least I hope we don’t,” Gray said. “I hope she’ll let me stay with her. Trent has his own place, I assume.”

Donovan frowned. “I’m going to give you some advice, Sloane. Don’t shut him out. It would be a mistake. You have the girl right now. You’re the one she’s chosen, but you know she’ll need him, too. If you aren’t ready to share her, don’t rub it in his face. Honor him if there’s any chance of him being your partner one day.”

Whoa. What were they talking about? I’d gotten sidetracked. I had that burger halfway down my throat.

“Is that what you did, Your Highness?” Gray sounded a tad bit sarcastic, as though he couldn’t imagine Donovan being truly kind, giving up his rightful place with the queen so some other dude wouldn't ache.

"No, it's what Devinshea did for me once." Donovan sounded almost wistful. "It was the first time I understood how serious he was, that our ménage could be about more than sex and possession. It was the first time I wondered if we could be a family."

Gray stepped back, nodding to the king, and when he spoke, his voice was serious. "I will think about it, Your Highness. And thank you."

I felt like I should have had something to say somewhere in there, but a girl's got to eat. Gray stopped in front of me, his lips curling up as I swallowed and tried to not look like a raging carnivore deprived of meat.

"I'll see if I can find us something for dinner." He leaned over and kissed my forehead. "I'll make sure to have enough for three. See that Trent shows up on time. I love you, Kelsey mine."

He walked out and I was left with half a cheeseburger, the King of all Vampire, and more than a few questions.

"What just happened?" I settled in. The king and I had a couple of things to talk about.

The king sat back. "I believe you started your journey on the happy road to ménage. Though expect there to be some road bumps. Sloane reminds me of myself. He'll struggle with it. Luckily, Trent won't give you trouble. He's been around us for far too long. Now tell me why you're intent on fucking up my day."

So arrogant. I took a long drag off my chocolate milk shake. Uncle Zack knew me well. "Why don't you tell me how my dad is."

The shake of his head told me I was a pain in his ass. The slight curling of his lips said he didn't mind too much. "Lee is going to be all right. He's struggling because he's between two worlds right now, but I've been assured that he'll be fine. We've had both a witch and Henri look him over. Physically, he's perfectly fine. Mentally, he's drifting in and out of the remnants of his old soul. The spell will wear off and he'll be at peace. Well, as at peace as he can be now."

I wanted to tell him. I wanted so much to shove this problem on Daniel Donovan's lap. He was kind of the be-all, end-all authority figure in my world and he wasn't a total asshole. He tried. I got Donovan. I understood him far better than I did the perpetually smooth Quinn or the always competent queen. But I believed Gray. He'd told me to beware the spawn, and that meant anyone who was under the wizard's spell. "I'm not going to talk about my reasons for signing the contract, Your Highness."

His brows came together. "Kelsey, I can help you. There's no need for this. Whatever Nemcox told you, there's another way out."

But I couldn't see it and if I tried to find it, I risked my father's life. "I believe him in this case. I do want to talk to you about something else though."

His brows rose. "Kelsey, I'm not going to allow you to sign a contract."

"You can try." I was sure he would. They all would. Now I had a bit of time and that meant there was some hope. Who knew? Maybe I would find some magical way to murder Nemcox. Of course, that would mean Donovan would likely have to have me executed, but I wouldn't be in Hell and my dad would be safe, so it might be a win.

But that was the old me talking. I needed to find a way out because I was kind of, sort of starting to want to live.

I had begun to see that Quinn was right. This plane needed me.

"You need to bring the demons to the table, Your Highness."

Of all the things I could have said, I could plainly see that Donovan hadn't expected me to say that. It was there in the length of his pause, in the way his brow furrowed with confusion and how his hands tightened into fists. I think that last part was because he had this fight regularly and he'd been sure he wouldn't have it with me.

Marcus had probably given him a hundred and one historical reasons why. Hugo would have pointed out all the legal ramifications. Some members of the Council would argue and debate over the economics of the situation.

I was going to do none of that.

"Have you thought about what not having a contract in place could mean?"

He huffed, an impatient sound. "Are you joking? Of course I've thought about it. I think about it all the time."

"Do you want to start a war, Daniel?" I meant to speak to the man and not the king, though I wasn't foolish enough to think the man was soft. But his stubbornness in this instance came from the man's emotions and had little to do with politics. I knew because I'd been in the same place.

"I don't intend to start a war, but I also have no plans to welcome the fuckers into my home. You did that. You're the one who's forcing me to let down my wards, and you won't even give me an explanation why. Is this your attempt to force my hand into some kind of negotiations with them?" Donovan seemed intent on playing the king.

I wasn't going to let up or be intimidated. I had just started to realize that this, this moment, this was why I was here. I didn't play politics. I wasn't looking to move up in the world. I lived in it in a way Donovan and his family didn't anymore. Couldn't. And that made it mine to protect. Even from him. "I met a woman today. She was Lester's good friend."

His eyes turned wary. "Are you talking about the prostitute?"

I stared at him.

His hands came up. "I'm sorry. I was trying for clarity. I'm sure she's a very nice prostitute."

"She seemed to be. What she truly was was scared. She was a halfling, one who took after her better nature. She followed the rules and yet Nemcox murdered her because she was talking to me. Those lines are being drawn in the sand and she was completely left out."

"If Nemcox is murdering on this plane, then we can bring him to justice."

"How? How do we do that when halflings have no status here?" It was one of the legalities that had lapsed with the contracts. "I begged her to come with me, but she was afraid of the Council. Daniel, she was afraid of you."

He sighed and I could see his weariness. "I've never willingly harmed a halfling. I know they're not all bad. I've had a halfling helping to raise my children for years."

"Yes, and Albert would be helpful in reaching the ones who are reluctant to seek us out. I've been thinking about this for days. I wanted revenge, but meeting my father made me want something more."

"What's that?" Daniel asked.

"A peaceful world for him to grow up in. I can't fix the injustices of yesterday, but I can do my damnedest to ensure more don't happen tomorrow. Have you thought about what happens if you do nothing?"

"I certainly have since that prophecy of Gray's. You think I don't want to avoid…how did he put it? Warfare unlike anything even the ancients have seen? Because I think we should probably avoid that."

Some of Gray's prophecy fell into place.

If you protect the man, you protect the child and the king.

By protecting my father, I was doing the same for Little Lee and Daniel. And that prophecy made it clear I shouldn't tell Donovan what I knew.

If he ever knows how Heaven tricked him, his fury will be a thunderstorm, punishing and never ending.

Heaven had tricked Merlin by hiding my father's soul in a new body. I had to protect that secret at all costs. But I also had to convince the king to meet with the demons and sign new contracts if I was going to save the world. Or at least our plane.

"Your Highness, the woman I met today wouldn't even come in to talk to me when she feared for her life. She can't go to the Hell plane because she's not royal and only royal halflings are given any consideration there. They have nowhere to go and no one to look out for them. They have no home. So I get to speak for them. I know a bit about what it feels like to not belong. They fear that if the war comes, they'll be the first to die for nothing more than the circumstances of their birth. Why did you take this job?"

"I took it because I could either rule or they would find a way to kill me." Donovan's head fell back and he groaned. When he looked back up at me, his shoulders fell. "But I also did it because I wanted to be better. I wanted to unite us."

"Sometimes the king has to put aside what feels right to him for the best of his kingdom," I said quietly because I knew I had him now. "For his family. Because Lee doesn't fit either and one day, he'll see himself in those halflings and wonder why his father didn't protect them."

"And he'll wonder if he's worthy, too." Donovan cursed under his breath. "Damn it. Fine. I hate it but I'll have Marcus open a dialogue. I've known I had to do this for a long time. My distaste has made me procrastinate. The halflings are creatures of the Earth plane. They should be welcome here."

I let loose a long sigh of relief. That had gone better than I'd thought. "Awesome. Hey, if I do end up signing a contract, maybe I can still go to the party. I've heard there's a big-ass party after the accords are signed."

"You're not signing a cont…" Donovan's eyes narrowed. "This is about Lee. When you left earlier you had zero interest in finding a condo on the Hell plane. You went and met with the prostitute who was then killed by Nemcox. Lee was with you. What did Nemcox do to him?"

Well, there was a reason he was the king, and it sure wasn't because the dude was dumb. "He didn't do anything."

Donovan sat up, far more animated than he'd been a few moments before. "No, I'm right. This is about Lee. Something happened there."

I stood up because I wasn't telling him a thing, but that meant getting out of here and fast. Donovan would keep poking and prodding, and I wasn't sure he wouldn't find the right answer. "I think I'll go and see what kind of progress Liv is making with Neil. I want to get that spell done as soon as possible. He's up in the penthouse. I'll say hi to your wife for you."

Donovan frowned. "Neil's not up there."

"Yes, he is. I sent him up there over an hour ago. He changed his mind about remembering his time on the Hell plane and Trent went up there with him." Now that I thought about it, I was surprised that Trent hadn't come back down to find me. Neil would be perfectly safe in the penthouse.

Or that wolf had snuck in a big lunch and not even invited me.

Donovan picked his phone. "Albert? Has Neil shown up? No. How about Trent? Okay. No, don't worry them. Thanks." He hung up. "Kelsey, Albert hasn't seen either one of them." He picked up the phone again. "Zack, I need you."

My uncle must have been standing outside in the lobby because he strode through the door seconds later.

"Why would Trent take Neil somewhere else?" I had my cell in hand, trying to get Trent on the line. It went straight to voice mail.

My gut went straight to churning with anxiety.

Zack took a deep breath, his eyes gleaming with a wolf-like stare. "Trent wasn't in here with you, but I catch his scent on this floor. He was here?"

"Yes. We were in the conference room down the hall," I began, but my uncle was already walking out of Donovan's office, turning toward the conference room.

Donovan and I followed.

Zack stopped right outside the room. "You were here with Sloane and his brother. I hate that smell. I've got Trent and Neil, too. They went this way."

"I need to know the addresses of any highborn halflings left here in Dallas." My mind was already on the worst-case scenario. Hopefully this was nothing more than two wolves who got a little hungry on their way and got distracted by the thought of burgers or steaks or something. With any luck we would find them in one of the shops and restaurants the building housed. They would be sitting there polishing off a snack, and I would feel like a moron for coming up with battle plans.

Donovan stopped and turned. "You two find Neil. I was supposed to have a meeting tonight with a halfling from Lester's family. He's a half brother. I agreed to meet with him to explain what happened to Lester. I'll call him and warn him to be on watch."

"Get me an address, just in case." I ran to keep up with my uncle.

Zack passed the elevators Neil and Trent should have used if they were going to the condo. He walked straight to the stairwell.

I got a bad feeling.

When Zack opened the door, I knew why. Trent was at the bottom of the flight of stairs leading down, his entire body covered in blood.

Chapter Fifteen

I ran down the stairs, my heart in my throat. He wasn't moving. Trent was a badass on the king's blood. I'd seen him take crazy damage and get his ass up a couple of minutes later.

I'd never once seen the man so still. Even in his sleep, he moved, but now he was completely still and I realized if he was dead, a part of me would be, too.

My wolf was howling inside as I dropped to my knees. "Please get Donovan."

Zack stared down as though he wasn't sure what to say. "Kelsey…"

I shook my head and put my hands on Trent. He was still warm. He wasn't icy cold yet and that meant someone could bring him back. "Get Donovan now."

Zack turned and ran back up the stairs.

What the hell had happened? Neil wasn't anywhere near as strong as Trent. God, I could barely recognize his face. I smoothed back his hair. It was matted with blood. I tried not to think about the hole in his chest.

"Don't cry."

I breathed a long sigh of relief at the sound of his tortured voice and let my head drop down to his. “Don’t fucking die.”

His body shuddered under my hand. “Bossy woman.”

I sniffled, trying not to give over to the need to wail. “Well, I was told to have you at dinner at the proper time or Gray will get his panties in a wad and he’ll probably serve us both salads or something.”

“He’ll probably serve me poison, baby. Fuck, that hurt.”

“What happened? Stop trying to move.”

He groaned and lay back. “It was Neil, but it wasn’t. There was a flash of light and then Neil wasn’t himself. He was the creature I remembered from all those years ago. I tried to stop him. He tried to pull out my heart. And now we’re here. Kelsey, something touched me. Not Neil, something else. It burned me from the inside out. I have no idea how I’m still alive.”

I was sure it was the king’s blood. I reached for his hand. His whole body was limp in my arms. “Hold on. Donovan will be here soon. It’s going to be okay.”

I knew I should be trying to find Neil, trying to identify this new threat, but all I cared about in that moment was making sure my almost lover lived. I lay down beside him, gently running my hands where I could. I didn’t care that I was getting covered in blood. All that mattered was my instinct in the moment. It told me to put hands on him, to give him the comfort of knowing he wasn’t alone.

I needed the comfort of knowing he was still breathing.

“Kelsey?”

“Hush, it’s okay. You’re going to be okay.”

“Loved you the moment I saw you. Knew it was you. Had almost given up.”

Tears made my vision go hazy. He wouldn’t be saying these things if he didn’t think he was dying. “You hold on.”

“No matter how pissed Gray is, I won’t leave. You need me.”

“Damn straight. So don’t die.”

“Hated that damn vampire.”

It was good to know that male jealousy was alive and well, even as I was fairly certain I could see his heart from that hole in his chest. "Please rest, Trent."

The door above came open and Donovan raced down.

"What the fuck happened?" He rolled up his sleeve and I watched as his fangs grew large.

It was an easy thing to put together in the end. Why else would Nemcox kill Larissa for her "loose lips"? She didn't work for him. From what I could tell, she didn't know the demon. Yet he'd shown up just as she was going to start talking.

I was dealing with a "stolen" weapon that came from the Heaven plane and a light that felt endless.

"I think an angel attacked Trent," I said quietly. I sat up and maneuvered so his head was in my lap. "I think an angel is controlling Neil, and I definitely think one of the angels is working with Nemcox, though I'm not sure he understands what's really going on. He seemed extremely upset that someone was using the connection to control Neil."

Donovan got to one knee and bit into his own wrist. "Come on, buddy. No time to do this in a proper, manly way. You're taking it straight from the tap today."

Trent frowned.

I looked down at him. "You will drink that blood and you will do it right fucking now, mister."

Trent growled, but when Donovan put his wrist down, he took the blood. Donovan winced as Trent's fangs came out and sank in, digging deeper.

Donovan's eyes tightened as he seemed intent to focus on something else. "Why would an angel care about whether or not I renew our contracts with the demons?"

It was getting a little hot in there. I know this sounds weird because I was watching my half-dead almost-boyfriend being saved by drinking another guy's blood, but you kind of have to be there to get it. There's something about the act of sharing blood that's physical, even sexual. I was sure if they'd had a choice, Donovan would have drained some of that blood into a thermos and passed it over, but we needed to move fast. Trent's hand came out, his fingers winding around mine, and I could feel him getting stronger.

"According to Marcus, if the plane fails to balance itself, Heaven will do it for us," I said. "What if we're dealing with a faction of Heaven that doesn't like the lower planes? They've been out of the action for a long time."

Trent finally let his head fall back. He looked past tired, but he was going to live. "Thank you, Your Highness. If it helps at all, I think I got a good swipe in on the bastard. Neil was in front of me and I couldn't see whoever showed up behind me, but I swiped back and I know I caught him with my claws."

"If it was an angel, then I'm not sure if those claws of yours are going to do much damage." Donovan straightened up. "Owens, we need to go. I have the address. We don't have much time."

Zack had moved in behind me. My uncle's arms went around me and I found myself caged in. "Daniel, do it now."

Trent got to his feet with a low groan. "What are you doing, Zack?"

I had a suspicion. I went still in my uncle's arms. Zack takes the king's blood, too, and it makes him super strong. Probably not stronger than me, but we were in close quarters and I didn't want to end up throwing him down fifteen flights of stairs. Of course, I also had zero plans to let him do what I thought he was going to do.

"I'm saving my niece. Daniel, I'll hold her. I can do it. All she needs is a little of your blood in her system," Zack explained, his voice tight.

Yep, we were back to that. I got ready to make my move. I would kick back and get out of his hold before Trent could help him. Trent had been right there in the "rah, rah let's hold Kelsey down and feed her vampire blood so she can't make her own mistakes" club.

Trent's skin was far paler than normal as he looked at me. "You sure you want to do this, baby?"

"I fucking don't want to do this." Trent and I were about to have our first real fight, and it would be a doozy.

He shook his head. "I mean you think you have to sign this contract. You have reasons you need to keep this option open?"

I nodded, not sure what was going on here.

"Daniel," Zack insisted.

Trent turned and placed his body in front of mine. "Over my dead body, Your Highness."

Daniel put a hand on Trent's shoulder. "You are a far quicker learner than I was, man. And Zack, I will never force her to do anything again. She is my trusted *Nex Apparatus*. If she says she's got her reasons, then I'm going to honor them. Now I need her to put her life on the line so we can try to save some halfling demon neither one of us has ever met. Let's go."

"Daniel, she's my niece," Zack said, but his hands loosened.

"And she's one of the smartest, strongest women I've ever met. She'll get out of this. Trust her, Zack." Donovan moved up the stairs. "We have to go."

I looked at Trent. "I thought you were going to make me do it."

He leaned over, letting his forehead find mine. "I won't put you in a cage, Kelsey. Ever. I was scared of losing you, but you aren't a safe woman to love. Probably wouldn't love you if you were. Now go and fuck that angel up, babe. I'll deal with your uncle and I'll make damn sure Gray isn't serving us salad tonight." He hugged me tight before stepping back. "Go."

He loved me.

He fucking loved me.

I wasn't even sure what to do or say. I simply ran up after Donovan, who seemed to be going to the top of the building. My mind was whirling.

Trent loved me. He'd loved me from the moment he'd seen me. It would have been nice if he hadn't maybe been such an ass then. Except now I could see he hadn't. He'd done everything he could to get to know me.

I got to the top of the building. Donovan stood there, the wind whipping through his hair.

"You never assigned him to follow me, did you?" I yelled the question because it was pretty loud up here and he hadn't even started up the helicopter yet.

The big bird that was one of Quinn's favorite toys sat on the landing site. I'd never flown in a chopper before. I hoped we would have somewhere to land.

"Not once," Donovan yelled back. "That was his own stalkery idea. Come on. We're going to have to move fast."

I jogged to him, wondering if we were waiting for a pilot. "Is Quinn on his way up? How exactly do you intend to land that sucker? Tell me we're not jumping out."

His arm went around my middle and for a minute I thought he'd tricked me. "Not jumping. Just flying. Hold on."

Worse. It was so much worse than jumping out of a perfectly good helicopter.

Donovan took off and I heard my own girly scream because wolves were not built for flight, and neither were humans or Hunters or any of the other things I could possibly be.

I closed my eyes because the ground was way too far away.

"Finally found something that scares you?" Donovan chuckled. "Don't flip out. I haven't lost anyone yet. And please, if you're going to puke…please don't puke."

I kept my eyes closed and thought of better things.

Like the fact that Trent was going to let me sign my soul away to Hell and never see me again.

Because he trusted me.

He let Donovan fly me into danger without any lecture other than to say he loved me.

He let me risk my life.

Because he trusted me.

I felt something settle deep inside me, something warm and secure.

Yes, letting me endanger my immortal soul was the single most romantic thing anyone had ever done for me.

I forced back my fear and opened my eyes. It took me a second, but I was ready to fly.

* * * *

Donovan's version of flying sucked, but he did manage a decent landing. My stomach was in my throat, but I felt so much better when there was ground beneath my feet. I found myself standing in the backyard of what looked like a mini mansion. There was a big pool with a fountain in front of me and it looked like an outdoor kitchen to my left. The massive two-story house looked like a Colonial.

It was perfectly quiet. That house looked like nothing bad had ever happened there.

Donovan strode forward toward the back door. A large wrought iron and glass door led into the house. "His name is something terrifically unpronounceable, but he goes by Ben."

"Let's hope he's still breathing because two halflings from the same family could be hard for a clan to take. What could they do?" I followed behind Donovan. At one point in time he'd been a thief, so I figured he had a way to get that door open if it was locked.

He did. He pulled it off its hinges and tossed it to the side like it weighed nothing. "They could cause a lot of flack for me when I try to negotiate. They could even deny negotiating at all unless the Council appoints a new leader. They couldn't take my crown, but they could force the Council to strip some of my powers. I would be placed in the position of giving up that power or letting the contracts lapse completely and risk all-out war. Which you so recently pointed out would be a bad idea."

I was starting to wonder if that wasn't the whole point of this exercise. The question was why would Nemcox want to help some angels go all postal on the Earth plane? I fully intended to find out the answer to that question because Papa Sloane wasn't an apocalypse junkie. He liked the status quo. He certainly didn't want to go to war with the Heaven plane, from what I could tell, and historically, Nemcox did his papa's bidding.

As I followed behind Donovan, the questions were playing through my head. Why would a demon like Nemcox play nice with an angel? Was he lying about not knowing what was happening with Neil Roberts? Or was Nemcox being played as a pawn, too?

The floor under me shook and rattled and there was a sick feeling in the pit of my stomach.

"No! What are you doing here? Get out of my house." A masculine voice was shouting.

Donovan took the stairs two at a time, but suddenly there was a terrible white light and he stopped.

My vision went fuzzy. There was something about the light. It made me physically ill, as though it could reach out and touch places that shouldn't be touched. Like my insides. Donovan had frozen in front of me and I smelled something burning. I watched in horror as I realized it was him. The light touched him and where it did, his skin charred and blackened.

I moved in because while the light made me want to vomit, I didn't go up in flames merely from walking into it. That made this my fight and not the king's. "Get back downstairs!"

His eyes were closed, but he took a step back.

I forced myself up those stairs, every step an agony. I could hear a weird humming. The light and the sound acted as a wall, attempting to bar me from moving forward. It was like moving through thick sand, but I kept on going. One step and then another. And another.

A sobbing sound caught in my ears and then I realized I was on the second floor. There was a massive ball of light in the middle of the room I found myself in. It glowed and shimmered, and all that sound and blinding glare was coming from there as though it was a massive spotlight, a perpetual flashbang that never calmed down.

I made out a figure beyond. Two, really. There was a fight going on but I wouldn't be able to help because that light and sound dragged at me.

Somewhere in the background I heard a scream, a crash.

The sound pulsed at me, making my bones shake. I was blind in that light, seeing only the vaguest outline of the center.

I had to turn off the light. If I didn't, I would die and soon. My eyes were failing me. My ears could barely handle the sounds.

So shut them off and trust your wolf. Trust your nose.

Trent was there in my head. He'd been pushing me over and over to get more in touch with my wolfy instincts.

I stopped trying to fight my way in by sight. I stilled and took a deep breath, letting the scents flow over my senses.

At first it was completely chaotic. I couldn't tell what I was smelling. Sunshine. Water. Grass. They overwhelmed me as though they were some sort of perfume meant to mask everything else. But I could go deeper. I could peel back the layers that covered the world around me. I let myself catalogue those initial smells and then shoved them aside, looking for the deeper truth.

Blood. I could smell blood. Blood and something odd. It was a scent from childhood, slightly vanilla. It was so evocative I could feel the dough in my hands, hear my brothers laugh as we pushed it through the toys. Our grandfather had given us a set for Christmas. The barber shop. I would use my hands to press the dough in and then we would cut the "hair" with big plastic scissors.

That was my scent. It was in exactly one place and that was the center of the light. That was the scent I would use to find my off switch.

I kept my eyes closed. I didn't need them. I followed that scent and let my instincts lead me. They told me when I was close, where I should hit. It was almost like I was in a trance. My fist came back and I put everything I had into it. Pain flared from my hand up through my arm as I made contact and the light completely snuffed out.

The cessation of light and sound seemed to stop everything in the room. It was like a curtain had been pulled down and I could see the truth again.

I was in what appeared to be a massive gameroom. As my eyes were able to focus, I could see a pool table and a big bar. It looked like there was a massive TV on the wall across from me.

And I wasn't alone.

My vision was still adjusting when I realized one of those blobby blurs that was stalking around the room was coming right at me.

There was a loud *thwack* as I felt something hit me hard, sending me to the floor. I found myself looking up into glowing, alien eyes and a familiar face. Neil Roberts was on top of me, snarling down. I wasn't dealing with a wolf though. Nope. While I could see that it was Roberts's face, it was changed. His eyes were red and his face had stretched slightly, giving him a lean look. He growled and I could see jagged teeth.

And those teeth were coming right at my throat.

My ears were still ringing, my eyesight a bit on the foggy side, but I had to keep those nasty teeth from ripping my throat out. I punched up, catching him on the jaw. The force didn't dislodge him, but it did give me enough space to bring my knee up. Hard.

He groaned on top of me and proved that even in some weird lizard form, Neil Roberts was still a male.

He moved and something fell from his hand, clattering to the floor.

"He's going to kill us all," a voice was saying. It came from somewhere in the distance.

I rolled away, getting to my feet and cursing the fact that Donovan hadn't stopped long enough for me to pick up Gladys. Or any kind of weapon. I'd spent most of the day in the Council rooms and those were weapon-free zones. The only thing I could find to try to take down a possessed werewolf/dragon demony thing was a pool cue. Sure that worked for Buffy on many an occasion, but I generally prefer my weapons to be, well, actual weapons.

"Please save me."

I glanced to my left and realized our potential victim was still alive and cowering. I didn't blame him. He'd probably been hanging out, having some supper and playing video games when the light of all Heaven invaded and spat out a lizard creature. That would make most people flip their shit a little.

I glanced back, looking toward Neil, but that was when I noticed what he'd dropped.

The sword. It was sitting on the floor behind Neil. All he had to do was turn and pick it up, but his eyes were on his prey.

"Stay back, Ben." I thought that was what Donovan had called him.

I needed that sword.

"I have no intention of moving ever again," he managed to say. "Is this what killed Les? How horrible."

Roberts was back on his feet, and it was super easy to see the dude was pissed. His hands had formed long claws he swiped out with. I jumped back, barely managing to avoid those talons.

"Neil Roberts!" I yelled his name, hoping to get some kind of hint of recognition.

He stopped, his whole body going still as a statue.

I stilled, too, unwilling to make a move. "Your name is Neil Roberts and you don't want to do this."

"No, you don't, buddy," Ben added.

Neil's head turned and he hissed, as though he'd remembered what he was supposed to be doing. He took off across the room, claws fully out. And that was when I realized he wasn't running to the cringing halfling. He was trying to get to the sword.

There was another body in the room, but whoever it was, he was on the floor and unmoving. I couldn't deal with him until I incapacitated Roberts.

Which would be hard because I couldn't kill him. Let me tell you something, battle is way easier when all options are on the table. Maiming and killing are perfectly valid battle plans, but taking down the dude who's trying to murder you without harming a hair on his head is a lot trickier.

They might have to forgive me for a little maiming. He was a wolf under all that lizardy goodness, so he should survive.

I hoped.

All I knew was I needed to get to that sword before he did because I was definitely certain that I wouldn't survive getting cleaved in two by the Sword of Justice.

He was far closer to it than I was, and I knew there was zero chance that I got to it first if I left this to a foot race. So I used what I had. I reared back, full-on Olympic athlete javelin style, and sent that pool cue flying.

If you've got a normal amount of strength, this move will do nothing but piss off whoever you threw a pool cue at, but I'm far stronger than that and I get even better when I let my arm change. I felt it tighten the way it always did when it transformed. I suddenly sported shiny demon skin on my dominant arm.

That was probably why the pool cue struck Roberts hard and sank into the flesh under his left shoulder blade.

A loud howl split the air, but I ignored it because I needed that damn sword. I ran for it, leaning over to grip it. I felt it singe my hands but for some reason it didn't burn into me the way I would have thought. I could hold it. It wasn't comfortable, but I had it.

Roberts pulled the pool cue out of his body and turned on me.

"Neil? Baby? Please don't do this," a new voice said.

Chad Thomas stood in the doorway and I realized night had fallen. The vamp wasn't even wearing shoes. He was normally a goth vision in leather or denim. He looked oddly young and somewhat vulnerable wearing a pair of pajama bottoms and a plain white T-shirt. His hair was twelve kinds of fucked up and I realized that was probably because Donovan had flown his ass here, and he hadn't done it slow. He must have gone easy with me and I wondered exactly how fast that man could fly.

Roberts stopped, his body doing that creepy statue thing again. It was so weird because while he wasn't moving, I could feel the menace coming off of him. He might not be moving at the moment, but when he decided to, he would go quickly, and I would be dead if I wasn't careful.

"Baby, you don't have to give in to this." Chad Thomas started to move in.

Donovan put a hand out. It was a kind of gross, bloody hand, but it seemed to still be functional. Donovan's body showed signs of what that light had done to him. His skin was burned in some places, and it was obvious he was taking his time to heal. Still, Donovan stood tall and steady. If he was in pain, I couldn't tell. "You can't get close to him when he's in this state."

"Then why the hell am I here?" Chad stepped out of Donovan's easy reach. "He's my husband and I'm not going to leave him like this. Neil, baby, it's me and I love you. I'm here. You can fight this."

A low hissing sound emanated from Roberts, though he hadn't moved at all.

"Do you think I should run now?" At some point in time, Ben had decided to take cover behind me. Like right behind me. I could feel him standing there. From the brief glimpse I'd gotten, he was much smaller than his recently deceased brother. He reminded me a bit of Harry Potter with his round glasses, youthful looks, and slightly shaggy brown hair.

"I think that would be a mistake." We needed to treat the threat in front of us like a snake waiting to strike. As long as we were still, he couldn't seem to figure out which way to move. There were so many of us in the room. His intended victim was behind me, Donovan and Chad Thomas flanked him to the left, and a few feet beyond lay the body of whoever had brought that light to the fight.

I had a bad feeling about what I would find when I finally got to that body. Something about that scent had been familiar.

We were all still, all waiting to see which way Roberts would go.

Or perhaps without the light to lead him, he wasn't sure what to do. He needed a push.

At some point in time his shirt had torn and it hung in rags on his body. I could see glimpses of the tattoo that had started all this trouble.

"I'm afraid Chad's right, Your Highness." I kept my eyes firmly on the threat in front of me. "I think he needs to get his hands on Neil. He needs to touch that dragon. Neil figured something out earlier today. The dragon is a part of him and the dragon recognizes its soul mate. He's suppressed it because he was afraid, but the dragon responds to you, Chad. I think if we can make that connection, can form the bond between the two of you, it will be harder for outside forces to take him over."

"If Chad survives getting close to him." Donovan seemed intent on being the Negative Nell of our group.

"So when the dude in the PJs gets close to the crazy lizard dude, that's when I should run?" Ben asked.

"Only if you want him to catch you," I replied. "I need you to pretend like you're in *Jurassic Park* and he's the T-rex who can't see you if you don't move. Can you do that for me, Ben? Can you play the still and quiet game for me?"

He went totally silent, proving he could.

"Talk to him, Chad." I needed to get this over with because I wasn't sure our other friend wouldn't wake up and flash that heavenly light around again. If it was as powerful as before and hit Donovan unaware, I wasn't sure I wouldn't lose him. I couldn't be the chick who got the king killed. It looks bad on a resume. "You have to connect to him."

Chad took a step forward and Roberts pivoted, his head tilting and taking in the man moving close to him. Chad's hands came out and he stopped. "Baby, it's me. We need to talk because you promised me breakfast in bed this evening. Do you remember? We stayed up late last night and watched *Game of Thrones* and we made out on the couch and you swore that when I woke up, you would be there."

Roberts's hands started shaking slightly. I could see where the blood dripped from the wounds there. It was where he'd held the sword that should have killed Ben.

Chad took another step. "Do you have any idea how long I've

wanted to touch you? Touch that part of you. I know you hate it and you think it's a sign of what that demon did to you, but I think that tat on your side is the sexiest thing I've ever seen. When I close my eyes and the dawn takes me, I dream about touching it, feeling it pulse under my hand because it's mine. Because you're mine. Not because I took you but because you gave yourself to me in love and passion and because our souls were born to be together."

The claws on Roberts's hands started to recede.

Another step and Chad could almost touch him. "I love all of you, Neil Roberts. Every inch of your flesh. Every part of your soul. Come back to me."

A single tear rolled from his red eyes and I knew we had him.

"Touch him," I said. "Put your hands right on that tat, Chad. Let it know you accept it. If it's anything at all like Gray's, it's been waiting and wanting, and I think the dragon's need might break through whatever's controlling your husband right now."

I saw Donovan tense, as though ready to step in at any second, but Chad didn't hesitate. He strode up to Neil and slid his hand through the slits of the shirt Neil was wearing. Neil's whole body tensed and then seemed to relax, the red in his eyes receding along with those nasty teeth and claws.

"I can feel it," Chad said with a wondrous look on his face. "I can feel it move. It's happy."

"Chad?" Neil shook his head and now he cried freely. "I heard you. I could hear you."

They held on to each other, clinging like the lovers they were.

Donovan took a deep breath and the whole room seemed to settle, the tension fleeing.

"Can I run now?" Ben asked.

Ben was starting to be a pain in my ass. I turned and faced him. "No, you can thank me and the king and you can come back to Council headquarters so this can't happen again."

He was just a kid. He looked like he couldn't be more than eighteen. He nodded. "Okay. I think that might be best. And I'll tell my mom that the *Nex Apparatus* saved me. That should impress her."

The king strode over, holding out a hand. "Ben, I'm sorry about your brother."

The kid nodded. "Me, too. Les was a good guy. I know you won't believe this but my mom isn't so bad. She's a succubus, but as long as she gets what she needs, she's very reasonable. She wants me to talk to you about her tribe. Without the contracts in place, they're suffering, Your Highness. They serve a function, sir."

Donovan nodded, but his focus changed. "I'll talk to her and I intend to open up a dialogue again. Come to the Council with us and we'll discuss it. But not before we figure out who's been controlling Neil."

Yeah, I had a feeling.

It had been that smell that made me wonder. He kept a small play area in the lobby of his office. The man on the floor saw patients of all kinds. He would never turn anyone away, and certainly not a child. He kept toys out there, too, and sometimes when I was running late for my appointment, I would catch him out there, rolling the dough out with his daughter or one of the others, making fun shapes for them.

"Felix?"

I'd never seen Donovan look so lost as that moment when he realized the man who had betrayed Neil was Felix Day.

Chapter Sixteen

I walked into my apartment feeling completely empty. Hollow might be a better word.

It hurt seeing my friends hurt. Which was funny because a couple of months before I wouldn't have said Donovan was a friend. Or Quinn or the queen. I'd looked at Felix Day as someone I had to get through so I could do my job, but over the months I'd grown to care about him and his family.

Zoey had broken down when Donovan had told her what we'd found. She'd said she couldn't believe it and I wasn't sure she did. Even seeing Felix hadn't helped because it wasn't like he could tell us what had happened.

Felix Day was in a coma. He was lying in a bed in Henri's hospital, his body still and only the beeping of the monitors to let us know he was alive. He'd taken wounds from his fight with Trent and those had been dealt with, but he hadn't woken up yet. His wife and daughter were praying, but I wasn't sure anything could help him now.

I'd stopped in at the king's condo and talked to my father. Well, tried to. He was kind of in and out of it. Soon he would be gone, settling back deep inside his new life, but I would know he was there.

I would save him if I died trying. Of course, dying wouldn't be so bad. Living in Hell would suck.

"Kelsey?" Gray walked out of the kitchen. He'd changed into a T-shirt and jeans and I could see his big feet because he was barefoot. Stupid sexy feet that I shouldn't have fixated on.

"Hey." I shrugged out of my jacket. "Sorry I'm late. I got caught up in the job."

He strode over to me, putting his hands on my shoulders. "I heard. I'm sorry about the doctor. I know you were friends with him. Did you get the sword?"

I nodded. "It's locked up in the armory and they've put all kinds of crazy wards everywhere. Apparently the king doesn't want the angels to get in and take it away without having a nice long talk with them."

I'd seen Marcus, too, and he'd been thrilled that the king was finally ready to open negotiations with the demons. He'd asked me to reconsider my contract, but I still couldn't see a way out of it.

I felt heavy and tired.

Would Nemcox renege on his offer now that I'd caught the person who had been manipulating Neil? Would I find myself right back where I'd started from?

I glanced up at Gray. He was so beautiful to me. Gray had dark brown hair and eyes so blue they were almost violet. He'd been the first man I'd ever loved. I could remember vividly the day he'd walked into my life, but I wondered who he would become when we lived in a place that was surrounded by evil.

And I knew I was going to miss Trent so much.

"What is it, baby?" Gray smoothed back my hair.

How could I tell him I was worried because I hadn't been able to find Trent? I'd spent the last hour searching the building for him. He wasn't at his place and I hadn't found him down in Ether. How could I tell the man I'd once planned to spend my whole life with in holy monogamy that I'd gone looking for another man and my heart wasn't whole without him? How did I tell him that I needed another man's arms around me?

"She's had a shit day and she needs a beer."

I held my breath as Trent strode out of the kitchen, too. He was wearing jeans and nothing else, his cut torso on full display and it was perfect and whole, with no signs of the damage Felix had done.

"I told you she would be twelve kinds of tired after what happened. Fighting takes a lot out of her because she can't physically change the way the rest of us can. She's gotta call on her inner wolf, but it takes a toll on her Hunter body." Trent had two beers in his hand and he offered me one. "You'll be happy to know he didn't even think of making a salad for dinner. Steak and potatoes. I managed to make the brownies."

Gray snorted. "Like they were hard. They're from a box. All you had to do was mix some stuff up."

I couldn't help it. I reached out and managed to get a hand on them both. I bit back a sob because they were both here and it had been a shitty day, and simply being in the same room with them made me happy. Happy in a stupid, Hollywood-romantic, everything-falls-into-place way that brought tears to my eyes.

Trent's arm immediately came around me, pulling me in. Gray took a few seconds, but it happened and I was drawn into them, caught between those big masculine bodies, and for the first time in forever I felt comfortable. Like this was where I belonged. Like I didn't have to fight for anything because I was safe.

I felt Gray's lips on my forehead, his hand soothing down my back as Trent put his nose into my neck and he breathed in, taking my scent into his body.

This was what I'd needed all day. This was the place I'd longed for. Warmth and welcome and love.

And I wasn't sure what happened next.

I stepped back, feeling awkward. "So when's dinner?"

"I think dinner can wait," Trent said. "I think you need to relax."

I took a long swig of beer. I wasn't sure how he expected me to relax. "I could probably take a nice long shower."

He stepped up, his hand going to the back of my neck. He looked down at me with warm eyes. "Or we could take you to bed and ease that restlessness I know you're feeling right now."

"Okay." I *was* feeling it. The future wasn't settled and that made me anxious. I might have bought myself a few days, but that contract was being written up and I would be forced to sign it if I couldn't find another way to protect my father.

Gray took a step back. "I'll handle dinner then. Let me know when you're ready to eat."

Trent's eyes closed briefly, but he took a deep breath as though fortifying himself. When he opened them again, he turned to Gray. "I thought we talked about this. You knew she would need to be touched and held and fucked when she came back. She needs sex on a base level."

"You know I could always go and have that shower and take care of myself." I wasn't sure I wanted to be "serviced."

Except I did. Because it kind of sounded a little hot.

Gray met his eyes. "And you seem ready to provide it for her. Maybe I can have a turn later tonight. I can sleep with her and you can come in and handle the day shift."

I stared at Gray because I didn't want to be serviced that much. "If this is a job to you, then I can definitely take care of myself."

I started toward the bedroom. The shower was sounding better and better.

A hand caught my elbow, stopping me and turning me around. Trent stood there, his jaw hard. "No. You don't walk away from this."

This wasn't how I'd pictured it at all. Well, I had. It was my worst-case scenario. "Having sex with me isn't a job. If Donovan assigned this duty to you, then walk away, buddy, because I can take care of myself."

"I never said it was a job to me, though you should know if it was, then I've been applying over and over again since the day you walked into my life. It's not a job, baby. It's a calling and I'm more than ready. You think those fingers of yours can do the trick?" Trent asked. "Because I don't think they can. If they did, you would be a lot sweeter to be around than you are. You need a man who can take care of you. Two of them." He turned to Gray. "I told you how this needs to go. Stop thinking. Kiss her. Show her you want her. Show her you love her so much you're willing to share her so she gets every single thing she needs."

Gray hesitated. "I do love her."

"Then what's the problem?"

I was still because this seemed to be Trent's fight. I was being too hard on him. We'd had that moment earlier when he'd given me what I needed. He'd told me he loved me and then proved it by standing up for me. He'd stood in front of his boss—a man he'd made a blood oath to—and chose me. I had to let him take control of this. It was my turn to trust him, and that meant standing back and trying to keep my sarcastic comments to myself.

Gray groaned and scrubbed a hand over his head. "It's weird."

"And spanking a girl isn't weird?" I didn't try very hard.

A brow rose over Trent's right eye. "Spanking? You spank her?"

I pointed his way. "It was just for fun. A little spanking and some bondage. Everyone does it these days, right?"

Trent's lips curled up in the sexiest smirk. "Oh, baby, if a bit of domestic discipline is on the table, my life is going to be so much easier."

Gray seemed a bit disconcerted by the banter. "It's not the same. And that was private, Kelsey."

"And it'll be private now," Trent assured him. "Are you worried about gossip?"

I thought I knew what he was worried about. "I think he's worried about sin."

"What?" Trent asked.

Gray shook his head. "You wouldn't understand. You weren't born into a demonic family. Do you think I didn't see things I shouldn't? I've been told all my life that it's only a matter of time before I give into my perverse impulses, and they were right. I do like to have some kink in my sex, but I kept it to one woman. And it's different with Kelsey. I intended to marry her. I intended to have a normal, happy marriage with her."

"That would keep you on the straight and narrow?" Trent asked.

"I have to watch myself. Always," Gray agreed.

Because he was practicing for his descent. There was only one problem I saw with it. "What would be wrong about this? Why would this be sinful?"

"It's not," Trent replied when Gray didn't. "There's nothing sinful about sex when it's loving and consensual. Hell, there's nothing wrong with it when it's not loving, as long as everyone respects their lovers. There is no normal, Gray. You're looking for some white picket fence to save you, but it won't. That white picket fence will do nothing but keep you from really living, and it will definitely keep you from giving her what she needs. Kiss her."

Gray didn't hesitate this time. He moved in and his hands came up to cup my face, his mouth descending on mine. I relaxed and let him take control. When I felt his tongue drag across my bottom lip, I opened for him. His tongue glided over mine, sliding and seducing. My body lit from within, every cell waking and readying.

And that was when I felt Trent at my back. His big hand traced down my spine and then he pushed my hair aside and placed his lips on the back of my neck.

I shivered at the feeling. His teeth scraped against my skin, an act of pure alpha wolf dominance that shot straight to my pussy. It made me want to get to my knees and offer him my body.

Gray stepped back, his eyes hooded with desire, but there was worry in them, too.

"Tell me you don't want her." Trent's hands slid over my hips and I could feel his cock against the curve of my ass. Yep. He was an alpha everywhere.

"I want her. I've always wanted her." Gray's voice had gone deep.

Trent's fingers found the hem of my T-shirt, playing with it, teasing Gray with hints of skin. "Tell me you don't want to be in charge of this. Tell me you don't want to order me to strip her bare and offer her up to you. Maybe you can watch. Do you honestly have no interest in sitting back and watching her come? In knowing all the while that she's putting on a show for you, that when she's done screaming, you'll make her scream all over again."

I could see plainly that he did. Gray's slacks had tented nicely and his hands fisted at his sides as though he was trying his hardest not to reach out.

"Take off her shirt."

"With pleasure." Trent's nose was on the back of my neck and I could feel him breathing in my scent. "Damn, you smell good. Do you know how long I've wanted that smell to be for me? I would show up on your doorstep with some dumb excuse and you would smell like this because no shower can completely get rid of the smell of sex."

Gray moved in and he closed his eyes, breathing in deeply. "She always smells like sunshine when she gets hot, but then I would get hit with that old Euro vamp smell."

"Hey." My protest was cut off by Trent dragging the T-shirt up and over my head.

"Yes, that was the problem," Trent agreed, ignoring me. Well, my words, at least. He paid attention to my bra because he had that thing handled in seconds. He was a pro when it came to getting a chick naked.

Gray's eyes opened and they were the same violet color that he got when he was emotional or horny as hell. "You smell a lot like her. The scents almost mingle. It doesn't bother me the way smelling the vampire on her did."

Trent eased the bra off and tossed it to the side. Cool air hit my skin and my nipples tightened. I was the one taking a steadying breath now because I was half naked in front of two stunningly gorgeous men. Trent's hands skimmed over my shoulders as though urging me to relax. "That's the werewolf part of her. You recognize that Kelsey and I smell alike because we're pack. She doesn't know it but she's got mad wolf pheromones. When we run, I've had to make it plain that she's not available."

"What?" I never spent any time with the male wolves when we ran. I kind of thought they all hated the fact that I wasn't a full-on wolf. "They don't like me."

"Cup her breasts," Gray ordered.

"Oh, they like the hell out of you because you smell like sex to them." Trent's big hands came around and cupped my breasts, making my heart race and my breath threaten to stop in my chest. "And I told them if I ever caught one of the fuckers sniffing around you, I would show them who the alpha is."

"I'm sure you were that polite about it." Gray pulled his T-shirt over his head.

"I might have used different wording." Trent's breath was hot on my neck, his hands gentle as he offered my breasts up. "Are you feeling better, Gray?"

"I'm telling myself that I was a fool to think you could stay near her and not take her," Gray admitted. "I was being selfish. I wanted someone who would watch over her but respect my claim. That wasn't fair to you."

"Or her. She needs us both." Trent rolled my nipples.

I could hear them talking, but I didn't care. They were negotiating and I knew I should have something to say about it, but all I cared about was the fact that I could see Gray's muscled chest and feel Trent's skin on mine. That was all that mattered.

Peace had settled over me, even as my body hummed with anticipation.

Gray moved closer. He reached out and brushed his fingers over my nipples. "You'll take care of her? When I can't, you'll protect her?"

The man had fucked me while impaled on a sword. I thought he'd already proven his devotion, but Gray dropped to his knees in front of me and I kept my mouth shut.

"I'll be your partner, Gray. I won't let either one of you down. I've spent years looking for her, waiting for her. I thought I would find a wife, but now I realize I was looking for a pack. You're my pack. The three of us."

"Then I'll be okay with this." Gray leaned over and licked my nipple.

I gasped at the sensation. He sucked the nipple into his mouth while his hands found my hips and held me tight. Not that I was going anywhere. I was trapped in between their big bodies and it was the best cage I'd ever been in. This cage was warm and happy and promised great pleasure.

I let my head fall back and I didn't need to hold myself up. Trent was there to do that for me. He rubbed his cheek against mine, letting me feel the brush of his five-o'clock shadow.

One of them undid the fly of my jeans and then started to work them down my hips. I didn't care who it was. Being naked with them seemed like a perfectly excellent idea.

Trent's hands roamed over my body as Gray helped me out of my shoes and then the jeans and undies. "And you'll watch over her if she has to go to the Hell plane? You'll find a way to take me too?"

I came slightly out of my haze. "What?"

Trent's arms wrapped around me, holding me tight. "No. I trusted you. You trust me."

Gray shook his head as he tossed my underwear aside. "It won't come to that. I promise you. I can handle my brother. I'll deal with it and we'll go on the way we planned. I won't let her go and I won't allow my brother to hold something over her head."

I didn't argue because Gray stood up and without another word to me, reached over and lifted me up like I weighed nothing at all. He brought me up to his chest and cradled me there.

He stared down at me, his eyes warm and soft. "I won't let anyone hurt you."

It was a silly, romantic thing to say since I was the *Nex Apparatus*, so getting hurt was part of the job description, but I knew what he meant. He would try to keep me safe.

And I would do the same for him and Trent. It was such a relief to look over Gray's broad shoulder and see him standing there. He followed us as Gray started walking toward the bedroom.

There were a whole lot of clothes on the floor.

For a moment I missed Marcus. I remembered the first time I'd seen him standing in this room.

But this was what he'd prepared me for. Oh, he'd trained me in everything from weapons to learning the ins and outs of the supernatural world, but this was what he'd truly worked toward. I finally understood why he'd been so important to me. Marcus had been the first man who could make me understand how much he cared. It had been there in the odd connection between Hunter and academic. I'd been able to feel his passion, and it made me a better woman, a more confident woman.

He'd made me strong enough to accept the two men I would need for the rest of my days. His gentle caring had given me the courage I needed to fight for the triad I required to survive.

I'd found myself in these rooms. It was time to find myself again, this time forever.

At least it felt like forever. I pushed aside the idea of the contract waiting for me. There wasn't a place for worrying here tonight. I had a few days and I would spend as much of them as I could with both my men because there was no way I was taking Trent with me if I had to go.

Troubles for another day.

Gray reached the bedroom and it looked like he'd already made himself comfy. His bag was in the corner and I could see he'd laid out his toiletries on the marbled bathroom counter.

"Moving in, are you?"

"I don't have much," he admitted. "I'm having my house packed up and my clothes delivered in a day or two. I want to stay with you as long as I can. Trent and I can share half the master closet. It's ridiculous. Seriously, how many clothes could one man require?"

"My apartment is roughly the size of that closet." Trent moved in behind me. "But we do agree on one thing."

"We're getting a bigger TV."

They managed to say that in stereo, and I wondered what kind of trouble I was in. Or maybe not. If the boys decided to become besties and spend their time playing video games and watching football, the good news was I liked both of those things.

But we were going to have to talk about the laundry.

Gray's mouth came down on mine and I forgot all about the laundry. All those domestic questions could wait. I needed this. It had been a horrible day and only their hands and mouths and yes, their cocks, could melt away the restless tension I was feeling.

He kissed me until I was drugged with the feeling. Gray overwhelmed and dominated, turning me into a submissive ball of goo. It was the only time I submitted to anyone. I tended to be the bane of authoritative figures, but when it came to this, I was more than willing to follow his lead.

I was completely breathless when Gray released me. Not that Trent cared because he immediately pulled me against his body. His lips curled up as they descended toward me.

"Do you have any idea how much I've dreamed about this?" Trent's body rolled against mine, bringing his pelvis in contact and our chests together. My nipples were rasped with the light hair that covered his chest. He kissed me, taking his time, as though learning every inch of my mouth with his tongue.

"Somehow, I doubt there was another dude in those dreams of yours," Gray said.

Trent ran his tongue over my lower lip. He didn't bother to look up, but I knew he was talking to Gray. "I don't have your problems with perversion, man. I don't see it as perversion. I don't need normal to be happy. I learned that a long time ago. Hell, as far as I can tell, trying to be 'normal' makes people more miserable than happy. And yes, I knew you would be here, Gray. I knew she loved you. I just wanted her to love me, too. And, Kelsey, I don't think our friend is going to understand how serious I am until we show him, baby. Why don't you give him some relief and we'll see if it makes him less of a sourpuss."

"I'm not a sourpuss," Gray complained.

Now Trent's head came up and he stared at Gray over my shoulder. "Do you want a blow job or not?"

"Ah, yes, I'm very sour," Gray replied quickly.

Trent winked down at me, and I realized how rarely he smiled so wide I caught sight of that heartbreaking dimple on the right side of his face. "See, that's how a partnership works. Go on, baby. Get on your knees. Take that big cock in your mouth and you might get a treat from me."

See, he said it wasn't perverted, but it felt totally perverted. I was turned from one gorgeous man to face another, and this one was naked. Gray had taken his clothes off, and I wasn't sure why he ever needed to wear them in the first place. He was a work of art. Gray was big and broad, and it had been far too long since we'd been naked together.

I stared for a moment, taking him in. He was a vision of masculinity and I loved everything about him. From the hard line of his jaw to the way his torso formed a V, and damn but I'd missed my dragon.

"Please touch me, Kelsey mine."

There was no question in my mind where he wanted me to touch. I placed my palm over the tattoo and I couldn't help but remember how beautiful that moment was when Neil Roberts had finally given over and let his husband bond with that piece of himself. This was a tangible piece of Gray's soul. Maybe it had been bound for the wrong reasons, but it was here and it was mine.

His eyes closed and I could feel the heat from the dragon, could sense it. It's an odd feeling, like a vibration that the eyes can't see, but it's palpable to the flesh. I got to my knees in front of him and leaned over to kiss the dragon.

"Fuck, you have no idea how good that feels," he whispered.

But I did. It was the way I felt when Trent touched me. There was a piece of my soul that I called my wolf and when Trent was close, she was content. I was content. If there was one thing I'd learned over the past couple of days it was that the world was a better place when she and I were one, when I accepted the whole of me.

As though he could sense what I was thinking, Trent put a warm palm on my shoulder. "Spread your legs wider, baby. I think Gray isn't the only one who needs to see how good this can be."

I wasn't sure what he was talking about since I thought it was going pretty well myself. Being surrounded by the most gorgeous men I'd ever met wasn't something I was going to complain about, but I did as Trent asked. Gray's legs were long and strong, like muscular tree trunks. I couldn't sit back on my heels. I was up on my knees and that brought me where I needed to go. That big gorgeous cock was right in front of me. I reached out and gripped it, feeling the soft skin that covered hard flesh.

I glanced up, a welcome rush of power running through me. The day had been spent with me feeling helpless, but this brought me back to a place where I was in control. Even as I gave it over to him, it was my choice. My choice to follow their directions, to allow them to give me pleasure.

The world fell away and seemed softer than it had been before. I leaned over and gave that cock a long lick, watching as Gray's jaw tightened and his eyes heated. A pulse of pre-come coated his cockhead and I couldn't help but suck it into my mouth. I loved the way Gray tasted. Gray had been the first man to teach me that there was nothing perverted about the sex act, not really. Not when you were in love. Before Gray, sex had been about forgetting. It had been about punishing myself, in some ways. Gray taught me how to make love. When you're in love, everything is on the table. The craziest sexual deviance is made loving and acceptable because you're in it together, pushing the boundaries and finding what works for you and your partner.

Oh, god. Partners. Partners. I couldn't breathe because Trent slid underneath me and raised his head so he could get at my pussy.

I felt the long, luxurious swipe of his tongue against my most sensitive flesh and it took everything I had not to scream because that felt good. And by good, I meant great. There is no one like a wolf to eat out your pussy. They don't play games and they enjoy the taste. At least Trent did. I won't claim another wolf lover, but I will tell you that with Trent there was no tentative "maybe I'll try this and see if it's okay" oral sex. There was only "eat me alive and make me scream until I come all over his tongue" oral.

"Don't you forget me." Gray's hands wound in my hair, tugging until he had my attention. I loved how that feeling flared over my scalp and made a shiver run down my spine. "If you stop taking care of me, Trent will stop what he's doing. Do I make myself clear?"

I showed him how clear he was by swallowing his monster cock. It was a thing I kind of loved to do because I am a girl who enjoys a challenge, and my mouth was a tiny bit too small for it to be really comfy. Fuck comfy. I wanted sexy, and sucking Gray's cock did it for me.

Of course, I'd never actually sucked a cock when a mega-hot crazy-sexy alpha wolf was running his tongue over my labia.

It was so hard to concentrate, and I think that was their point. They were teaming up on me and it was perfectly fine in my book because I loved both. I loved the way Gray filled my mouth and how his strong hands tugged on my hair, lighting up my scalp, and there was no way I couldn't appreciate the talented tongue and mouth currently eating out my pussy.

I worked Gray's cock, sucking and whirling my tongue over and around and back and down. Every second I lit up Gray's dick, Trent pulled on my hips, dragging me down so he could fuck me with his tongue.

Gray's hands tugged at my hair, letting me know he was done with playing and ready to take over. It was time for me to relax and let him use my mouth. It was easy because Trent was doing crazy things underneath me. Even as I felt Gray's cock swelling inside my mouth, Trent was suckling my clitoris, and I couldn't help but moan because every drag of his tongue and pull of his lips brought me closer and closer to the edge of something amazing.

"You feel like heaven, Kelsey mine. I can't hold out as long as I'd like. Trent, make her come. I want to feel it in my cock. Make her come hard."

Trent sucked at my clit and then pressed down with the flat of his tongue, and the only reason I didn't come off Gray's cock was the sturdy hold he had on my hair. Instead, I moaned and whimpered and nearly screamed around the cock that filled my mouth.

Gray shuddered and thrust inside. "That's what I wanted. Here it comes, baby. All for you."

His cock pulsed and then my mouth was filled with his taste. I sucked him down while Trent licked and laved my pussy as though he couldn't get enough.

Gray let go of my hair and stepped back. "Love you. Now give me a show."

Trent shifted and I found myself lifted up and moved down his body. Seriously, supernatural dudes are strong and limber and can do sex things like nobody's business. I barely had a chance to realize what was happening before I felt his cock between my legs.

"Whoa, birth control." I had to point that out because we lived in a building with not one but two fertility gods, and I didn't think our brand new threesome needed a baby.

Trent was staring up at me, his eyes distinctly wolfish. His wolf is always there, but I could tell the alpha part of the wolf was in control now. "I put it on before I started in on your pussy. Ride me, Kelsey. I want you to ride my cock until you scream again."

That sounded perfectly fine to me. Once wasn't enough. I needed more. I needed to stay in this soft place where the world slipped away and all I had to do was please my men and let them please me.

And it pleased me to ride that hunk of werewolf underneath me. I lowered myself down on Trent's cock, his hands circling my waist. His jaw was tight as I worked my way down inch by inch, loving how he filled me.

I was in control this time and it did something for me, too. This was one more thing Trent could give me that Gray would struggle with. Gray needed control, but Trent seemed happy to share it with me.

His hands moved up, tracing my curves as I took my time, taking him in slow passes. He cupped my breasts and his eyes trailed down, watching the place where his cock was disappearing into my pussy.

I kept it up, the slow sweet grind of my body on his. All the helplessness I'd felt earlier in the day melted away because I was powerful here.

I glanced up and my eyes met Gray's. He was standing back, watching. His face was a careful blank even though his cock was hard again, pressed up against his body.

"Bring him in," Trent whispered. "Make him a part of this."

At least one of us knew what he was doing. I supposed years and years of living around a happy threesome had taught Trent a thing or two.

"Please come and kiss me." I kept moving, but I looked to Gray, pleading with my eyes. "I want to feel your mouth on me, your hands on me."

Gray hesitated for a moment and then moved to me, dropping down to his knees and leaning over to kiss me. Our mouths meshed together even as I could feel Trent move under me. His hips tilted up and he started stroking some magical place deep inside me.

Gray looked down, watching as I fucked Trent, but now he seemed warmer, more open to the experience. "It's sexy. I didn't think it would be. I thought I would want to hurt him."

Trent reached out with one hand. "You don't have to hurt me. I would never cut you out. You're my partner."

Trent's hand brushed over the dragon tat and I swear I saw it flash before he covered it with his big palm. Gray gasped and his hand came over Trent's, holding it to his side as he gritted his teeth. He held Trent's hand down, keeping it over his dragon.

I couldn't hold out a second longer. I lost my careful rhythm and slammed down on Trent. My whole body tightened and I could feel Trent's cock swelling inside me. It was all I needed. I came again. Gray leaned in, kissing me and drinking down my cries of pleasure. I was with both the men I loved.

Loved. I loved them and that felt good and right, and it scared me in the best way possible.

Gray fell back onto the soft carpet, his chest heaving as much as Trent's was.

My wolf smiled up at me, his whole body relaxed. "That was worth waiting a lifetime for. Damn, man. What the fuck was that? That was spectacular."

Gray stared up at the ceiling.

I rolled off Trent and moved in between them. "What are you talking about?"

My body was humming with pleasure, with peace. I reached out so I had a hand on both of them.

"My dragon," Gray began. He went silent for a moment and then he burst into laughter. "I think my dragon's bi."

Trent started laughing and I couldn't hold back.

We lay there, laughing and together for the first time.

I didn't realize it might be the last.

Chapter Seventeen

I woke up to the click of a door closing. It was a soft sound, but it still startled me awake. I rolled over and realized one of my men had left the room. Gray's side of the bed was empty, though I could still feel the heat of his body there.

"Give him a little time." Trent turned over on his side.

A glint of daylight from where we hadn't completely closed the curtains allowed me to see his outline, and I rolled toward him but not before I'd seen the clock. It was a couple of minutes after one in the afternoon. We hadn't gone to bed until well after dawn. Gray should have stayed asleep for hours, and that worried me. "I think I should talk to him."

"I think you should let him have some space." Trent's hand found my hair, smoothing it back. "He gave us a lot tonight. This was hard on him. He needs to process. He hasn't been planning this for a year the way I have."

I couldn't help but shake my head at that statement. "Yeah, Gray's not the only one having trouble processing. I thought you couldn't stand me."

"I was disconcerted at first," Trent admitted. "I think deep down in my soul I didn't believe the myths."

"The myths?"

"That there was one perfect mate out there in the world for me."

It was a myth that wolf parents told their sons and daughters sometimes. And sometimes they told their sons and daughters that it was complete shit and they should simply attempt to find a mate they could procreate with as soon as possible. Since he'd brought it up, it gave me a really good reason to ask him a few questions. "You obviously didn't believe it before since you were married."

"I was." He scooted closer to me, his hand running under the covers to stroke along my side. "I told you I didn't marry my wife for the reasons you thought I did. Honestly, it still feels weird to call Lissa my wife."

"Can you tell me the reasons or is it a big secret?" I didn't want the day to start. I wanted to stay warm and safe and here in bed until someone dragged me out of it.

He pulled me into his arms. "It's not a big deal."

I laid my head on his chest, loving how I could hear his heart beating. "It's a big deal to me. I would tell you about my prior relationships but they mostly involved tequila and one-night stands."

He chuckled. "Yeah, I've had a few of those. Melissa wasn't one of them. And I meant it's not a big secret. I'm not ashamed of it. I just don't talk about it much, but I meant what I said. You're my true mate, Kelsey. Everything I have, whether it be a material possession or the story of my life, I'll share it with you."

I hoped he couldn't see how his words made me tear up. I pressed forward because I did need to hear this particular story. Come to think of it, I wanted all of his stories. "She was your wife? You had to be young when you married her."

"I was barely eighteen and we'd recently finished what our group considered high school. Melissa was my best friend." Trent's hands moved over my back, stroking me like it gave him comfort. "Her mother and mine were as close as sisters and they managed to get pregnant within months of one another. In the wolf world, that means something."

Because fertility was a problem for the wolves. It certainly had been before Devinshea Quinn and the queen had started performing fertility rituals. Any child was seen as a blessing, but two friends having children close together would have been seen as something special. "You grew up together?"

"We did. Lissa and I were the only kids in our pack for a long time. I think the next child to come along was four years behind us. It made us close. Close enough that she was willing to tell me her secret."

I could guess. There was only one truly scandalous secret in the wolf world. Wolves are shockingly tolerant. Drugs? That's what kids do. Teen sex? Just hormones. Don't bother with condoms. Criminal activity? Don't get caught and everything's cool, baby. But one thing will get a wolf parent twelve kinds of freaked out. "She liked girls. She was gay."

Trent rested his head against mine. "She was. Lissa always knew it, but her parents were in denial. The trouble really started when we moved. I sometimes wonder if they knew and that's why we all moved. You have to understand that some of the more rural packs are different from what you'll find in the city. Lissa and I spent our first twelve years with the Boston pack. I had an uncle on my father's side who was the beta. I loved him, but he and my father fought a lot and over the years my dad became more and more certain that any human interaction would harm the pack. But the Boston pack was a city pack, very mainstream, integrated with the other supernaturals. So our parents decided to move deep into the woods."

I'd heard rumors of packs that isolated themselves. They were more than a little cult-like. "You were Lupus Solum?"

It was what they called themselves. Wolves Alone. I'd never dealt with them but Marcus had told me they were rare, but troublesome to the Council. They attempted to free themselves of outside influences. No humans allowed. No other supernaturals. They kept to themselves and did as little business as possible with outsiders. I found it hard to believe that Trent had grown up in one of those backward, intolerant communities.

"My parents were. I never was. I hated it and so did Lissa. The other kids our age had grown up in the group. They were true believers and the first thing they believed was that female wolves started trying to get pregnant as soon as they could. Lupus Solum relies on female wolves having babies. Often the men of the group will take fertile females into their beds with or without their permission. There's only one way to stop it once the female turns eighteen. Before that, they're careful because no matter how isolated they try to be, there are always police or family services who will come and look around the community if they aren't careful."

"That's horrible." But I did understand. I'd grown up with a man who called himself my father and who would make sure his abuse of my person came in the form of denial and verbal abuse no one could arrest him for.

"There was one way out for me."

"The Army." He'd gone in at a young age. "That's where you met my dad."

His voice changed and I could hear his smile. "I met your dad years after he'd left the service. Your dad was a legend, but mostly for his deep desire to stick it to the man, as he would have put it. I did however serve under the same CO who commanded your father's unit. That's how I knew him. Our unit was close-knit and even after a wolf left, he could call on any of us and we would answer."

"The all werewolf unit?"

"Yes. They would send in a senior officer to meet the new recruits and a few of us found ourselves pulled into specialty units," he explained. "But I knew before I left that I couldn't leave Lissa behind. We ran away under cover of night and when we made it to Boston, I married her. It was the only way I could get her out."

Now I understood. "They would have found a way to keep her without your claim. They would have married her to one of the males, and she would have been treated like breeding stock."

"Oh yes." He kissed my nose and cheeks. "But the marriage license meant we had some cover from the traditional packs. Like I said, we snuck out one night, got married, and I swore my fealty to the head of the Boston pack. Because we were married, when Lissa's parents came and tried to take her back, our alpha refused."

It had been an act of kindness on Trent's part. By marrying his best friend, he cut himself off from everything else. "Wolves don't divorce. You must have loved her to be willing to give up the rest of your life."

"She was the only person who knew me, the real me," he whispered. "She was my sister in every way that counted. I couldn't leave her there to be raped and used. This is what I meant, Kelsey. I know what normal means to some people and how destructive it can be. We weren't born to conform. We were born to live, and for me that meant saving my friend. Even though in the end, I couldn't."

Because despite all of his efforts, she'd still died. "What happened to her?"

He was quiet for a moment, but I felt his hands on me, taking comfort from me. I moved against that touch, letting him know how each stroke warmed me, made me feel happy and comfortable in my own skin. This was what I'd missed. There was nothing inherently sexual in his touch. This was one wolf displaying his love and affection for another. "Lissa was reckless in those days. I went into the Army because I could support her that way. And honestly, I wanted to see something outside of Boston and the tiny town we grew up in. I wanted to see the world. I shouldn't have left her."

"She got into trouble?"

"A ton of it. She was all right when I was close, most of the time, but I got sent on my first deployment and she decided to try to save the younger girls. She would sneak back into the woods and meet with a few of the young girls to try to convince them to run away before they were married to whoever the alpha deemed worthy. On one of those trips, they were waiting for her."

I wrapped myself around him, knowing this was hard for him to talk about. "Who is they?"

"Lupus Solum has packs across the country. Small, but they can be nasty when they want to be. Apparently Lissa and me successfully getting out caused trouble with some of the younger wolves. They wanted to leave, too, and the elders decided to send a message. One of the girls Lissa was trying to save betrayed her."

I could only imagine what happened next. "They killed her?"

"Only after they tortured her. And because Lissa had been actively causing trouble, my uncle felt like he couldn't help us. Politics, he said. We'd broken their laws and at that point in time no one cared about a small group of wolves that could basically be called a cult. If it happened now, I could go to the Council and petition for relief, but back then we were very insular."

"What did you do?" He wouldn't have let it pass.

"I came home and buried her. I tried to get the Boston pack to listen to me and when they wouldn't, I decided to take care of it all on my own. One night right after the full moon, I snuck back in. On a new moon, adult Lupus Solum packs hold prayer rituals. They leave the children and gather together and pray for fertility. I burned the village down starting with their gathering space," Trent admitted. "I probably killed my own parents, but I don't know. It was chaos. I have no idea how many of them got out and I didn't care. Still don't. I spared the children. Everyone else was fair game. I couldn't let it stand."

"Of course you couldn't." I rubbed my cheek against his chest. It didn't bother me at all that he'd gone back.

"So that's the story of my marriage. My never consummated marriage. You're the first woman I ever felt the spark with, likely the only one I'll ever feel it with, so if you go to Hell, I want to go with you."

That made me sit up. "Trent…"

The door came open and Gray was standing there. "Kelsey, the queen is here. She wants you to come upstairs with her. She says your father is lucid, but he won't last long. He wants to say good-bye to you."

I was up and out of bed in a heartbeat.

* * * *

"He begged Liv for five minutes," Zoey explained as we walked into her condo. "I should have had Sarah do it, but she won't leave Felix's side."

Because their happily ever after hadn't lasted as long as it should have. I certainly got that. Felix Day had left Heaven to be with his wife. It made a girl wonder why he would give it all up to kill a couple of demons. "Liv used a spell to keep my dad awake and in control of his body?"

"I did." Liv stood in the hallway. "But it's white magic, Kelsey. It's perfectly safe so it won't last long, and I believe once it wears off the old soul will be resettled. I know that's probably not what you want to hear."

I hugged my bestie. "I want the best for both of them and that means allowing Lee to have the life Heaven wanted for him. My father lived his lone wolf life. This is his chance for something better. But I do thank you for letting me say good-bye to him."

Liv sighed and hugged me back. "I'm so sorry you have to say good-bye at all."

But I was feeling so much more optimistic. It's surprising what hours of sex with two hot men followed by steak and potatoes and brownies can do to a girl's outlook on life. "I'm happy to have met him."

"Kelsey, Gray and Trent are here," Liv whispered. "And they have that possessive caveman look but they're not beating on each other. Should I be worried?"

I stepped back, a smile on my face. They really did have possessive caveman looks. "I tried to explain to them that I could walk to the condo on my own, but alas, they worry."

"I would worry less if you didn't run around promising to sign demon contracts," Trent admitted.

Gray wasn't about to let that go without some input. "Yeah, for me it's all the fights that she manages to find. More and more I see the pros of having a partner who can help keep her out of trouble."

"We are so talking later," Liv promised as I moved down the hallway and into the room Lee shared with his brother. Lee was wrapped in a blanket on his bed. Donovan paced while Quinn sat with Lee.

"We're trying to keep it from the other kids," the queen explained. "I don't know that they would understand. It's best to tell them Lee's sick and we're watching over him."

"They know." Kids knew everything. "They know something's wrong but kids are resilient. Once Lee is back to normal they'll probably forget anything happened at all."

"Well, I hope you're right. I'm going to check in on the others. Mia's here. Sarah didn't want her to try to sleep in the hospital so I let the kids stay up. They don't have school so I'm going to let them sleep." The queen smiled at Lee. "Here she is, old friend." She leaned over and kissed his forehead. "I miss you."

Lee looked up, his eyes so much older than normal. "Did I ever tell you how happy I am to be your son?"

"And I to be your mom." Tears dripped from the queen's eyes. "Rest well. I'll take care of you."

He nodded her way and then looked around the room. "Can I have a moment alone with my daughter?"

Quinn took his wife's hand. "Of course. Thank you, Lee. For everything."

Lee winked up at him. "Go easy on the kid. It can be hard to be the only human in the family."

Donovan held out a hand as Quinn and the queen walked out. "Good-bye, Lee."

Lee held the king's hand between both of his small ones. "Don't forget."

"Never." It sounded like a promise. "You're my son. I will never forget."

He walked out the door, his eyes suspiciously bright.

"What is he not supposed to forget?" I had to ask.

My dad shook his head. "It's a problem for another day. Don't worry about it. Let me look at you. You're the single most beautiful thing I've ever seen. You should be glad you take after your momma."

There were those tears again. "I'm glad I got to meet you."

"Oh, darlin', I wish I'd been with you all those years."

But now I realized in some ways he had. "Did I ever tell you about the dreams I had when I was a kid?"

He shook his head. "No. I can't imagine how great they were given the father you did have. I looked him up in the Council records. He was a true monster, Kelsey. I can't believe I left you with him."

I didn't want to spend our last few moments wrapped in guilt. "You didn't know. I don't blame you and honestly, I've started to think that these things happen for a reason. If I'd had you for a dad, I'd probably be all soft and mushy."

"You would not," he grumbled. "But you would have been loved."

And that's where I had him. "When I was young, well, even through about a year ago, I had these dreams and in them I was running. It was always night, but there was nothing scary about the darkness. It was like I knew that forest was where I belonged. Even on the darkest night, I could see. I could see the forest and hear the harmony there. I would run and I was so free in those dreams. There were times when I felt so bad about my real life that I prayed for bedtime because I knew I could be free in my dreams."

"That was your wolf, darlin'," my father said. "She was with you even back then. Long before you felt her manifest, she was there."

"But so were you because I never ran alone. I ran with this huge brown wolf. I don't remember a time he wasn't in my dreams. He would run beside me and I knew I was safe. He would show me all the beauty of the forest and all the best places to see. I knew he was my father. My real father."

Lee reached out for my hand, squeezing it. "Don't sign that

contract. Baby girl, you have to know that I don't care what happens to me. I don't fully understand what went on between you and that demon, but you can't go with him. I'll figure something out."

"Daddy, you're nine." It was probably the strangest sentence I would ever say, but it was true. "You can barely put yourself to bed. Have some faith. I'll find a way to make this work. Somehow I always do."

He twitched, his body shuddering, and he put a hand to his head.

"It's wearing off. Come here and let me hold you." He opened his arms.

I sat beside him and wrapped my arms around him. This time with him had been brief and possibly the most precious of my life. I'd gotten to meet my dad and he'd loved me. Now I got to protect him. I got to ensure that he grew up and had a happy life.

"I don't want to leave you." His head rested on my shoulder.

"You'll still be here." I would know he was somewhere deep inside his new body. I would know my father loved me. It was something no one could ever take from me.

"But I won't be able to protect you."

I had to laugh a bit at that statement. "Then it's a damn good thing that you made it so I can protect myself. Dad, I'm strong because your blood runs through my veins. I'm a warrior because I'm your daughter. Not his. Never his. Always yours. Even when I didn't know you existed."

"Love you, baby girl," he said, his voice oddly rough. "Tell those men if they don't take care of you I'll kick their asses. Yeah, I know about Sloane. Tell him to get along with Trent and take care of you."

"I love you, Dad." I wasn't going to let something silly like embarrassment hold me back. And when I thought about it, I wasn't embarrassed about my new ménage.

"Kelsey?"

"Yes?"

He hesitated for a moment. "If something happens to me, promise me one thing."

"Nothing is going to happen to you." I was going to make sure of it.

"But if it does, I need you to promise me," he said insistently.

"What?"

He was quiet for a moment and I worried he was gone. Finally he spoke, his voice a low whisper. "Don't leave my body behind. No matter what. No matter where it is. If I die, bring my body home."

A chill went through me, like I'd heard some prophecy I didn't want to acknowledge. "Dad, that is not going to happen."

"Promise me."

"I promise." I fought back the urge to shudder as I had a vision of my father's body still and broken. Would it be the wizard who killed him? Because I hadn't been strong enough to go through with the contract? Or because Nemcox would find a way to have his cake and kill my father, too?

He laid his head back down and was quiet for a moment. When he looked back up, it was with confused eyes. "Kelsey? What's going on?"

Not my dad. That voice was young and tremulous. My heart ached, but it was all right. This was how it was supposed to be. "Hey, buddy. You've been fighting a fever. You feeling okay now? Should I get your mom?"

He rubbed his eyes and looked around the room. "I had a weird dream."

I sat up. "It must have been the fever, but it seems to have broken so you'll be fine."

The queen must have been hovering outside the door, not that I blamed her. She stepped inside, an anxious look on her face. "Lee?"

He perked up. "I'm totally feeling better, Mom, but I could use a Dr Pepper."

Zoey rushed over to him, wrapping her baby boy up in a hug as Quinn strode into the room. "You know what, screw the sugar rule. Tomorrow you can have Dr Pepper and we'll have Albert make cupcakes."

Quinn stood over them both. "Chocolate, your favorite."

I stood up, my heart both heavy and light. Heavy because I knew I wouldn't see my dad again and light because he was happy. So happy. He was happy and loved and unburdened with the weight of his previous responsibilities.

Donovan was waiting outside the door. "Kelsey, thank you for everything you're doing for him."

"He's my dad." I sniffled and swore to myself I wasn't going to blubber all over the king.

"Lee is special."

"I know."

Donovan shook his head. "You can't know. I'm struggling. I don't want to allow you to sign that damn contract. I talked to Nemcox, offered him other options, but he will only take you."

He'd talked to Nemcox? As far as I knew he hadn't said a word to the demon in years before today. Now he was negotiating with him. "I don't want anyone else to take my place."

"I understand that you have your reasons for not talking to me about this and I'm not going to force you. I trust you, Kelsey. Lee cannot fall into anyone else's hands." Donovan seemed to be speaking carefully, as though he was worried to say too much. "It's very important."

"I don't intend to allow it to happen."

He scrubbed a hand over his head, a weary gesture. "I'm trying to figure out how to deal with Nemcox. He's a full blood, Kelsey. If I thought I could kill him, I would, but he's immortal. I would only hasten a war. I would ask one of the angels, but they aren't known for assassination attempts. Well, most of them aren't. I don't even understand what's happening with Felix."

I held up a hand. The king needed to stay out of this. "I'll handle it. Gray is working on the problem. In the meantime, I need you to help Henri find any way at all to get Felix Day awake and talking. The angels are going to figure out we have that sword soon. Have you tried your blood?"

He shook his head. “Not yet. I’ve been too busy with Lee, but I promise I will. I can’t believe that Felix would do this. He gave up Heaven for Sarah. He wouldn’t risk it. Felix is the least violent being I’ve ever met. Someone was controlling him.”

“Well, we need to figure out who it was because the demons are going to find out that Felix was there and they’ll want blood. Unless you intend to make sure our young demon friend doesn’t talk.”

“I can’t. I’m flanked on all sides and I’m not sure how to wiggle out of this trap.”

“That’s what you’ve got me for. I’m a wiggler. Buy me some time.” I saw Liv move in the living room. I needed to talk to her. “Now go and be with your son.”

He briefly touched my shoulder and disappeared into Lee’s room. I moved down the hallway. Liv was the answer to at least one of my problems. I needed Neil Roberts to remember his past. If he remembered his past, pulled the veil aside on his memory, he might know something about who had been controlling him. He could tell me once and for all whether it was Felix Day or if the fallen angel had been nothing but one more pawn in a game I didn’t know the rules to. Now that Neil was more willing to remember, a white spell could work.

I just needed to make sure Lee was far, far away.

I started walking down the hall, thinking about my plans for the day. I noticed someone had left the game room door open and realized those kids were not asleep.

I got a brief glimpse of Rhys before he slipped back into the room.

“They’re all in my room. I think Lee’s okay,” he whispered.

The rest of the house was quiet so when I went still and concentrated, I could hear him.

“I don’t think he was sick,” Rhys was saying. “I think it was something magical. He wasn’t himself. He told me I needed to change my underwear or I would get crotch rot. Why would he say that? Like he remembers to shower.”

"Do you think it's the same thing as my dad?" A young girl's voice broke through the silence.

I saw Liv stop her pacing at the end of the hallway. She stared at me, but I held up a hand. I wanted to know what the kids were thinking. Unlike the queen, I knew damn well they weren't fooled by some story of a cold.

"Maybe," Rhys replied. "Be quieter. You'll wake up Evan and she can cry real loud."

I had to lean in to hear the rest.

"Do you really think your friend is the one who hurt your dad?"

A chill went up my spine.

"Mom told me he was imaginary, but I saw him, Rhys. He glowed super bright and he called me his cousin."

"Tell me again what he told you to do," Rhys said. "I won't tell if you don't want me to, but once Lee is Lee again, we'll figure this out. I promise."

"Lee is good at figuring stuff out," another voice said. Sean Quinn. He was Dev Quinn's nephew and the son of the future king of the Fae. A bit on the arrogant side, but he was more open than his father and hyper loyal to the small group of kids he was growing up with. "I believe you. Your mother is wrong and this person exists. Once we find out who he is, I will take him down with my bow."

But again, arrogant like his father Declan Quinn.

Mia sniffled. Mia Day was the daughter of Felix and Sarah and I'd been told she was quite a bright companion. Bright enough to compare to Zoey and Evan, but in my mind she was simply a little girl who wanted her father to be well again. "I know you would try, but I think he's dangerous. I didn't at first. I thought he was my friend. He glowed so beautifully and he only wanted to talk. But then he asked me to go into my dad's office and break something."

What? That was the question I wanted to ask. Still, I stood there, unwilling to give them a reason to stop talking amongst themselves.

"I thought he told you to steal something," Rhys said.

"I was supposed to steal it and then break it," Mia acknowledged.

"He said he couldn't help me until I broke the seal. He said my dad was afraid of him but he shouldn't be. I think I killed my dad."

I heard her start to weep and I couldn't hold back. It didn't matter that they might clam up. It didn't matter that they weren't my kids. I was the *Nex Apparatus*. Sure some people will say that's a term for the warrior who protects the king, but I tend to make things my own. I worked for the king as long as he worked and fought for what was right. If he stopped, then he would find his death machine turning on his ass. But I knew one thing. Those babies were innocent and I wasn't about to let sweet Mia Day, who was all of nine and three quarters years old, believe that she'd willfully hurt her father.

And if I let it go, my dad in his nine-year-old body would try to solve the case and we'd all be in trouble.

Oh, god. I shook my head as I stood outside that door and realized what it meant to love me. I vowed to go a bit easier on Gray and Trent and my brothers and Liv. Even Casey, since he had to deal with me. I was stubborn and difficult and I wasn't changing any time soon.

I opened the door and was faced with three shocked preteens and a peacefully sleeping four-year-old who might grow up to be the woman who took my place with Marcus. For now she was a sweet baby, sleeping in a *My Little Pony* sleeping bag and looking as cherubic as her ancestry would have her be.

"Kelsey?" Rhys stood up, obviously taking the leadership role. "We were about to go to sleep."

"No, you weren't. You were about to tell me what's going on so I can take out the bad guy." I moved into the room and sat down with them, getting on their level. "Mia, what's been happening?"

Even in the low light, I could see the way she paled. "It wasn't my dad."

My every instinct told me she was right and that she had the answers I needed, but I had to be gentle with her. The key to successfully interrogating anyone is knowing what they want and how to properly give or withhold the desired outcome. Mia felt guilty, likely terrified that she'd done something wrong. I needed to be on her side. "I know that, but I have to figure out how to prove it. That's my job. I figure out who the bad guys are and I save the good guys."

It was a gross oversimplification of what I did, but it would serve for now.

Mia hesitated and I realized how scared she was.

"You haven't told your mother what happened, did you?"

Tears rolled from her eyes and she shook her head.

Rhys moved, sitting down beside her. "I think we should tell Kelsey. You know how she always helps Lee and she never tells on us."

Oh, I would have to break that promise because this wasn't catching them sneaking sodas from behind the bar or feeding visiting hellhounds under the table. "Mia, your father's life is at stake. He's being accused of something serious."

"Of killing demons," she said quietly. "My father would never kill anyone."

"You know that and I know that, but there are witnesses who saw him at the scene. And Mia, he did nearly kill Trent. The question is was he in control of his body when he did it or was something else controlling him." It made me wonder when he'd made those wards. Felicity had seemed so shocked that he had them. How recent was his distrust of his former family? "Do you remember your father acting weird recently?"

Mia's mouth closed.

"Mia, you can trust her."

I turned and Lee was standing in the doorway. I caught a brief glimpse of the queen but when I shook my head she seemed to understand and she moved out of the line of sight. I was sure the whole royal triad was listening but they were allowing me to control the encounter.

Lee walked in and sat down beside Mia.

She turned toward him, her eyes wide. "Are you better?"

He nodded and opened his arms. Mia practically fell on him,

sobbing as though she'd lost everything, and when I thought about it, she nearly had. For Mia, that loss was mere moments away. This was the first time the perfection of her world had been challenged, and I couldn't help but tear up because she was a lucky girl. She had no siblings of her own, but she had this group. Watching Rhys and even Sean move in and surround her reminded me that I hadn't been alone. When John Atwood would make me feel like less than dirt, my brothers would sneak into my room and poke and prod me until I felt better.

And now I had two men who loved me, two men who I could count on, and I had Marcus to thank for that.

I glanced over at Evangeline, promising myself I would shield that child as fiercely as I would Lee because she could be the key to Marcus's happiness.

I let Mia cry, allowed her all the time she needed because I knew where she was. I hadn't been the kid to cry, again a gift Marcus had given me. I'd been the kid who shoved it all down and pretended it wasn't there. Mia didn't need that.

She finally looked up at me and leaned into Lee as though she found some comfort from merely being close to him. "A couple of weeks ago I met someone. Something, really. I thought it was all a dream at first, but it wasn't."

"What did it look like?" I asked.

"Light," she replied quietly. "It was this beautiful light and I felt good. I'd had a bad day at school and I thought I was stupid, but the light made me feel better. It wasn't very big. It fit under my bed and it whispered to me."

A shiver went up my spine because I was going to have to deal with that light. "What did it say?"

She hesitated again, but Lee reached for her hand. She nodded and turned back to me. "At first it just wanted to know how my day was and it told me that it was a secret, a present from my cousins. It didn't feel wrong."

"Of course it didn't, sweetheart." If "it" was who I thought it was, he was supposed to be all that was right and good in the world. "This isn't your fault. It tricked you, but I'm here to make sure it can't trick anyone else. Tell me what happened. You're not going to get into trouble. I promise."

"But my mom will be so mad at me." Her tears started again.

"She won't. I know your mom and all she wants is for you to be safe." I would have to be careful because Sarah Day *would* want her child to be safe, but she would want some serious vengeance, too. Unlike her husband, the former dark arts witch wasn't a pacifist. "She won't be angry. She'll be thrilled that you're brave enough to save your dad."

That seemed to mean something to her. Her spine straightened and she took a deep breath. "It wanted me to hide something in our house."

I could guess. "Was it a sword?"

Mia nodded. "Yes, a big one. It was heavy, but I managed to get it inside the closet where we keep our Christmas decorations. No one goes in there."

He'd used a child because she was a companion and she could touch the sword without burning herself. Son of a bitch. Well, not literally, since angels weren't born in that fashion. Maybe if the fucker had a mom he wouldn't have turned into an evil piece of shit. "Did you see your dad with the sword?"

Mia leaned against Lee. "Only once. It was a couple of days ago. I saw him putting it back but his eyes were weird. He told me never to mention it again and he went to his office."

"Did the light ask you to do anything else?"

She nodded slowly and sighed. "It asked me to find Daddy's necklace and showed me how to scratch off a piece of it."

The ward. Felix had made a ward and his daughter had rendered it useless. A ward had to be intact for the magic to work. I was sure she'd scratched off some tiny piece that Felix wouldn't have noticed. He thought it was still working.

I stood up and put a hand on Mia's head. "It's going to be okay.

I'm going to fix this. Get some sleep because everything is going to be back to normal soon and you'll have schoolwork to do. Don't you ever think you're stupid, baby girl. And if someone says that to you, you remind them that you're friends with the *Nex Apparatus* and she doesn't take kindly to anyone saying nasty things to her friends. You tell them I'll be on their doorstep if they mess with you. Any of you."

Donovan was grinning as I walked out of the room. "You're going to make a whole bunch of school bullies shit themselves, you know."

"Hey, what's the point of being the boogeyman if I can't help out my friends." I looked to the queen. "You heard?"

She nodded, her mouth tight with worry. "I did and I think we all know who it is."

"Yes, so I need Hugo to figure out how I deal with this legally." I walked out into the living room where Gray, Trent, and Liv were waiting for me. Albert stood in the background as though waiting to be of service. "Okay, here's what I need. Gray, I need to talk to your brother because he knows something about this he's not telling me. See if you can get him here sometime this afternoon. Liv, I need you to work that spell on Neil Roberts. I need an eyewitness because there's no way Lester's family doesn't want some justice. Your Highness, keep that sword under wraps. We can't lose it. Trent, I need you to get the chick who runs the tattoo and piercing parlor on five. I'm going to need some ink."

Calliope House was a white witch who specialized in healing "ornamentation," as she called it. I needed a ward no one could easily scratch off.

Trent nodded my way. "Are we warding against below or above?"

"Let's go for broke and do both." I walked up to Gray and slid an arm around his waist. "If I go to the Hell plane, getting rid of my ward can be my first fun bit of torture."

He frowned. "I don't even want to joke about that."

"Then you should have picked another girl, buddy. I've got a dark sense of humor." I went on my toes and kissed him before the next part. "And I need you to call Jacob. I need to know everything he can tell me about the Sword of Light."

"Gladys?" Quinn asked. "Your sword? Why do you need it if we keep hold of the Sword of Justice?"

Donovan shook his head. "She won't be allowed to use the Sword of Justice in battle, but Gladys is hers."

"Battle?" Gray asked.

Yep. I was going into the ring again, and this time I would have to take down an immortal angel. Never let it be said I don't like a challenge.

I sent Albert a smile. "You have the most important job of all."

The big demon bowed, but not before I saw his grin. "I have already begun breakfast. I made all the bacon we have."

He was a lifesaver.

And *I* had a plane to save.

Chapter Eighteen

Despite my misspent youth, I didn't have a ton of tats. None, actually, since tattoos were somewhat expensive and I'd been super broke most of my life. By the time I had some cash from this job, I'd outgrown the need to ink a Wonder Woman symbol above my cootch, so this was my first tat.

Ink stings. Like bee stings all over your skin. I didn't particularly like this pain since I was fairly certain it wouldn't end in a screaming orgasm, but it also wasn't so bad that I stopped eating.

Trent held out the milkshake Albert had made me. It was one of those breakfast smoothies, but Al knew how to make a wolf happy, so along with the protein powder there was real chocolate to make my day bright. I sucked down a nice bit and then frowned Trent's way when he took a drag off it, too.

Though I do admit I liked the intimacy of sharing it with him, but he was going to have to be the one to refill it.

"He made more," Trent assured me as he offered me a piece of bacon. "Do you want this? Are you going to be nice to me?"

I let him stuff the excellent bacon in my face.

"Okay, see this is why I'm a vegan," Calliope said with a

shudder. "Sorry. I'm not usually around werewolves because of the whole 'can't keep a tat on' thing. My usual clientele is witches who want to paint their flesh with the goddess, and vampires who are trying to look way cooler than they are. I did the king's tat."

That was some gossip I hadn't heard. "The king has a tat?"

Trent touched his right pec. "You know the symbol on the queen's necklace? He's got it right here. I heard he lost a bet a long time ago. You sure you don't want that on your lower back. It would be pretty sexy."

The ward against angelic influence was going on my right shoulder blade. I'd decided to put the ward against demonic influence on my left. Like wings except not. Trent kept trying to get something inked on my butt. I think he mostly wanted to see my butt.

"All right, the outside is finished. I need to switch colors if you want to take a break." Calliope's hand moved over my shoulder and I felt a surge of warmth as she completed it with a bit of magic. She'd explained that all her ink was imbued with white magic. I had also been given a lecture on the fact that pigs were alive, too, but I didn't listen to that part.

The door opened and I was happy to have that break. Gray walked in with his brother in tow. Nemcox was in the same body he'd been in before, and I wondered what the poor dude had done to deserve being worn by a demon, aside from the fact that he was very "Nemcox." Gray's brother liked his clothes young, male, and startlingly handsome, but not too far on the masculine side.

"Hello, Kelsey dear," he began with a gracious smile that quickly became a frown as he realized who was sitting at the edge of the chair, holding my milkshake. "What is he doing here?"

I sat up, readjusting my shirt.

Calliope was staring at the newcomer, her arms covering her chest as though she could protect herself. "Is that what I think it is?"

"Why don't you go into the kitchen and help Liv prep for the ritual? We can start up again in a few minutes." It was easy to see the witch wasn't happy to find herself in the same room as a full-on possessing demon.

She nodded. "I'll get things ready. And maybe you should think about some other wards as well. You seem to need them."

She hurried off, her sandals slapping across the floors.

"Hippie witches," Nemcox said dismissively. "You smell of patchouli and desperation, little girl." He turned toward me. "And you smell like a whore."

Trent stood up but I had this one. "And I took a whore's bath and everything. Guess I'll try harder."

"Brother, I won't put up with you talking about her like that." Gray stepped in front of his brother.

Nemcox waved him off. "So much testosterone for one room. Grayson, why haven't you killed the wolf? Do I have to do it for you?"

"I'd love to see you try." Trent punctuated his statement with a low growl.

It was actually pretty hot, but I didn't have time to indulge his alpha instincts. I turned around on the chair Trent had dragged down along with Calliope. "Why don't you go and see how lunch is coming?"

Breakfast wasn't totally done yet, but I stress eat and Albert knows it. He'd already promised me some of his famous tacos for lunch.

Trent frowned my way. "How about I stay here and make sure the demon behaves himself?"

"Do you think I can't handle my own brother?" Gray asked, obviously annoyed by all of it. "I won't let him hurt her, but he's going to be easier to deal with if he's not staring at you and trying to decide the best way to murder you."

"I already planned it out. But for you, I'll make it a surprise," Nemcox purred.

Trent's jaw clenched but he moved toward the kitchen.

And he took my milkshake. Damn it. I was carbo-loading. Also, I really liked Albert's shakes. The minute we were "alone," I turned to the demon. I only use the quotes because Donovan was somewhere in the condo and his hearing was superlative, so I was fairly certain he was listening in. "Who is the angel you've been working with?"

Nemcox managed a look that conveyed both startled shock and the tiniest hint of insult. "Angel? I would never work with an angel."

Gray sighed. "I told you. It's not in his personality to work with someone he would consider the enemy. It could get him in serious trouble with our father."

He looked up to his brother. "I'm loyal and you know it. It's precisely why I'm doing what I'm doing now and why you should listen to me."

"I can't and won't allow you to sign a contract with the woman I love," Gray replied. "You know what my wishes are concerning her."

"I know that you'll feel differently when you come home," Nemcox insisted.

Gray wouldn't have a choice, but that was an argument for another day. "Put the contract aside for now. If you aren't working with an angel, then why did you murder Larissa Dymone? She was going to talk to me about the murder of Lester Hixalnaxendallixxxba, which I've tracked back to angelic influence, so either you were working with the angel who killed Les or you had another reason to murder her and I need to hear that now."

Nemcox went still. "I thought the person who killed Les was my puppy. I thought perhaps the king had his reasons and was using his powers to call wolves to control him somehow. Are you telling me some fucking angel managed to control Neil? Are you saying he forced Neil to do things?"

Even I could feel the righteous heat coming off him. This wasn't some acting job. He was pissed. His eyes shone red. It was a good thing. If I got him emotional, I might get an honest answer out of him. "That is exactly what I'm saying. And I would bet that the same angel who is manipulating the man you love so much that you dragged him to Hell and raped him for years is the same angel who protected you from me."

"What are you talking about, Kelsey?" Gray asked.

"I tried calling him to my hand for months," I admitted. "I had all the incantations right and I know his name. I should have had my showdown, but somehow your brother avoided me every single time. I wasn't wrong. I did everything properly but Nemcox here had an ace up his sleeve. He had an angel working some nice mojo to keep him safe. I'm going to assume from the horrified look on that borrowed face that you didn't realize what kind of price you were paying for that protection. What did the angel require from you and how did my hooker friend connect to all of this?"

"Nem?" Gray turned to his brother, his face going ashen. It had to be hard to see all the possibilities of the world except the ones that affected him directly. A prophet shouldn't get blindsided, but it seemed to be the story of Gray's life. "Is she right?"

"Well, what did you expect me to do, brother? I couldn't allow your bride-to-be to try to kill me. It wouldn't have turned out the way she wanted it to. I wasn't going to kill your lover but she was quite insistent about murdering me."

Gray shook his head.

But Nemcox was right on this one. "Nah, I was totally going to kill him. Or at least do something nasty if I couldn't figure out how to off him. I thought seriously about cutting off his head and putting it in a box so I could make sure his body didn't grow back."

There was an ick factor to that plan, but sometimes a girl's gotta do what a girl's gotta do.

"There, you see." Nemcox pointed my way. "I had to find a way to stop that. She was going to force me to hurt her, and I couldn't do that to you, brother. I know all too well what it means to love someone who is stubborn."

"Which angel are we talking about?" I had a hint of who it was from the way Mia described how the light had made her feel, but I needed a name because I didn't intend to fight all three of those suckers.

He opened his mouth and then it shut again. He frowned and his hands fisted at his sides. He shook his head. "I can't. I can't even say…" His jaw slammed shut.

He couldn't even give me an indication if we were talking about a male or a female. Yeah, Heaven can work some mojo. "You had to agree to some things to gain protection, didn't you?"

His whole body went stiff and I could see the anger welling in his eyes.

"What did they do to you?" Gray asked.

Gray was too invested to see that Nemcox deserved everything he was getting, but I could make some educated guesses. "An angel came to you at some point after that first time I called you. You held me off that time, but you knew it wouldn't work forever. I was going to catch you."

The demon snorted, an oddly elegant sound. "As if you could. You have no real idea what it means to kill a full blood."

Except I'd managed to do in a Hell lord, and his ass wasn't coming back. "Abbas Hiberna might argue with you if he was still alive. So either you got scared and called the Heaven plane version of 911 or an angel contacted you."

His face flushed and he swallowed twice before he answered. "I certainly didn't call anyone."

Now we were getting somewhere. "So this angel offered you help in holding me off, but only if you gave him something in return."

Gray sank down to the sofa. "I can tell you what it was. Only one thing could allow someone else to control the dragon tied to Roberts's soul and that's the original incantation and the blood of the family who bound him. What were you thinking, brother?"

"I thought I was saving my own skin and never did I believe…" He went silent again, the spell working its magic.

I was actually surprised. "You didn't think the angel would do anything bad with it? Who's naïve now? What else could he have done with that incantation?"

Gray turned to his brother, his eyes going wide. "You thought he was going to unbind Neil." Gray stood again, facing his brother. "You were trading your love to save mine."

Nemcox's eyes seemed to water. "My love left me long ago. He was pulled from my arms by one of them. Whatever that first angel did made it so I couldn't call him home. I finally accepted that he wasn't coming back, but I can save you from the same fate. Kill the wolf."

Gray shook his head. "I can't."

So now I had the whys and wherefores and I could guess the who. "Larissa was the go between?"

Nemcox groaned. "I can't even nod my bloody head."

That was good enough for me. "It's nice to know the Heaven plane uses hookers, too. All right. I think that's all I need. Gray, could you tell Calliope we can continue with the session?"

Nemcox stepped in between us. "What are you planning on doing?"

"It's none of your business," I replied.

"She's going to look into it," Gray assured his brother. "I'll help her. I'm not so far from my old job that I don't remember how to solve a crime. Between Kelsey, Trent, and I, we'll find a way to prove this was angelic influence and not the king, and the negotiations will continue. That's what this is really about. Someone on the Heaven plane wants us at the vampires' throats."

Nemcox shook his head. "I hadn't considered it. I truly thought it was Donovan who's been killing the halflings. He seemed determined to start a war."

"And now he's planning on renewing our contracts," I pointed out. "Gray's right. I think this was an attempt to push our planes to war. We have to prove that Neil and Felix were under angelic influence when they committed the crimes or Lester's family will push the issue."

"Several families will protest," Nemcox agreed. "There are rumblings on the Hell plane that since Donovan's taken so long, we should do what we were meant to do and bring about the end of days. It's insanity."

"And what does Lucifer say?" Gray asked the question with no irony in his voice, the same way one might ask "hey, what's Uncle Maurice's take on how the Cowboys' line is this year?"

"He says nothing," Nemcox replied. "Lucifer says it will play out as it will and he has his own plans which he shares with no one."

Lucifer was a smart one. "Then it's up to me."

Nemcox pointed my way. "You see, that makes it sound like you are planning on doing something spectacularly stupid."

"Wouldn't be a Tuesday if I didn't."

"You can't think to take on a heavenly host." Nemcox managed to sound truly shocked.

"Of course she's not…" Gray's eyes narrowed. "Kelsey?"

"Dude's not going to kill himself." I wasn't sure what they expected me to do. I couldn't let him come down to my plane and get away with shit. If I did that then everyone would try it. "Why do you think I'm getting this sweet tat, babe? Now the asshole angel can't pull any mojo on me."

"No, he can pull a fucking sword on you," Gray pointed out.

"Then it's a good thing I have a sword of my own. You know Gladys spent some time on the Heaven plane." She might not be as big as the Sword of Justice, but she was still badass.

"It's not the same," Nemcox insisted. "If you attempt to go up against an angel, you'll die."

"Like I haven't heard that one before."

"Kelsey, we need to talk about this," Gray said, obviously shaken. "I had no idea you intended to go up against this person."

Then he either didn't know me as well as he thought he did or becoming a dark prophet had ruined his brain. Trent had already talked to me about getting some sword training in. He knew what I was planning on doing.

"I'm going to talk to some people, and by people I mean the one angel I know who I'm fairly certain isn't a psychotic whack job. I've already got a call in, but I suspect I'm going to be told I have to handle this myself. If Heaven wants to deal with it, great. But if it comes down to it, then I'll do my job."

"Or you'll be in Hell tonight because I'm putting a contract in front of you," Nemcox promised.

"It won't work." Donovan walked into the room, his lazy strides letting me know he intended to stay calm and collected. "The contract can't be signed for another forty-eight hours. Your father agreed that she is a protected member of the Council, therefore she falls under the seventy-two-hour rule. And that will be upheld everywhere, Nemcox. Would you like to see the agreement? We signed it as a part of the opening negotiations between this plane and the Hell plane. You can't even start negotiating that contract for another two days. Unless you would like to come to me directly and explain what you have on my son."

Nemcox's face went a nice shade of red and I watched as he forced himself to take control again. "Don't think for a second I'm letting her out of the trap."

"If she's forced to fight, we'll do it here," Donovan explained. "You'll be invited as a witness, but don't show up in a meat suit. It won't be allowed. Demonic forms only for those full bloods who can't mask up."

Even I winced because that would embarrass the hell out of Nemcox. His inability to change his form was considered a weakness.

"You would let your precious *Nex Apparatus* die for you?" Nemcox hissed the question.

"I don't think she'll die at all," Donovan replied. "I think she'll show Heaven that we can take care of ourselves. Now I would like you to get out of my home. I might have to welcome you for the negotiations, since it looks like your father will be the one representing Hell, but you're not welcome near my family. You've done enough damage to us for a few lifetimes."

The demon turned toward me, leaning in. "Know that if you die, I'll eat that child's soul myself. If you even attempt to step out of line, I'll ensure he never sees another day and can no longer harm my master in any way. Am I clear on that, whore?"

"Brother!" Gray pushed his brother's borrowed form away from me. "How dare you."

"I dare much for our family." Nemcox straightened his clothes and made for the front door. "If you can't be strong enough to take your fate into your own hands, then I shall do it for you. I'll be here, Your Highness. I'll be here in all my glory."

"I'll look forward to it," Donovan promised.

He moved to the door and stopped, his hand on the knob. "Kelsey?"

"Yep?" I was ready for just about anything to come out of his mouth.

"You're right about that sword of yours," Nemcox said. "The secret's in the blood and the line. Blood will unlock blood and unleash the true strength of the sword, but only the strongest of the line will do. There's a reason the vampires took the sword from their companions. They were afraid."

He slammed the door behind him and I was left with a million questions.

The good news was I knew who to ask.

Chapter Nineteen

"She's inside, *bella*...I mean Kelsey," Marcus said with a sad smile. "I'm sorry. It will take me weeks to change the habit."

We were standing in the small waiting room of Henri's mini hospital. There were only three beds, an exam room, and an autopsy room, which got used way more often than the rest of the rooms.

Luckily I'd managed to talk Trent and Gray into staying outside, giving them the "let's not spook away the only person who might help us" excuse. I didn't need any more testosterone or masculine martyrdom. I'd gotten a ton of the former from Trent, who wanted to go after Nemcox, and the latter from Gray, who'd decided he should be the one to face the angel if it came down to it.

I was intent on ignoring them both. After all this was done, I was sitting down with the queen, a bottle of tequila, and some nachos and asking her for advice on how to deal with two men. The sex was awesome. I wasn't sure about the rest of it yet.

"Don't worry about it. I was thinking earlier that it's weird to be in the apartment without you." And now it was awkward to be here with him. I couldn't get comfortable with Marcus any way I went. I still loved him, but it wasn't the same. The passion I'd felt in the beginning had softened to something like friendship. And yet I can remember so vividly how this man had made me feel—loved and wanted and beautiful for the first time in my life.

And it had nothing on the passion I'd felt the night before when I'd been between Gray and Trent.

"Somehow I don't think you had time to worry too much about it," he said wistfully. "Don't blush. I'm happy for you. I can see how calm you are. You're facing something terrible and you're perfectly confident. That is what I wished for you, for you to understand and accept your power. To know that you deserve the power you've been given and that you're worthy. You should expect to be cared for by the men who love you."

I was getting teary. "You could have warned me that once I was all healed and stuff I would leak a lot."

He smiled, a brilliant expression, and held out his arms. "Your emotions are a part of you, *bella.* They're another beautiful part of you, and I'm glad you can embrace them fully now."

Because of him. I hugged him close, the scent of him bringing back memories of how well he'd loved me. "I wished I'd been a little less stellar a student on the feelings part because it hurts to let you go."

He sighed and his arms tightened. "It does, but it also is right. I can see how you need Trent. I know he doesn't know it yet, but I believe Grayson needs him as well."

I pulled away reluctantly, but knew it was time. I couldn't help but think about the fact that his dragon reacted to Trent, and not in a platonic way. "Trent wants to go with me if I sign the contract."

He reached out and brushed away the tears I'd shed. "You won't. I've thought about this and realized that I believe in you. I believe you need to protect your father, but you'll find a way out or someone will do it for you. You weren't meant to descend. You were always meant to bring light to our plane. I am going to do something I haven't done in a long time."

"What's that?"

"I'm going to have faith." He stepped back and somehow he seemed calmer as well. "I'm going to believe that things work out for a reason."

"What happened to Marcus and who are you?"

He smiled again. "I don't know. I feel better than I have in a long time. You're going to think it foolish of me, but I think that painting in Daniel's office is some kind of magic meant for me, meant to lift me up."

"Is she getting closer?" If he needed a girl in a painting to make him feel better, then I would cheer for her.

"She is, and I can't wait to see what happens," he admitted. "Sometimes, it's the little things that bring us joy. I'll be sad when the story is over, but it's reminded me that life is worth living. After this, I believe I shall travel for a while. There are parts of the world I haven't seen in many, many years."

"Could take you fifteen years or so to see all of it properly." In fifteen years, Evangeline would be of age.

He shook his head. "No, it will be twenty at least. Then we should know."

He would give her time to mature, to be able to make her own decision. "I promise I'll watch after her in any way I can."

"And I will keep you in my heart." He bowed in that formal way of his that reminded me of lords and ladies and royalty. "Now, the angel is in there with Felix and she's agreed to speak with you. She's also given Hugo some pointers on how this should proceed from a legal standpoint. The king was correct. If this is to happen, it will happen on this plane, and it will be decided by combat."

I'd known that all along. "Nemcox told me something about my sword. Can you look into it? Gray hasn't been able to get in touch with Jacob, but I thought you might know some people. He said that originally the Council took the sword from the companions because they were afraid."

"It was before my time, but there were rumors that the sword the *Nex Apparatus* uses was originally handed down to the queen of the companions. It had much power, and the original vampires were worried because of the way it seemed to hunger for blood."

"Nemcox said there was a secret and that blood had something to do with it. Blood and the line. I assume he meant either bloodline or the lineage of *Nex Apparatuses*. I remember this part verbatim. 'Blood will unlock blood and unleash the true strength of the sword, but only the strongest of the line will do.' Any thoughts? I could use a stronger sword."

"I don't think he's talking about a line of Death Machines. They aren't connected by blood, merely by ability. I believe he is talking about the companion line. They are hereditary and Zoey is the strongest I've ever seen, though I believe her daughter will pass her in time. I will think on it and see if I can find out anything about the lore of the sword. I've always wondered what it did with all that blood. Perhaps we can find out." He glanced at the door. "Please be careful with her. She's the kindest of the three, but she's still dangerous."

I glanced in and saw her standing over Felix's bed. She was dressed in a pretty sheath; her hair and makeup model perfect, but there was a sadness I couldn't deny.

"I'll handle her. And Marcus, did I ever thank you for everything?"

He stepped back. "Every time you save the plane, *bella*. Be safe."

I walked into the hospital with a lighter heart. Marcus and I would be cool. Better than that. I strode up to Felicity Day and felt not a single effect from her legendary powers.

Except I did feel for her because she was crying. That wasn't her power. It was all that stupid humanity I'd found. It made me weak and it made me so very strong.

"Ms. Day?"

She looked up and stared at me for a moment. "Kelsey, dear. I'm sorry to have to see you at a time like this." She looked back down at Felix. "He looks like he's sleeping."

"In some ways he is."

She took a deep breath and looked up at me. "But he's not. He's in between, and whether he lives or moves on depends on what you do next."

"I get that a lot." As long as I had a heavenly being here and she was talking, I might as well ask a few questions. "Does it ever get easier? The whole 'fate of the world on my back' thing."

She smiled, a fraction of her usual, and reached out to put a hand on my shoulder. "I can feel that it already is because you've accepted your gifts."

"My wolf?"

She shook her head. "No, your men, dear. Your wolf was a part of you the moment you were born. She was an act set in motion long ago, but those two men are the gifts of a loving deity who believes we must be allowed to choose. Even when we make the wrong choice."

"Like Jude?" Jude, the betrayer. Jude, who embodied faith and had used it against us all.

Tears fell from her eyes like diamonds raining down. "Yes, like Jude. I'm surprised you figured that out. I assume he meant for the blame to fall on Oliver."

But he'd made a mistake. He'd used a child, and her honesty had led me straight to him. "He went to Mia and convinced her to betray her father. She told me that when his light was close to her, she knew how smart she was, how worthy. It was what I felt when I was close to him."

"He didn't realize how clever you can be. He underestimates humans." She sniffled and went back to Felix. "He's my brother, you know."

"Jude?"

She smoothed back Felix's hair with her hand. "Felix. We were made of the same clay, split by our maker's hand because he said he'd pinched off a bit too much. Oliver came before us and Jude after, but there wasn't a moment of my life that I didn't know and love Felix."

"Can you save him?"

She shook her head. "Only you can do that, dear. When Felix fell he became human. He's under angelic magic, and only by killing Jude can he be made free. That's what I'm struggling to accept. He knew what it meant for Felix to make this decision."

"The decision to fall? It must have been difficult."

She turned to me. "Not at all. He knew from the moment Sarah's soul came into being that she was half of him. This was not something Felix struggled with. He knew he would fall, and he welcomed it with joy in his heart because this is what we all wish for."

Even with the ward protecting me, I couldn't help but watch Felicity Day. She was beautiful without her angelic glow. "You want to fall?"

She turned bright eyes on me. "We want to feel. At least many of us do. To love is the highest purpose we have. It's what we were built for. Our father made us out of love and he made us to love, to experience it in all of its forms, and Felix knew it was his time to be a husband and a parent. He helped me to understand what time I am going through."

"What time is that?"

The saddest smile crossed her face. "Unrequited love is difficult, but once accepted, it makes us better beings. It brings us closer to understanding what love is and how it works. I've been the angelic manifestation of love for millennia and I'm still learning, still growing. Love is the destination and it is also the journey. Being loved in return is merely winning the lottery."

I was quiet for a moment, letting it sink in and giving her a bit of space. "I'm truly sorry about your brother. I know him. He's my therapist and he's amazing. He helps people."

"It was what he wanted to do," she said. "He wanted to come here to the Earth plane and experience everything. We're isolated in Heaven. Some say it's because God favors us, but I worry it's because we're not ready. Being human is hard. I often wonder which of us God thinks of as the more advanced of his children. Would it surprise you to know the reason I want to fall? I hope to experience physical love and to have a child."

My heart constricted because we had a few things in common.

"That doesn't surprise me at all. I want to have my own babies. *That* surprises me."

"Stay on your path and those children will come to you. You are very brave, Kelsey Owens. You would risk everything to make things right for others. I've found that kind of bravery is often rewarded by my father, though he sometimes takes his time." She turned again and seemed more resolute. "I can feel the ward you placed on your body."

"I can't allow him to influence me."

She nodded. "I understand, though it makes me sad because our influence often has purpose. Our influence, when well placed, can allow our charges to move mountains."

But I could now see that I'd been given other influences. "I think that's what Marcus was for in the beginning. And now Gray and Trent will take that role. It's like Dev said. I will be provided with the tools I need. I merely have to be smart enough to see them and have enough faith to use them."

"Then you are ready," Felicity said. "I'll tell you how to call him. From there you are on your own, though know that I will pray for you."

"Why did Jude do this? Do you know?"

She leaned over and kissed Felix's forehead before stepping back and finding one of the chairs in the room. She sank into it before speaking. "We've been on our own for a while. It's not like the creator keeps office hours. We can feel his love, but not all choose to live inside it. It's much like all the planes, when you think about it. We're given the tools we need, but we must both find them and accept them and be smart enough to use them properly. It doesn't mean he loves us less. It merely means we should try again. I often think his highest principles are patience and fortitude."

"I thought you said they were love."

"Ah, but patience and fortitude are the foundations of love. All rests on those two virtues. Anyway, there is a faction in Heaven that has become restless again. It's cyclical, from what I can tell. We've received several souls from the lower planes who worked to ascend, and that tends to make some ready to descend, in a perverse way."

That was news to me. "You can move from Hell to Heaven?"

"Of course. What would be the point of Hell if there wasn't a way to get to Heaven? Do you think my father loves less than yours? It's why I want a child so badly. I want to know that love, the love that is purely selfless, the one that requires nothing from the receiver except existence. No, my father leaves no one truly behind, and Armageddon won't go the way some believe. If you had a child, could that child do anything that would make you damn him or her for all eternity?"

I knew the answer. "No. I would still love my child."

"And so it is in Heaven. What Hell doesn't understand is that it is merely a way station, and one day…oh, one glorious day it will not be required and my father will open his arms and welcome them all home."

"Even Lucifer?"

"Well, I didn't say it would be tomorrow," she admitted. "My father plans things out, and his version of a timeline is a bit on the endless scale. He's a long-term planner. As for Jude, he has become ambitious. He believes we should rule the planes in our father's stead, but he cannot simply lead an army. He doesn't have enough who believe."

"Hence he's sowing dissent between the Earth and Hell planes," I surmised. "A war between the planes would almost certainly disrupt the humans, and then it would be easy to convince the others that angelic intervention is required."

She nodded approvingly. "See, a smart girl. Yes, Oliver and I believe this is what he has done and what he has planned. They already speak of it in Heaven. The talk will cease if you kill Jude. It will be seen as our father's will. I am so sorry we can't help you. We used up much of our power a few years ago. It's not endless and it takes years for us to recharge when we do something big."

I could guess. "Something like pulling a soul out of Hell?"

She smoothed her hair back. "Oh, yes. Years ago, when the

queen was taken by the head of the corrupt Council, she was left alone when the king smuggled Devinshea out of the compound. I had a hand in that. He is my charge, you see. In exchange, I offered my power, my strength, and my influence to help Oliver's charge."

"The queen." I'd heard that story. The gruff and grumpy angel watched over the queen.

"She needed someone with her, someone to lift her up, and it couldn't be her husbands. So Oliver and I freed the little wolf. We wiped his memory clean and gave him the means to find his friend. We could not break the seal placed on his soul, but we could protect him from being dragged to Hell again."

Whoa. That was definitely some news I wished I'd heard earlier in the game. "Seriously? Neil can't go back to Hell?"

She smiled beatifically. "No. He is safe from the demon."

"You might have mentioned that to him. I think he's been worried about it for flipping years."

She seemed to think about that for a second. "Huh. I suppose it slipped my mind. So many things to do, you know."

I had some other questions. About a million actually, but I settled on the most immediate one. "If he can't be influenced that way anymore, how is your brother doing it?"

"When we pulled him out of Hell, we did it through the dragon. Think of it as a portal to his soul. Now that portal is open to angelic influence, though most Earth plane beings are. Neither Oliver nor I would ever have used it in such a way." She moved to me and put a hand on my shoulder. "You must be resolute and brave. You must set Jude free of this life."

"You're calm about me killing your brother."

"Kill is a hard word, and not truly fitting. You are ending one life and allowing him the chance to choose again," she explained. "Nothing is ever wasted. Certainly not a soul. Do what we cannot do, Hunter. Set Jude free and bring Felix back to us. Everything you need is here. The battle should take place somewhere you feel comfortable."

"Can my sword kill him?" I knew she wasn't fond of the word, but it was kind of the point of me.

"The Sword of Light can kill anything if it's properly prepared. It's angelic so its power isn't endless, and it has been gone from the Heaven plane for a long time. But it also hasn't been used in forever."

That was where she was wrong. "I used it just the other day."

She shook her head. "Not the way it was meant to be used. Not the way the original caretakers would have used it. What do you think it drinks?"

"Blood." Which was fitting of the current caretakers.

"Oh, but there is strength in blood, and that is what it gathers. It gathers strength so the warrior can call on all of the tribe. When the strongest gives her blood, the chosen warrior is complete and the tribe empowers her to save them. It is how the companions survived in the beginning. They were not the strongest, but together they could move mountains. They could use the blood of their enemies against them."

A chill went down my spine because I thought I'd figured out what she was saying. "And it hasn't been used this way in millennia?"

"No, dear. All that power, waiting for you." She leaned over again and kissed Felix's forehead. "Like I said. My father always provides. Good luck, Kelsey, and I'm so sorry."

"Sorry?"

"As I explained, I watch over Devinshea and Oliver protects Zoey. I apologize that the angel directed to watch you turned out to be so very incapable."

So I got a guardian angel and he turned out to be a dud. Story of my life. "Well, he's about to get his angelic ass fired."

Felicity winked out of existence and almost immediately Sarah Day rushed into the room as though she'd been standing outside, waiting for the chance to come in again.

I nodded her way and wished her well.

I had work to do.

Chapter Twenty

By late afternoon I'd read up on everything Marcus could find about the Sword of Light, also known as Gladys. I'd also been briefed on how the trial would go. This wasn't a trial that included a jury, who would likely not appreciate the fact that some heavenly host had been causing trouble. No. That would be far too easy. Hugo had laid it all out for me. The "trial" of Jude, the Faithful Motherfucking Betrayer, would be decided by combat with the champion of the sword. Not any sword, but the Sword of Light. Only a sword forged in Heaven could be used in this particular battle, and Excalibur was now considered to be an Earth plane sword due to the magicks worked on it by Merlin. Donovan had tried that line of reasoning. I kind of thought he just wanted to kill something, but it turned out yet again that when bad shit happened on the Earth plane, it was my responsibility to deal with it.

The trial/me potentially getting my ass kicked was to occur at one of the in-between times. Donovan decided on midnight rather than dawn since he believed night would favor my wolf. I wasn't so sure about that, but I was going with it. There was a whole ritual thing that involved the owner of the sword, and then right before everything went down we would use Zoey's blood to unleash Gladys. And then we would see if I would live or die.

Just another Tuesday.

"Hey, you okay?" Gray walked out of the bedroom wearing nothing but a pair of sweatpants.

That totally made me feel better. Damn that man was fine. I didn't hesitate the way I might have in the past. Something about getting my ass kicked time and time again to save the freaking plane made me think I deserved any pleasure I could get. I fought. I bled. I deserved this.

I let my hands roam over his cut torso, pausing to pet that dragon. "Better now."

"I have dinner almost ready. If you want to eat," he offered.

"I pretty much always want to eat." It was something he needed to get used to if he was going to hang around. I wasn't sure Trent had any idea how to make something that didn't come from a box, and I was not Martha Stewart. It was up to Gray to make sure I ate anything that didn't come from Ether or the coffee shop on the sixth floor.

"Good." He was speaking blandly, as though trying hard to keep things as normal as possible. "Should be about twenty minutes. Can I get you a beer?"

"I think I will skip the beer until later." I would probably need it and a lot of pain meds since I couldn't take vamp blood. "How did things go with Neil and Liv?"

He shook his head. "Still working on it, from what I understand. She's worried about what could happen when he does remember. It would be nice if the doc was able to be there."

But our shrink was currently in a coma, and he might never wake up if I didn't win this fight. That weighed heavily on me. Felix Day had fallen and he should have been looking forward to a nice long life on the Earth plane with his love and their daughter, but he wouldn't see them again if I didn't make it happen. "Yeah, well, a session with Felix is going to have to wait. If Liv wants to put off trying again until we can bring Felix in, we should know something shortly after midnight."

Because I didn't think this fight would take long. I would win or lose and we would know Felix's fate.

"You don't have to do this, Kelsey mine." His hands found my hair. "We can walk away and not come back. This isn't on you."

"Isn't it? I know you can't see futures that directly involve you, but tell me what you see if this doesn't happen tonight. Look at it from an intellectual standpoint. Forget that it's me. Think about what happens to the supernatural world. What happens if there is no trial for Jude, the Faithful Asshat?"

"Can we put that on a T-shirt?" Trent stepped through the kitchen door and leaned against the bar, a smile on his face. He wasn't wearing a shirt either, and I wondered what the boys had been doing while I was gone.

I do not mind saying I kind of hoped it was something dirty.

"I thought she was the sarcastic one," Gray said with a shake of his head. His eyes rolled back and became the full-on black that came with his prophecy powers. His body stiffened and I could feel a fine shudder go through him.

"You can never have enough sarcasm." Trent moved in behind me, resting his head on my shoulder. His arms wrapped around my waist. We were connected, the three of us.

Gray came out of it with a sigh. "War. Death. Unbalance."

Trent kissed the nape of my neck. It seemed to be a place he loved to nuzzle and kiss, and I couldn't help but think about how dominant and alpha the gesture was. Or that he'd probably not been this affectionate with a woman ever. He'd waited for me, and now that we were together he seemed incapable of keeping his hands off me.

I liked it.

"That sounds like a job for Super Kelsey," Trent murmured against my skin. "I would have thought you might be a bit restless."

I smiled at the thought. He wanted to make sure I didn't need anything from him, maybe something that could calm me down like a couple of screaming orgasms. "Oh, make no doubt, I've got about four hours before this thing goes down. I intend to spend some of that time in bed, but I'm good, babe. I am neither pulling my hair out with worry or morosely waiting for my death."

I'd done both in the past. Now I was calm and ready for the fight, ready to get it over with so I could move on to the next problem. I still had the threat of Hell looming over my head, but that was a problem for another day.

Gray stepped back. "Well, I'm glad you're calm because I'm sure as hell not. Have you thought for two seconds about what happens if you die?"

"I try not to." Because that would free Nemcox to talk about my dad.

Trent groaned behind me and then strode over to the couch. "I told you, she's good at this. You have to have some faith in her or you'll go crazy. I've watched it time and time again with the king and Devinshea. They always flip out when the queen wants to do something stupid and they forbid it, and she does it anyway and everything turns out all right except that no one gets any sex for a couple of weeks because they're all mad at each other. I say we do it better than they do and accept that Kelsey can handle things."

I got the feeling this wasn't a new discussion. The idea that they'd sat around and tried to figure out how to handle me probably should have worried me, but I kind of liked the idea. I'd spent so much of my life without the feeling that I was cared about.

"How many times have you had to watch her almost die? Because it's been a few for me," Gray grumbled.

"I watched her in the arena when she first came to the Council. I watched her against an alpha and his two betas and it was one of the most magnificent things I've ever seen," Trent said quietly.

Ah, good times. That had been my first battle in the arena. I'd been fighting to protect a herd of does from a power-hungry wolf pack. That had been my "morosely waiting for my own death" period. It had been before my training with Marcus and I'd been so alone.

Gray stared at Trent. "I don't understand how you can claim to care about her and then watch her nearly kill herself."

Trent's eyes narrowed, and I could feel the irritation rolling off of him. "She didn't nearly kill herself. She fought hard and she fucking won. Stop being such a prissy prick. You think she needs to be safe, but that's never what this woman is going to settle for. You fell in love with her why? I can tell you why I did. I fell for her because I saw the strongest, fiercest, most beautiful bitch I'd ever seen stand in the arena when everyone was against her. She didn't back off or back down, and despite the fact that she didn't even have her full powers at that point, she still won. She was bloody and broken and utterly defiant. She could barely hold her arms up but she let the king know exactly how she felt. I knew in that moment that I wouldn't be happy until I was worthy to be called her mate. When did you fall for her?"

"He saw me in a vision." I said the words as blandly as possible, trying not to let Trent know how deeply I was affected. The bitch part is a wolf thing. I didn't take it as anything but pride and affection. The wolf inside me knew she was a bad bitch, but hearing her mate say it made her curl with pleasure. It also made me wonder about Gray because if Trent had fallen for me at my worst/best, then Gray had fallen for a vision that might not exist. "I was in a wedding dress and we were starting our honeymoon. Even before he was an official prophet, he had visions."

Gray looked at me and shook his head. "Don't you even think that. After everything we've been through, I don't see you as some doll to protect. I might have in the beginning, but I don't anymore. I might have thought we could have something normal where I go off to work and you stay home and raise our kids, but if you haven't noticed, I left that fucking dream behind."

My heart ached for him because I did know how much he'd longed for a world where he could marry and be a Ranger and not have to worry about descending into Hell. Becoming the Earth plane's only dark prophet hadn't been Gray's idea, and I wondered if he missed his house and his job. Before he'd met me, he'd had some semblance of normalcy. Did he miss my brother, who had been his best friend? But mostly I wondered if he blamed me for much of it. "I don't know that I'll ever be that woman in a white dress, Gray. I think you've been looking for her for a long time and you might never find her. She was a possibility that might have been left behind long ago."

He took me by the shoulders, looking down into my eyes. "I don't give a shit if we never make it to that hotel. You think you're the one left behind? I can't even conceive of myself ever being the happy asshole I was in that vision. I know it's dead and I'm still here because while that vision might never happen, I'll fight for us. I'll fight you for us because nothing in my life is as important to me as you."

Sweet words and words I'd been longing for. "Then stay with me. Stop this bullshit about how bad you are for me and let us be."

He reached out and lifted me up like I didn't weigh a thing. He brought me up so I could wrap my arms around his neck. "I won't ever willingly leave you again. I might have to one day, but it will not be my choice."

He kissed me and I could feel his passion, his will. He was with me this time, and though we might have a million barriers in our way, I would find a way to keep this man with me.

Gray lowered me down and rested his forehead against mine. "And I don't think I'll be able to get rid of that one. He seems dug in."

One of Trent's arms pulled me back against his body but the other found Gray's tat and I felt the moment they connected. Gray gasped slightly, but he didn't pull away.

"Very dug in. Like a tick," Trent replied with a husky chuckle, as though he enjoyed the effect he had on both of us.

Considering how he spent a good deal of his time, I wrinkled my nose. "Pick a better metaphor, babe. I will delouse you if I have to."

He did spend large parts of his life running around the woods.

I couldn't help but wonder how different that would be now. We would run through the woods together and when he was done he could return to his human form and we would make love there, too. I would wake up wound around him, naked and feeling alive.

"You'll never have to," he promised. "I'm a very clean wolf. Well, except when you want me dirty. Then I can get filthy for you, baby. I promise. I'll dirty up real nice."

The room was heating up perfectly. I sighed, already getting used to having four hands on me. Gray leaned over and kissed me.

After a moment, Gray released me and turned me toward Trent. "Kiss him. Give me a show, Kelsey mine. I find I like watching you."

Trent smiled down as his hands tangled in my hair. "He's giving in to his perverted side. He's going to be so much happier that way. I like watching you, too, and damn but I've waited my whole life to be able to kiss you."

He kissed me, a long, luscious exploration of my mouth that had me panting. When he finally released me, I looked back at Gray. His eyes had gone dark violet and he moved to join us.

"Yes, dinner can definitely wait. I'm hungry for something else." Gray picked me up and headed for the bedroom.

* * * *

Two hours later, I looked at Neil Roberts, who seemed like a completely different person from the one I'd tried to basically arrest a few days before. This Neil Roberts was calm and oozed self-confidence. He stood in the middle of that gorgeous penthouse and held court, laughing and smiling and yes, every now and then he got a little teary. It was as if he'd come back from a place he'd been stuck in for years.

It was not the reaction I'd expected.

"I'm surprised," I whispered to Liv, who'd managed to get the ritual done on her own. I could tell she was pleased with herself. The spell had done wonders for Roberts, but it had done something for Liv, too. "I expected him to be upset. Remembering all that time in Hell would have fucked up a lot of people."

"It must have been how smooth and easy that spell went down." There was a smirk on Liv's face I hadn't seen in years. Not since long before Scott and their epic engagement that had ended a few months before. This was the Liv who'd taken on the mosh pits at rock concerts and boldly asked guys out. The one who never gave up and always had my back.

That ritual must have been a hell of a thing.

And I didn't feel at all bad about missing it since my whole body hummed with how perfectly those two men fed my every hunger.

Besides, it wasn't like she'd been completely alone.

"Don't believe it," Casey said. "It wasn't easy and it was damn lucky she had me since I'd recently been out to a site on the web that talked specifically about the spell she needed."

She wrinkled her nose the vampire's way. "Casey might have figured out I was using the wrong amount of periwinkle. Though I do think you were right about Neil being more receptive. It worked quickly once the formula was right."

Casey nodded and his arm started up like it was going around her shoulder.

She turned and stared at him, and he tried unconvincingly to turn the motion into a stretch.

"Not there yet, buddy," Liv said with a shake of her head.

Casey's whole face lit up. He was grinning down at her, and in that moment I could actually see the appeal. Casey was tall and muscular, in a lean way. "You said yet."

She sighed. "I did. Now go and get me a glass of wine. I'm going to need it if I have to watch Kelsey get her ass kicked again."

Casey practically ran toward the kitchen.

"Yet?"

She flushed but that smirk was back. "Yeah. I kind of like him. He's not a complete ass. He's actually quite sweet and he's surprisingly helpful. I think I could train him. Is that a horrible thing to want to do?"

"Nope. I think a spot of training would go a long way with that one." I went back to watching Neil. His husband was staring at him like he was the only person in the world. When I glanced around the room, though, I caught Gray staring at me the same way. And Trent.

Gray was proving a very bossy lover, and damn if Trent didn't let him. They were rapidly finding their places, and I was surprised that didn't worry me at all.

Losing them both worried me. It worried the hell out of me.

Liv turned my way. "And how is the ménage going? I thought you were a lucky girl when you were doing the vampire. Jeez, Kelsey, how are you going to manage those two?"

I shrugged. "I might not have to. When you think about it, I'll probably die in the arena or I'll get dragged to Hell by Gray's brother, and despite what Trent thinks, I won't bring him with me and then I'll only have to deal with Gray, who will likely go mad because of his descent. But it's okay because I've been assured I'll go wolf loco without Trent's sweet loving, so we'll all be bonkers."

Liv stared my way. "That is not helpful."

Yeah, maybe my morose phase wasn't entirely over. Now that we were literally an hour away from calling Jude, I couldn't help but think about the truth that even if I survived this fight, I would have to deal with the fact that I owed Nemcox my soul. Mine in exchange for my father's.

I shoved the thought aside. I would deal with that problem another night. Tonight was all about survival. "Do you have the spell to call Jude?"

Liv nodded, but she'd paled a bit. "*Dico Angelus*. That is the name of this spell. Felicity assures me it will work. I've been granted the equivalency of an approved heavenly bounty hunter, so he has to answer my call. Once he's here, Felicity and Oliver will announce the trial and the winner gets the Sword of Justice. By the way, you've agreed to give the sword back to Oliver in exchange for him waking Felix up."

"He can wake Felix up?"

"Only if Jude is in transition," she explained. "I'm not supposed to call it death. When Jude's soul is parted from his body, the ability to right the wrongs he's done on this plane transfers to the angel who embodies justice. Oliver will wake Felix up, but he can't bring back the dead. We already asked about potentially bringing back the halflings Jude had murdered. That was a no go. The king has to deal with that on his own, but I heard he's already planning to meet with the families of the halflings and open talks."

Marcus was going to be able to get his politics on.

And then he would roam the world until his promised love was old enough to decide.

I was going to miss him so much.

I would miss them all if the next ritual didn't go well.

"And what have you learned about the sword ritual?"

Liv frowned. "Very little. I had Casey look around and he couldn't find much either. The lore about that sword was lost, or someone got rid of it. I don't know which. I do know that the sword is ancient. It's older than Christ."

"Jacob was the first prophet to walk the Earth plane, so that makes sense. According to Felicity, he gave the sword to the group we now call the companions." Which didn't make sense. "Do you think they were always known as companions?"

Liv shrugged. "No idea. I'm surprised they were once some kind of tribe. Even after the king freed the slaves, they don't seem eager to get back together. I know the queen has some friends who are companions, but when a group of them gets together they kind of watch each other warily."

Millenia of enslavement could change whole classes of people.

"Your wine, my lady." Casey offered Liv a glass of red wine with a flourish.

She took it but shook her head my way. "Forgive him. We're watching *Game of Thrones*. He's a dork."

"You're a dork, too. She's totally obsessed with that show," Casey said, still grinning like a loon.

"I need you to be obsessed with that sword," Liv shot back.

"We've got another hour or so."

Casey saluted. "As you wish. I've got a few theories I'm trying to track down. What do I get if I save the day?"

"Dude, you get to live on a peaceful plane," I replied.

Liv smiled a secretive smile. "We'll see. But you have to come through big time."

He ran off down the hall and I heard the door open and close.

He wouldn't take much training if his eagerness was any indicator. "That boy has the hots for you."

"It feels good to have someone interested in me," Liv admitted. "Though I'll also admit that I'm enjoying living on my own. I got one of the open apartments with a terrace. It's weird not to have a full garden, but I'm learning how to grow my herbs in pots. And I've got more time to study. It's been good for me. I feel more like me than I have in years, so I'm not going to take this fast with the vamp."

Slow was a good idea. Just not for me. I had little time left, and that meant getting in all the hot, soul-filling sex I could.

Chad poured a glass of champagne and passed it over to his husband as Neil continued with his story.

I could see the whole thing was making Gray uncomfortable, but he'd insisted on coming.

The queen stood and hugged her bestie and then looked over at me. She tilted her head toward the kitchen before she started walking that way.

It was time. The kitchen was probably as good a place as any to do this.

The minute I started moving, Gray stood up, but Trent got up as well and put a hand on his arm. Trent whispered something and Gray nodded. They both started to move, but not my way. They walked out to the balcony.

How did I handle Gray before Trent? If he hadn't been around, I would have been fighting to get some privacy. We'd decided to keep this ritual as private as possible. We had no idea if it would work, and if it did the fewer people who knew the queen's blood unlocked some magical property in the sword, the better. It was me and Liv, the royals, and Evangeline.

Which made me stop and look around because my dad could be sneaky. I listened carefully and heard both Rhys and Lee talking, and then the quiet sounds of Mia saying something I barely could hear.

At least I didn't have to worry about Lee.

I walked into the kitchen and Donovan was there with the queen, their daughter in his arms.

Gladys was sitting on the counter, Dev having brought her up from the armory. He stood behind the queen, a frown on his handsome face.

"I don't like it," he said.

Donovan sighed. "It's only a little blood. She'll barely feel it."

"She's so young." Quinn walked to his daughter and put a hand on her head.

"Unfortunately, she's also incredibly strong, according to the angels," Liv explained as she picked up the sword and brought it to the island in the center of the kitchen. She laid it carefully in the middle. "They didn't tell me much. This was a secret ritual among the companions. I was told that the queen's blood would unlock the sword but also that the companions would crown the strongest queen. Zoey's title comes from the vampires, not the companions."

"Because we're a sad-sack group that serves our masters now," Zoey grumbled. "We're not a tribe at all."

"Yeah, baby, you serve me so often," Donovan replied. "You're so submissive."

Dev's lips curled up. "Well, she can be."

The queen sent him a look that would have frozen fire. "Discretion, Dev." She looked down at the sword. "I can't help thinking about the fact that we were once powerful. I spent so much of my life without any power, but I come from a line of women who had it."

"And who owned this sword once," I murmured. There was something odd about being in a room with the queen and her daughter and Gladys. It made me realize I'd rarely been so close to the queen when I had my sword. Something felt…powerful about being with them, and I knew instinctively the sword recognized either Zoey or Evan.

The queen touched the sword, her fingers skimming over it. "It hums for me."

Something we had in common. "Me, too. Sometimes when I'm fighting with her, I can feel her pull me this way or that. Just a bit. Just enough that I know what she wants me to do."

"That's so cool." The queen was looking at the sword like she wished she could hold it, fight with it.

"You can pick her up." If the lore was true, Gladys was as much the queen's as mine. If we'd been back a couple of thousand years before, it would have been the queen and not the king to invest its power in me.

For a second I thought she would pick it up, but then she stepped back. "I'm afraid my warrior queen days are done. Besides, according to the lore Marcus gave me, the queen didn't use the sword herself. She appointed a warrior. Who wants to bet that's where the vampires got the idea for the *Nex Apparatus*?" She glanced Liv's way. "Does the sword react to all females?"

Liv shook her head. "I felt nothing. When I picked it up all I thought was Kelsey's got amazing upper-body strength because that sucker is heavy."

"I find it interesting that Kelsey can feel the sword but Liv can't," Dev said. "It makes you wonder."

"If the Hunters and the companions have something in common?" Donovan asked, shifting Evangeline in his arms. The girl was trying to reach down toward the sword. "Yes, I was wondering that myself. Companions are humans descended from fallen angels. Hunters are demon fighters. They kind of go together. What if Hunters are another class of companions?"

"Well, we'll never know." I didn't glow the way a companion did so I seriously doubted I had angelic blood running through my veins.

"Let Evan touch the hilt. She can't hurt herself on that. We're asking her to bleed for that sword. The least she can do is touch it."

Donovan snorted slightly. "I suppose you're right. I don't like the idea of hurting her though."

Evan shook her red curls. "I'm not scared." Her eyes hadn't left the sword. "It's pretty, Mama."

"It is, baby." The queen took her out of Donovan's arms and lowered her down. "Once it was ours. Once it belonged to a whole tribe of women like us."

"Still. Still," Evan said as she reached for it. She stared at the sword with pure fascination on her face.

"It won't move, sweetie." Dev hovered close, as though ready to clutch his daughter from the jaws of evil if he had to. "I promise it will stay still for you."

But Evan wasn't scared. She tried to wind her tiny hand around the sword's hilt. She grinned, her face lighting up. "She feels fizzy. I like her." She looked up at me. "She likes you."

"Good, my daughter likes weapons. Daddy's girl." Donovan sobered. "Let's do this. I want it done long before that angelic asshole can know what's happening." He held out a hand and popped a claw as elegantly as any alpha wolf. "Who's first?"

Zoey looked at her daughter. "You ready to help your Auntie Kelsey?"

That damn near brought a tear to my eye. I loved those kids.

Evan held her hand out, looking back at Quinn. "It's only blood, Papa."

Donovan nicked her palm and she flinched a little, but shed not a tear.

"Squeeze the blood on the sword and watch her drink it up," Zoey whispered. "Our blood can make her strong so Aunt Kelsey can fight the bad man."

Evan squeezed her small fist tight and droplets of blood hit the blade. They disappeared almost instantly.

The queen held her hand out and did the same, dripping her blood over the blade and allowing Gladys to soak in her strength.

We stood back and waited.

Nothing. The sword was perfectly silent.

“Should it glow or something?” Quinn asked.

I picked her up and tried to sense some change in her. She hummed against my palm but otherwise was silent. “Feels normal to me. If I’m supposed to feel some kind of power, I don’t.”

Liv frowned. “Perhaps it won’t show up until battle. The problem is we have so little information about it. I don’t know what it’s supposed to do when it’s primed.”

“Because the vampires wiped out the information,” Zoey said sullenly.

Donovan sighed. “I didn’t do that personally, Z.”

She looked up at him. “I know, babe. I’m sorry I’m being difficult. It feels like there should be more. It feels like I should do something more. Cut me again. Let’s give it another try. It’s all right. I’ll heal.”

Donovan nicked her again and I stood back, praying this would work.

Chapter Twenty-One

I stood at the edge of the arena and couldn't help but think back to that first time I'd walked into this place. It hadn't been so long ago and yet it felt like ages. I was older, some might say wiser, but I felt a bit like the girl who'd stood at the edge of the sandy arena floor wondering if she would live to see the next day.

Of course, I found it interesting that this time the aisles weren't filled with wolves and deer. This time I was being watched by Heaven and Hell.

It was easy to pick them out. The angels were the ones who sat in perfect silence, their odd silvery eyes shining in the low light. They each wore white, and I wondered if this wasn't a part of the ritual for them. I picked out Felicity from the silent crowd. She sat next to Oliver, her hand in his. He looked paler than before and I wondered what being parted from his sword was doing to him.

The demons, on the other hand, weren't silent at all. And they wore no uniform. They were here in their natural forms. For some that meant almost human looking. I picked out Gray's father in a tailored business suit. He was with a group of men who looked an awful lot like him. Power suits and serious expressions. I assume they were some of Hell's heavy hitters because they could hold their human forms naturally, a rule Donovan had put in place for any demon attending this ritual battle. So we had a nicely dressed portion of the contingent. For others, well, I was glad I didn't have to be the one to clean up because some of them oozed slime.

I caught sight of Nemcox. I knew it was him because he was staring directly at me, his black eyes watching. When he wasn't possessing a human body, he was a medium-sized, red-skinned devil, as I liked to call them. Demons come in many shapes and forms, but Nemcox was mostly human, if one forgave the cloven hooves, red demon skin, and flowing horns. He was the classic demon and I couldn't help but wonder how many like him I would be surrounded by if I was forced to descend.

"Don't pay attention to him," Donovan said, coming to stand beside me. "I'll make sure he doesn't interfere. None of them will, demon or angel. Focus on killing the betrayer and I'll take care of everything else."

I wasn't sure what else he intended to take care of. As far as I knew if I killed Jude, everything would be all right, but it didn't matter because the clock chimed midnight and it was time.

Liv stood in the center of the arena, a book in her hand. She wore a white gown that made her look somewhat like our angelic audience. Her auburn hair was piled high in an elegant bun as she said a bunch of stuff in Latin. Naturally I understood none of it, so I gazed up into the crowd again. I was looking for their faces because I so needed to see them again, to know that they were here with me.

Trent and Gray sat in the royal section below the angels. The royal trio had a box with the best view, and they kept their Council friends close around them. Trent and Gray were seated next to the queen and Devinshea, with Jamie on Gray's other side. My uncle was there with his wife. The academics were all together in a row, but I saw the moment Marcus realized I had stepped out into the arena.

He nodded my way, his smile genuinely warm, and though I couldn't hear him I saw him mouth the word. *Bella.*

And I said good-bye silently, understanding that our connection was gone forever but our friendship might remain. I'd needed the sexual connection with Marcus in the beginning, but now I had another bond, a tighter one that I would need for the rest of my perhaps short life.

There was a crack and a wave of energy went through the arena, and I felt the ground tremble beneath me. Liv took a step back as the world seemed filled with light.

Donovan cursed as a blinding white light flashed through the arena. I glanced up and saw the king's skin smoke and char.

It dimmed almost immediately and two winged angels stood in front of Liv. They were both male, their wings gloriously white and spread in a show of power and grace and beauty. All around me the crowd was whispering.

I watched as Donovan's skin began to heal.

"Fucking angels." He started toward the center of the arena.

I followed, Gladys humming in my hand. She hadn't done anything special and I was sincerely hoping she was waiting for the main event to start to unveil her secret abilities. Whatever they were.

The whole place had gone quiet, even the demons seeming to realize this was serious shit. I stuck close to the king, watching the two angels ahead of me.

Jude the Betrayer looked perfectly pouty. I have to admit in some ways he reminded me of a teen pop star with his floppy hair and dreamy, youthful face, and now he looked even more teen-idol like because he had that air of complete ennui, the-world-is-so-boring look on his face.

The second angel didn't look bored at all. He was taller than Jude, his broad body masculine and strong. His hair was dark, his eyes finding mine, and I swear I saw a flare of recognition there. I didn't know the man, had definitely not met this angel before, but I would have sworn he knew me.

Jude looked around the arena. "Who thinks to call me to this lesser plane?"

Liv stood there, looking at the two heavenly beings she'd summoned. She'd gone a nice shade of white. I had to poke her to get her to talk. "Me. I mean, it was I."

I frowned her way because there was a whole lot of ritual that was supposed to happen here.

Liv nodded and stood up straighter. "I, Olivia Carey, a witch of the Earth plane, have called this trial by combat in the name of the king of the Earth plane and all its creatures. Our plane has been defiled. I demand that Jude the Faithful meet our champion and that justice be served. May I know the archangel's name?"

By calling Jude to a trial by combat, we got an archangel, too. One of the seven archangels would come and serve as witness, ensuring no funny business went on. I was sure he would have some long-winded description of his job, but I rather thought he was there to make sure no one cheated.

The gorgeous, shining man bowed, a courtly gesture. "I am Raphael and I am at your service." He reached out and his fingers brushed over the burnished gold medallion that marked Liv as working for the angels and imbued her with the magic to power her spell. "And I see Felicity has invested you with this power."

He turned toward the crowd as though he could feel her presence.

Felicity stood.

"You have heard the evidence, Felicity Delictio? This is your will?" Raphael asked, his voice low, and yet somehow I was certain everyone in the arena could hear it.

"It is *our* will, Raphael." She reached down and clutched her brother's hand. "I accuse Jude the Faithful of seeking to disrupt the balance on the Earth plane. He stole our brother's sword and caused him imbalance as well."

Angels are serious about balance.

Raphael turned to Jude. "And do you wish to answer this accusation?"

Jude bent his head slightly. "I seek purpose for our plane. The king of the Earth plane has pushed them almost to the brink of war.

Soon there will be no way to keep our father's favored humans from knowing the truth of our worlds. It is our appointed time, Raphael, and I am not the only one who believes this. Yes, I used the demons and the earth creatures to further my own agenda, which is to bring our kind into our proper place—dominion over the lesser planes. They are corrupt and require correction."

"Oh, my brother, they are not the only ones who are corrupt." Raphael reached out and touched Jude's chin, bringing it up so their eyes met. "You seek to bring about something that only our father can. Armageddon is his, and he will choose the day and the hour of his dominion. His. Not yours. Not ours. I am going to allow this trial and his will shall be done."

A savage smile lit Jude's face. "It shall, brother."

I'm going to be honest here. That smile freaked me out. Like nearly wet my pants freak me out. It was all there in his face. He was going to rip me apart and he would enjoy it. My death would be his righteous triumph. My blood would prove him right.

Raphael turned to Liv. "I assume our Felicity has apprised you of the rules. Who possesses a sword forged on the Heaven plane? Who will be your champion?"

Liv stepped back, giving up her place to Donovan.

"I am the King of all Vampire and this is my *Nex Apparatus*. Kelsey Owens possesses a proper sword. The Sword of Light." Donovan put a hand on my shoulder. "She is the champion of the Earth plane and we invest our future in her."

No pressure or anything.

Raphael turned those endless eyes on me. He looked down at the sword and held out a hand.

I frowned and tightened my grip.

"Kelsey." Donovan managed to make my name sound like an admonition.

But luckily the archangel chuckled, a smile creasing his face. "I'm not offended, King Daniel. She is descended from a long line of warriors and they would not be parted with their weapons either.

Come, child, and allow me to inspect the sword. I promise not to disappear with her. It has been many years since I was in her presence."

It was the way he called Gladys her that made me hand her over. "You can look at her, but she's mine."

"Yes, your kind can be possessive, too." He held the sword in his hand and sighed as though the contact was something pleasant to him. "Yes, I haven't seen her since my brother gifted it to the tribe on the banks of the Thermodon. Such a beauty of a weapon, and she holds so much power for one who can wield her." He glanced back at Jude. "You can call this trial off. You can apologize and attempt to make reparations. I will grant you mercy if you admit to your mistakes."

Jude's shoulders were straight, his wings relaxed as he spoke. "Apologize to these creatures? Never. They are beneath us, brother. I was not created before Jacob, the prophet who handed the sword over to the warrior women, but I know this one cannot wield it properly. She might have come from that line, but they're all mongrels now. There is no purity on this plane. They fight and war with each other over scraps. They don't even remember who they were. The queen sits in the audience, submitting to her king and never understanding who she is. This one…oh, I can't tell you how pathetic this one is. You think you're being kind by allowing their existence, but I feel them. I feel their hopelessness and their pain. I feel hers. Putting her down will be a mercy as our father once showed this plane mercy by flooding it and allowing them all to begin again."

Raphael sighed and passed Gladys back to me. "Brother, you know nothing. Their impurities, as you call them, are exactly why our father adores them. They're nothing without their struggles. Their pain builds them into something new and different, something that pleases our father and inspires the best of us. You were made to bring them hope, to give them strength when they have none."

"They never have strength," Jude insisted.

"You're about to see mine." I gripped Gladys, ready to get on with it.

Jude turned to me, his eyes silvery and shining. So alien to me. "You think I haven't seen you, child? You think I haven't watched you every day of your life? I've seen you at your best and it wasn't impressive. Every bit of strength you have has come from someone else."

From Marcus. From Gray and Trent. I glanced up and saw Felicity still standing there. She'd told me some truths and they'd sunken deep inside me. "Yes, I've used the tools I was given and I made something of them."

"You've made nothing but a whore of yourself," Jude said, and oddly, the words didn't seem unkind. It was as though he was simply pointing out some inescapable truth. "You kill and fornicate and eat and drink. You have no thoughts to higher purposes."

Raphael held up a hand. "You've made your feelings about the Earth plane and its inhabitants clear. I have one question. Why attempt to frame your brother?"

Jude's face went cold, jaw setting in an arrogant mask. "Oliver the Just is much like those he serves. He should be fallen. He curses and gambles and watches these beings with amusement. He is the one who is unworthy."

I bit back a chuckle because Oliver was sitting in the audience, his middle finger shoved up Jude's way. Felicity shook her head, trying to cover her brother's action, but I kind of thought he was awesome.

Raphael sighed. "Then we should begin. Our laws require that whoever the sword belongs to come forth and state your purpose."

Donovan stepped up. "The Sword of Light now belongs to Vampire and the Council. I give you my *Nex Apparatus* as champion. She will fight for this plane and when Jude the Faithful is defeated, we will have no more trouble with Heaven."

Raphael looked at me. "Is this true, child? Is the king your master?"

Well, he did have the power to put me in jail. Something made me look back at the queen. Some odd impulse, but I forced my gaze back to Raphael. "Sure."

"All right, then. The trial may begin and when it is over, the Sword of Justice will be returned to its rightful owner." It wasn't a question from Raphael.

Donovan inclined his head slightly. "It will."

Raphael stared at him for a moment as though he was trying to see into Donovan's head. A long moment passed and I couldn't help but think some unnamed conversation was happening between the two men. Well, the archangel and vampire, who both happened to be male.

Finally Raphael stepped back. "Of course, no matter what happens you will need a few moments to process the trial. You will have half an hour to return the sword."

I watched Donovan's eyes flare as though he was surprised, but his face quickly went blank again. "I thank you."

Raphael waved him off. "There is no need, King Daniel. When one seeks justice, one will find help from the Heaven plane. We are not at cross-purposes in this, but my brother is correct in one thing. You must bring peace between the lesser planes."

"My *Nex Apparatus* has already convinced me of this truth," Donovan admitted. "I have a plan in place that will bring justice and maintain our ability to deal with the lower plane."

"Then she is much more than a mere death machine, and the vampires have chosen wisely," Raphael said.

It was one of those moments where I was pretty sure there was some serious subtext going on that I didn't understand. I certainly wasn't going to analyze the convo now. I was too busy looking at Jude, the Dude Most Likely to Murder Me, and counting the claws on his wings. Yeah, he had those. They were almost impossible to see because they were pearly white like the feathers that covered the wings, but I caught sight of them. There seemed to be four of them, two on the bottoms and two at the highest part of the wings.

They gleamed in the low light and I knew they wouldn't be shiny white for long. They would seek blood. Mine.

Raphael turned to the demons, his head tilting slightly. "And welcome to you, beings of the lower plane. I bid hello to my brothers and sisters."

They sneered and laughed his way, and if it bothered him, he didn't show it.

He bowed his head. "Let the battle for justice begin."

And then he disappeared. He and Donovan and Liv were there one moment and gone the next. When I looked up, Donovan was seated next to the queen, Liv beside Casey, and Raphael was with Felicity and the angelic crowd.

That was when I heard the horn that signaled the beginning.

Jude stretched those mighty wings of his, the span seeming endless for a moment. He stretched them out, hovering over the sand of the arena and blotting out the light for a moment so I was in shadows. "Walk away, child. Bend your knee and beg my mercy and you shall find it."

Yeah, I wasn't good at begging. Well, not in a non-sexual fashion. "I was told you've watched me since I was born. What do you think I'm going to do?"

Adrenaline flooded my veins, a welcome drug. I started to seek to open the connection between my human self and my wolf, but it was already there. She was me and I was her. I might still call her my wolf, but after this day it was habit only and not any kind of truth. My strength was right there, tapped in a way I'd never been able to use it before.

I chose not to change my dominant arm. Before that moment, I didn't have a choice. That demon-skinned arm showed up when I was in danger. But this time I knew it wouldn't unless I called on it.

Which was a good thing because I wasn't sure how Gladys would handle demon skin.

But despite the fact that my arm remained perfectly human, the sword was silent.

Jude rose a bit more, his sandaled feet hovering above the sand. He practically had a halo of light around his head and I wondered if he practiced that shit in a mirror or if it was all part of the angel mystique. "I know what your instinct is, child, and it will be my greatest mercy to put you down. Isn't that what you've wanted all your life, Hunter? Do you think I don't remember that moment when you realized no one would ever love you? If your own father saw the abomination that you are, how would anyone else find a place for you?"

I'd thought those exact things. Even the word. I'd thought the word that day so long ago. Abomination. I'd thought the word before I'd picked up the knife when I was sixteen and couldn't understand what I was. Abomination. I'd felt that word in my soul as I'd tried to take away my pain.

Betrayal didn't begin to cover what this being had done to me.

"You were supposed to be my guardian angel." He was supposed to be the one who whispered to me, sweet words that gave me faith. He'd done the opposite and it had only been my own God-given nature that had saved me. I'd been built to survive. I'd healed, my body working so much faster than my mind.

I realized something else. Felicity had been right. Every single time I was in trouble, I'd been sent the tools to survive. That terrible day when even my angel had betrayed me, my "abomination" of a body had saved me, and Liv had come and my brother, Nate. They'd held me and whispered words that drove out Jude's.

At night, some force in the universe had sent me dreams of my real father.

I'd fought so hard against becoming the *Nex Apparatus*, but it gave me purpose. Jude was wrong. I did have a higher purpose.

To protect my world and my people from assholes who thought they were better than us.

"I realized what you were," Jude replied, wings stretching. "I knew you deserved no faith. You are the product of illicit fornication between your mother and a dog. You are the daughter of a long forgotten warrior tribe. Now all whores. It's time to end this. End this plane. End this experiment. End you."

This was the moment when I would usually charge in, but he was a fucking asshole coward who was floating way above my ability to jump. "Why don't you come down here and fight me, then."

He shook his head sadly. "No, as I said, there will only be mercy from my touch."

I heard a great whooshing sound, the wind from his mighty wings whipping my hair back, and then he was flying so fast I almost couldn't track him. He was a white bullet headed my way and I barely managed to duck.

And not all the way. I bit back a scream as one of those razor-sharp claws scraped against my shoulder. The cotton of my T-shirt gave way and he managed to slice into my left shoulder.

First blood went to the angel.

I held my left arm in close. I needed a bit of time to heal. It had been weeks since I had taken any vamp blood so I had to rely on my own abilities to fix the damage. They would work quickly but not as fast as vamp blood, and the more damage I took, the longer the healing would take.

I moved back, trying to put some distance between us. I'd fought a couple of things that could fly, but Jude was large when his wings were spread. So fast.

He floated above me, still in a way only pure predators can be. He stared at me and I at him, though my brain was working about a million miles an hour.

Gladys hummed insistently in my hand, but she wasn't doing anything spectacular. There was no grand rush of energy coming from her. There was no spark coming off her. In fact, if I had to describe what I was feeling from that damn sword, I would say she was anxious. Antsy.

We'd missed something. We'd done something wrong. There was power inside her, but we hadn't properly brought it out. We'd skipped some step or messed up on how we'd offered her blood.

I couldn't beat Jude if I didn't have the Sword of Light on my side. She couldn't be on my side when we hadn't primed her properly.

She wanted. I felt that. She longed to be unleashed the way she was meant to be, but there were rules and rituals to be followed and we had not.

Those mighty wings flapped and I knew I was in trouble.

I hit the ground as he dove low, trying to get out of the way of his sword. He held the Sword of Faith in his left hand, his right reaching out and down. I tasted sand as I tried to evade him, but he caught me by the ankle and I was being lifted into the air.

"I would like to know how my powers are not affecting you," he said calmly, as though we were having a mere conversation about the weather.

He held me upside down and it took everything I had not to lose my sword. Almost immediately I was nauseous. I could see the floor of the arena and wished Donovan hadn't had it built with such high vaulted ceilings. I had to be fifty feet off the damn floor. "I don't know what you're talking about."

Keep him talking. That was always a good play in battle, especially when one was getting one's ass kicked.

I glanced down below, trying to see Gray and Trent, but I couldn't twist and orient myself so I could see them.

Jude's hand tightened around my ankle and I wondered if he was going to break the bone. "I mean I've been using my angelic influence on you and I've gotten nothing back. It makes me wonder if you've done something you shouldn't. Where is the ward?"

Fuck. If he clawed that ward off, I would be in a world of hurt and I would be the one hurting myself. If he truly turned the influence on, he could make me do his work for him. It was precisely why I hadn't trusted a ward that wasn't tattooed onto my body. It would be far too easy for my angelic opponent to pull an amulet from around my neck. I hadn't even thought about the fact that those talons could literally rip the flesh that held my ward against him. The angelic ward was on my right shoulder blade. I wasn't sure how close he'd come to scratching the demonic ward, but I knew I had to protect the angelic one.

He shook me, my whole body jarring and my stomach turning again. I clutched the sword and knew he could start clawing at any minute. When he realized the ward wasn't coming off easily, he would start in on my clothes, and then he would find what I'd done.

I had to get out of that hold. He shook me again and when he pulled me up, I swung my body up, forcing the sword into the nearest part of his body I could get to. Gladys sliced into the angel's torso, cutting up and through his side. I pulled to the left and drew her out, leaving him with a gaping hole in his side.

And then I was falling. I tried shifting and moving my body because that sand was coming fast and I was going to crash right on my damn head. Gladys slipped from my hand and I barely managed to avoid breaking my neck.

Not that it didn't hurt like hell. I slammed into the sand and couldn't breathe for a moment. If I'd hit concrete I would have broken every bone in my body, so as much as I'd cursed the sand before, I was grateful for it.

Someone screamed out my name, but I was a little on the disoriented side. My vision had gone fuzzy and trying to move made me want to get sick. Still, I had to find my sword. I had to get her back in my hands.

I started to twist to my side, but a strong hand went around my throat. So strong. Jude lifted me off the ground and back into the air. My feet dangled and I felt him squeeze. He didn't need two hands to strangle me. One worked just fine.

Silver eyes stared into mine, so cold. "Did you brand yourself against me? I shouldn't be shocked that you would defile your body. You so often defile your soul. Like all your kind. There will be a reckoning for them. Doubt it not. For you, the time is now."

That was the moment he shoved a sword through my gut.

I fell back to the sand, blood gushing from my abdomen. I put my hand over the wound. Getting gutted really fucking hurts. Warm liquid coated my hand. My own blood. How long would it take for my body to start healing? Would it heal from a heavenly sword?

I wanted to see them. I wanted to see Trent and Gray. I wanted their arms around me so badly in that moment.

What would happen to my dad? Tears blurred my eyesight. I couldn't give up. If I did, he died and everything he'd gone through would have been for nothing. If I failed, they might all die. Raphael might view my death as his father's will and the angels could take Jude's side. I didn't want to be the chick who caused Armageddon. That was supposed to be the queen's job.

It's funny the things that go through your head when you're dying. Regret. I really regretted that we didn't do that spell right. We'd given Gladys blood and Donovan had introduced her to Raphael.

Donovan had. Because Gladys belonged to Vampire.

What if Gladys didn't want to belong to Vampire? What if she resented the fact that she had been stolen and forced into service? What if she wanted her true mistress to claim her? To give her to the warrior?

What if she was a badass bitch of a sword and we had disrespected her by allowing a male to own her?

What had he meant? Raphael had said I came from a long line of warrior women. Felicity said we had once had another name.

I hadn't fed Gladys properly. Not at all. I hadn't respected her or myself. I might be the king's *Nex Apparatus* but that wasn't what made me protect this plane. It wasn't what made me stand in this arena the first time and risk my life for a bunch of people who turned into deer on full moon nights. Being forced into this role hadn't made me take on a duke of Hell, and it hadn't truly caused me to pit myself against an angel.

I did that. I did that because something deep inside me couldn't abide injustice. I did it because I couldn't do anything else. Because I am Kelsey Owens and I will never back down when I'm needed.

Who was my leader? I didn't like authority figures, but once my father had followed one. Once my father had thrown aside all ritual and tradition and he'd sworn a blood oath to a companion with no power.

With a groan I rolled to my side, trying to find my sword. I would do better. I would do it right this time. The battle should never have begun because it hadn't been started properly.

She was there. I reached out and almost had her in my hand when I felt wind rushing over my body.

Jude stood over me, sword in hand. "I'll send you home, child."

He raised the sword again and I knew I had one play left in my book.

"Raphael!"

I screamed his name as the sword began to descend.

Chapter Twenty-Two

I waited for the sword to strike. This time it was coming for my heart, and I was certain there would be no healing from that wound. Right before the sword pierced my chest, Jude stopped. His body went completely still and so did the air around me.

"Yes, child?"

Raphael stood above me. From my vantage point the angel looked about ten feet tall. I took in a short breath, trying not to move an inch because while Jude wasn't pressing that sword down, it was awfully close to my heart. If I lifted up for even a second, I would pierce my own flesh.

"Any way we can have this conversation without a sword pressed to my chest?" I was feeling a bit better so either my healing abilities had kicked in or the whole time-stopping thing was good for blood loss.

He tilted his head and dropped to one knee. "I'm sorry. Without proper reasoning I can't stop this fight more than I already have. Do you have a confession to make? I will take it, child, though you should know our father already sees you."

That was good to know. "I don't want to confess."

He sighed. "Then we should get on with it."

"Whoa. I mean I do want to confess. I definitely need to confess." If it bought me a moment of his time, we could call this whole thing a confession.

His lips quirked up and I wondered how often an archangel got to smile. "Excellent. I am listening, though you know I will have to continue this fight at some point." He sat down on the sand, crossing his legs and looking relaxed. "But we have some time. They'll wait for us."

"I confess I lied to you."

One brow rose over his right eye. "Really? We haven't spoken much. I'm not sure what you could have lied about."

"I lied about the king. He isn't my master. Not even close. I serve the sword and the sword does not acknowledge the King of all Vampire." It was a desperate play, but the only one I had. If it didn't work, that sword was going to take out my heart and then a whole nasty set of dominoes would start to fall.

"Is that how you want to play this?" The question was asked with a hint of menace, as though my day could get worse if I didn't answer him properly.

"I'm not playing, Raphael. I didn't realize it until a moment ago. I call myself the *Nex Apparatus*, but I was forced into this job. The king is a good man, and I don't mind working with him, but he is not my master. No man is my master."

"Figured it out, did you?" Raphael asked, the menace gone. "I hoped you would. Will you take back your power?"

I would take back any power I possibly could. "I will."

"Do you pledge yourself to the sword?"

To the Sword of Light? "Fuck, yeah."

"Then do things properly this time." Raphael stood. "I cannot fix you, child, but the Sword of Light might help to hold you together. I can merely send both you and Jude to your corners and allow you another beginning. Do you understand? And do you know what you must do?"

I did. I knew enough about history to figure it out. "Yeah, but her husbands are going to be pissed. I'll have to take that chance."

"I think the queen won't mind. Well, except for the hideous pain, but then she's known that before." He clapped his hands.

And I found myself on my feet, yards away from Jude. Gladys hummed happily in my right hand and I kind of held myself together with my left. I watched as Jude's sword plunged in and found only sand. I heard the confusion of the crowd and I saw Trent putting a hand on Gray's shoulder, as though letting him know he could look again.

Jude glanced up and scowled as he saw Raphael standing beside me. "What is the meaning of this, brother?"

I kind of stood there bleeding and hoped this was going to work. If I was wrong, this time there would be no coming back.

God, I hoped I was right or I was about to put the queen through something shitty and I would die anyway.

Raphael held up a hand. "It has been pointed out that mistakes were made in the opening ritual of this battle. I seek merely to ensure there is no question of fairness and balance."

"There was no mistake," Jude snarled.

Raphael reached out and touched Gladys, his finger skimming over the flat of the blade. "No, there was. The Light has always refused to serve the vampires. She has done her duty, but never served her purpose. She speaks to us, brother. You can hear her, too, and you know she denies that the king is her owner."

I saw the moment Jude hesitated. It wasn't more than a tightening around his eyes, but I saw how that fact made him question what he was doing. He'd known I didn't have full use of the sword. He'd known and not said a word because he didn't want a fair fight.

He looked me over, taking in the way I was coated in my own blood. He might be able to see through my gut to the other side of the arena. I was a fucking mess.

"Do it, Raphael, and I'll kill the abomination anyway," he vowed.

The archangel turned toward the royals. "I'll ask again, who does the Sword of Light answer to."

Donovan stood but before he could speak, Zoey Donovan-Quinn was on her feet.

"She belongs to me." The queen moved quickly. She looked down to Trent, who picked her up and lowered her to the arena floor.

Donovan and Quinn followed, but it was easy to see the queen had figured out our mistake as well. She paid them no heed as she moved toward the archangel.

"I am the Queen of the Companions." Her voice rang out and I saw more than one woman in the audience stand up as though backing her. Kimberly, Henri's companion, got to her feet and watched her queen. Liv wasn't a companion, but she stood, as did Sarah Day. Most of the women of our world stood, though they were not companions. There are so few companions left that I thought it must have felt good for the queen to know how many women stood behind her.

"That is not the proper name for your tribe, Queen Zoey," Raphael said solemnly, "but I will forgive your ignorance. That knowledge has passed from the plane and times must change. Companion will do. Who do you choose as your champion?" He looked over at me and back to Zoey. "There is still time for you to choose another. This warrior is wounded. I will allow a substitute."

I was going to argue against that, but Zoey didn't hesitate.

"Kelsey Owens is now and shall always be my champion, for as long as she chooses." She moved in front of me. She was wearing jeans and a white silk blouse that was totally going to get ruined. It was all very modern, but in that moment I could see a different Zoey. I could see a warrior queen. "Kelsey Owens, I am your queen. Will you serve me in this?"

As my father had all those years before, I answered her. "I will."

Jude snorted. "You see how ridiculous they are, Raphael? She is offered the choice of an unwounded warrior and selects the one who is half dead already?"

The queen turned to him. "I would choose a half-dead Kelsey

over a fully healed warrior every single time. Her family has always served me with courage, and above all, with faith. I give that faith back to them. She will win this battle. I know it. "

I hoped she meant that. "That's not the end of the ritual is it, Raphael?"

"You can't tell her," Jude argued.

Raphael stepped back. "I cannot tell them, but I believe the sword will. Follow your instincts. She will inform you."

"Zoey, I have to…" I began.

The queen reached out and grabbed the blade, letting it slice her hand. Blood began to coat the blade, though Gladys drank it up quickly.

Dev started to reach for his wife, but Donovan held him back.

"Don't." Donovan nodded my way as though he knew what I would have to do. "This is woman's work, Dev. Let her take back the power that was stolen. Let her be the queen she was born to be, the one we love and serve and offer up our lives to. Give this to her."

Zoey's eyes met mine and I saw the recognition there. "Is it true? What she's whispering to me? What we were?"

I nodded because I believed. I believed that somehow this sword had been waiting for us. That she had been captured and kept from her true life because this moment was her purpose. Raphael was right. The truth of our beginnings had passed into legend, but the Light knew. She'd been there when our tribe was born. She'd seen us through wars, but couldn't save us from enslavement. Zoey had done that, and Gladys was ready to serve another queen, to be the hand of another Hunter champion. "Say it, Queen Zoey. Say what we were. Say what we could be again and then I'll do what we have to. I'll do what the sword requires. But name us first. Let all here know our true name."

Zoey held out her arms as though offering up her body and blood and soul to the cause. "Amazon. We were Amazon. We are Amazon."

It was what Gladys had tried to tell me every time I held her. She'd hummed in my hand because it had been so long since she'd been fed, since she'd been lovingly fed by her queen. Now the images came fast and furious. The truth of who we'd began as hit me. I could see us training on the banks of the Thermodon, see us bowing to a queen with one breast because she sacrificed when the time came.

As my queen was going to sacrifice for me.

"Do it," she said, her voice harsh.

"Zoey…" Even Donovan sounded nervous now.

Her eyes never left mine, her will a palpable thing in that moment. "I am your queen and I command you to do your duty. Bring us together. Unleash our power."

I brought Gladys back and then shoved her straight through the queen's heart. I kept going until I'd bisected her body and the hilt of the Light was planted firmly in her breast. It was a blow that would kill any human, but my queen was something more. Far more.

My mind flashed with the knowledge of how the vampires first became necessary. Before the vampires, our queen gave her life to win the battle. After we made our deal with the vampires, she didn't need to die, but we'd made a deal with the devil because it would lead to our oppression.

Zoey looked down and when she looked back up she was grinning, a droplet of blood on the corner of her mouth. "Hold on, Kelsey. This is going to be wild."

I wasn't sure what she meant until the world seemed to tremble. At first I thought we were experiencing some sort of earthquake, but when I looked around no one else was moving. They were watching us, all eyes on the crazy chicks with all the blood.

Light flashed out from Zoey's body. Golden and bright, I felt that light like a crazy, gloriously happy wave shooting into my body, flooding my veins. Gladys was happy, so fucking happy, and she was ready to release all the power she'd gained.

Millennia of power shot into my soul, filling me to the point that I couldn't contain a scream. It was too much, far too much, but I held on. Zoey reached out even as her body must have been on the verge of death. She reached out and completed the circle our tribe had formed long before on that ancient river. Queen and champion and sword all sworn to protect and defend. We were the warriors of the Earth plane. All that history flooded through me, so much I couldn't possibly understand it all.

Our history and the blood history that Gladys had gathered. She'd soaked up blood and in doing so, she had taken in the power of those she'd tasted. She didn't have to kill a being to soak in its strength. Ancient power flowed through my veins and I had hints of monstrous beings. They came from all the planes. Visions of mighty frost giants and an army of red-capped Fae played in my brain. This sword had fought demons and angels and vampires back when they were monsters who frightened everyone who caught sight of them. She'd fought armies of men.

I felt the moment the king's power struck me. He'd nicked himself once and Gladys had sucked it all down. That tiny bit of blood showed me how damn good it must feel to be Daniel Donovan.

And then I felt him. My wolf. Trent's easy power rushed over me and I could feel something else. I felt his passion, his devotion. It was there in his blood, or it had somehow transferred through the long hours he'd spent with the blade in his side.

Trent was with me not because Donovan had required it. I wasn't a job to him. I was his mate and he would die for me.

That meant I was damn straight going to live for him.

A final blast of pure energy hit me, shoving me back away from the queen. The sword came out of her body, somehow staying in my grasp even though I swear I'd lost control of my grip during that moment. Gladys stayed with me and I watched the queen begin to fall back.

She didn't hit the sand. Donovan was there in the blink of an eye, lifting his wife up and hauling her close. Devinshea ran for the stands, trying to keep up as Donovan rushed toward his box. Before I could take another breath, he had the queen on his lap, feeding her the rich blood that would fix all that damage I'd done.

"It doesn't matter, abomination. I will still triumph."

Yeah, fucking Jude was still there, but I wasn't afraid of him anymore. I was still bleeding, still covered in it, though now the queen's blood mingled with my own. None of it mattered because I glowed with power. I could see it coming off my skin. It pulsed through me. The only question was which power I should use, which one would win the battle quickly so I could go back to real life.

"Now we are set," Raphael said. "You may resume your trial, brother."

He was gone and Jude was obviously not playing anymore. He sideswiped me with that massive wing of his, knocking me over. I turned into a roll, using his own motion against him. He couldn't shift that wing on a dime and it allowed me access to his back.

I kicked up, wincing and praying my guts stayed where they were supposed to. Something way harder and more insistent than adrenaline was riding me now. The sword moved my hand. I twirled her in a way that would have had my weapons teacher panting. I didn't have to think. I gave over and let the part of me that fought instinctively merge with Gladys. It was good and right to do it.

This was what I'd been born to do. I wasn't merely the demon hunter the vamps had turned my kind into. I guarded this plane from all comers. You want to disrupt the balance here, you gotta go through me and my kind.

I kicked out, trying to force him off balance. My foot met the small of his back and I got him to stumble. He hit his knees and I charged. He swept back, his wing catching me again, and then he was in the air.

Fucker. I tried to track him, but he was fast. He soared up to the highest point in the arena and then he was a bullet coming my way. He tucked his wings in and dove. I ran, trying to make myself a harder target, but when I was sure he would hit the ground, he unfurled those wings and caught me up in them. The whole world went white and soft and then I felt that claw scratch deep across my face and I saw blood.

I dropped down and avoided him slitting my throat.

So much blood. Despite all that power, I was getting woozy. My time was going to be up soon.

I held on to Gladys with everything I had.

Jude floated above me, an arrogant look on his face. "I think I only have to wait here for that body of yours to give in. The bodies on this plane are as weak as the souls. You weren't ready for all that power were you, abomination?"

I was still shaking from it, but my mind was racing. It wasn't mere power and strength I'd gotten. It was so much more, but there was too much. Too many different sources to pull from. It was a storm in my brain.

It didn't take long to realize that I would die here if I didn't think of something. I let it flow over me, trying to figure out what to do, what power to choose. Donovan's strength meant nothing if I couldn't get my hands on Jude. It whispered through my brain that Donovan could fly and that meant I could for now, but that seemed super risky. I needed power and strength that I could control with little learning curve. If I fell again, I was probably done for.

A storm. It was like a storm in my brain.

The Ala. She was here. Gladys hummed her assent, approving of my choice.

"Your plane will run red with blood. Purification will be only the first step." Jude was having a grand old time talking about the coming apocalypse. He was totally playing to his audience. He glanced over at the demons. "And then we shall come for the lowest plane."

The demons didn't like that idea, but I couldn't think about it now. I was pulling together the Ala's power. It was fresh and I could see how to use it. Gladys pulsed in my hand as I envisioned a mighty storm. Localized, of course. I didn't want to rain baseball-sized hail down on anyone except my target.

"The demons shall be destroyed." Jude's wings flapped slowly. "You will not be needed in the new order and not tolerated for a moment more."

There was a mighty crack and the arena shook as the sky above

Jude opened up and rained down on him. Huge chunks of ice fell from the black cloud that had formed. I concentrated on every single one hitting his ass.

Or any part of his body I could get at.

A big, nasty piece hit his wing and I heard it crack, saw the blood begin to flow, and he was falling. He managed to steer himself down, falling to his knees and protecting his head with the cover of those wings. They wound around him, sheltering him.

I couldn't let that happen. I needed more.

Lightning flashed through the arena, striking near the angel. My aim could be better, but I did manage to get him to come out of protective mode. He drew his wings back, cradling his injured wing. His eyes stared through me and I knew what hate looked like. He hated me, hated this plane, hated everything he didn't understand fully. Only one way would ever make sense to this version of Jude and I understood what Felicity had told me. Angels fell when their time was right. Jude wasn't ready for an angelic existence. It was time to allow him to transform.

All my anger fled and an odd sympathy crept through me as Jude lifted his sword and ran my way. I had just figured out my place and there was comfort in that. He'd said I had no higher purpose, but I had the greatest one of all. To protect the ones I loved. To force myself to care about even those I couldn't stand. It was my mission.

What had Donovan called it? Woman's work. Yes. He would play the king and rule with authority, but when it came to compromising, to bending and protecting the weakest among us, it would be me and the queen who were called upon.

And I had a job to do now.

Jude charged, his face a mask of rage, and I called down a lightning strike, this time my aim proving true. That bolt of pure energy struck the top of his head, and I watched as his body shook and shook. I could hear the angels weeping and the demons cheering, but I didn't feel triumphant. There was happiness that Felix would awaken and I could reunite a family, that Neil wouldn't have to worry about being a crazy sleeper agent again, that we would all be safe. But I felt for him. Maybe it was Gladys or maybe I was becoming a more well-rounded assassin, but all I could think of in that moment was how much promise he'd wasted.

Raphael was suddenly at my side. "It's time, child. It's all right. Do your duty and have no guilt in the action."

The lightning let him go and Jude fell to his knees. It was easy to see how spent he was. Perhaps I was bloodier, but he'd taken a shit ton of voltage and it had been imbued with Gladys's unique energy. His wings drooped and I knew I should make it quick.

"Choose better next time."

Gladys guided my hand as I brought her up and down and separated Jude the Faithful's head from his body. Before his head could hit the ground, it turned to ash and was gone. His body stayed visible for a mere moment before it too turned and floated away.

I stared at the spot and hoped that like my father, he found a happier existence next time around.

Then the world started to go fuzzy again. I could hear the crowd screaming, cheering me, but it seemed to come from somewhere far away. Gladys fell from my hand and the minute I lost her, weakness sent me to my knees.

The sand was warm under me. Warm and soft and I realized why. I'd started bleeding again. The pain hit me now that I'd used the power. I was bleeding from multiple sources, each and every one aching like a motherfucker. I could feel where he'd split open a good portion of my face.

"Your friends are coming," Raphael said, kneeling beside me. "They'll take care of you now. I thank you for setting my brother free and for balancing out the king's more aggressive instincts. Perhaps he will listen to you and your queen more often now that he knows where her crown truly comes from. Hold on. They're almost here. Let Donovan know I'll come for my brother's sword in due time."

He blinked away and I couldn't even hold my head up.

"Donovan!"

Gray was shouting. He sank into the sand beside me, reaching for me. Trent knelt down and looked me over.

"Don't worry, baby." Trent managed something of a smile. "The king is on his way, along with the academics. There is going to be so much blood to heal you. You won't even remember how bad it feels right now. Gray, we're going to need to hold her skin together or I'm worried how it will heal."

I will give it to my wolf. He's calm in a crisis. Must have been his military training. His voice stayed even, but I knew what he was talking about. He was worried that if they didn't hold my skin together I would heal with parts of me on the outside. That's how broken I was.

"Give me some room." The king strode across the sand. Zoey ran beside him, her clothes bloodied but otherwise perfectly well. That's what vamp blood will do for you. The blood left over was the only sign Zoey had suffered at all.

"Liv, can you get Kelsey's face? Hold it together so it heals right," Trent asked. "Gray and I will make sure her belly heals properly and Jamie can pull the skin back over her clavicle."

Damn, I was fucked up. I couldn't wait until that blood started working its magic and I felt whole again. Everything hurt. My body was a massive wound that wouldn't stop bleeding.

"No," a dark voice said.

Gray's head went up. "Brother?"

I forced my eyes open and Nemcox was standing there, his father at his side.

"I said no vampire blood," the demon insisted. He stared down at me with pitch black eyes. "We agreed to it."

"But she's dying." Gray smoothed my hair back. "She's not going to last long enough for her body to heal."

"We've got a couple of minutes, maybe," Trent agreed. "There's not even time for a healing spell to work. Vampire blood is the only thing that will save her."

"And it will mark her as the property of Vampire and then she can't sign a contract." Nemcox looked me over as though academically assessing my wounds.

I felt Trent move, but I was too weak to say anything. There was a crowd around me, blocking out the light.

"Did you not see what the rest of us saw?" the king asked. "I think we can safely say Kelsey is her own person. Let me save her and we'll talk. You can't haul her off to Hell if she dies."

The demon grinned and held up a piece of paper. "I can if she signs this. It gives me her soul after death. I think you'll find there is no clause in our contracts that prevents anyone from signing away their soul after they die. All of your language is strictly to protect the living."

Lord Sloane chuckled. "You need better lawyers, Donovan."

Nemcox shoved a piece of paper toward me. I could bet what it would say. It would ensure my descent into Hell after my soul left my body. Which wouldn't be long now. "Here you go, dear. You can sign now or I'll tell my father the truth."

"You can't do this," Gray said, sounding utterly horrified. "She's mine. I make the decisions concerning her."

"Not when you make such horrible ones," his brother replied. "You'll thank me later."

I wanted to say something but I was so tired. So fucking tired. I wasn't sure if I would be able to sign my name to the document Nemcox was holding up for me.

"Father, talk to him," Gray begged.

Lord Sloane shook his head. "He won't be reasonable about this and honestly, I don't care. I think I would rather know the secret. The girl is valuable in a breeding fashion, but I think she'll still be trouble. If I have to choose, I pick knowing her secret. And yet your brother won't tell me."

So my father was still safe. Nemcox hadn't broken our deal.

"Sign, dear, and we can be done." Nemcox started to lean over. "Or simply say the words. Say 'I give my immortal soul to you, Lord Nemcox, and wish to dwell with you forever.' Then you can die in peace."

"I don't want her to die." Gray looked up to the king. "Do something. She's your *Nex Apparatus*. Or you, Queen Zoey. Please. I need time. I can make him see reason, but not if Kelsey's dead."

Where was Trent?

I wanted to see him one last time. I wasn't sure how long I had. Donovan was arguing with Lord Sloane about something and Gray was pleading with the queen. Jamie had gotten to his feet and was yelling for Marcus to come and help me and Liv was trying her hardest to say some spell that would start my healing process.

"Gray?" I tried to squeeze his hand.

He was looking up at the queen. "Talk to him. Please, you can't let this happen."

"I'm not going to," Zoey was saying.

It was chaos all around me. They were all talking and arguing and nearly coming to blows.

"Say the words, Hunter." Nemcox's voice was a snake in my ear, slithering and tempting. "Tell me you're mine and you can die knowing your father is safe. If you don't, you'll go into eternity knowing you'll never see him again. I won't merely kill him. I'll annihilate his soul."

I looked past him and saw a flash of silver and then Nemcox stiffened, his midnight eyes going wide. There was the sickening sound of flesh versus blade, and Nemcox was staring down at the hole in his chest.

He stood there for a moment and then his body turned to dust, forming a pile on the ground.

All those years of life, of evil, nothing but a pile of ash.

The world seemed still for a moment, and I wasn't exactly certain what had happened. I heard someone shouting. It was Gray, and he wasn't holding my hand anymore. It was Zoey Donovan-Quinn at my side.

"Drink up, Kelsey. Do it now. I'm not taking no for an answer," she said, nodding at her husband.

What had happened? I'd seen a glimpse of metal and I could have sworn Trent had been the one holding a sword. I'd seen a flash of his serious face right before Nemcox had started to bleed.

Only a heavenly sword could kill an immortal demon, and then only when he was in his full form.

What had Donovan done?

He was shoving his wrist at my mouth and I found myself held down. I looked up and the king was staring at me. "I know I promised, but I can't allow you to die. I can't. And I won't allow you to descend."

His blood was already flowing into my mouth and there was nothing I could do to stop it. Hell, I didn't want to stop it. The minute I tasted that rich, dark velvet blood, all I wanted was more. Strength immediately flowed through my veins and I wasn't lying there weakly. I was sucking it down.

"That's right," Donovan encouraged. "That sword Jude used on you was heavenly. The wounds are much worse than anything you've taken before. Take what you need." He leaned over. "I wasn't going to let you descend to protect my son. He needs you here. We need you here."

He'd planned this. It hadn't been Gladys Trent had wielded. It was worse. Nemcox might have had a shot with Gladys, since she wasn't being used by a favored tribe member. But Trent had used the Sword of Justice. No one could survive that.

It was why Donovan had insisted on all demons coming in full form, no possessions allowed. It was why Donovan had made the trial public, to lure Nemcox to the one place where he would feel safe but be vulnerable. It was why Raphael hadn't taken the sword immediately.

Trent had killed Nemcox.

Trent had killed Gray's brother.

Shit.

I shoved up, able to move now. Trent had murdered a full-blooded demon in front of a mass audience of demons. They wouldn't give a fuck that he'd done it for love. They would tear him apart, and Gray might lead the charge.

"What have you done?" I nearly shouted the question at Donovan.

"What I had to do," he replied.

"They'll kill him." I scrambled, looking for Gladys. I couldn't let them tear Trent apart.

Donovan was back on his feet and I realized with great relief that Trent wasn't being eviscerated. A thick vine snaked around him, forming a protective circle. He stood in the middle, the Sword of Justice in his hand. Quinn stood, his back to the Council crowd as he moved the thickly thorned vine this way and that, wielding it as a weapon against the throng of demons surrounding my wolf.

"Dev can handle them for now," Donovan promised.

Zoey shook her head. "I begged him to let someone else do it, but Trent didn't trust anyone else."

My heart was in my throat. I didn't realize how terrified I could be until that moment. It was totally different to be the person in the middle of a blood-thirsty crowd than it was to be the one watching a person you love in the same position. I would have done anything to have switched places with him.

I pushed my way through the crowd and was horrified to find Gray at the front. His horns had come out, his fangs curving and claws ready to tear into his opponent's flesh. Unfortunately, that flesh belonged to our third, and I wasn't about to let that happen.

"What are you doing?" I pulled at Gray's arm.

He didn't look back. "Get out of here, Kelsey."

Trent had caught sight of me. Some kind of slime demon put a hand on my arm and Trent started toward us.

I put up a hand. "Don't you fucking dare leave that circle, you massive sneaky asshole." I shoved an elbow back, catching the stinky thing in its…parts… You can almost never tell with slime demons. It could have been his balls for all I knew, but it did the trick.

"Baby, I did it for us," Trent yelled. "Gray, forgive me. You know he wasn't going to back down."

"I could have talked to him," Gray insisted. "Come out here, you coward."

"I'm not afraid of you," Trent replied. "But she's a different story. I really am afraid of her."

He better be. "Stay that way. Don't you dare step outside that circle until I find a way to fix this."

Gray turned to me and his pain was so plain I wanted to reach out and put my arms around him. "There is no fixing this. He killed my brother."

"Who was planning on torturing our woman," Trent shot back. "I know you're hurting, brother, but you have to see why I did this."

"Never call me that," Gray roared and surged toward Trent, but the Green Man's vine smacked him back.

A strong hand wound around my arm, pulling me outside the fray. Lord Sloane wasn't playing around. He dragged me until we were behind the line of fire.

"I hope you're a truly spectacular lay because this is a fucking mess," he snarled down at me. "You do understand that I'm in a position to require the werewolf's head. We recently agreed to negotiate with the Council and now I have to execute the queen's trusted bodyguard. That's what got us into this fucking position in the fucking first place. I hope you enjoy this. I have no choice."

"You do." My mind was whirling, but I wasn't good at politics. "You can forgive him in an attempt to keep the balance on the plane. You know what happens when Heaven decides we're not handling our shit."

"Yes, and we were almost free." Lord Sloane smoothed down his jacket. "Now, because my son can't keep it in his pants around you, and my other son couldn't stop plotting, we're right back where we were. All that pain you just went through was for nothing. I can't back down without reason. I have to look strong."

I couldn't allow this to happen. I couldn't save the damn day only to lose Trent. He'd been willing to go to Hell with me. He wasn't going to be executed. I had to find a way.

Lord Sloane put up a hand and the demons quieted immediately. Well, except for Gray. He had two men in suits—his father's contingent—holding him back and he was still trying to get at Trent.

"You know he's in a rage, right?" The queen stood beside me. "When demons get particularly emotional, it's hard for them to reason. Don't judge Gray too harshly. If he had hurt Trent, he would almost certainly have regretted it."

Gray didn't look like he would regret anything. "Why would you sacrifice Trent? After everything he's done for you."

I would plead with the queen, lay on the guilt, do anything I had to do to stop Trent from being executed.

"I have no intentions of sacrificing him," the queen replied. "Though I don't doubt there will be some punishment. Wait. Trust me. Please."

"King Daniel, I request your presence." Lord Sloane looked calm and cool, almost as though requesting justice for his son was a real drag on his day. Despite the fact that Nemcox had been a prick who'd threatened my father and me and who'd been more than willing to let me die to further his own agenda, I couldn't help but feel for Gray. With this ass for a father, I was sure Nemcox had seemed like a loving brother. "Your animal has offended me. He killed my beloved son and has turned my other son into a raging beast. Seriously, Grayson, have some decorum."

Donovan stepped up. Devinshea was beside him, his hand still controlling the plant he'd turned into a weapon. I'd heard a rumor that the gorgeous ivies and ferns that decorated the arena were actually there as a defense mechanism, but I hadn't believed it until today.

"I believe you'll find my servant was trying to protect his lover from being forced into signing a contract," Donovan explained. The demon hoard hissed and booed. "Your son was also keeping her from receiving healing from her king, which is her right."

"And Nemcox was an asshole." The queen wasn't above putting in her two cents.

"Zoey, please," Donovan said with a sigh. "I know you came into an enormous amount of power tonight, but let me handle the politics. I'll allow you and the *Nex Apparatus* to defend the Earth plane."

Zoey stood up taller. "It's a deal."

It was good to know the night had worked out for someone. I attempted to step forward. "Trent was trying to protect me."

Zoey put a hand on my arm. "No, Daniel is right. Let him handle this. All this talking and whining and complaining, that's men's work. And he's totally good at it."

I saw Donovan's head shake but he was right back to royal in a second. "I think we can negotiate, Lord Sloane."

Sloane's eyes had narrowed. "I find it interesting that the wolf was able to handle the sword at all. You can call wolves, can't you, Your Highness? You can control them."

"It isn't a power I use lightly," Donovan explained. "And he was far too fast for me."

"Somehow, I sincerely doubt that," Sloane replied. "I demand a new trial. Unless you will agree to give me the head of the wolf who killed my precious son."

Donovan rolled his eyes. "He was so precious to you. I can see that."

Sloane's fangs came out. "He was my blood and I will have vengeance."

"I will have justice, as well, Lord Sloane," a new voice said.

Zoey squeezed my arm and I realized they had planned this as well. So much careful preparation and I had been left out of it all. It wasn't that I blamed them. Not truly. I just didn't know what they were planning and I hated being left in the dark.

But I'm also a horrible actress, so I get it.

Neil Roberts stepped up, his husband at his side. "I have something to say. Demand, really. You see, if I don't get what I want out of this, I intend to call a satan."

Lord Sloane's hands went to his hips, staring the wolf down. "What? Why would you need a satan? You don't have a contract."

"Yes," Neil said. "That would be my point."

Donovan nodded toward the lord of Hell. "I believe my citizen claimed the right to a satan."

Satans are the lawyers of the demonic world. You don't call on one if you don't think you know they're going to go your way. Their word is the be-all, end-all of contracts.

Lord Sloane held out a hand despite the fact that his other son was still in a state of complete insanity. Gray was fighting his keepers, howling and yelling his rage. "There's no reason for him to call in a satan. We can deal with this here and now."

"He says that because he knows what the satan would say." Chad Thomas was dressed in his normal leather pants and white shirt. "My husband was taken without a contract. He clearly belonged to Vampire and he was taken to Hell against his will, and we can demand justice."

I finally realized what they'd done. They had planned everything carefully, right down to how they were going to save Trent.

I was shit at politics, but Donovan and Quinn were damn fucking good.

"I was the servant of Daniel Donovan when the demon Nemcox dragged me to Hell against my will." Neil Roberts stood tall and proud against an army of demons. "I was held in Hell for nearly thirty years, though the equivalent on the Earth plane was mere months. During those years, I aged and my life-span shortened. I have less years with my love than I should have and I demand payment. I never gave in. Not once. I was raped over and over by Lord Sloane's precious son and because he is gone, my justice will come from his family."

Sloane turned Neil's way, suddenly taking him seriously. "What do you expect me to do? He's dead. I can't exactly hand over his balls. The wolf made sure they're dust."

Yes, he was aching over his loss.

"I demand reparations in the form of your servitude, Lord Sloane," Neil replied. "You will serve the Council as I served your son. You'll find this form of recompense is all laid out in the documents signed by your kind years ago."

"I'm not going to serve anyone." Sloane shook his head as though trying to comprehend what was happening. "I'm certainly not serving on the Earth plane."

"Then I suppose I'll call the satan and see what he has to say," Donovan offered.

Sloane moved in close, his voice going low. "I'm not an idiot. What do you want?"

"Pardon my servant." Donovan sprang his trap.

Yes. That was what I wanted. I would deal with Gray. If what Zoey said was the truth, then he would calm down at some point and be more reasonable. He would see that this had been the only way.

Sloane grimaced. "I can spare his life, but there must be punishment. I can't allow this to pass without some form of punishment. I would lose my power and it will start a war on my plane to see who takes my place. Negotiate with me. Give me lead on the meeting between our planes and banish the wolf. He is to no longer be welcome in Council-held lands and we have a deal. Otherwise, call the satan and unbalance the demonic plane. See how that works for you."

I shook my head. "No. You can't banish Trent."

"I'm not going to banish my servant for delivering justice," Donovan replied.

Sloane thought for a moment and then nodded. "Call the satan. If there was no angelic interference, you will almost certainly win. If there was…well, I'll call for a separate hearing concerning Neil Roberts. I believe Louis Marini was the head of the Council at the time. He had the power. If Neil Roberts's contract is deemed just, then it is Hell that will ask for a trial and perhaps compensation."

Even I knew that time was a murky part of history. Louis Marini had been the head of the Council and Donovan had been marked as an outlaw for months before he finally took over the Council. Could we win? They might not be able to drag Neil back to Hell, but they could put the king in a bad place when it came to negotiations. I'd begged him. I'd been the one who changed his mind and now it was my situation that placed the Council in harm's way.

I saw the moment Donovan realized this wasn't going to be perfect, but then he'd probably planned for that, too.

"And if I declare my former servant to be outcast, unknown to the Council due to his crimes, would that serve you?" Donovan would never give up his wife's best friend. And he couldn't go into negotiations in a submissive position. Even I knew that.

But to declare Trent an outcast? He wouldn't be allowed on Council land. Wouldn't be recognized by the king or his Council. He would be alone in the world. He would have to run because no one would protect him.

Sloane held out a hand. "I am the lead on the negotiations with the Earth plane and this will be done. I shall demand no vengeance but you will give the outcast no succor."

Donovan's eyes closed briefly and when he opened them I knew his decision, and I also knew that it sucked to be the king. "Agreed."

He'd saved me and the plane, but Trent was outcast.

Sloane shook his hand and the deal was done.

The demons stepped back and Dev was allowed to release the vine. It slithered back underground and I ran to Trent.

His arms wound around me. Gray was still being held away from us, but I hated the look in his eyes as I hugged Trent.

"I'll go with you." I wasn't going to leave him alone.

His hands came up, cupping my face. "No. I knew what would happen when I agreed to do this. Take care of Gray. Take care of that wolf inside you. She's the strongest, bravest bitch I've ever known. I love you. Take those words into your soul, baby, because they won't stop if I die. I'll love you forever."

They pulled him out of my arms, tears clouding my eyes, and I wondered if it was the last time I would ever see him.

Chapter Twenty-Three

Three weeks later

"I thought you would be taller." Liv was grinning as she looked at me. "Being an Amazon and all. And the queen is even shorter than you."

"I don't think height is a requirement." I wasn't exactly tiny or anything. I was a respectable five foot six. I wasn't petite like the queen.

"Still, I think it's interesting." Liv sat back on the couch. "Any word on Trent?"

The very name made my heart ache. "The last I heard he was on the run. He isn't allowed in the normal wolf packs. They're considered Council and apparently the word succor means help."

Trent wasn't allowed any aid from Council members, and that included the wolf packs that accepted protection. Pretty much all of them accepted protection. Trent was on his own and I didn't know if he was dead or alive.

"Hey, do you two need a snack?" Gray stepped out of the kitchen. He looked wholly masculine in a clingy T and jeans. He'd chilled out exactly the way the queen had said he would with the singular exception of I wasn't allowed to even speak Trent's name. He was counseling the king on the upcoming negotiations, but he wouldn't speak about our werewolf. He wouldn't acknowledge that he'd ever existed at all.

Liv had shown up thirty minutes before, smiling and bringing me gossip and news. I'd been holed up for weeks, mourning my loss, processing what had happened. Marcus had come several times and spent hours with me. He'd talked to me like a therapist, asking me to confess my emotions and telling me about his. Somehow when it wasn't simply me talking, I could do it. When Marcus would tell me about the girl in the painting and how she kept moving across the field, I could talk to him about how much I missed Trent.

I could feel the loss of him like a limb torn from my body, but I couldn't talk about it with Gray.

"I'm good. Thanks, babe. But I could use another beer." It was kind of how I processed.

He frowned but disappeared back into the kitchen. I was well aware my lack of appetite was worrisome for him, and I vowed to eat whatever he put in front of me for dinner tonight. It was the first full moon since I'd lost Trent and I couldn't help but wonder where he was, who was after him. I knew no one was taking care of him.

Liv put a hand on my arm. "Kelsey, you two have to talk about what happened."

"He won't." It wasn't like I hadn't tried. "He kind of pretends it didn't happen at all. He decided to go back to work. So I'm learning what it means to be a cop's girlfriend. Jamie shows up in the middle of the day or night and Gray will be gone for days at a time."

In some ways, it felt like I'd lost both of them. Gray was still here most of the time. He made love to me every chance he got, but there was a distance between us.

So I spent my time working. I was in a bit of a lull. No grand murders to solve. I'd taken to training Justin to do more than play around on the computer and answer the phone. He'd helped me track down a couple of runaways, catch the kid who was stealing from the bakery on the sixth floor, and prepared dossiers on the bigwig demons who would be coming in for the contract negotiations in the upcoming months.

And yes, it totally was Lee who stole the cookies and that whole pan of brownies. He claimed he was merely trying to keep up his skills, but I'm pretty sure once the queen got over her initial freak-out, the no-sugar rule went back into effect.

I worked. I worried.

"You seem awfully calm for all this drama," Liv said quietly.

I was. "I know he's out there. I know he wants to be with me. And I know if there's any way for the king to bring him back, he will."

"Do you think that's why you're calm? Because you trust you'll see him again?" Liv asked.

I ached for him, but I also knew if he could find a way, he would come back to me. "I do trust him and I have some faith that it's going to turn out all right."

Funny how I'd killed an angel who specialized in faith and found a bit of my own.

According to Donovan, bringing Trent home would be top on his agenda when he sat down with the demons. I trusted the king, but that was months away and anything could happen. I wanted to talk to him. Needed to know he was all right.

Perhaps it was time to start quietly looking.

"Enough about me. Tell me about how Felix is doing. I saw him right after he came out of the coma, but he's not seeing patients again yet. I heard he took his wife and daughter on a vacation."

Liv nodded. "Yeah, they're on some island the royals own. I've talked to Sarah a couple of times and she says he's doing well. Apparently Felicity and Oliver went to see him and they worked some things out. So now they get a new angel of faith and Felix gets on with his life."

Justice had been done. Neil Roberts was safe. Felix was well and whole again. The plane was free of angelic influence.

My dad's secret was safe for now.

"Everyone wins." Except Trent.

Liv seemed to know what I was thinking. She leaned over. "I can try to find him for you."

I shook my head. She could get in serious trouble for doing that. Trent was my responsibility. Besides, I had another job for my bestie. "I need you and Casey working on that other problem."

Finding the wizard known as Myrddin. I wanted to know everything about the man who had plotted to kill my father, and I definitely wanted to know about the prophecy that had led him to do it. Only Liv and Casey knew anything about my quest to find Merlin, and I intended to keep it that way.

For now.

We talked for another twenty minutes and then I hugged my friend. She was going to a meeting with the higher-ups in her coven. Liv was going places after stepping in for Sarah Day.

I closed the door with a sigh. It would be another long night, broken up only when Gray would reach for me and I would forget for an hour or so.

Well, not forget, but if I closed my eyes I could feel Trent there with us.

"Don't lock that," Gray said. He stood in the doorway dressed in slacks and a Western shirt. He'd put on a bolo tie and his cowboy boots. He picked up his Stetson and the keys to his truck.

"Are you going to work?" Those neatly pressed Western clothes were perfectly acceptable uniforms in the world of the Texas Rangers.

"I've got a couple of open cases that need some attention, but I thought I'd take you out first." He settled the hat on his head and opened the door.

I sighed. The night would be far longer than I'd thought. Perhaps I would go back to the office as well. "It's okay, babe. Like I said. I'm not hungry."

Or I could go down to Ether and see if the queen needed a

drinking buddy. We'd gotten a lot closer in the last couple of weeks. Funny how violence and a hidden history could do that for a couple of girls.

Gray stopped, turning my chin up so I had to look into his eyes. "I know and that's why I'm doing this. Come with me, Kelsey mine. Please."

It was the first time he'd asked me for anything since the arena. I couldn't turn him down.

I found myself following him, sitting beside him in the cab of his big F-150. I hummed along to Luke Bryan and watched as we left the city. For some reason I didn't question him at all. I let the miles roll by as we moved from concrete to suburban perfection to the wild thicket of the forest. An hour and a half passed before he pulled off the road and onto a dirt path.

"I don't think there's a restaurant out here, Gray." But my wolf was breathing in the pine scent of the air. Was he going to try to run with me? Was he taking me to the pack for the night?

He stopped the truck. "No, but he is. I'll be back to pick you up in the morning. I love you, Kelsey mine. I can't talk to him. But I've made sure he has what he needs because I know what it would do to you if he died."

I sat up, my heart starting to pound as a shadow pulled away from the tree line and I saw Trent for the first time in weeks. I turned to Gray. His face was tight and he looked ahead.

I leaned in. Now I was the one who forced him to look at me. "I love you, Grayson Sloane. Thank you."

He nodded. "Be here at dawn. Tell him he better keep you safe and I'll have another shipment with me."

"Shipment?"

He shrugged. "The guy's gotta eat. He's staying at a cabin I bought a few years back. It's only because you would worry if he was in a tent somewhere, and the food is practical. People will talk if they suddenly see a bunch of dead deer carcasses lying around."

Sure it was. My heart surged with love for them both. "Thank you, Gray. I'll be here at dawn."

I kissed him and practically jumped out of the car. This was why I'd been calm. Deep down, I trusted Gray. I finally understood that he loved me and he would do anything for me. Including hand me off to the other man I loved.

I ran and Trent caught me in his arms. He pulled me into a hug that nearly cracked my spine, but I didn't mind. His mouth found mine and he kissed me.

By the time he was done, Gray's truck was gone. But again, I could feel him there with us.

"Wanna run with me?" Trent asked.

I nodded. I took his hand and we ran, the forest all around us and the full moon above.

I ran with my love and for a moment I was free.

Kelsey, Gray, Trent, and the whole Thieves family will return in *Outcast*.

Author's Note

I'm often asked by generous readers how they can help get the word out about a book they enjoyed. There are so many ways to help an author you like. Leave a review. If your e-reader allows you to lend a book to a friend, please share it. Go to Goodreads and connect with others. Recommend the books you love because stories are meant to be shared. Thank you so much for reading this book and for supporting all the authors you love!

Sign up for Lexi Blake's newsletter
and be entered to win a $25 gift certificate
to the bookseller of your choice.

Join us for news, fun and exclusive content
including free Thieves short stories.

There's a new contest every month!

Go to www.LexiBlake.net for more information.

At Your Service

Masters and Mercenaries~Topped, Book 4
By Lexi Blake
Coming November 14, 2017

Juliana O'Neil's promising future was burned away in the heat of battle. She had been an officer with a bright future in the military, but now she is struggling to survive. Her husband gone and her career in shambles, she finds a job at Top as a hostess and tries to put together the pieces of her life. The last thing she needs is any kind of male attention, but she can't help but be amused at her neighbor and coworker's lothario antics. Not that she would have anything to do with him, at least not for more than one night.

Javier Leones doesn't understand monogamy. No woman could ever be enough for his endless libido, but he has to admit Juliana has his attention. For reasons he doesn't fully understand, he can't seem to get the gorgeous redhead with the sad eyes out of his head. After one scorching night together, he realizes he'll never be able to get her out of his system. But with his reputation, he fears she'll never see him as more than a one-night stand.

When their passions collide, these new lovers will be forced to confront Juliana's past and come to terms with Javier's present. Will they find their way or will this reservation be canceled at the last minute?

* * * *

All alone with the storm. Maybe she should call Kai. And ask him to get out in the middle of this? That seemed pretty selfish especially since she knew exactly how poorly driving in storms could go.

A hard flash of white light made her jump back.

Nope. She wasn't going there. She was going to stay in the here and now, and that meant finding a flashlight and trying to get some candles lit. Someone was out there working on getting the power back on, and then she would ride out the storm watching rom coms and falling asleep on the couch. It was going to be okay. Deep breath. It was going to be okay.

A few moments later she'd found her one flashlight and had a nice set of candles out, and she was faced with the problem of lighting the suckers. Oh, she had a big box of matches, but she'd never struck a match without her left hand.

A lighter would be easier. She could figure out a lighter maybe. Jules tried holding the box against the table with her stump while she struck the match with her right hand. She fumbled, the action so unnatural it made her slip up and break the match.

And the second one.

And the third one.

Tears pierced her eyes, but she wasn't going to shed them. She was going to figure this out or she would make due with the flashlight. It was all about adapting. That was what she had to do. Adapt.

She wasn't going to let this beat her. Normally she was tough. It had happened and she dealt with it, but between the storm and the conversation with Suzanne the day before about her mother and the sweetness of flirting with a handsome man she couldn't have, she was feeling awfully vulnerable. She wasn't going to sit here in the dark and cry.

A knock on the door made her gasp and jump.

Fuck. She wasn't like this. She hated this…this anxiety she got when it rained. It was weakness and she couldn't abide it.

If you walk away from this you'll ruin your life, Juliana. Don't think I'll watch you do it. You go through with this and you do it on your own. Am I understood?

Sometimes she felt like she was still seven years old, and if she could just get her mom's attention everything would be okay.

Jules gripped the flashlight and walked across her apartment to the door. It was likely one of the neighbors coming to check on her. Actually, that was an excellent idea. She could go down and see if Mrs. Gleeson needed some company. There were some elderly residents she could check on and a single mom she'd met at the end of the hall. She could see if she could be of any assistance and that would get her through the night.

She opened the door expecting to see anyone but the man she saw standing there.

Javier Leones. He had a flashlight in one hand and a bottle of wine in the other. He was wearing jeans and a button down that he'd left undone enough she could see a nice swath of golden brown skin. His hair was deliciously mussed, as though he'd taken a shower and simply rubbed a towel over it to get it dry.

He was big and male and so sexy it hurt to look at him, and Jules realized she could do something else to take her mind off things.

Those plump, sensual lips of his broke into a bright smile. "I thought you might like some company. I know I would. I actually don't have any candles, so I was sitting in my living room with this sad one flashlight. You look like a woman who likes some candles."

But she couldn't light them. She hadn't figured that part out.

His face fell and he walked into her place, closing and locking the door behind him. "Hey, what's wrong? It's okay if you don't have any candles. It's cool. Two flashlights are better than one."

He set the flashlight and wine bottle down and moved into her space, his hands coming up to cup her shoulders. "Jules, what's wrong?"

She had to be stronger than this. She shook her head. "Nothing. I'm fine."

His jaw tightened. "Don't. Please don't. I live with a stubborn asshole who won't let me help him in any way. I get that we've only known each other for a few weeks, but I thought we were friends. You help me out all the time. You're kind to me. Fucking let me be kind to you. I spend every day trying to help someone who won't let me. Please let me feel like I'm worth something."

If he'd said anything else, joked about the weather or told her to suck it up, she could have, but he'd opened a door. He'd been vulnerable and honest, and she found she couldn't pay that back with stubbornness.

"I have candles and I can't figure out how to light them." Tears rolled down her face. She *was* vulnerable. All the time. Even when she pretended like she wasn't.

"You can't…" he began and then he looked down. Instead of stepping back and giving her space, he drew his hand down her arm, warming her skin where he touched her. It was dark but the moon was full and gave enough light to see the outline of his face. There was no look of horror there. He caressed her arm until he got to the place where she'd been split apart and sewn back together unwhole. He brought it up and wrapped it against his palm, his fingers closing around it until the whole thing was surrounded with his warmth. "You haven't figured out how to do it yet. Probably hasn't come up or you would know what to do. How long since you lost your hand?"

"A year and a half," she said. He was touching her there. No one had touched her there except her doctors and therapists.

Come to think of it, no one had touched her at all since before the accident. Had it really been so long since she'd felt warm flesh against her own? He was so close, close enough that all she would have to do was go up on her toes to brush her lips against his.

Would that be wrong? As long as she remembered who she was dealing with, why couldn't she take a few moments of respite for herself? If he wanted her.

About Lexi Blake

Lexi Blake lives in North Texas with her husband, three kids, and the laziest rescue dog in the world. She began writing at a young age, concentrating on plays and journalism. It wasn't until she started writing romance that she found success. She likes to find humor in the strangest places. Lexi believes in happy endings no matter how odd the couple, threesome or foursome may seem. She also writes contemporary Western ménage as Sophie Oak.

Connect with Lexi online:

Facebook: Lexi Blake
Twitter: https://twitter.com/authorlexiblake
Website: www.LexiBlake.net

Sign up for Lexi's free newsletter here.

Made in the USA
Lexington, KY
10 December 2017